Aden's Chance

An Alternate American History Time Travel Novel

Pale Rider Series Book 4

By

Michael Roberts

D1521234

Copyright 2022 Michael Roberts and Michelle Deerwester-Dalrymple

ISBN: 9798838740823

Imprint: Independently published

Proofreading by Phoenix Book Promo

All rights reserved. In accordance with the U.S. Copyright Act of 1976, the scanning, uploading, distribution, or electronic sharing of any part of this book without the permission of the author constitutes unlawful piracy of the author's intellectual property. If you would like to use the material from this book, other than for review purposes, prior authorization from the author must be obtained. Copies of this text can be made for personal use only. No mass distribution of copies of this text is permitted.

This book is a work of fiction. Names, dates, places, and events are products of the author's imagination or used factiously. Any similarity or resemblance to any person living or dead, place, or event is purely coincidental.

silver and Joint bookbinders.

Chapter One Chauncey

September 18, 1814

Chauncey stood a whole five foot eleven, weighed one hundred and sixty pounds soaking wet, and was perched on his makeshift chair – a white wooden shipping crate he'd found on the docks weeks ago. He had set it on its end and sat it in front of a decrepit brown table in the back of a shack he called home when he was not on the ship and at sea. One of the table legs was loose and the table wobbled, and he hadn't bothered to stick a shim under it for balance. The wobbling didn't bother him.

Chauncey didn't have a last name or, at least, not one that he knew of. His father had been an insignificant pirate of no renown, killed in a knife fight in a dark alley before Chauncey was ever born. His mother, conversely, was a well-known whore in Baton Rouge.

Chauncey was born and raised in the same house of ill repute where his mother had worked, until she, too, was killed by an angry drunk who accused her of pinching his purse.

Chauncey had been all of twelve years old at the time but old enough to stick that drunk lecher in the back with a large kitchen knife, slaying him mere feet from his own dead mother.

Chauncey had later found the man's purse on the floor where he'd dropped it. Without his mother working for their keep, the owner of the brothel kicked Chauncey out, and he was forced to grow up stealing and begging on the streets of Baton Rouge.

Once he was old enough, he traveled to New Orleans and signed on for a new life as a sailor for a privateer. It didn't take long for him to follow in his unknown father's footsteps and turn to the more libertine and rewarding life of piracy. He presently sailed with a disagreeable master by the name of Captain Burlington, a man not known for his intelligence but for his violence and ruthlessness. Chauncey was by far smarter than Captain Burlington.

By his own account, Chauncey should be captain of his own ship, with Burlington answering to him and not the other way around. Chauncey had been born a small, starving child, and although he grew tall, he remained thin and sickly-looking. He used violence if it didn't involve a fair fight, but he learned long ago not to rely on brawn he didn't possess. Rather, he survived by his wits and cunning. As a planner, he always searched for a good deal and fast coin.

And he was sure that last night he'd finally found it. He found his leprechaun that would lead him to his pot of gold.

Chauncey studied the unconscious man on the floor, this leprechaun of his. The man laid on his side in the fetal position, facing away from Chauncey where Chauncey had tied him up. This man was a stranger in New Orleans, and strange in other ways. Captain Burlington had instructed Chauncey to find more crewmen for the ship, so Chauncey and a few others hurried down to the docks to locate a few healthy-looking drunkards they could talk into joining Burlington's crew.

Chauncey had spotted this strange man with another man in one of the taverns. He spied on them, waiting to see if they were well inebriated or not when he overheard them speak. They spoke English but in an odd dialect, one he hadn't heard before. Chauncey had a refined ear but this time he couldn't figure out where they might have been from. His eyes narrowed at their fat purses and the peculiar flintlock this strange one stowed under his cloak, almost hidden out of sight.

Chauncey and his friends had jumped the two men on the docks with the intention of killing them, but the other, older stranger had escaped. Chauncey had knocked this man, his leprechaun, out with a cudgel, and now he had questions for the man. He was bursting with questions, and he hoped the man would wake up soon, if at all. He had killed a man once accidentally by hitting him too hard in the back of the head, and he hoped that was not the case this time.

Chauncey's mates were pleased to split the purse and the few items that they'd grabbed from the man, but not Chauncey. He knew there was more to be had. He could smell it. The man's satchel, sword, knife, and powder horn now sat on the rough table in front of Chauncey.

He turned the stranger's odd-looking flintlock over in his hands. Before running away, his mates had made off with the man's fine leather boots, thick black vest with its large brass buttons, and his heavy brown cloak. They had no doubt given the items to Captain Burlington as gifts for his forgiveness in failing to return with new men for his crew. The coins they had probably kept for themselves, neglecting to tell the captain about *those*.

Chauncey shifted his gaze from the man on the floor to

the flintlock in his hand as he turned the weapon over, studying it from different angles. It was made entirely of steel except the wooden grips on the sides of the handle. There was no wooden frame to hold the barrel, and this was the first flintlock Chauncey had ever seen without a wooden frame. A cylinder rotated as the user pulled the hammer back. The hammer, barrel, and trigger were the only parts of the flintlock that Chauncey recognized for what they were. The name *Webley* was engraved in the metal. Was that the strange man's name? When Chauncey had fired the flintlock, the first thing he had noticed was the lack of thick cloud of gunpowder smoke. This weapon used a new kind of smokeless powder. That alone was worth a fortune.

On a whim, he had pulled back the hammer again and then the trigger to see if the flintlock might fire again without priming, and it had. That's when he figured out the six chambers spun around every time the hammer was pulled back. The six chambers each held a preloaded shot. He discharged the flintlock four more times before it stopped firing. For the life of him, he couldn't figure out how to load the flintlock. He had found two dozen small brass containers, each less than an inch long and holding what appeared to be lead inside of them. They were the same type of containers as those in the flintlock's cylinder. Chauncey grinned to himself – he recognized value when he saw it, and this strange weapon would be worth a king's fortune to any army.

He also happened to be familiar with an unreputable man known for selling information to both the British and the French. Tomorrow, Chauncey planned on finding the man and requestion he set up a meeting with representatives from both countries. Once Chauncey described what he had to sell, they would come. They would come with gold or promissory notes or whatever they had, because neither country wanted their enemy to possess such a weapon.

He would sell the flintlock to the highest bidder, and that country could mass produce it. In no time at all, they would have the most powerful army in the world. No army would be able to stand on a field of battle against a force armed with weapons such as this. And though it seemed a horrific image, none of that mattered to Chauncey, who would be so rich that he could go anywhere he wanted with his own ship, far from any country or their army.

Chauncey wondered if this design might be used to build a better rifle – a rifle that held six preloaded shots. This weapon would change warfare. One man could kill six with a weapon like this. The more he studied it, the more questions flooded his head. Why had Chauncey never seen or heard of this weapon before now? And what was this man doing with it? Who was he to possess a weapon that Chauncey had never dreamed of? A leprechaun indeed.

Chauncey set the flintlock back on the table and assessed the different and peculiar items he had found in the satchel and on the stranger. In the satchel, he found items that he couldn't identify but did not seem to serve any purpose. The powder horn, for instance, was empty and appeared clean, as if it had never had any powder in it. The knife and sword were made of no metal he'd ever seen before. They were the finest made weapons he had ever encountered. The steel was strong but lighter than most swords he had held.

He briefly considered keeping them, but they were worth too much money to keep for himself, and he didn't have his own king's fortune yet. He needed the money that these weapons would bring, since he couldn't return to the ship. Captain Burlington would want to know about the man they had sacked and the items Chauncey had found.

The man's body moved as he gave out a low, half-conscious moan. He was waking up slowly. His eyes fluttered opened then closed as he squeezed them shut. The light in the room wasn't bright, but after a head injury, it didn't take much light to cause pain. Chauncey expected the man to have a bad headache at the least, after the blow to the back of his skull. After some slow blinking, the man finally managed to open his eyes. He tried to lift his hands to his face before he realized that they were tied together in front of him with a thin strip of leather. The man's eyes widened, and then he looked around, apparently to figure out where he was. His legs moved, and he discovered his feet were also tied together.

"You're awake, leprechaun," Chauncey said from behind the man. "Is your name Webley?"

The man's body twitched in surprise at Chauncey's words. Then he slowly rolled on his back so that he could see Chauncey clearly, stirring dust from the floor into the air as he moved.

"Who are you?" the man asked, blinking dust out of his eyes.

He sounded confused but not afraid. Chauncey's lip lifted in a nearly unconscious sneer. He hated his own voice. Men like Captain Burlington or Jean Lafitte struck fear in a person with a few words – quiet or loud. This man was tied up, yet Chauncey's voice did nothing to scare him.

Chauncey stood up in a flush of anger, and with one step, he kicked the man's ribs. The man barked out in pain and that made Chauncey feel better.

"I'll ask the questions," Chauncey commanded, trying to make his voice sound more powerful than it was. He couldn't think of a question, so he repeated the man's words. "Who are you, leprechaun? Are you Webley?"

"Webley?" the man asked. "No. My name is Aden Steel. I'm from Washington City. Why did you call me leprechaun?"

Chauncey may not have been intimidating but he did have the talent of knowing when people were lying to him, and this man was lying. Chauncey was not sure if he was lying about his name or about being from Washington City, but he was lying. He'd let it go for now, because he wanted to know about the strange flintlock more than who this man really was.

"Where am I?" Aden asked, squinting as he glanced around. "You knocked me out? Why? What do you want?"

"I want my pot of gold," Chauncey said, holding up the flintlock. "And I want to know more about this."

...erwriter and joint bookmark...

Chapter Two What Went Wrong?

October 15, 1782
One Month Later

An hour ago, an old friend of mine from the twenty-first century showed up, banging on my front door in the middle of the night. *In the year 1782.* How had that happened?

Jake Mendoza was not only a friend of mine, but also the pilot of the blue alien ship that brought me through time, back to this century from 2021. He was about fifty years old, a little overweight and reminded me of the actor Anthony Quinn when Anthony Quinn was in his fifties.

Despite my shock, I invited him inside. We sat in my eclectic home office, drinking strong black coffee that Annie had made for us out of her *special-for-guests-only*, white bone porcelain teacups. I had briefly introduced Annie to Jake, and she could tell that we were uncomfortable talking in front of her. With a polite smile, she had quickly excused herself to give us privacy.

To Jake, it may have looked like a polite smile, but I had

been married to this special woman for the last four years. I knew her irritated look, especially when she painted a smile over it. No matter how big or beautiful her smile was, when she grasped her apron in her strong fingers like she wanted instead to wring my neck, I always knew I'd pay dearly later for whatever unforgivable and unknowing act I had committed. The first opportunity she found to get me alone, she would question me like the Spanish inquisition, wanting to know every detail about Jake and what he wanted of me.

The fireplace in my office had burnt down to glowing red coals. I tossed a few small logs onto them to help warm up the room.

"God, it's good to see you," I said, my mind still reeling from seeing his face. "It's been five years from my point of view. How long ago from yours?"

"About two years," he answered slowly as he sat down across from me. He pointed to my facial hair. "I like the beard."

"I hate it," I said laughing, scratching my fingers through it. "Annie likes it, so I keep it for her."

"That's sweet," Jake said. "But I didn't come here to talk about your beard."

"I didn't think you had. Didn't it work? Didn't I change history?" I asked.

"Oh, it worked," he said, taking a sip of coffee. "You did your job well."

My jaw clenched. "Then why are you here? And where is the ship?"

"The ship is in your workshop," Jake said, pointing toward the barns. "I'm here because Aden needs your help. He's stuck in the year 1814, and I need your help to rescue him."

"1814? The ship is in my workshop? How the fuck did you get the ship in my workshop without me noticing? And

13

what do you mean, Aden's stuck in 1814? What the hell's going on?"

"Aden bought this land," Jake explained. "Or he will, in the future. In fact, he bought the whole Cain's Striker company. Congratulations, by the way. Your company becomes one of the world's largest match companies. Well, until the invention of the lighter, but your company ends up making lighters, too."

"What's that got to do with anything?" I asked. I hated it when people got side-tracked over important business.

"Your grandchildren turned this property into a museum. More of a tribute to you and Annie. It looks almost the same in 2023 as it does now. Aden bought the entire company, and we had the ship moved into the workshop. That way we'd know it was a safe place to go through time. There's another wall with double doors inside the workshop that's not there now. According to our records, you never used that space and never allowed anyone to see behind those doors. The doors were big enough for us to roll the ship through. The weird thing was that you built that wall and designed the doors to only open from the inside. I was surprised to find they weren't there when I arrived. It's one of the many mysteries surrounding the famous Thomas Cain. And why we chose the workshop as our landing point, if you will."

I blinked, trying to absorb all this fantastical information. "Famous Thomas Cain?" I raised an eyebrow at him.

He nodded. "Aden was convinced you were Thomas Nelson. The famous Pale Rider."

"I was. I mean I am. You got me talking about myself like I'm dead. Knock it off."

"Sorry," Jake said, taking another sip of coffee. "It's just so cool, that you're really him. There are so many stories about you, so many theories, the history books mention you in passing but it's all so vague. There's one book written about you that seems creditable."

He pointed to the wall behind me. "And one thing that's different. Later, your grandkids, put up a famous painting by an artist named Hicks on that wall. It's a painting of the British surrendering at Yorktown. You're in the painting on a horse between General Washington and a French guy . . ."

"Lafayette," I finished for him.

"Yeah," he said. "That's the name."

Jake dug into his satchel, pulled out a photograph, and handed it to me. It was a small, three by five-inch photograph of a painting. Sure enough, it was a painting of George Washington on his horse Nelson, and I was next to him on Little Joe with Lafayette on the far side of me. A flood of emotions hit me as I recalled that day.

The smell of the ocean, the cry of the seagulls, the sounds of feet hitting the ground as thousands of British troops marched by, not in disgrace but pure fatigue and wanting to go home. Their musicians playing the tune, *The World Turned Upside Down*. The pain in my leg where I had been stabbed. The pride Washington made me feel for ending the battle without the additional loss of thousands of lives. Most of all, the feeling of relief that I had accomplished my mission and could go back to Annie and live the rest of my days raising my children and not killing people.

This was most likely the only painting of Washington, Lafayette, and myself together. If it wasn't for Jake, I never would have known about this painting. I was grateful that my descendants would have the chance to see it.

I breathed out my heavy emotions to refocus on the reason Jake was here. "What's Aden doing in the year 1814?"

"When I left you and went back to our century," Jake

15

answered as he rotated his right hand in the air, "some things had changed, but the British still rule the States. Not as much of the world as you remember though. You set them back about fifty years, I'd say. Germany is still a free country, holding out. Russia and China are not nearly as close to giving in as they were before. You won the war, and the United States was recognized as a country. And your friend George Washington was elected the first President of the United States, or he will be in a few years."

While my chest fluttered at hearing Washington would become a president, I was disheartened to say the least. Literally, years of my life, the suffering, the killing, and in the end, it had all been for nothing. Why were the British still in control? Could nothing bring them to heel?

"What went wrong?" I asked, shaking my head.

"The War of 1812," Jake answered. "Remember, the timeline had changed, and Aden didn't know about you going back in time. I found Aden, like he'd told me to, and showed him the videos on the cell phone. He thought I was crazy at first, but he went with me to see the ship. After that he was onboard. Aden was always one to see an opportunity. He compared the history he knew from his new timeline to the history on my cell phone, from our timeline."

Jake leaned forward and pressed his hand between his knees. "After studying everything, Aden was sure the War of 1812 is where things went wrong. The British came back and managed to take over the States again. In August of 1814, they attacked Washington D.C., they even burned down the presidential mansion."

"Presidential Mansion?" I asked, not understanding. "What is a *Presidential Mansion*?"

"It's where the different presidents live while in office,"

he explained, shaking his head to dismiss my question. "Anyways, they burned down the mansion, most the government and military buildings, and the Capital building. Aden was even more excited this time than he was last time. After learning that in our timeline he'd sent you back and that you were the Pale Rider, he had the realization that history *could* be changed. That you had changed it and had stopped the British, initially. When he saw for himself what the alien ship could do, we started the whole operation over. This time he was determined to go slow and do everything right. You'll remember we were worried about the government finding out last time? This time, no one was looking for us. We had plenty of time to go slow and do things right."

I sat across with him dumbfounded, my mouth hanging open. To hear all the changes, even though I knew in my head there had to be changes, but to sit in my office and *listen* to it all made my brain numb.

"Aden was so happy that you or a version of you was still alive that he bought your company," Jake continued as if he wasn't shifting the world under my feet. "And we used this place as our headquarters. Better than taking off from a random field. Aden wanted to go back and help the Americans win that war the same way you helped them win the Revolutionary War."

I groaned. Aden was a great guy, but he was a businessman, an entrepreneur. What had he been thinking?

"What happened to Aden?" I asked, afraid of the answer.

"He wasn't as good at it as you were," Jake answered, his voice softening to lessen the blow of the news. "Sorry, I mean to say as good at it as you *are*. Damn past tense and present tense. It's confusing, you know. Bottom line is that he was captured. I didn't know what else to do, so I came here to find you. On the upside, we really did do things right this time. Last time, with you, we were in a rush and had little time to prepare. Everything was just … thrown together. This time we spend two years learning how to control the ship and obtaining the best equipment we could think of."

"So now you want me to go to the year 1814 and save Aden?" I asked slowly, as if trying to make sense of the question myself.

"Save Aden and help the Americans win *that* war," Jake answered. "Aden had a modern pistol, among other items. If the British get their hands on it, who knows what damage it would do to the timeline. I was afraid to go forward in time. Who knows what I would have found? Going back in time was my only choice. So, I came back in time to you for help."

My body ached from hearing him suggest this task, and I rubbed my shoulder where a scar marked my skin jagged and red from a bayonet that had sliced clean through my shoulder. The old injury still throbbed with changes in the weather. And it throbbed now at the memory. All my aches and pains did. I'd thought I was done with this. The prospect of more fighting . . .

Yet, Aden was my best friend, and I owed him everything. If it wasn't for him, I never would have met Annie, never had a family, children, this business . . . Worse, if his gear was compromised, then he may have made things worse than before I had left.

Freaking timelines.

"What kind of pistol did he have?" I asked.

"He took a Webley, 45-caliber, six shot revolver."

That was a fine revolver as far as revolvers went. A little outdated but a reliable pistol. What kind of damage could the British do if they got their hands on it? I rubbed my forehead where a headache was starting to form, along with a plan.

Annie was *not* going to be happy. Knowing I'd have to

suffer her tongue-lashing didn't help my headache at all. I rose and stood behind my desk.

"I'll need new gear and supplies."

"Oh, don't worry," Jake gushed with a big smile on his face as he rose from his chair. "The ship's filled with gear. Aden made sure to have extra gear loaded up in case anything went wrong."

Of course he had. The always pragmatic Aden. I had a dozen questions to ask my friend from the future, but the biggest question right now was, should I tell Annie the truth or lie to her? I spoke the words aloud as I weighed my options, all of which sucked.

"Can't help you there, bud," Jake commented, his right hand twisting a wedding ring around his ring finger. "Your wife, your decision."

Jake had a habit of twisting his wedding ring whenever he thought about his family. The British were responsible for the loss of his wife and kids, as they were responsible for the loss of my first wife. He was doing his part of this mission for the same reason I was. And like me, a different version of him existed in our timeline. I didn't want to ask about his family yet, but if we had saved them, they would be with the alternate version of himself and not with him.

"Then what good are you?" I asked him with a hint of sarcasm before I drained the last of my coffee, hoping to distract him from sad thoughts.

"I fly the ship," he answered with a slight smile as he let go of his ring. "Well, not really fly the ship, I mean it doesn't seem to physically move. But I'm the one who pushes the buttons."

I had some decisions to make but needed more information first. "Then, tell me about this War of 1812," I said, setting my empty coffee cup down on my flat-top colonial desk. "And why Aden went back to the year 1814 and not 1812 or 1811 to prevent it?"

"Tensions between America and England were extremely volatile," Jake said, sipping more of his coffee. He then moved his cup to set it next to mine. "Aden was convinced that the war was inevitable. There was no preventing it. The war was bound to happen eventually, one way or another. There was nothing to change. So, he focused on finding a way to end it that would be most beneficial to the Americans."

I wanted to see the ship again while we talked, so with a motion of my head, I signaled for Jake to follow me out of my office.

"Let's walk and talk," I said, lighting a lantern with one of my matches. "I want to see the Second Chance."

"The British were fighting on too many fronts," Jake continued, as he followed me out of the office. "The mad king was losing the war against Napoleon, so he was trying to negotiate peace with the United States through strength. The king sent thousands of troops to force the Americans into coming back to the Empire."

"Different war, same playbook," I interrupted, walking out the front door.

The cold, crisp night air hit us as we stepped out onto the porch.

"After the Battle of Baltimore, the British signed the Treaty of Ghent," Jake continued, following me out the door. "The war had formally ended on December 24th, 1814. The Americans had once again beaten the British."

"I don't understand," I said, stopping to face Jake. "Who is Napoleon? And if the Americans won the war, then why did Aden go back in time?"

"I'll tell you about Napoleon later," Jake said. "He's not important right now."

Something about *that* rang hollow. "Then tell me why Aden went back to fix something that apparently wasn't broken."

"The Americans won the war of 1812," Jake answered, turning to face me. "But the Treaty of Ghent was signed in the United Netherlands, later to be called Belgium. It would take months for the Empire to notify its officers here in America."

"What happened?" I asked, dropping my head as I walked, not really wanting to know.

"The British were losing in the north, so they attacked the south before the king was able to notify them that the war was over," Jake answered. "In January 1815, the British managed to take control of New Orleans. They moved east from there. When the king was notified about the taking of Louisiana, then Florida, and that his forces controlled these states, he denied knowing anything about the treaty and continued sending more soldiers."

"What happened next?" I asked. We had reached the barn and I paused to pay attention.

"The war continued for another six years," Jake said. "The American President and Congress signed a new treaty. The Treaty of Reunification, which would eventually bring us back into British control. President Monroe was the last freely elected American President."

My hands stopped at the two large double doors. "What was Aden's plan?"

"Aden and I went down to New Orleans. Aden believed that if we defeated the British there, the king would honor the treaty and the war would truly be over."

"Why did the Americans lose at New Orleans?" I asked.

"According to the history books," Jake answered. "The General arrived late. He got to New Orleans after the British. He didn't have enough men, and he was short on cannon fuses or cannonball fuses, I can't remember which, to make his cannons effective."

"I know how that feels," I mumbled, thinking back on a time when I had cannons and cannonballs but no fuses for them.

"What? How is that?" Jake asked.

"Nothing," I said, opening one of the doors to the barn. "I'll tell you about it later. Long story about a short battle."

Jake pulled the second door open with me. "Most of the battles around New Orleans were fought in the swamp, along the Mississippi, or up close in the fog. The Americans were better shots with their longer muskets, but that didn't matter because most of the fighting was close up or with cannons. The British had the advantage of numbers and more disciplined men. They were also in defensive positions, while the General was forced to attack New Orleans and try to overwhelm the British, even though he had less men."

As the barn doors slid open, the oddly familiar alien ship sat at the far end of the barn, in the glow of my lantern's light as if it had a way of attracting, even pulling the light to itself. Aden's experts had determined the ship was made of some sort of metal which looked like blue rock. It was seamless and appeared to have been created of one piece of the mysterious blue material, with a pointy nose that widened like a tear drop, then thinned to about six feet. Good old-fashioned earth steel had been wrapped around the back portion of the broken craft. A bulkhead had been welded to the steel wrapped around the craft, closing off the broken, open compartment. An oval shaped door, three feet wide and five feet long and in the middle of the human made bulkhead, was closed.

Last time I had seen this ship streaks of dried slime, barnacles, and red coral covered it. Now the whole ship had been scraped clean and looked shinier, newer even. When we'd found the ship at the bottom of the ocean, we had no idea how many hundreds or thousands of years it had sat there. I stood frozen in place as if seeing it for the first time.

"Come on," Jake said, pushing me towards the alien craft.

"Why didn't this General have enough men?" I asked, stepping into my barn. If I was going to do anything to help Aden, I needed to focus less on the shiny ship and more on what needed to be accomplished. "If he knew he was going up against the British, why didn't the President give him more men?"

"He would have had twice as many men and might have gotten there before the British, if it wasn't for some battle in Florida," Jake answered, walking next to me as we neared the ship. "Pensacola, Florida, I think."

I stopped to face him. "What happened in Pensacola?"

"The General fought the British there on his way to New Orleans," Jake said. "There was a Spanish fort that the British had taken over. The General attacked and the British retreated."

"Sounds good so far," I interjected, knowing there was a *but* coming.

"But," Jake said right on cue, "the British blew up the fort when their men were running out and the General's men were running in. General Jackson lost half his men and spent weeks taking care of the wounded before he continued to New Orleans. He didn't have enough men to retake the city, and if he'd gotten there before the British, he never could have held it. The General and his men were killed."

"How'd they blow up the fort?" Though my gaze was on

the ship, my mind worked, trying to envision what had happened with this General that had led to disaster.

"No idea," Jake said, shaking his head. "The history books said that the *brave* British had tricked the General and blew it up."

"So why don't I go back to the day you guys got there and stop you?" I asked as I slowly walked around the alien craft, studying it.

"Can't," Jake said, and let that one word set in. "The craft doesn't work that way. I can't pick a day. We've been experimenting with the controls. One dial sets the ship in sixty-one-year leaps as you remember, and we managed to figure out the next controls smaller, ten-year jumps. The last dial sets it in two-year skips. I can only get it down to a two-year interval at best."

I reached out my left hand and let it trail along the edge of the cool blue ship, like the caress of a long-lost lover. "And?"

"Aden was captured a month ago," Jake said. "It took me that long to ride from New Orleans to here. We went back in time, two months ago from my point of view. So, when we go back it will be over a month later from Aden's point of view. Unless you want to hide the ship and wait two years. Then I might be able to get you there before Aden."

"No," I answered and shook my head. "Too many things could go wrong. Someone might find the ship and start asking questions. We leave tonight."

I didn't understand this time travel crap the last time I climbed into that ship. I didn't see any reason why I would understand it any better now, and this time more variables made it even more confusing.

"You said you had equipment on board?" I asked, lifting my right hand to touch the craft with both hands.

Jake stepped up and turned a single handle which opened the rear hatch. As the steel hatch silently swung open on its three freshly greased hinges, I came around to peer inside. The two same seats sat in the middle of the compartment up front. Military grade equipment boxes were stacked on the left side of the seats and in the back. The controls for the ship were in easy reach of the front of the seats and to the right.

Jake climbed in and started handing the boxes out to me. The name *Pelican* was imprinted on the boxes. They looked like standard, impact-resistant, waterproof containers that I was used to, but I had never heard of this name brand. In the timeline I came from, the Royal Tough name brand was the most common equipment case used. Maybe this was one of the changes caused by my fiddling with time. I had to wonder what else I had changed.

I stacked the boxes up on the work benches so I could get a look at everything they had brought.

Opening the boxes one by one, I eagerly examined the twenty-first century gear. I was familiar with what I was looking at, but Jake explained everything as we went, in case of any changes. The first box we opened contained a sword and had an empty spot in the cushion for what must have been a matching blade. Two large hunting knives were next to them, with two empty spots for identical knives. The two knives matched the ones I had brought and recently lost a few months ago. Aden must have employed the same blacksmith. Two brass knuckles laid flat in the dark gray foam cutouts.

"Aden brought two of everything he could think of, and I have one of the knives," Jake told me.

"If that's true, then out of all these weapons, he only took a sword and one knife," I said.

"Yes," Jake responded. "He didn't take much. He wasn't

planning on fighting. He wanted to organize a militia months before this General Jackson ever arrived."

The sword resembled my musketeer's sword, but Jake explained that, like my old knives, they were made from titanium. I had seen swords break before, so it seemed like a sound idea. And this sword was lighter than mine.

In the next box, I found what looked like two matching, beautiful redwood flintlocks, with brass caps on the butt. They were not standard flintlocks – these were modern, twenty-first century pistols disguised to look like eighteenth century flintlocks. The one I had used before ran out of ammunition, and I had destroyed it to avoid it being discovered. It had been a rebuilt Tec-9 pistol constructed into a real German flintlock.

These were a little bigger, and the wooden frame felt wrong. Ten loaded magazines were nestled in cut-outs, five magazines or thirty rounds for each of the two pistols. The magazines were the same size as my old ones, and each magazine held six rounds, as mine had.

"Aden spent a small fortune on these two babies," Jake said, lifting one of the twin redwood and brass pieces of art out of the box. "I think he spent more money on these two pistols than I spent on my new, two-story house. They're not rebuilt Tec-9s, like yours was. They're unique. Based on the same mechanics of the Tec-9, but totally custom and built into a hard red polymer resin body, not wood. The frame is about ten times stronger than a real wooden frame, but the caps are brass. They operate like your pistol did, but with a new upgrade."

He twisted his wrist to the right, flipping the pistol to the side so I could see what he was doing. I shifted over for a better view. Above his thumb was a button. Only it didn't look like a button – it looked like small imperfection in the frame, disguised to look like a protruding wooden knot. His thumb moved up and pushed on the nub.

"It has a laser sight," he said. "Can't see it with the naked eye. Only with the night vision goggles."

"The barrel looks wrong," I said, leaning in closer to examine it.

He tapped on the gun. "The whole barrel is a suppressor. No more screwing it on or off. These are always on."

"I'm sold," I said. "I'll take it. Why did Aden spend so much money on them and then not take one of these?"

"He planned on using one until the last minute," he answered, pointing to the next box in line. "You must remember Aden wasn't raised around or trained in violence like you were. He wasn't trained in a dozen different weapons. He was never comfortable shooting guns like you. He couldn't get the hang of them, so he took one of those instead."

"I had taken at least twice as much ammunition last time," I commented, counting in my head. "I'll have to make do with the sixty rounds. This is a quick mission. Should be more than enough."

The next box held a Webley 45-caliber six shot revolver. A space was cut out for a matching Webley, but that space was empty.

"He really took a Webley?" I asked, shaking my head as my jaw clenched. Seeing the ship had made me forget my headache, but now it returned with a vengeance. "So much for not liking the guns. You fuckers have undone everything I've fought for. This is why Aden never should have gone."

"Yeah. The Webley and thirty rounds of ammunition. He didn't think he'd need a gun at all, but if he did, he wanted it to be something he'd used before."

The Webley company was one of the oldest gun companies still in operation in the twenty-first century. In my time, Webley had set the standard for revolvers. It was a British based company that had been around forever. If the British got their hands on a Webley revolver, they would have the single greatest leap forward in warfare that the world had ever known.

I pinched the bridge of my nose as I cursed under my breath then aloud.

"Damn fool. Smartest man I have ever known, but a damn fool. Let's pray he didn't make things worse. If the Empire gets their hands on that pistol, they'll reverse engineer it and rule the world even sooner than they did before. We'll have accomplished the opposite of what we've been trying to do."

"I know," Jake said, rubbing his hands together nervously. "That's why I was afraid of going back and had to come to you. I was afraid of what I might find."

The next box was a longer rifle case. Inside were two matching Lewis and Sons over-under, double-barrel, hammerless shotguns. They operated on a two-trigger system, not side-by-side triggers but a forward and rear trigger. They had matching, thick, tan leather slings which had stamp impressions of flying ducks on them. I had seen these same shotguns before. Aden and I had shot clay pigeons with them at one of the expensive gentlemen's clubs that he was a member of. British law in the twenty-first century allowed the wealthy, like Aden, to own shotguns if they paid a stamp tax on them and kept them at a club with a royally sanctioned armory.

Two black leather bandoliers rested between the two shotguns. Ten red double-odd buck shells, five green slug shells, and two black shells were tucked in the bandolier.

"The black shells are armor piercing incendiary slugs," Jake explained pointing to the twin black shotgun shells.

"Why did you bring these in the first place?" I asked bewildered as I pointed to the two fine shotguns. "And if Aden took a Webley, why didn't he take one of these as well? I mean, if you're going to fuck up and do something as stupid as bring a Webley, you might as well go all the way. Right?"

"He'd planned on taking one of the shotguns," Jake admitted as he dropped his gaze to his feet, obviously embarrassed to have been part of the whole debacle. "He wanted simple-to-operate weapons that he'd used before and knew how to use. He decided against it at the last minute, saying they were too long and bulky. He couldn't hide it like he could the Webley."

Thank God for small favors, I added silently.

In the next case, I found a black, bullet-proof vest. It looked like my old one, but thicker, and I knew it at once was for me. Between gunshots and water damage, my old vest was not so bullet-proof anymore. This one had two C4 charges in the shape of large buttons like mine once had years ago. I would have to attach the three throwing knives from my old vest to this one. A birthday gift from Annie years ago, the three, six inches long, double-edged knives were solid black steel except for the razor-sharp edges that shined. How she had found a blacksmith on this side of the ocean to make perfectly balanced blades was beyond me. But that was my beautiful wife – loving, considerate, practical, and relentless.

And understanding, I hoped.

"The inside has a thick layer of self-sealing gel," Jake said as he held up the vest and opened it to show me the inside. "Cuts down on and spreads out kinetic energy. Getting shot doesn't hurt as much. Or so they tell me."

The next box was a wooden military crate. I smiled as I recognized it as the same kind of crate that held six grenades last time. Opening the lid with a smile on my face, I was disappointed to find only two grenades in the box, next to four empty slots.

"Aden took four grenades with him?" I asked in surprise.

Jake held up two fingers after setting the vest back down. "Just two. The other two he used to practice throwing. He'd never thrown one before."

I cussed under my breath again.

We spent hours going through the equipment as I pulled out what I wanted and put back everything I didn't. I was able to locate a single box of twenty 30-30 rounds for my Thompson Contender. That made me smile, since I only had two rounds left from my original stash.

"Did Aden take a GPS tracker with him like I did?" I asked as I laid out what I wanted.

"Yeah," he said, nodding his head. "Same kind of tracker. Looks like a powder horn. The battery will last about four months so you can track him with it. But without satellites in the sky, you must be within half a mile to pick it up."

I looked around at the equipment. "Where's the receiver?"

"It's an app on the smart phone," he answered. "I'll show you later."

As we evaluated my selected weapons, I thought about how Jake described the fighting in New Orleans as up close and in the fog or the swamps. I had been to Louisiana once with my father as a boy, and to Florida several times with Aden on business, so I already knew how foggy it could get.

I held up one of the twin Tec-9s to Jake. "Can you shoot a gun?"

"Can I? Yes. Am I any good at it? No."

I set the Tec-9 back in the box, selected one of the double barrel shotguns, and strolled over to my work bench with the built-in vise.

"I noticed a red toolbox behind the seats in the ship," I said, as I tightened the shotgun in the vise. "Tell me you have a hacksaw blade in there."

"Yeah," Jake answered and walked over to the back of the ship and reached in. "As a matter of fact, I do."

Jake pulled out the large red toolbox and placed it onto one of the work benches. He opened the lid and dug through it until he found the hacksaw, then handed it to me. I went to work cutting off first the barrels right where the wooden forearm ended. Next, I cut the wooden stock down, leaving only the curved pistol grip. The whole shotgun was now under two feet long. It would kick like a mule, but it would be easier to hide.

I handed the shotgun to Jake with one of the bandoleers.

"If you have to shoot this, use both hands," I instructed, demonstrating for him. "Hold the front end down with your left hand or the barrel will come up and knock out your teeth."

I had finished picking out the equipment I wanted to keep and was organizing it as Jake loaded up the items I wasn't using back into the ship. My mind was on my work, so the distinct sound of the barn door closing behind me made me freeze in place and cringe. Jake was in front of me, and he also froze, his back and neck muscles bunching up as if understanding what that sound truly meant. I slowly turned around in fear, already knowing what I would see.

Annie stood in front of the now closed barn door, a pot of coffee in one hand and two of her fancy porcelain teacups slung on a finger of her other hand. Her eyes were shocked blue saucers, and her mouth hung open. The two teacups dropped from her hand as she raised her shaking hand and pointed to the ship. As the two teacups shattered against the cobblestone, flinging white chips everywhere, her fingers gave out in her right hand, dropping the pot of coffee. The pot tumbled with a clatter, spraying hot coffee in our direction.

Her shock was not surprising. The ship must have looked like a giant hollowed-out blue boulder to her, and why would such an oddity be in the barn?

"Hi, honey," I said casually and raised my hands to stop her from screaming. "I'll explain everything to you. Please stay calm."

I slowly moved over to her and grabbed her by the shoulders. She allowed herself to be guided to a chair and dropped down into it. A heavy sigh welled in my chest. The damage was done and the choice of whether or not to tell her had been taken from me. I was going to have to tell her the truth and hope for the best.

Two hours and at least fifty questions later, Annie started to believe the truth. She didn't want to believe that I was from the future. And why would she? That her husband, the man she loved and married, was somehow *alien*. She also couldn't come up with a better explanation for the blue alien ship that had somehow ended up in our barn overnight.

Her biggest question was why I had come to this timeline in the first place. Though the answer rolled easily off my tongue, it was more complicated than anything I might tell her. I answered her questions with all the patience in the world, finally getting to the part about the British tyranny in the future.

When I explained to her how the British Empire would one day end up ruling the world, that determined glint came to her eyes and she vowed to help us in any way she could. Considering what we were telling her, I thought she took it very well. She seemed to handle the information we gave her better than I had when I first learned of the alien craft.

Then I told her I was going to need to leave again. That determined glint became an angry glare, and to say she was not happy about me leaving was an understatement. At first, she insisted on going with us until the realization of I might not live to come back sunk in. She needed to raise our children and continue the business if I didn't return.

"Is there anything I can do to help?" she asked as the angry tinge in her voice faded. She grabbed a crescent wrench from Jake's toolbox and studied it like it was a magic wand.

In fact, there was something she could do. I handed her my new vest and asked her to remove the three throwing knives from my old vest and stitch their sheaths on to the left side of this new vest.

"Anything else?" Annie asked.

I tugged on my beard. "You could help shave this off. Not having it helps me feel more like . . . him."

"You mean more like the Pale Rider?"

I nodded my head, hesitant to speak the words in front of her. She seemed more comfortable about saying I was the Pale Rider than I was, as if saying his name aloud invited danger right to our door.

"I'll fetch the razor and a pair of scissors," Annie told me and rose from the chair. She left the barn and returned shortly with her necessaries.

As Jake loaded the unused equipment boxes into the ship, Annie gave me a fresh haircut and shave. I had never grown accustomed to using the straight razor, and every time I shaved, I worried about cutting my own throat. It was the other reason that I let the beard grow.

Annie, however, had a steady hand and confidence with the razor, and I closed my eyes to enjoy the feel of her tender fingers on my skin. When Annie was all done with me and my face was smooth again, for the first time in a year, I started donning my new equipment. I tugged on my original black leather combat boots and wore a pair of black pants specially made for me, complete with homemade cargo pockets sewn onto them. I topped it all off with a loose white shirt.

My new black bullet-proof vest was next, then my shoulder holster and Thompson. The sensation of wearing the vest again gave me mixed feelings, like an old friend I didn't really miss. My own black sword belt with a leather loop for my pistol and three pockets for extra magazines went on over the vest. My brown low cut buckskin coat slipped over it all, covering my shoulder holster nicely.

The buckskin coat had been a gift from Daniel Boone two months ago. We had remained good friends and he came through this area now and then, always stopping for dinner. He'd given me the coat as a gift when I rescued him, after he had been captured by some British in one of the very last battles of the war. They were calling it the Battle of Blue Licks. That had also been when I'd used my last three rounds for my Tec-9, all but two rounds for my Thompson, and I'd lost my two hunting knives.

As was my normal routine, I placed one of my new titanium knives on my belt in the small of my back and the second one in the front on my left hip. It was nice to have them on me, like old friends returned to me, and these ones were welcome.

Annie tried to hand me a hat to cover my recognizable forehead scar.

"No," I said, shaking my head. "No one is looking for the man with a scar this time. I don't need to hide it. Plus, you know I don't like wearing hats."

Annie laughed lightly as she dropped my hat onto the floor and reached up to rub her hands over my now smooth face.

"I miss the beard already," Annie told me with a sigh. Her brogue had thickened because her emotions were strained, to say the least.

"It'll grow back," I reassured her.

Jake wore brown pants and a white shirt. His boots looked like mine but smaller and newer. He had on a brown cloak and liked to wear the hood over his head as though he believed himself as some kind of spy.

He carried a matching satchel, one of the knives, and the shotgun. He also had a smart phone, solar charger, first aid kit, and a purse heavy with gold coins.

I handed Annie a diagram of an add-on wall and told her to have the workers build it while I was gone. I drew the diagram based on what Jake had told me he'd seen in the museum barn before coming to this timeline. Then I pointed to show her where I wanted the new wall added.

"Thomas," Annie said suddenly, grabbing my right arm and stopping me.

Looking into her glistening eyes, I already knew what she was going to say.

"I know," I told her in a low voice. "I'll be extra careful. I promise."

"Don't you dare," Annie said with a scowl on her face and heat in her voice.

I pulled back a little in surprise. "What?"

Her strong hands gripped mine. "You once told me that being too careful meant hesitating. And that hesitation leads to death."

She took a calming breath to start over in her patient way that she used to handle me. "Did I ever tell you what I think of every time I hear the name Pale Rider?"

"No," I answered, not understanding what that question had to do with anything.

"I think about that night on the Johnson's farm when you saved my two little girls from Captain Bonifield. I think about when I left the girls with the horses and ran back to the farm to check on you."

I had no idea where she was going with this, but I was smart enough to keep my mouth shut and allow her to finish what she wanted to say without interruption.

"I remember crossing that wooden bridge," Annie continued, with sadness in her eyes and her voice thick. "The house was on fire, the barn a blaze, horses running in all directions, screaming, and dead British soldiers littered the ground like weeds. Captain Bonifield sat on his horse without even a saddle, running away from the death that had come for him in the form of a lone bloody man with a bayonet still sticking out of his shoulder. I had never seen a sight like that before or since. It was fear and chaos mixed with mayhem and violence. You had killed all but three of his men, and he knew he was next. He looked in your eyes and saw vengeance."

"I killed all but four of his men," I said. "You killed one and saved my life in the doing."

"My point is this." Annie slapped my chest to let me

know she was serious. "That man was the unstoppable force that the British named the Pale Rider. That man called death itself to his side and made it heal like a trained dog. That man caused kings to tremble and armies to run in fear. That man sacked British warships and crossed an ocean to pull off an impossible assassination. *That* man is who your friend now needs."

My chin trembled at the force of her words. I pulled her into my chest and kissed the top of her head without saying anything. I breathed in deeply through my nose, smelling the flowery scent in her hair, hoping I would never forget what it smelled like.

"And now I need that man to do whatever is necessary to bring my husband back to me." Her muffled voice broke, and her tears soaked through my shirt. "I know it's wrong for me to say, but I don't care what you need to do to come back. *You do it.*"

"If that's who I must become again to return to you, then that is who I will become. And God help any man who tries to stop me from returning to you," I said simply. Anything more and my voice would have broken.

We stood in the barn holding one another as time slipped by without notice. This was one of those tender moments in life that comes to your mind when you think of the person you love. Every time I looked in her eyes from now on, I knew this moment between us would flash in my mind.

After waking the kids up, Annie and I explained that I had to go on a business trip, then I kissed them goodbye. Not wanting to appear in the year 1814 in broad daylight, we rushed to leave that night. Annie insisted joining us to watch the ship disappear, so she knew she was not going mad. We climbed into the ship and closed and locked the back hatch.

Jake turned a switch in the back with an audible click,

and four mounted lights flickered on, flooding the compartment in soft red light. Then Jake took his seat and reached down, grabbing seatbelts I had not noticed before, and buckled the seatbelt around his waist. Although the ship didn't physically move, this seemed like a reasonable addition to the ship's safety equipment, so I snapped mine on as well.

Jake turned the second and third dials. The last time I had been in the ship, we avoided touching those dials and stuck to the first dial only. When he pressed what he called *the enter button*, a blinding white light flashed just like last time, and I flung my arm across my eyes.

And, like last time, the air grew thick, and I tasted ozone in my mouth as my fillings vibrated in my teeth.

screenwriter and joint bookrunner.

Chapter Three New Orleans

September 19, 1814

Chauncey strode to the blacksmith's shop, stopping across the street and a few shops down, where he had a good view of the front door and two picture windows. The streets bustled with people buying or selling their mostly stolen goods. This area of the city always smelled like piss, yet it still smelled better than other parts of the city. Two flies refused to leave him alone. They kept landing on his ear with an annoying buzz, and he missed when he tried to slap them away.

It was broad daylight and he searched around for any familiar faces. He had started to feel like a man with a price on his head. Captain Burlington would be the only person looking for him and he didn't know yet why Chauncey was hiding. The others must have told the captain about the stranger they'd sacked, and that Chauncey chose not to kill the man and roll his body into the water. Burlington would demand answers to why, that much was certain.

Chauncey gripped his new sword and knife in his left hand and wore the man's satchel across his body. The man's flintlock was hidden in the satchel. He had his own flintlock in the front of his belt, but he'd not need to draw it once he was inside the blacksmith's shop.

If he was going to keep this Aden stranger hidden from everyone while managing to stay hidden from Captain Burlington himself, he was going to need more coin. The shop looked busy, and Chauncey heard hammering over the buzz of conversation, of hawkers selling their goods, and of the flies. The hammering meant Granger was in his shop working away at some stupid piece of metal over hot coals.

Chauncey had never heard the immense blacksmith talk. He wasn't sure the man *could* speak, but he figured the smith must be French like the two Lafitte brothers. The good news was that he didn't see Captain Burlington or any of the men from the ship.

The bad news was that he'd not seen Pierre Lafitte either. Chauncey didn't want to be seen in the shop until he knew for certain that Pierre was present. If Burlington was looking for him, word would get back to him quickly that Chauncey was at the shop. He needed to be fast and that meant not sitting around in the shop waiting for Pierre or his brother to return.

Chauncey hovered inside the doorway of Johnson's butcher shop. Slaughtered pigs hung upside down behind the counter so the customers could see the meat was fresh. Mr. Johnson was busy with a customer, but he'd been watching Chauncey like a hawk. Most likely Johnson would kick Chauncey out if he didn't buy something soon. Chauncey didn't think he had ever stolen from Mr. Johnson, but Chauncey had a reputation of having loose fingers.

Chauncey waved a hand in front of his face, shoeing away a fat fly that had landed on his nose, when Pierre Lafitte appeared, sauntering down the street. The older of the two Lafitte brothers, he was dressed in expensive clothing, as usual, and walked with a finely etched, bone-topped cane he did not need to use. He carried a sword on his hip and was well skilled with it, but Chauncey knew firsthand that Pierre preferred to use the cane as a weapon. The cane looked like a thin piece of dark wood, but it was actually a thin steel bar forged by the giant blacksmith, painted to look like wood. Most people didn't expect Pierre to use the cane and were surprised when he chose the cane to attack. Pierre sauntered straight into the blacksmith shop like he owned the place, which he in fact did.

Chauncey glanced around the street again for any shipmates who might be searching for him, and when he didn't see any he stepped out of the Butcher's shop, crossing over as fast as he could without running or bringing attention to himself.

Chauncey entered the blacksmith shop, and a wave of heat from the furnace struck him as soon as he entered the doorway. He searched the shop but didn't see Pierre. Grim-faced Granger, clad in a leather apron, was striking a piece of glowing red-hot metal with an oversized hammer. It looked like he was banging out a large knife. Sweat poured from the man's bald head and down his stern face. Swinging that hammer every day gave the man arms larger than Chauncey's thighs. Granger hit the glowing piece of metal again with an ear-splitting clang, and as he brought the hammer back up, he paused to level a flat look at Chauncey.

Disregarding Chauncey, he returned his attention to the piece of metal he was working on, and the hammer slammed back down. Granger had seen Chauncey in the shop enough to know he was there to sell some stolen property to Pierre, so

Granger dismissed him.

Chauncey ambled past Granger as the man ignored Chauncey as he always did. Granger was known for being overly protective about Pierre, and Chauncey hated that Granger never saw him as a threat.

Chauncey strode to the back office where he knew Pierre would be. He didn't knock on the open door but lingered in the doorway, waiting to be noticed by Pierre who sat at his desk and read some papers while drinking wine. His lieutenants, Oliver, Pete, and Henry, leaned against the far wall. They watched Chauncey as though they didn't trust him, but none of them said a word. They were parasites, licking the Lafitte brother's boots, scrambling for whatever scraps were thrown their way.

"Burlington is looking for you," Pierre intoned in his French accent. He sipped his wine while still reading, not looking up at Chauncey.

Though Burlington was the captain of his own ship, many captains in the New Orleans worked for the Lafitte brothers in one way or another. It only made sense that Burlington came by the night before or this morning, looking for Chauncey. Or one of his shipmates to let Pierre know that Burlington was looking for him.

Chauncey still loitered in the doorway and ignored Pierre's comment. "I have something special for you."

"For me?" Pierre asked in a bored tone, keeping his gaze on his papers. "Or to sell to me? If it's to sell to me, then it's not for me, it's for you. *Oui?*"

"Yes," Chauncey said. "To sell to you. But like I said, it's special."

Pierre finally raised his annoyed gaze up at him. Chauncey lifted his left hand, displaying the sword and knife, and told him about how he came upon the items.

"Who's the gentleman you sacked?" Pierre asked. One eyebrow on his narrow face shifted higher than the other, revealing his piqued interest. "Is he dead? Can I sell them, or do I need to put them in the warehouse for a few months? Your mates reported that he had a friend who got away."

"No," Chauncey said, not wanting to lie to this man. He knew what came of that poor decision. He walked into the office and stood directly in front of Pierre's desk with the weapons, so Pierre might get a better look at them. "He's alive but not a problem. I don't know who his friend was, so yes, the warehouse is a good idea."

...rewriter and joint bookbinders.

Chapter Four Collecting a Debt

October 16, 1814

The surge of bright light ended as fast as it had appeared, and we were again bathed in red light. Jake unbuckled his seat belt and moved to the rear of the ship, and I followed. Turning off all the lights, he touched something. The sound of a lock click came to my ears and the door opened. There wasn't any direct light outside, but it was less dark. We were obviously still in my workshop, but it was somehow *different*. A desk sat against the wall with an old dusty lantern atop it. A new wall stood a few feet from the ship that had not been present a few minutes ago when we'd left. Annie must have had the workers build it like I had asked. Cobwebs covered the desk, lantern, and walls.

The place looked abandoned.

Pulling one of my strikers out of my vest coin pocket, I lit the dusty lantern and examined the new brick wall and wooden, double barn doors. As Jake had told me, a drop down bolt had been constructed on the inside of the doors. The room appeared as if it had been untouched for decades, except for two sets of footprints that marked a trail in the thick layer of dust on the floor. I grabbed Jake's arm, stopping him, and pointed down to the footprints.

"That's from Aden and I, three months ago when we first arrived," Jake explained.

Jake lifted the bolt and opened the doors. I followed him out of the room, as he mostly closed the doors and then, using a knife between the two doors, he forced the bolt up shutting the doors the rest of the way. Lowering his knife, he locked the bolt into place. We made our way to the main doors of the workshop and crept outside as quietly as possible. I saw the outline of my house from where I stood and briefly wondered if Annie was asleep next to a different and much older version of me.

The rest of the property hadn't changed much either. Next to us was the horse barn, and I moved quietly over to look inside. The door opened easily enough and didn't creek on it hinges. It was reassuring to know that the farm was still well-kept. Slipping inside the barn, I peered into the darkness, looking for my old friend that I hoped to see.

The name *Little Joe* was painted on his stall door in bright yellow letters. Under his name in smaller letters was the name *Buttercup*, what the girls had called him. But I didn't see my horse. The stall was empty, cleared of everything, including hay. A tear ran down my cheek as I acknowledged the meaning of this.

Little Joe was gone. He had been my first friend when I stepped off the ship in 1777. I had killed his owner, a British soldier who tried to kill me, took Little Joe for myself, and we bonded more than I thought possible for a horse and rider. In my head, I knew he would be still waiting for me when I returned to the year 1782, but right now in this year, he waited for me no longer. My chest hitched as I stared into the empty stall.

I didn't know if I had painted the name Little Joe on the door, marking it as forever his, or if Annie and the girls had done that for me. The girls never stopped calling the cowardly horse Buttercup. I liked the thought that he would always have a place here in this barn. The other horses began to stir at my presence, and I slipped out before they made a racket.

"What were you doing in there?" Jake whispered to me.

"Just needed to check on something," I told him as I wiped the tear that ran down my face.

We needed to get to Philadelphia, but I was not willing to steal my own horses, so we were going to have to walk. It was only a few miles, and I had ridden to town many times with Little Joe, so I knew the way by heart. Once we trudged into town, we wanted to ensure we did not run into anybody who knew me, so we searched for an inn that had been recently built.

After paying for one room for the both of us, we sat down at the rickety table in the room to plan. We decided to secure a ship to New Orleans, which would be faster and easier than us riding horses the whole way down. Before going anywhere, I wanted to go to Washington City that Jake had told me about. We needed to locate information, and I figured that city would be the best place to start. Using Jake's smart phone, I researched my friends to determine who was still here and might be best to help us.

General George Washington had died in 1799, which saddened me greatly. He had been a great man despite our disagreements, and I would never forget the day I met him in that tavern. If I made it back to the year 1782, I would have to remember to take a trip and visit him one more time. A part of me was happy that the country appreciated my friend General Washington enough to name not only a city after him, but the capital of the country.

I then looked up Marie Lafayette and discovered that he had returned to France and assisted in their own revolution. My lips curled up at that. I was sure he'd done more than *assist*. He would not be able to help us, but I wondered what kind of adventures he had been up to since last I saw him. I had to admit, I really missed Marie and his wry personality.

I considered Daniel Boone. This type of . . . whatever you would call what we were doing, mission perhaps . . . was right up the old trailblazer's alley. But if he was still alive, he wouldn't have the kind of information I needed, and he'd be too old to help us. I was sure he would have been willing to try, but he was probably living in a log cabin somewhere in the mountains of middle-of-nowhere Kentucky. It might take me longer to find Daniel than to find Aden. I wasn't a mathematician, but even I could add up *those* numbers.

Alexander Hamilton, like General Washington, was also deceased. He had been killed in a pistol duel in 1804 by a lawyer and upstart politician named Aaron Burr. I had never heard of this Aaron Burr before, but the article said he fought in the war so I may have run across him. I found myself briefly wondering if I should look him up and seek revenge before considering that Hamilton had always been opinionated and may have gotten himself into his own trouble. Don't get me wrong – I liked the guy, he was always nice to me, and Washington had a soft spot for him – but I liked him a little less after Jake had told me that Aden figured out I was Thomas Nelson after reading a book called *The Pale Rider* written by, yes, Alexander Hamilton.

The little shit.

Only one name remained that I could think of who might still be alive and help. It turned out that he was alive and now a member of Congress, representing the state of

Connecticut. He was also the President of a bank called the Phoenix Bank, and conveniently enough, Washington City had a bank branch, almost. The branch wouldn't officially open until 1815, so I gambled on the odds that he might be there, overseeing the construction of the bank.

The next morning, we bought two horses and headed for Washington City.

"I don't like this, Thomas," Jake announced from the back of his horse as we rode.

"What's to like?" I asked, glancing back at him, trying to figure out what he wanted from me.

"I'm worried about Aden," he said. He kicked his horse to ride up alongside of me. "He was captured a month ago. I don't think we have time to go to Washington City. We need to ride straight to New Orleans. We don't even know if he's still alive or not."

"He was captured a month ago," I said. "We'll be going by boat, so it will only take us half that time to get there. We could spend a year down there looking for him. This way we might get some useful information that will help us find him."

It took us several days to get to Washington City, and that gave Jake and I some time to catch up on our lives when I was able to distract him long enough from worrying about Aden. Jake did not tell me right away, but I had pressured him to tell me about Jenny. It turned out that history had repeated itself, and Jenny had been assaulted and murdered in the new timeline as well as the old. When I inquired why Aden had not asked the alternate version of me to go to New Orleans instead of himself, Jake informed me that in the new timeline, I was not released from military custody but was hanged.

Ouch.

Having heard enough of *that* timeline, I regaled Jake with

48

stories about Annie, Molly, Regan, George, and little Marie. I was afraid I insensitively talked too much about them and how happy I was in my new life. At times, when I found myself prattling on about my life, family, and happiness, Jake grew quiet and his eyes filled with sadness and tears, as I presumed he thought about his own family lost at the hands of the British.

I didn't ask Jake about his family at all but decided to wait and let him bring the topic up. Either the timeline had not changed for them, and they were still dead, or it had changed, and his wife was now married to a different version of him, and his children called *that* man their father. Either way, he had to be heartbroken over it and must have felt alone.

The days spent riding were otherwise uneventful. We rode at a manageable pace, staying at inns when we could, sleeping under the stars when we couldn't. Jake had asked about General Washington and what kind of man he was, and that sent me into another whirlwind of tales. Then he asked about being the Pale Rider and wanted to know the real story behind the name.

That was even more of a story, and I gave him all the details.

We were only a day away from Washington City when Jake pulled on his reins, stopping his horse. He seemed to want to talk again, so I turned my mount around and came up beside him.

"What's on your mind?" I asked.

"Are you happy?" Jake asked, looking over his horse's head at me. "In your new life, I mean."

"Yes," I told him honestly with a smile. "Very happy. I have Annie and the kids."

"Good," Jake responded, nodding his head. "I'm happy for you. You deserve it. I'm glad you were able to build a new life here."

I gave him a sardonic half-smile. "Don't get me wrong. There's a lot about the twenty-first century that I miss."

"Not the traffic or smog," Jake joked.

"No, not the traffic or smog," I confirmed. "I do miss indoor plumbing. I'd kill for a toilet in the house. I still hate having to walk to the outhouse in the rain."

Jake nodded. "I can understand that. Anything else?"

"God, yes," I said, almost gushing. "Movies, hotdogs, phones, and dentists. A real dentist, I mean. Here, you're lucky if you can find a doctor who doubles as a dentist. Hell, you're lucky if you can find a doctor who doesn't want to put leeches on you for everything that hurts. I once had food poisoning. Annie was scared and called for the doctor. The bastard brought in a jar full of leeches. I had to pull a knife on the man to get him to leave me alone."

"You know, you could come back with us, if you chose to. I mean back to the year 2023. Or we could take you to 2021 when you left," Jake said quietly.

I shook my head slowly. "No. Even with the stuff I miss, I'm happier here and now. I have my farm, my family, and my new business. Ever since the war ended, life has been nice and quiet."

"I get that. I knew you'd say no. But I had to ask."

"What about you?" I asked, pointing at him. "Are you happy?"

Jake twisted his wedding ring around his finger. "I'm happy to be here. I'm happy to be helping you and Aden hurt the Empire."

"But?" I asked.

"I don't belong here in this timeline," Jake admitted. "And with the alternate me back there, I feel like a copy of a person in the new timeline. I'm a man without a home, Thomas. I have no family or timeline that I belong to."

"I'm sorry, Jake," I said. "I didn't think…"

Jake waved off my apology. "Aden took me in. He took me in and gave me a purpose. We spent these last two years planning his mission, wanting to do it right. He gave me something to focus on besides my problems."

I realized in that moment that Aden had become Jake's lifeline to sanity, which was why Jake seemed so desperate to save him. And in light of Jake's few comments about his own family, either dead or alive, I understood that they were no longer his.

Jake's sadness reminded me of why I came here in the first place. Why history needed to change. It stoked the flames inside me that had cooled these past three years, smothered by contentment and happiness.

"My family is alive, Thomas," Jake said, as a tear ran down his cheek. "I saw them. All of them. I almost ran to them but…"

"The alternate you was there with them," I finished for him.

He didn't answer but nodded his head.

"I had the same dream over and over my first year here," I told him as I ran my fingers through my hair. "It was that same scenario. I truly can imagine how you felt."

"They looked so happy," he said, wiping tears with the pad of his palm. "I couldn't confuse them by intruding."

"At least they're alive," I told him. "You can find comfort in that."

We finished riding the last day to Washington City in silence.

What we found in this metropolis called Washington City horrified me. Government and military buildings had been broken into, ransacked, and burnt to the ground. Civilian businesses and homes had also been destroyed, razed to nothing. The entire city stank of wet, burnt wood. Jake said that he and Aden had traveled through the city right before the British had attacked it. The fires had been so out of control it was only by the grace of God that a storm came through, and rainstorms put out the fires.

"This looks like a raid more than an attack," I said, pointing to destroyed structures. "What did the British hope to accomplish?"

"Aden thought they were trying to pull American troops away from the Canadian border," Jake answered. "The British didn't like us being so close and there were several incidents up there."

American soldiers and civilians alike were trying to rebuild the city and hauling burnt timber away in wagons, while others rebuilt the structures with brick rather than wood. After questioning a few soldiers, we received directions to the Phoenix Bank and made our way to it. Many of the streets were blocked off, either from lumber being hauled away, or new buildings being built. The streets ran with rumors that the President had fled the city, or that he'd returned and planned an attack on the

British. I had no idea what the truth was, nor did I care. I was here to save Aden this time, not some short President named Madison.

Jake and I sat on a bench and watched the half-built bank's front doors for about an hour before a man in his sixties strode out. His short gray hair, fancy black suit, and white shirt with ruffles in the front that protruded between his open coat, told me all I needed to know.

He strolled with a fancy, silver-handled wooden cane with a brass tip at the end. Two younger men in their 30s followed several feet behind him. They were rough looking men in cheap suits. Bodyguards. As they marched behind the older man like former soldiers, I caught the glint of flintlock in their belts under their jackets.

"Is that him?" Jake asked, pointing to the old man.

I slapped Jake's hand down "Yes. Don't point."

"Who are the two men with him?" he asked, rubbing the back of his hand where I'd slapped him.

"Footmen would be my best guess."

"Footmen?"

"Bodyguards," I explained.

A fancy open carriage pulled by two white horses pulled up to the front of the bank. The carriage driver didn't move but one of the cheaply dressed footmen stepped forward and opened the door to the carriage for the old man. After he climbed into the carriage, the two footmen followed, slamming the door behind them. Jake and I mounted our horses and followed at a distance as the carriage rolled out of the financial district and into an expensive, upper-class residential neighborhood.

The carriage rode up to what could only be described as a mansion on at least five acres of land. It was a white, two-story plantation-style mansion with giant white columns in the front entrance. An eight-foot rock and mortar wall wound around the whole property with ornate wrought iron at the front gate. It was the only property in the neighborhood that had a wall. Most of the properties appeared friendly and welcoming. A few brick houses boasted decorative, three-foot wooden fences around them, but this was the only property with a solid wall. Two soldiers stood guard at the gate as sentries.

The added security made sense. The man was a member of Congress, and Washington City had been attacked by the British six weeks ago. Seeing American soldiers at the front gate was not too surprising.

"What now?" Jake asked, lifting his chin at the soldiers. "Do we go up to the gate and ask to speak to your friend?"

"No. I don't think he'll want to talk to me. We'll have to come back after dark and come in uninvited."

"Well, would it be ok if we went and got something to eat while we waited for it to get dark?" Jake asked.

I smiled at him. "Sure. No harm in us getting some food while we wait."

We sat at a corner restaurant, drinking wine and eating quail, carrots, and cornbread as the sun went down. We took our time riding back towards the white mansion. When we got close, I noticed the sentries had been replaced by different soldiers. We didn't go near the front gate but instead rode around the property to the back portion of the wall. The grass was high, and trees clustered the property behind the mansion, making for good cover.

Standing on our horses' saddles, we were able to sit down on the wall, throw our legs over and drop down onto the grass between two large rose bushes. A second house was behind the main house, most likely servants' living quarters.

The back wall was about four hundred feet from the rear house, and the entire property was dark. The wall, trees, and houses blocked most of the moonlight. It was the perfect opportunity to put on my new night vision goggles. When I did, the yard lit up in the same green hue that my old pair had, but clearer. This newer pair cost Aden thirty thousand dollars each, according to Jake, and was worth every penny. This pair was also not as bulky as my old pair, resembling skiing goggles. They had two settings, night vision and thermal. Aden took one pair, and I now wore the other. Jake had to rely on me, since he didn't have a pair.

We crept around the rear house, not knowing if any of the servants were awake or not. With the goggles on, I could see one of the two bodyguards from earlier sitting in a chair on the back patio of the main house. He was obviously guarding the rear door while he smoked a pipe. If I didn't have night vision goggles on, I might not have seen him until it was too late. I signaled for Jake to wait against the wall while I dealt with the bodyguard.

I stayed in the darkest reaches of the yard and made my way past the back of the house, coming to the side of it. Creeping slowly and quietly, I made my way to the back patio. With a quick peek around the corner, I watched the bodyguard pack more tobacco into his pipe and puff on it to keep the tobacco lit. In the green haze of the night vision, his pipe lit up like a beacon. The sweet smell of burning tobacco reached my nose, as I started moving towards the man, one slow step at a time. Every step was placed carefully, heel to toe, the way Daniel Boone had taught me.

I kept moving until I was right behind him, stopping a mere two feet away.

I had gone up against men who did not need to hear or

see me to sense I was present. Thank goodness this man did not have that ability.

And in that moment, it was like the last three years fell away and everything came back to me as though I had done just this sort of thing yesterday.

My right arm shot out like a snake and around his neck. My right hand secured my left bicep as I tightened my arm, and his throat pressed into the bend of my elbow. My head was turned to the left, chin down, the side of my head pushing against the back of his, to prevent him from head butting me. My hand had knocked the pipe out of his mouth, and it skidded across the ground, sending tiny sparks of lit tobacco onto the patio.

His hands rose up in surprise and panic, grasping my right arm and trying to pull me off his throat as he struggled to stand. I pulled back and down, using my weight to keep him in his seat as my bicep and forearm squeezed on his carotid arteries on both sides of his neck, cutting off the blood flow to his brain. Three seconds later, he was unconscious; hands dropped to his sides and his whole body went limp, nice and quiet.

I lowered him to the ground. trying not to cause any more damage, placing him onto his stomach. I whistled for Jake, and he ran up.

"That was awesome," Jake whispered excitedly, looking down at the unconscious man. "He had no idea what was happening until it was too late."

I ignored his childlike excitement. "Get that duct tape out of your satchel. Tape his hands and feet together and put a piece across his mouth."

As Jake taped up the bodyguard, I made my way to the double doors to find that they were locked. Using one of my throwing knives, I was able to force the lock open. With a creak of wood and a squeal from the hinges, the doors opened outward.

We found ourselves in the dark, empty kitchen. Moving through the doorway and into the hall, I noticed illuminated lanterns in what had to be the parlor and main room of the house. The light was too much for my night vision goggles and canceled them out, so I turned them off and tucked them back in my satchel. We moved to the stairs and I pointed to the floorboards next to the wall, indicating for Jake to walk up the stairs as close to the wall as possible to prevent creaking floorboards. We made it to a hallway at the top of the stairs with several rooms but only one with an open door and a lantern lit inside.

Two men were talking in that room, accompanied by the sound of a pendulum swinging from a clock. We slowly made our way to the door and peeked around the open doorway. The back of the second bodyguard was visible. He sat in a chair on this side of the desk and spoke to somebody on the far side. He sat high enough up that his body blocked out the other person, but his voice was familiar enough to me that I knew this was the man I sought. A dark brown bookcase filled with books lined one wall to my right. A tall grandfather clock was against the opposite wall, ticking away as the pendulum swung back and forth.

Withdrawing my Tec-9, I quietly stepped in the room behind the bodyguard. I flipped the pistol in the air and caught it upside down by the barrel at the halfway point.

The bodyguard either sensed or heard me and turned around as I swung my pistol down to strike the man in the head. He dropped out of the chair and onto the floor like a sack of potatoes.

Blood flowed into his hairline, but I could see his chest

heaving so I figured he would live.

The older man sitting at the desk jumped to his feet and shoved his chair backwards. His eyes locked on me, bulging. His mouth hung open and his face drained of its blood. He flopped back into his chair, not able to talk or take his eyes off me. Jake had walked into the room behind me, but I did not think he noticed Jake.

"Good evening, Benjamin," I said casually as I sat in a chair across from him, in front of his desk. "How have you been? You're well, I hope."

Benjamin Tallmadge cringed in his chair with terror in his eyes, as if he was looking at a ghost. From his point of view, I guess he was.

"You," Tallmadge sputtered, pushing back in his chair even more. "Are you real? Is it really you?"

"Yes, Benjamin. I'm real. It's really me."

Tallmadge shook his head, disbelieving. "This can't be. You look the same as you did thirty years ago."

"Thirty-two years ago," I corrected, slipping my pistol back into my belt loop. "But who's counting?"

"You haven't aged a day. How is that possible?" Tallmadge jabbed his right forefinger at me.

"We can talk about that later," I said and pulled a torn piece of map out of my pocket, setting it on his desk. "Did Washington give you a message for me after Yorktown?"

"He said you wanted to talk to me," Tallmadge answered as he leaned slightly over his desk and looked down at the unconscious bodyguard. "I believe he implied you were upset with me and that I might not survive the conversation. Why do you think I've had protection with me all these years? Why do you think I built a wall around my property? Had soldiers at my gate?"

I flapped my hand at him, though I already knew the answer. "You tell me."

"Knowing my name was on the Pale Rider's list of people to kill is somewhat unnerving," he explained.

"I need something from you." I spoke as levelly as I could so as to not overwhelm him more then he already was.

Tallmadge tilted his head, noticing Jake for the first time, and then gave me a suspicious look. "Who's your friend?"

"An old friend," I said. "Don't worry about him."

"Spanish?" Tallmadge asked, examining Jake from head to toe.

Jake wasn't dark-haired or Spanish in any strong sense, at least in my opinion, but his skin was more tanned than my pale body. His grandfather had originally come from Spain, and Jake retained many of the Spanish traits, like thick eyebrows and deep age lines. Jake also spoke Spanish fluently, not that Tallmadge knew that.

"I was born here in the colonies," Jake answered him in his naturally perfect English.

I rapped my knuckles on Tallmadge's desk, bringing his attention back to me. "I'll give you a choice of two options. One, we can talk about that piece of map with your initial on it that I've kept all these years, and about the map Captain Brant had with him when he kidnapped my wife. Or two, you can write a letter of introduction for me and provide me with some information."

In reality, I had only kept the torn piece of map for a year now, though as far as he knew, I had kept it for the past thirty-three years. I could see how that might look a little obsessive, which was the impression I wanted to give.

"Who do I write the letter to?" He sat up straight in his chair. "And what information do you need?"

I'd had a feeling he would not want to discuss the map issue. I needed him, so I was going to let him skate by without discussing it. If he had admitted out loud that he had provided the map to Brant, I would have killed him without hesitation. I don't think I could have stopped myself, information or no information.

"Who did the President send to New Orleans to stop the British?" I asked. It was an easy question as I already knew the answer, but I wanted to see if he would tell me the truth.

"New Orleans?" he asked, his eyebrows furling as he tried to figure out what that had to do with me. "How would I know? I'm a member of Congress, yes, but the President does not confide in me."

My jaw clenched, and I stabbed my finger toward him. "You were Washington's master spy. I doubt this President wipes his ass without you learning what color his shit was."

"Yes, well," Tallmadge stuttered as he straightened his coat to stall for time. "I'm not a spy these days."

I didn't say a word and kept my level stare locked onto him. It didn't take long.

"The President ordered the Secretary of War, James Monroe, to send Andrew Jackson to protect and defend New Orleans from any and all enemy forces." He finally broke the silence. "He ordered General Jackson to go there and stop the British's advance. How do you know about that? It's a secret."

"Then that is who you will write to," I told him as I slid his ink bottle and quill pen closer to him. "Write a letter to this Jackson fellow. Tell him that I represent Congress in this matter and should be given every courtesy. That he should consider me your personal eyes and ears until the British are defeated."

He crossed his arms over his chest. "I will write no such letter. I don't have that authority, and more importantly, you don't represent Congress in any manner."

I closed my eyes, and reaching up with my right hand, I pinched the bridge of my nose as the grandfather clock got louder and louder, *tick tock, tick tock, tick tock.*

"Fine," I said, with a flip of my hand, opening my eyes again. "I respect and admire you for that."

I flattened out the torn piece of map and shoved it across his desk to him with my index finger.

"However," I said, releasing the torn piece of map as I leaned back and crossed my arms, mimicking him, "you played a dangerous game with the devil years ago. Now the devil will have his due. You'll pay what you owe me. Let's talk about how Captain Brant had one of *your* maps in his possession."

Tallmadge stared at the torn piece of map with the letter *T* written on it. The torn piece of paper had been ripped from one of Tallmadge's personal maps in 1781 and matched a map that a man named Joseph Brant had with him when he kidnapped my wife. Brant's goal was to bait me into coming for him, as he had been sent by the king of England to kill me.

Unfortunately for him, his plan partially worked, and I had gone to him. I thought I had killed the man, but later learned through General Washington that he had somehow survived.

The grandfather clock kept ticking away as his face tightened and he considered his options. *Tick tock, tick tock, tick tock.*

Without another word, Tallmadge reached into his desk and pulled out a piece of fancy, thick paper and an equally fancy envelope. When Tallmadge was done writing the letter, he blew on it a few times to dry the ink and handed it to me. I read the letter, and when I was satisfied, I tri-folded it and placed it in the envelope. The envelope I tucked in the inside pocket of my vest.

"Are we done here?" Tallmadge asked as he stood up, eager to escort me out.

"No," I said. "I still need some information."

He dropped back down into his seat, crestfallen. "About?"

"The British. I have a friend who was captured down south, in New Orleans. I need to know where the British are camped."

"As far as I know, the British aren't down there yet," he stated, appearing confused. "You must be mistaken."

"I'm not. They must have a small advance party somewhere down there. My friend was captured last month."

"Not by the British," Jake interrupted.

Tallmadge and I turned our heads together to look at Jake.

"What?" I asked.

Jake shifted from one foot to the other. "I never said he was captured by the British."

I held up my finger to Tallmadge, indicating that I needed a moment. I rose from my chair and stepped towards Jake. Then I grabbed him by the arm and yanked him a few feet away from the desk.

"What the hell do you mean, he wasn't taken by the British?" I asked, leaning close to his ear, and whispering harshly. "You're making me look stupid in front of this man."

"I mean, he wasn't taken by the British," Jake said defensively. Repeating himself was not helping.

"When you said he was captured, I assumed you meant by the British. If it wasn't the British, then who captured him?"

"Pirates," Jake said.

I gripped his arm hard enough to leave marks. "Pirates? How did he get captured by pirates? Were you guys on some sort of ocean cruise?"

Jake shook his head hard. "No. We weren't on some sort of ocean cruise. We were, in fact, in New Orleans trying to recruit men for the war and buy some canon fuses."

He wasn't making any sense. "If you weren't on a ship, then how was he captured by pirates?" I asked.

"Aden insisted on recruiting men from the harbor. We got jumped. One of the men whacked Aden in the head with a stick, knocking him out. They came at me, but I ran and was able to get away. But I saw them clear as day and I'm telling you, they were pirates. Not soldiers. He was abducted."

"And you never thought to mention this before now?" I complained.

"Who else would have captured him in New Orleans? The British aren't even there yet. I thought pirates was implied."

Letting go of Jake's arm, I blew out a long breath. I stepped back to the desk and resumed my place in the chair.

"It seems you are correct, Benjamin," I admitted through gritted teeth. "My friend was not taken by British soldiers after all, he was taken by... pirates. Abducted as it was. Any idea who would have done that?"

"If it was pirates," Tallmadge drawled, his face showing no surprise to the new information, "and it was in New Orleans, then you will be wanting to speak to the Laffite brothers."

"Who?"

Tallmadge's fingers fanned out across the surface of his desk. "Jean and Pierre Laffite. "They're pirates. They do most of the privateering down in those waters. Jean is the brains and the brawn of the operation. Pierre is the older of the two and the face of their operations. He owns a blacksmith shop in New Orleans and runs a warehouse of stolen goods that they sell. Pierre is the broker of the operation. They may have nothing to do with your friend's disappearance, but if not, they'd know who did."

"How do you know of them?" I asked.

"Like you said," he answered. "It's my job to know these things. Plus, they have about a thousand pirates in total working for them. It seemed wise to know who they were."

"A thousand?"

"Maybe not working directly for them," he clarified. "But at least a thousand pirates come to them to sell their pirated goods. To say they have influence over a thousand pirates may be more correct. Your friend will either be dead or chained up, impressed into work on one of those ships. Jean Laffite would most likely know but he's harder to find. He'll be on his ship out at sea or in their hideout, fortress really. Pierre Laffite should be easier to find. He'll probably be in the city."

I let this information process for a few moments. "Anything else you can tell me?"

"I can tell you that Pierre Laffite is only motivated by money," Tallmadge said.

"And his brother?"

"If I remember correctly, he has certain *desires*," Tallmadge said. "Unusual desires for a pirate. He's a man without a country. From what I understand, he wants to belong to something, to somewhere."

"Then you will write one more letter for me," I told him.

"To whom?" Tallmadge picked up his quill.

"To Jackson again," I answered. "Telling Jackson that the President is offering a pardon for all crimes to any man who joins the good general in the fight against the British. He will need the manpower. It may motivate this Jean Lafitte to join in with his men. Later, you can claim to the President that you did this in his name or deny it. I don't care. I need those criminals to join in the fight."

"Are you sure that's a good idea Thomas?" Jake piped up from behind me. "Are these the kind of men we want on our side?"

"They are today," I told him over my shoulder. "Criminals know how to fight, and we need fighting men."

"Can they be trusted?" Jake asked.

"Only if there is something in it for them." I turned my head back to Tallmadge.

"Very well," Jake sighed. "If you're sure."

I grew irritated by the interruptions. "Thank you, Jake."

"That might work," Tallmadge added, bringing our attentions back to himself. He grinned. "The General will offer the pardons. If it works, the President can't publicly admit that it wasn't his idea, and if it doesn't work, Jackson will be dead and unable to confirm that he got a letter from me in the first place. Even if he survives, he'll never admit that he was tricked. Other than some hurt feelings, I'll be free of any accusations. Most criminals who do agree to fight will likely not survive any military engagement against the British, anyways."

The old spy was so happy to be scheming and plotting again, he seemed to have forgotten that I wanted to kill him.

"I'm happy you approve, Benjamin," I said sourly. "Now, please write the letter."

After the letter was written, folded, and placed in my vest next to the first one, Benjamin stood up again.

"Is our business now concluded?" he asked, reaching down to pick up the torn piece of map.

"Yes, Benjamin," I answered. "If these footmen are with you because of me, then you can sleep sound at night without them."

"Then allow me to walk you out," the old spy said, his grin widening as he strode around his desk and stepped over his unconscious footman with a look of disdain, as if he was forced to step over refuse.

"Don't bother." I held up a hand to stop him as I still did not trust the man. "In fact, you'll wait here in your office for five minutes. We can see ourselves out."

"What about Fredrick?" Tallmadge asked.

"Who?"

"Fredrick?"

I turned to exit the office. "I didn't ask his name, but if that's the name of your second footman, you'll find him tied up outside your back door."

"Alive?" Tallmadge clarified, narrowing his eyes.

"Why would we tie him up if he was dead?" I responded. Foolish question.

Tallmadge poked me in the back with a finger. I spun around again, my hands coming up ready to defend myself.

He raised his hands to stop me from hitting him and quickly spoke. "Just wanted to make sure you were real and not a ghost. I still don't understand how you haven't aged."

"Life's full of mysteries that we'll never know the answers to," I quipped as I strolled out the door with Jake on my heels.

"Does the Bringer of Death ride again?" Tallmadge yelled behind me as I shuffled quickly down the stairs. "Has the Pale Rider returned?"

...kewriter and Joint bookmarks.

Chapter Five Alligators

October 21, 1814

Jake and I got another room at the Inn and rested a day before resuming our journey. We spent the next two days riding south down to and along the Potomac River to the city of Alexandria, to locate a captain willing to sell us passage down to the Potomac River to the mouth of the Chesapeake Bay. We'd spoken to about ten different boat captains along the riverbank, none of whom were willing to take us all the way to the Atlantic Ocean.

Captain Waters captained a thirty-two-foot-long fishing boat. A surly old man with unkempt gray hair and a limp, he kept an unlit pipe in his mouth and cussed a lot. The expression, *cusses like a sailor*, may have come about because of this man. He and his crew of four younger men made their living making round trips from a place called Cape Charles to up to Alexandria.

Nets and crab cages lined the hull of the boat. Every day,

they caught their fill of crabs and sometimes fish from the coast, then returned to Alexandria and sold their catch to buyers, mostly chefs or restaurant owners. The boat had four rowing oars and one main sail in the middle to catch the wind and help move the boat. His ship was empty of cargo as he readied the ship to sail back to Cape Charles, and he was willing to take us with him for a small enough price. The captain said that we might catch a ship at Cape Charles to sail us south to Florida.

Captain Waters and his crew sailed the boat down river throughout the day. The sail did most of the work, but when the wind died down, Captain Waters started yelling at his crew, and they eventually picked up the oars while they ignored their captain's insults. We tied up on shore when it was too dark to safely sail down the river. Jake and I volunteered to stay awake and on guard so that the crew could sleep.

The next morning, Jake and I slept while the crew continued our trip. We followed this routine all the next day, and on the morning of the third day, after only getting a few hours of sleep, I woke up to the throbbing pain in my left shoulder where I had been stabbed by a bayonet years ago. It usually only hurt on cold nights, so I guess sleeping on a boat going down Potomac River at night counted as being cold enough for that old pain to return. I swallowed a pain killer, replenished from Jake's supply, and went through the motions of stretching out my shoulder. After twenty minutes, the pain disappeared.

By the time I was done stretching and looked around to see where we were, I noted our boat was sailing across the mouth of the Chesapeake Bay. The Atlantic Ocean was on our right, and Virginia laid straight ahead of us. Captain Waters was good to his word, as Cape Charles had several large schooners anchored out in the ocean past the surf.

At Cape Charles, and after an introduction from Captain

Waters, we paid for a meal and located a captain who accepted payment for passage on a schooner at the same inn. Our ship was a hundred and sixty-foot schooner named *The Lucy*. Her captain, John Lawton, sailed up and down the east coast with passengers and cargo. He'd also been commissioned by President Madison as a Lieutenant and as a privateer against any British ships located on the sea. He agreed to take us as far as some place called Saint Marcos but refused to sail any closer to New Orleans.

"Too many pirates and British war ships sailing those waters these days," the captain explained. "And a new pirate has everyone scared. I don't know much about him, and I don't want to."

The Lucy had three large masts with huge, billowing sails. The ship was a mess of sails. Besides the three giant ones, I counted six more smaller sails tied in the riggings. John Paul Jones would have lost his mind if he saw this ship. This vessel was built for speed, and though it had been four years since I had been out on the open ocean, my sea legs returned quickly.

Captain Lawton explained that although he would be forced to attack any British ships we came across with his six carriage guns, he was in good standing with the Spanish. With only six guns on her, I hoped he was boasting about attacking any British ships. The smallest British war ship would sink *The Lucy* in the first volley of shots. But I had no doubt she could outrun any large warship, if the captain was smart enough to run.

Tallmadge had better information on these two criminals than history had. We were unable to find any additional information on them. They may have been important in 1814, but it seemed they played no important part of history and were forgotten about.

A few times when the day went smoothly and the men

were bored, they would sing. I smiled as I thought back to a time when I sailed with John Paul Jones, and Lafayette had encouraged me to distract the crew. I started singing sailor songs, of all things. In fairness to myself, it had been a resounding success – the men had been distracted and their spirits lifted.

On the morning of the third day, we pulled into port of the Spanish-governed town of Saint Augustine. The Spanish controlled the harbor but permitted us to tie up to the pier without being molested. Near the town was the Spanish fort Castillo de San Marcos. As Jake fortunately spoke Spanish, he translated that for me, *Saint Mark's Castle*. One of the sailors informed us that the fort had stood here since the late sixteen hundreds. The Spanish really had picked the perfect spot to build a fort. It was in a good position to guard the harbor with its cannons, and the small islands that laid close to shore prevented most ships from attacking at night.

"What do you gentlemen know about these parts?" Captain Lawton asked us as we prepared to disembark for a few hours while he off-loaded his cargo.

"Nothing," Jake said before I could think of a safer answer.

"The Spanish and the colonists east of here don't get along," he told us as he pointed to the massive stone fort several hundred yards from the small town where we docked. "Their small war is over, but there are still some bad relations. My only advice is don't get mistaken as Spanish with the self-proclaimed Patriots, or vice versa. Either party is likely to shoot first and find out who you are later."

The soldiers in the town didn't appear overly hostile or abusive like the British soldiers had been with the colonists. In fact, the villagers smiled and waved to the soldiers in what had to be a symbiotic relationship. Many Spanish soldiers marched around in their elegant blue uniforms and over-sized hats. In my opinion, the British had fancy uniforms and dumb hats, but these soldiers took uniforms to a whole new level. Like the British, the officers here bore flintlocks and long swords. The only difference was the Spanish swords curved more than the straight swords of the British officers. The enlisted carried long muskets with two-foot-long mounted bayonets. Some of the soldiers had longer wooden spears with shiny steel blades at the tips. I had been in this timeline five years now, but I didn't remember ever seeing soldiers with spears.

Jake wanted to get a better look at the fort, and I didn't see the harm in exploring the area, as long as we made it back in time to board *The Lucy* before she sailed again. I also wanted to see how the Spanish built their forts and any potential weak spots. We stayed on the dirt trail, and the vegetation around us quickly thickened and grew lush. Agitated by our presence, birds chirped louder and more aggressively than I'd heard in the north.

As we trekked around the area, alligators became a common sight, swimming through the water, part snake and part torpedo, or crawling down the dirt roads as if they feared nothing. They were the apex killers in this neighborhood, and they knew it. Not for the first time, I was glad I carried my Thompson Contender. The 30-30 Winchester rifle rounds would be more effective against their thick hides then the nine-millimeter rounds of my Tec-9. Then again, I was planning on staying as far from them as I could. I had no intention of ever needing to shoot one, or on becoming alligator food.

A large group of soldiers passed us coming from the fort and heading to the village. Two officers on horseback lead them. We stepped out of the way to let them pass, and I noticed that the horses' legs and the officers' boots were wet. They halted, and the officers looked us up and down, taking in our appearance. An older officer with gray hair and a neatly trimmed gray beard that ended at a fine point said something to us in Spanish, and Jake responded with a few words in return. I stood smiling and pretending I knew what was being said, while they carried on their short conversation.

After they marched by, Jake explained that the older officer was Captain Sanchez, commander of Saint Augustine and the fort. Some of the cargo being off-loaded from *The Lucy* belonged to Captain Sanchez himself, and he was on his way to pick it up. The captain wanted to know how long we would be in Saint Augustine. Jake had told him that we were from *The Lucy* and taking a walk while she off-loaded cargo. Jake mentioned we would be leaving with *The Lucy* and heading out as soon as the ship was ready, but smartly kept any actual timelines vague. The captain seemed satisfied with that answer and nodded his approval.

After the soldiers continued down the trail, we started walking again. A few minutes later we crossed a twenty-foot rope bridge that extended over a wide marsh in a shallow depression. The marsh burst with green plant life but reeked of decay. Several large white birds ambled around the muck, jabbing their thin long beaks in the water like spears, trying to stab small fish the lived in and under the watery vegetation.

The bridge was constructed simply, with two ropes tied to trees that reached across the marsh about seven feet above the water, with wooden boards tied to them to walk on. Two more ropes were secured to trees four feet higher, meant to be used as handholds or a railing.

My first thought was that the bridge was overkill for water that was barely knee deep, and I assumed that the soldiers were worried about their dressy uniforms. This explained the officers' wet boots. The officers rode around the bridge while the soldiers crossed it – the bridge never would have held the weight of an officer on a horse. Yet, no marks scarred the ground showing where the horses came up. The officers must have gone down in the marsh and came back up in a different location. The bank was steep, but the horses could have made it.

I continued to study the bridge – something didn't feel right about it. I stopped to investigate my surroundings. A half dozen or more alligators lounged under the bridge, hiding in the reeds sticking up in the marsh. They didn't as much as blink. Their dead eyes stared up at me while their bodies held completely still with their mouths fully open, like they hoped we were foolish enough to get near them. This was their land, and the soldiers wisely decided to build a bridge over them rather than try to convince the giant apex lizards to habituate elsewhere. Now I knew why the Spanish officers went far around to a spot where it was safer to cross.

When we neared the fort, four Spanish soldiers approached us, speaking Spanish. Jake told me that they were inquiring why we were at the fort. Jake must have appeared to be Spanish and didn't really draw their attention. I however did, which was ironic because I had spent so much time worried about Jake standing out.

Two of the soldiers carried those metal-tipped spears in their hands and swords on their belts. Their comrades held muskets in their hands and flintlocks on their sides. They were not as satisfied with Jake's answers as the captain had been. They asked a lot of questions that I was depending on Jake to answer in ways that didn't get us into hot water. The four of them looked us up and down, taking in our weapons and satchels. In the end, Jake said something that seemed to satisfy them, and they marched toward the village.

Only then did I breathe a sigh of relief.

The massive fort did indeed look like a squat castle. The whole fort was the shape of a four-pointed throwing star, and its twenty feet high walls had sharp angles and were thick. I thought about how many men would have to die to take this fort. It was well designed and strongly built. Jake didn't focus on the structure as much as he was fascinated by walking through history.

Armed guards stood at every entrance of the fort and on top of the battlements. None stopped us or asked what we were doing, but I could feel their critical gaze on us as we walked. They had seen their Captain march down the same road we came from, so the natural assumption would be that we'd received permission to be there. But they'd still keep a steady eye on us, just in case.

The firing ports were only six inches wide on the outside but widened to two feet on the inside. The design allowed the men inside the ability to aim muskets out the long rectangle port, in what I was guessing was a ninety-degree field of fire from left to right.

The walls around the ports had to be two feet wide. My grenades would not put a scratch on the walls, or rather only scratch the walls at most. It would take a bundle of dynamite to blow the smallest holes in these walls. A cannonball might chip away at them. Three or four direct hits in the same area should do the trick. It was good knowledge to store in the back of my mind for future use.

These walls would break wave after wave of men as they attacked. As best I could tell, there were only two ways to take a fort like this. Starve the soldiers out, or the use of cannons to open a hole wide enough to flood the fort with men.

Jake was onto something – it was a fascinating study in

history.

On our walk back to the village, we crossed over the same creaky bridge. When we reached the midpoint, two of the four soldiers we had spoken to appeared on the trail, those with the spears, stepped out of the vegetation and blocked the end of the bridge.

We froze in our tracks, with Jake on the left and me on the right. I slowly swiveled my head to peer behind us. As expected, the two soldiers with muskets appeared from nowhere like the first two, blocking the end of the bridge behind us.

"What exactly did you tell them?" I asked Jake.

"Not much," Jake said defensively. "They thought we were the colonist patriots we were warned about. They wanted to look in our satchels, and I thought that would be bad, so I told them that you were an important person and that they should show you respect."

I licked my lips. "Who did you tell them I was?" I asked, looking from one end of the bridge to the other.

"I wanted them to think you were too important to mess with," Jake answered in a hushed voice. "You know, so they wouldn't detain us. I told them that you were from Washington City, here on behalf of the government."

"So, they think we're spies. That's great."

"No," Jake said. "I think they just want our money."

So much better.

The two men with muskets started moving forward across the bridge towards us. The two in front waited where they were, waving us to them. One of them yelled something in Spanish.

"He says for us to lay down our weapons," Jake translated. "They want our purses as well."

"I don't think so," I said through my teeth.

They didn't want to kill us while we were on the bridge. If we fell over the side, our purses would go with us, then they would have to deal with the alligators. If I went for my pistol, they would fire their muskets, money or no money. I might survive it if they hit my vest, but if they hit Jake, he might not. Even if we both survived, the musket shots would alert the soldiers at the fort, and we would never make it back to the ship before it sailed.

I motioned with my head for Jake to move forward with me. As we stepped towards the end of the bridge, I slowly removed my satchel over my head and Jake did the same, and we held them out as gifts.

Jake began speaking to them as we moved. First, he took a friendly tone which turned to yelling as though he was trying to scare them. I didn't understand a single word, but I understood their body language, and they were not buying whatever Jake was selling.

We had reached the end of the bridge when the man in front of Jake stabbed the butt of his spear into the ground so he could grab our satchels out of our hands. The man in front of me yelled while pointing his spear point at my sword and pistol. I didn't need Jake to translate to know what he wanted of me.

"Have it your own way, pal," I bit out through clinched teeth and smiling lips. "Don't say we didn't warn you."

I nodded my head in understanding and lifted my sword belt that went across my body over my head with my left hand. My Tec-9 hung in the loop on the sword belt, so it went with my sword. I bent over, setting my sword belt onto the ground in front of the man pointing his spear. The two soldiers laughed, and as I bent over, I glanced back behind me. I could see the two soldiers behind us were now at the halfway point on the bridge, muskets still pointing our way.

My right hand moved a few inches and caught the handle of one of my three throwing knives. They were only six inches long but double-edged and extremely sharp. The right-side rope of the rope bridge rested over the ground near my right foot, so when I pulled my throwing knife, I slashed through the rope in the same movement as I stood up.

I clutched the soldier's spear shaft behind the point with my left hand, pushing it up and away from my body as I shifted into the soldier's personal space. My right hand slashed across the soldier's throat. My blade bit deep and opened a gaping, bloody gash. His hand flexed, and he dropped his spear, stumbled backwards, and fell, all with a look of horror on his face.

The two soldiers on the bridge screamed for help as the other soldier in front of me froze with indecision, his spear butt grounded in the dirt and our satchels in his frozen right hand.

To his credit, Jake used what he'd learned in high school and dove forward like a linebacker, tackling the man to the ground. The spear and satchels dropped from the surprised soldier's hands. As Jake and the soldier rolled around on the mushy ground like they were in a schoolhouse fight trying to punch one another, I looked back at what was left of the bridge.

When I had cut the lower rope holding the boards, the whole right side of the bridge released, causing the soldiers to fall. They had wisely dropped their muskets and clung onto one of the upper handhold ropes, reminding me of kids on the monkey bars. Their weight caused the ropes to plummet several feet more, and their legs dangled four feet above the marsh.

The alligators, no longer content lying in wait, rose up on their front legs, mouths snapping open as high as they could get them. The bottom of the alligator's throats vibrated as they made horrible sounds, something between a snake hissing and a dog growling. It sent a shiver down my spine, and without realizing it, I stepped away from the edge.

I retrieved my sword belt, slung it over my head, and positioned it back in place. Jake was holding his own with the soldier, so I didn't rush. Jake sat on top of the soldier, but he was still trying to punch him and didn't seem to understand what was necessary to prevail. The soldier took the punches while his right hand slid down to his side to clasp his knife. In a smooth, practiced movement, I withdrew my Tec-9 and kicked Jake in his side and off the soldier. The soldier's mouth was a round *O* at my help until I put two rounds into his chest. The man's face went slack.

Jake jumped up and glared at me. "Why did you do that?"

"Do what?" I asked, sliding my Tec-9 back into its leather loop. "Kick you or kill him?"

He regained his feet and stood up. "Both," he demanded.

"I kicked you to get you off of him so I could kill him," I explained as my voice grew louder. "I killed him because you weren't going to, and he was pulling his knife. Why were you punching him? Why didn't you pull your knife first? This isn't a game, Jake. There're no rules except the rules of survival."

He stared at me with his mouth open, but nothing came out.

"You're not a killer, Jake," I continued in a softer tone. "Neither is Aden. That's why I made the first trip. Because I'm capable of doing what needs to be done. And that's why you and Aden never should have come here. This world doesn't care about kindness or compassion. It cares more about might and power. You should go home, Jake. I'll find Aden by myself."

"Not on your life," Jake countered, brushing dirt off

himself. "I'm here to stay. You can go fuck yourself if you think you can just send me back."

Screaming interrupted our conversation. The two soldiers hanging on the rope were yelling at us.

"What are we going to do about them?" Jake asked, jerking his thumb at the two soldiers.

"What're they yelling?"

"They are yelling that we'll die for this," Jake translated. "They say we'll hang, and they'll watch us die."

I doubted that. The knife on the front of my belt came out fast, slicing through the air and the upper rope. Jake jumped as the two men hanging from that rope tumbled straight down, shrieking.

A splash of water followed, then the screaming got louder and abruptly stopped as the splashing became vigorous, and the sound of what might have been the teeth of a steel beartrap slapped closed. But there were no bear traps. Only the jaws and teeth of huge hungry alligators were the traps in the marsh. Well . . . not so hungry anymore.

Jake stood in shock, unable to take his eyes off the carnage below. I had to pull him away from the edge and force him a few feet down the trail. I went back to the stream bank and rolled the two dead bodies over the edge, into the marsh below. The alligators didn't seem to notice the new meat right away. They were . . . busy. But they would find the fresh meat soon enough.

We made it back to the ship minutes before it drew away from the mooring. From the safety of ship aft, we watched Captain Sanchez and his men march back to their garrison with a dozen small crates. It wouldn't take long for them to make it to the bridge, or what was left of it. I didn't see any other vessels tied to the docks, so they wouldn't be able to come after us right away if he figured out that we had killed his men. He might buy that one of his men tumbled into the alligator pit, but not four. The captain had gotten a good look at us, and a man of my size with my short hair, scars, and weapons wasn't exactly easy to forget.

"I could have done it," Jake said, out of the blue as he stood fixed next to me, watching the Spanish soldiers march toward the sun that had sunk low in the sky.

"No," I said, keeping my own gaze fixed straight ahead. "You never thought about pulling your knife. He did. And he would have killed you. It doesn't make you weak, Jake. It makes you more human. It makes you a better person than me or most of the people in this world."

He seemed satisfied by my answer but didn't respond. He stayed quiet for most of the trip.

Our trip south along the Florida coast, around the tip of Florida, and back north along the west coast to Saint Marcos took us another six days. The trip was thankfully uneventful and easier than I had any right to expect.

We disembarked, and I asked the captain for a minute of his time. It was not fair to let him sail off not knowing what had happened with the Spanish soldiers and the alligators. He might have returned to the same harbor not realizing how upset the commander of the fort was going to be. However, I wasn't a fool. I wasn't going to confide in him while we were on his ship surrounded by his men. The captain was understandably upset, but after he threw his hat at me and hollered at us, he eventually calmed down and was grateful for the truth. He understood what would have happened if we hadn't owned up to it.

After leaving the upset but appreciative captain, we made our way to one of the trading posts that also served food and alcohol. The large two-story white clapboard building displayed several alligator skins hanging and drying on wooden frames. Shifting my side gaze from the skins to Jake, I could see that he was remembering how the soldier's limbs were ripped off while they were still alive. Neither of us would ever look at an alligator in the same way again.

Our attention was brought back to the present as a passed-out man laid in the grass, moaning, while face down in his own yellow vomit, and we pressed on into the post. We strode into a loud, smoke-filled room, filled almost to bursting with rough-looking sailors. Most of the men were barefooted, though some wore cheap shoes Two young barmaids in .their twenties served drinks, but they also had a hard look to them. This wasn't a place for the timid or weak-willed. The air itself was thick and acrid, tasting of sweat and liquor.

We snaked around the tables to the far side of the room. Finding an empty table, I sat in the chair, placing my back against the wall. Every man in the room carried either a sword, a flintlock, or both in plain sight. Some men rested their flintlocks on the table to have them in reach, or to let the room know that they wished to be left alone.

One of the barmaids sashayed her way over to us and stood expectantly at our table without saying a word.

"Food," I said, not glancing up at her but scanning the room. "And water. Clean water, if you please."

"Whiskey?" she asked with a smile on her face and meaning in that one word.

Maybe she was afraid of trouble when the local patrons saw that we were not drinking whisky or beer, or maybe she feared what her boss would say when he found out we weren't buying their overpriced, watered-down alcohol.

"Food, water, and whiskey, please," Jake said sagely, speaking up for the first time and handing the woman a coin before she sauntered away.

About thirty men crammed into the room, sitting at tables or at what passed for a bar. A few men sat by themselves to drink their troubles away, while most were in groups of three or four. One older man wore an eye patch covering his left eye, and one of the sailors was missing a hand. I childishly expected a hook or something, but maybe I had watched too many movies as a kid. Everyone in the room seemed to be missing several teeth.

Two of the tables were occupied by colonists. Their skin had tanned from being out in the sun, and they wore more colorful shirts than most sailors. Three of the tables were filled with darker skinned men who sounded like they were perhaps Jamaicans. These men were as hard looking like the rest of the room but laughed louder, as if they were somehow more pleased with their day. A couple of tables had Spanish sailors who spoke Spanish. By their dress, they appeared to be pirates like the rest, not Spanish Navy, and they didn't seem apprehensive about the colonists. Between the light conversation and bursts of laughter, there didn't seem to be any animosity between the different groups. Somehow, these criminals seemed to overlook their differences in a way their mother countries never could.

More than one set of eyes openly watched us. We were new blood, and they were trying to determine if we were a threat or an opportunity.

Jake leaned in close to me and whispered, "The group to our right are talking about a pirate that's been sacking a lot of ships."

The group was a set of Spanish sailors talking loud and fast, and I could only pick out a few words. Then the oldest sailor at the table, a gray-haired man with a ponytail and two hooped, gold earrings in one of his ears, spoke two words in loud, perfect English, two words I did not want to hear.

"Pale Rider," he called out, waving his hands in the air. "Pale Rider!"

Did the man recognize me? He was old enough to have seen me years ago on any one of the many ships I had sailed on. I didn't recognize him and didn't know of any Spanish sailors I might have sailed with.

In reflex to the spoken name, I drew my Tec-9 before I realized that my hand had moved, but the man was not pointing at me or even looking my way. My eyes narrowed. I searched the room and had the attention of more than a few sailors wondering who I was going to kill. Hands grabbed flintlocks on the tables or dashed under the tables to grab flintlocks in belts. The room became quieter as the men who had noticed my movements had stopped talking. The whole room was instantly electrified and ready to explode in violence.

"Not you," Jake whispered louder, holding his hand against my arm to stop me. "He's not talking about you."

My eyes went from the older man to Jake who was trying to stop me. Jake flicked his eyes back and forth, from me to the sailor.

"The new pirate," Jake continued in a rapid whisper. "He's talking about the new pirate captain. He says the new captain is the Pale Rider."

This made no sense to me. *I* was the Pale Rider.

"He says that his ship was sacked," Jake whispered quickly. "He saw the captain and swears it was you. Well, not you, but the Pale Rider."

I set my Tec-9 on top of the table as if I was keeping my pistol within hand's reach and nothing more. The room seemed to physically relax as men around the room released their flintlocks or brought their hands back up from their laps. No one was openly staring at us now, but more eyes watched us surreptitiously, under lowered lips and with brief glances. The noise level rose as men started talking again.

Jake painted a wide, fake grin on his face, as if nothing unusual was going on. Our barmaid returned with a large tray. She slapped down two glasses of whiskey, two wooden cups of not so clean water, two plates of cooked meat, and a plate of brown bread. I sniffed the meat and crinkled my nose. By the look and color of the meat, I was betting it came from one of the alligators hanging out front.

"Any of those ships sailing for New Orleans?" I asked her, nudging my chin in the direction of the pier.

"Most sail back and forth, if you know what I mean," she answered without looking. "I can ask round for you and see if any are making for port today. Captain Smith is an honest man. I'll ask him first."

She smiled and waited expectantly, until I nodded to Jake who dug into his purse and produced a silver coin, as if she was doing us a favor by speaking with an honest sailor. She surprised us when she snagged the coin with her right hand and with the same movement, leaned forward and then kissed the top of Jake's head, thinning hair and all. As she bent over, her loose blouse sank forward, opening farther and giving Jake a view of her ample breasts that the poor guy hadn't expected.

"Think she's into me?" Jake asked, turning red in the face as the young lady strolled away smiling.

I jabbed my finger towards the leather purse filled with coins. "No, I think she knows you control the money."

Jake turned his head to stare at the barmaid as she moved away.

"Maybe when this is all over, I might come back here and settle down like you did," Jake said, still focused on the barmaid's backside like a lovesick puppy.

"The woman shows you her chest and now you're in love?" I asked. I rolled my eyes.

We were half finished with our surprisingly delicious alligator when I asked Jake to invite the Spanish sailor over for a drink. The man whose name was Audres, remained wary and suspicious until we pushed our two drinks to the open chair. Jake explained to him that we only wanted a little information, which had always been a valued currency since the beginning of time. He eyed our table, then accepted our request as a fair trade for the two free drinks.

Jake spoke to him while I continued eating my butter-fried Mississippi alligator. I instructed Jake to ask about the Pale Rider, and Audres was excited to talk about his experience.

"Audres says that he's not from these parts," Jake translated. "His ship had sailed for New Orleans with a hull full of coffee beans. They were attacked and boarded by pirates before they made it to port. The pirates killed five of the crew when they attacked, and they were upset about the cargo being coffee."

"Why?" I asked. "They could sell stolen coffee as easy as any other plunder."

"He says that pirates don't like moving heavy bags," Jake answered, looking from Audres to me. "The bags were also marked and easy to distinguish. The pirates were hoping for cargo that was easier to move and sell."

"Why didn't the pirates kill them and scuttle the ship?" I asked.

"If they did that, then who would ever surrender to them?" the man answered me via Jake's translation. "This way, the word spreads, and future crews know that if they give up the cargo, they'll keep their lives."

That makes good business sense, I thought as I chewed and nodded my head. Our barmaid was off to the side, speaking to one of the sailors and pointing towards our table. The man slipped a coin into her cleavage before she moved away. The hairs on the back of my neck stood on end at their interaction.

"Why did he say the captain was the Pale Rider?" I asked, trying to focus on the man who stole my name.

"Three reasons," Jake translated as Audres spoke. "First, the man called himself the Pale Rider. Second, the man had on a black vest, and Audres had once seen the Pale Rider in the Port of Le Havre, many years ago."

Jake asked where the Port of Le Havre was, and Audres and I answered *France* at the same time.

"This man dressed the same," Audres continued with Jake translating. "Third, when the pirates boarded our ship, my captain shot this man in the chest. The man went down hard onto his back but stood back up. With a scream of anger, the man drew his sword and ran my captain through the stomach, killing him. Then the man threw our captain's body overboard for the sharks to feed on. Who else could do these things? Who else feeds the sharks with his enemies?"

I nearly choked on my alligator. Yeah, that last part was my own fault. You hang one person over a group of sharks in a feeding frenzy and the rumors take on a life of their own. I had never *actually* fed anyone to a shark. Well, that wasn't true – I had. But I never fed a *live* person to a shark.

After Audres left, leaving us with more questions than answers, the sailor I noticed with our barmaid sauntered up and coughed exaggeratedly into his hand to get our attention.

With a wide smile and only a few missing teeth, he introduced himself as Captain Smith. Jake gave his real name, but I stuck with the name General Washington had mistakenly given me, Thomas Nelson, not wanting Thomas Cain associated with anything that might arise.

Captain Smith seemed a pleasant enough fellow, but as someone who used an alias, I had to wonder if that was *his* real name. He bore the look of a colonist in his worn brown pants and indigo blue shirt and carried a sword on his hip and a flintlock tucked into his belt. He appeared to be about forty years old, but like most sailors he had sun-aged skin. His eyes kept shifting to the scar on my head and the chunk of missing ear that I no longer thought about unless I noticed someone looking at it. He was marking me as a man who had seen violence and lived.

"I'm told you wish to buy passage to New Orleans," Captain Smith inquired, leaning forward, his hands on our table to hold himself up.

Jake quickly smiled. "Yes, we are."

"Can you pay?" the man asked, shifting in his chair to address Jake.

"We can," I answered.

"Just the two of you?" Smith asked, shifting back to me. "Or are there more?"

"Just the two of us," I said, pointing a finger at Jake then myself.

"Fine," he said, standing again. "That's just fine. My ship's *The Shining Star*. She's a sloop. One hundred and ten feet long with two masts and eighteen guns, so you don't have to worry about any pirates thinking us easy prey and attacking us. We sail before sunset."

It was as simple as that.

~ ...crwriter and John Bookfraun...

Chapter Six Taking Command

November 06, 1814

We pulled away from Saint Marcos and headed out into the Gulf of Mexico with the captain and his crew of about sixty men. A ship this size could hold a complement of twice that, so that told me this ship stayed local and didn't go sail from home. One of the crew, an old man in his late fifties or early sixties, dropped a bucket of water when we came on board. His mouth fell open, and his eyes bulged. He looked familiar somehow, but I couldn't place him. He quickly picked up the bucket and scampered off below deck. The rest of the crew looked dirty and wore tattered and filthy cotton clothes, which was odd. Captain Smith didn't seem like the kind of man to allow his crew to go unclean.

The sun was near to setting, and the captain said he would have us in New Orleans by morning. As we sailed out to sea, our sails billowed, filling with wind, and the land started to disappear behind us until the shore nothing more than a line on the dark horizon. A mild breeze blew in from the east, and seagulls followed us high above. The water darkened to a deep green-blue, and the white tips of the waves were more noticeable. I loved my home and farm, but I could see the appeal the ocean had on a man, and why sailors chose to do what they did.

"What are we going to do about this Pale Rider imposter?" Jake asked, leaning closer to me and breaking my train of thought.

"Do?" I asked him, confused. "What do you mean, what are we going to do?"

"Someone is using your good name to commit piracy," he said. He sounded insulted for me.

I tried to think of the best way to explain this to him. "Right now, we are going to do nothing about him. I appreciate you being worried about the good name of the Pale Rider. But the Pale Rider was an assassin. The name was never that good. It's not our problem. Finding Aden is the mission. Stay focused on that."

The truth was the name Pale Rider was nothing more than a means to an end, but at the same time, I didn't like a pirate picking up the mantel and acting in the Pale Rider's name to rob and kill. I wanted to do something about this man, but we had bigger fish to fry.

"What about the story the sailor told us?" he asked. "This pirate was shot in the chest and stood back up."

"Yeah," I said, rubbing my chin, pondering his words. "I've been thinking about that. I can tell you firsthand that rumors take on a life of their own. For instance, I never fed anyone alive to sharks, but that's not what people say about me. This could be a tall tale like that was."

"Yeah," Jake said. "Tall tale. You say you never fed

anyone to a shark, but I witnessed you feed two men to a bunch of alligators. And those men were alive at the time."

"And?" I asked, lifting my eyebrow. "What's your point?"

"And what if it's not a tall tale?" he asked. "What if he has Aden's vest?"

I glanced down at my watch band with the small compass attached to it. "First, we find Aden. If we find the vest with him, then we know it was a story. If we don't find the vest, then we'll deal with it then. One problem at a time. Our first problem is dealing with the crew of this ship."

The crew on ship had kept their distance, and when they did look at us from under low eyelids, it was with pity or contempt. Those men who weren't openly drinking rum from bottles, that was.

Jake swiveled his head, looking around the deck. "What do you mean by that?"

Before I could answer Jake's question, Captain Smith strolled up to us, a wide smile plastered on his face. He had both arms extended to hand us two cups of wine.

"You men should find a place to lay down," he said pleasantly, his gaze touching on my sword and the Tec-9 pistol. "I'll wake you before we get to port."

"Thank you, Captain," Jake said, taking one of the cups from Smith and gulping a drink.

I grasped the remaining cup. "Captain, what do you know about this Pale Rider person that we keep hearing about? We were told he sails in these waters."

"I know he's not the Pale Rider," he said chuckling. "No, the Pale Rider was a famous pirate who had a flare for stealing British war ships during the revolution. Some say he was an assassin. Others say he worked for General Washington himself.

I have an old crewman named Mr. Task who claims to have sailed with the Pale Rider to France and back many years ago."

My stomach jumped. Task? Lieutenant Task? He had been Captain Jones's first mate. Was he the old crewman? He was the right age. Gone from serving in the Navy to a life of piracy? He would not be the first.

"No, that pirate is not the Pale Rider," Smith continued. "I know the man. His name is Captain Burlington, and I've gotten drunk with the man more times than I can count. Burlington isn't his real name either. His real name is Timothy Butterfield. He claims to be the illegitimate child of a British General named Burlington, so he took the General's name, hoping for recognition. Unfortunately for him, he never received it. The recognition that is. Now he pretends to be the legend, dead and gone, back from who knows where. He's convinced people that he's the Pale Rider returned. Wears a black vest and carries two pistols. Fear can be the greatest weapon of all, and a name can hold great power."

His astute eyes dropped to my vest visible through my open coat. He was right about names having power. The name did hold power, in a way. There were times, years ago, when I could feel men's eyes on me, knowing they wanted to kill me for the bounty on my head. But they had been afraid to act because of the name. Maybe Jake was right. Did I need to take up the name again? Tallmadge had seemed to think so.

"So, he's a fraud?" Jake asked, taking another sip of his wine before I could stop him. Wine loosened lips and I needed him focused.

Smith leaned on the side rail. "No, he's a very dangerous man to be sure. Very skilled with the knife and sword, but he's not the Pale Rider. The name Captain Burlington doesn't strike fear into the enemy the same way the name Pale Rider does." He shifted to lean on his elbow and look at me directly. "Why do you ask about him?"

"He may have something that belongs to me," I said. "We need to find him so that I can ask for it back."

"I see," the captain said and fixed his eyes on the three throwing knives on my vest. "That won't be easy. Whatever he has of yours, you should know he can be a very violent man."

Jake took another drink of his wine and then yawned.

"You're tired," the captain commented. "We can talk more in the morning. Go rest for tonight."

As the captain moved away smiling, I grabbed Jake's arm and shoved him forward.

"Where are we going?" Jake asked as he yawned again.

"To the aft of the ship," I told him. I tossed my cup over the side railing and into the water below.

"Why are we going to the aft?" Jake asked groggily, as his arm dropped to his side, and his cup slipped from his now open hand, struck the deck, and rolled away.

"Because I need to find a safe place for you to lay down." I lifted his arm around my neck and held up his weight. "New Orleans is due west of here and we are sailing due south."

"So?" Jake mumbled.

"That mixed with the fact that these men are pirates and you've been drugged tells me they're going to rob and kill us," I answered. "I need room to fight, and I want the ocean at my back when they come for us."

"How would they know to rob us?" Jake asked. "They don't know how much gold we have on us."

"I don't know, Jake," I answered, my frustrations growing as I shuffled him down the deck. "Maybe that nice barmaid who kissed you on the head while distracting you with her chest so she could get a good look at that fat purse of yours told them."

"If you knew the wine was drugged, why didn't you stop me from drinking it?" Jake asked in his slurred voice.

"Do I have to tell you not to take candy from strangers? If the nice captain had asked you to get into his windowless van, would you have done it?"

Jake argued about the barmaid's virtue as we climbed a damp set of steps to the aft of the ship. He swore that she was a good woman and would never betray us. Then he asked me if I remembered her name.

A large landing extended from the top of the stairs with plenty of room to move around. I set Jake down with his back against the railing, and he tilted against the hull and quickly fell asleep, his head falling to the side, his legs outstretched.

The sun bloomed in a bright liquid ball of fire as the last sliver of light sunk into the ocean to the west. The crew kept their distance from us as they waited for me to lie down and fall asleep.

My compass indicated that we were still sailing south as the lanterns were lit high up in the crow's nest and up front at the bow. The lanterns put out large circles of light up high and to the front, but the bubbles of light didn't reach the main deck of the ship. No one came to light the fancy, black, wrought iron and glass lantern mounted to the railing above Jake's head. It was also painfully obvious that they were leaving the two larger, oversized glass lanterns on the main deck untouched.

I took off my deer skin coat and satchel so to have freer movement for the fight I knew was coming. I also wanted my combatants to see the Thompson under my arm, hoping it might make them think twice. The first seven to come up those steps were going to die quick if it didn't. I made myself comfortable and leaned back against the railing, crossed my arms, and faced the midship to let the crew know that I was staying awake and watching them. The waves were small tonight, but the ship bobbed up and down with them, like an old, comforting rocking chair. I took the moment to appreciate spending the prior week on the ocean, regaining my sea legs. I knew I would need my sea legs for what was to come.

The pirates waited for the blanket of full night to cover us, then as the sky filled with twinkling stars, a dozen men crept up from below. Captain Smith was one of those men. It was dark, but I could make out the old man I'd seen earlier, now pulling on Smith's arm.

"You're making a mistake, Captain," the old man advised in a loud whisper as the sailors spread out on the main deck. "Don't do this, Captain. I implore you."

"Stop acting a fool," Smith hissed in a stern voice. He shook off the old man's hand. "If you really sailed with the man, he'd be in his sixties now."

The old man *was* Task.

"I tell you, it's him," Task pressed. "I don't know how but it's him."

Smith pushed the old man away. "Step away if you're afraid, but you forfeit your share of the purse."

"Dead men can't spend gold, Captain," Task said ominously, pointing a finger at his captain and stepping back.

I reached into my satchel and withdrew my night vision goggles, slipped them on my head, and turned them on. As dark as it was tonight, and as small as these new goggles were, I didn't think the crew would be able to see them.

Smith walked up the stairs to where I stood. In the green light of the night vision, I counted ten men. The first two and last two carried muskets, three had swords, and the rest held glinting knives in their hands. Task continued to back away from the group, not wanting to have any part of the violence that he knew was to come.

Smart man.

Although it was dark, Smith noted my outline and paused directly in front of me. In the dark, he might have thought I could not see his smile was no longer there, having been replaced with a scowl. The rum on his breath cut through the sea air to my nose. He'd been drinking since I last saw him – working up his courage, maybe.

"You didn't drink the wine," he said. "This would have been so much easier if you had."

"Easier for you," I retorted. "I don't think it would have been easier for me."

"If you suspected something, why did you board my ship?" he asked.

My hand drifted to my Tec-9.

"It's only a trap if you don't know about it. Plus, I don't really want to go to New Orleans. Not right away at least. I was afraid you'd say no if I told you where I really wanted to go. I need your ship and your crew. But I don't need you, so think carefully before you make your next move."

"Mr. Task thinks you are the real Pale Rider," Smith said with another fake chuckle. "You certainly have the balls of the Pale Rider. Unfortunately, like the real Pale Rider, after tonight you'll never be seen again."

He sounded afraid and tried to hide it behind a laugh. The shine in his eyes shifted up to my scar again.

"Task has a good memory for faces," I said in a low tone. "We sailed together on The Ariel with Captain John Paul Jones. Captain Jones later became Admiral Jones. We went through the worst storm I'd ever sailed in, and Task was promoted to first mate that night after we lost Lieutenant James.

We were hit by a rogue wave that took the good Lieutenant off his feet and over the side. I remember it like it was yesterday."

His eyes widened as I talked, and he stepped back from me as he realized the truth of it. In the dark, I pulled out my Tec-9 and switched on the laser sight. A thin green beam, invisible to the naked eye, shot out from the pistol grip to the deck. He didn't think I could see his hand moving slowly to his sword.

"Like my dad used to say," I said loudly for all to hear, "let's kick this dog in the ass and see which way he runs."

I stepped forward with a sudden and violent burst of energy, kicking out with my right foot. My kick hit the surprised Captain Smith in the center of his chest. The man never saw it coming and flew backwards off the landing to the deck below, arms and legs floundering.

My father also taught me, if you're not cheating, you're not trying. Smith landed on his back on the main deck as the four sailors with muskets cocked their hammers back with their thumbs. They brought the stocks into their shoulders and the barrels swung down in my direction.

I smoothly raised my pistol, leveling the green laser on the chest of the first man and fired. The slide moved back and then forward again. The thunk of the slide moving back and forth and the small cough of the bullet were the only sounds the gun made. The first sailor with the musket tumbled backwards onto the deck, like he'd been punched in the chest by an invisible force, his musket clattering against the wooden deck. I stepped to the right as two of the muskets fired at my outline, or where my outline had been a second ago. In the dark of night when aiming in on a dark silhouette, it takes the brain a half second to register when your target moves.

The fourth sailor had not fired yet and managed to track

my movements. I swung my pistol around to his direction, settling the green laser on his chest like I had done to the first man. He managed to fire first, and I was spun around when his musket let out a loud boom. Its lead ball struck me on the right side of my chest.

My new vest held up as advertised. The kinetic energy of the impact was absorbed by the gel lining of the vest. Don't get me wrong, it *hurt*, but it felt like I was hit by a rubber mallet this time, not by a sledgehammer. The gel lining of the vest was the greatest thing for my injury ravaged body since sliced bread.

I spun back around and fired three quick rounds into the man who had shot me. The remaining two sailors with muskets were busy reloading as fast as they could while the sailors with swords and knives moved forward and up the stairs.

Firing my last two rounds, I killed the two reloading their muskets and holstered my pistol. My left hand slid across my body, drawing the knife on the front of my belt as my right hand reached behind me, drawing the knife behind my back. I loved this new Tec-9, but nothing beat good old solid steel blades for terrifying the enemy. Or in my case, titanium blades. Guns were great, but a knife fight was where I was really in my element.

I didn't want to wait for them to climb the stairs and fight on this deck, what with Jake helpless the way he was, so I took the fight to them. I leaped down to the main deck, driving my two knives into the chest of the last man who hadn't reached the stairs yet. As dark as it was, I don't think he ever saw me. My blades sunk deep, straight down into his flesh, their handle hilts hitting his chest. Then I immediately released them, knowing it would take time and effort to get them out, as deep as they were. As my feet landed on the deck, I followed through with the momentum and rolled over my left shoulder in a combat roll.

Continuing my roll, I smoothly came up to my feet,

pulling my sword with my right hand and yanking off my goggles with my left. I had the advantage with the goggles when fighting with the pistol, but with the sword, I feared the tunnel vision that they also gave me. I slipped the goggles into my cargo pocket.

The five men on the stairs spun around as their friend emitted a single bloody scream and collapsed on the deck. They came back down the steps, coming at me in a rush. Smith also quickly regained his feet, shook his head, then pulled his own sword.

The first man to reach me slammed down on his face, dropping his sword after taking my blade in the throat. The last four, not wanting to follow his lead, raced around me, keeping their distance and surrounding me.

None of them were in arm's reach, and that was by design. Men started yelling below deck, and footsteps pounded as they ran up the stairs behind me, investigating the musket fire they heard. Torch light pushed back the shadows and the newcomers could see six of their comrades laying on the deck – dead. Someone lit the two large lanterns on the main deck near us, bathing the whole deck in a flickering yellow light.

The four around me waited for the right moment to step in and slash. They were hoping one of the others would move in first. Not that it mattered – a few of the newcomers would have flintlocks and not need to get near me.

"Let the captain kill him!" a voice I recognized as Mr. Task's yelled out. "The captain should do it. He brought these men on board and now six of our brothers are dead. I warned him not to tangle with this man."

A man, or woman for that matter, didn't become captain by displaying fear in front of their crew. They needed to be the toughest and smartest on their ship if they hoped to keep command. Additional voices spoke up, calling for Smith to kill me. Task had given me a chance by putting Smith on the spot in front of his men. Smith stood behind one of his men, sword in hand, panting hard from anger and his fall. The four men closest to me looked to him for an answer.

"How about it, Smith?" I asked. "I've already killed six of your men. How many more have to die before you and I cross swords?"

Furious, Smith stepped up, shoving the man in front of him out of his way. He faced off with me, then sliced his sword through the air several times, making a swooshing sound. I didn't know if he did this to intimidate me or bolster his own courage, but it didn't seem to serve any real possible function.

I raised my sword. "I warned you to think carefully before you made your next move. You should have listened to Mr. Task."

He lunged forward, thrusting his sword toward my chest. Several of the crew yelled out with excitement at the fight. I stepped back and twisted my wrist, bringing my sword around in an arc, and deflected his sword. He chopped down with his sword, once, twice, then a third time. I brought my sword up and blocked his attacks. He stepped back then shifted forward again.

I quickly learned that dueling at night in the dark was vastly different than dueling in the daylight. In the dark of night, it is harder to see your opponent's thin blade. If you're lucky, torchlight might shine on or reflect off the blade and make it stand out for a second as it moves. Barring that, you're going off the man's movements and must think of the sword as an extension of his hand, realizing that where his arm moves, his sword follows. The upside is that your opponent has the same problem and has to guess where your blade is.

Smith led with another thrust, but this time when I brought my sword around to block his, he allowed my sword to swing his in a circular path. As our swords circled one another, the sound of blade scraping blade filled the air between us. The two blades continued around in their arc, and our guards slid closer and closer until they collided like bulls locking horns.

He twisted his body, telegraphing his left hand as it shot forward for my side. When our swords had circled one another, I knew he had drawn his knife with his left hand, and he now tried to stick me in the side. I jumped back, disengaging our swords and causing his knife to miss all but air.

My feet landed, and I immediately leaped forward again, forcing him to parry my attack. As our swords clanged together, I pushed forward, getting closer and my left fist erupted out for his jaw. The clap of bone hitting bone caused the onlookers to grimace and shout. Smith was knocked backwards, stumbled, and then landed flat on his back.

I stepped forward to finish him while he was still on his back, but one of the onlookers to my right found the courage and the opportunity to move directly in my path, sword in hand. He was one of the four who had surrounded me a minute ago. Without thought or hesitation, my sword sliced through the air and across his face with a *swoosh* sound. Blood sprayed the others next to him, as I cut a deep laceration across his cheeks. My blade had also sliced through his nose, connecting the two cheek cuts. His sword clanged to the deck as his hands rose to his nose that was now grotesquely split open at the bridge and profusely bleeding down his face. Blood poured between his fingers, and one of his friends yanked him out of my reach and slapped a rag on his face. He was in no danger of dying, but he would be paying double at whatever whore house he normally spent his stolen money at.

Another pirate leaped at me from my left side, emitting a high-pitched scream, his knife in his right hand. Torchlight bounced off the blade which shot straight out like a spear, coming at me in a stabbing motion. I shifted to the side and though he missed my stomach, my left hand snapped out like a striking serpent, wrapping itself around his wrist in a vise-like grip. Twisting my body towards the man, I brought my sword up into his stomach, pushing hard until my sword guard struck his shirt. My thin blade glided through his body and out his back with little resistance.

He grunted and his steamy, tobacco-scented breath expelled from his lungs, hitting me in the face. I held onto his knife as his fingers opened, and he slid backwards off my blade and onto the deck.

I turned to face Smith who was again standing and moving forward for another attack. I was breathing hard but was ready for his attack. We sprang forward at the same time and met each other in the middle. The crew screamed their encouragement, as they were caught up in the fight, bloodlust filling their veins.

Like two gladiators in the arena, surrounded by the cheers of a blood hungry crowd, we started circling one another and our swords clashed over and over. We took turns attacking and defending as our swords danced violently in the night. Neither of us were willing to get close enough to use our knives. Not with our swords slicing through the air and bouncing off the other's blade. He wasn't the best swordsman I had ever fought, but he was every bit as good as me. We clashed together and then withdrew. Over and over again, we attacked and defended, always circling to the left or to the right, constantly trading roles and trying to slip under the other's guard. The first to make a misstep would be the one to die. There was no yielding tonight, no mercy or forgiveness. One of us had to die so that the other could live. Moving together and away, our swords clashed in some kind of sick dance of the blades.

We started slipping a little in the fresh blood soaking the deck, and we had to put significant effort into where we placed our feet and our balance as we did our sword work. Sweat dripped down my face, staining my shirt. Our muscles started to tire as we slowed our attacks, but his men still screamed encouragement, wanting the fight to go on. Several of the crew were yelling for me now. I could hear men who sounded Australian yelling for me.

Smith became impatient and began swinging as fast as he could while screaming for me to die. Whether it was the alcohol he had drunk while waiting for me to fall asleep, or he was losing control of his temper, or the fact that some of his crew were turning on him, throwing their support towards me, he was fighting more aggressively and less effectively. He made the mistake of lunging with a thrust at the wrong time. He slipped on some blood, and I parried his blade with mine while he struggled to regain his balance. His arms flailed in the air, and I stepped in close and drove my knife blade hard in between his ribs, right under his raised sword arm, three inches below his arm pit.

I broke off the attack thrusting back, leaving my knife in his ribs. He froze in his place, and I imagine he was in too much pain to move. I had impaled his lung, and blood sprayed from his mouth as he coughed. With his eyes open and blood pouring down his chin, he collapsed forward, face first onto the blood-slicked, wooden deck of his own ship.

One of the crewmen stepped forward, crouched on one knee, and checked on his captain.

"Dead," the pirate pronounced, looking up at me.

I thought this was good news for me until the *click, click, click* sound of a hammer being cocked back on a flintlock came from behind me.

I slowly turned around to find one of the crew standing against the railing, pointing a flintlock at me. At my head, to be exact. The bastard smiled at me as his hand tightened on the flintlock grip finger to squeeze the trigger.

My mind flashed that I was about to die, and there wasn't a thing I could do about it.

Instead, I jumped as a boom twice as loud as I expected broke the night, and the pirate holding the flintlock disappeared as he flew backwards over the railing into the darkness and then splashed into the water below.

Everyone and I spun to see Jake standing at the top of the stairs, holding his shotgun in both hands as he leaned heavily against the railing, barely able to hold himself up.

"I told you I could do it," Jake announced. His eyes drooped only to be forced open again as he tried to focus.

Ignoring Jake for the moment, I took advantage of everyone's shock to shift my sword to my left hand and draw my Thompson with my right.

The tension in the air was thick. The crew wanted to kill me, but none of them wanted to be the first to try. I couldn't watch everyone at once, so I had to hope Jake could stay awake long enough to watch my back.

"Who are you?" a voice in the crowd yelled out.

The question came from a tall blond man with deeply suntanned skin and what sounded like an Australian accent. I thought he might have been one of the men who had thrown their support behind me.

"My name is Thomas Nelson," I said in a tempered voice, my attempt to quiet them down if they wanted to hear me.

"Lads," a voice called out from the riggings, "that there is the *real* Pale Rider."

I looked over and saw Mr. Task a few feet up in the riggings, holding a flintlock pointed at his own crew. I was impressed that he could still climb into the riggings at his age. He perched with his feet balanced on a rope, holding himself steady with his left hand while grasping the already cocked-back flintlock with his right.

"New Orleans already has a Pale Rider," another sailor in the crowd argued.

"Aye," I said. "That's part of the reason I've returned. This Captain Burlington has taken my name and must die for that."

I was lying. I had no intention of ever meeting Captain Burlington but needed a reason for being there. Revenge was an emotion these men could respect and believe.

"You men know me," Mr. Task yelled out. "You've all heard the stories I've told about the Pale Rider. I tell you this true. That man is him. I can't say how he looks the same as he did thirty years ago. Sent back from hell is my only guess. Look at the eight dead men at his feet, Captain Smith among them, if you aren't convinced."

By this time, all I wanted was to get to my first stop and then to New Orleans alive with Jake.

"Who's the first mate?" I asked, wanting to know who the captain of this ship was now.

"Jude!" a voice shouted.

"Where's Jude?" I asked, scanning around the group of men. "Speak up. Where's this Jude?"

"Your friend sent Jude over the side with that monstrous flintlock of his," a new voice in the crowd said.

"Then the ship is mine," I told them coldly and I turned

in a circle, trying to look as many of them in the eyes as I could in the flickering light of the torches. "Unless someone wishes to challenge me for it?"

Buzzing of mumbles sounded among the men. None of them were happy about me claiming the ship, but none were rushing to challenge me, not with so many dead bodies lying between us.

"Mr. Task," I yelled out as I peered up into the riggings.

"Yes, Captain!" Tasked answered, shouting out the title of captain for the whole crew to hear.

"If any man wishes to challenge me, let me know," I instructed. "In the meantime, you are first mate. Set course for Pensacola, and then after you have a few of these men throw the dead overboard, meet me in the captain's quarters."

I sheathed my sword, holstered my pistol, and turned my back on the crowd of pirates. I felt naked as I walked towards Jake. I waited for a knife blade to stab me between the shoulder blades, but it was necessary to show my confidence and assurance that no one would dare attack me, even if I didn't feel confident.

Grabbing Jake by his left arm, so his right arm holding the shotgun was still free to shoot anyone stepping in our way, I slipped his arm over my neck again. I held up his weight, and we made our way to the captain's quarters with what felt like every pair of eyes on us.

"I told you I could do it," Jake mumbled again, turning his face to look at me with his drooping eyes and smug grin.

"That you did buddy," I assured him. "You did good."

Men began talking again, the din of their conversations filling the air, and Mr. Task yelling out orders to distract them. He shouted out names and instructed them to throw the dead over the side of the ship. This didn't go over well, as the dead had been friends of the men presently throwing them overboard – or whatever passed as friends in the pirate world. Shipmates I guessed would be more accurate. Once we entered the room and shut the door, the thick wood managed to block out most of the sounds of the men grumbling their displeasure in their new captain. Two lanterns were already lit in the quarters and filled the entire room with enough light to see by.

The captain didn't have a hammock, he had a real bed. It was small, the size of a modern single bed, in the far back corner of the room, but it was a real bed. Ropes were tied to the four corners, hanging the bed from the ceiling like a hammock, and it swung lightly back and forth with the motion of the ship. I dumped Jake onto the bed and grabbed his shotgun out of his hand before he dropped it. Once he relaxed, he was back asleep in minutes.

"Leave or die!" a high-pitched voice yelled from behind me. "Leave or die!"

I swiveled my head sharply to the large desk behind me which crowded the other corner of the room. Two chairs were positioned on this side of it and another, more ornate one, was on the far side. The three chairs were of a set, but not the same set as the desk. Whereas the desk was dark red oak, the three chairs looked to be of cheap white pine. The far chair backed to the window and faced the captain's door. But the desk itself wasn't what attracted my attention.

On the desk was a large red parrot, bobbing up and down. He had blue on the tips of his wings, a white face and beak, and black lines breaking up his red body feathers.

It took me a moment to register what I was seeing.

A parrot?

He appeared harmless, if loud. I had larger concerns than this bird.

Grabbing a shotgun shell from Jake's bandoleer, I broke open the shotgun and replaced the used shell with the new one. I walked over to a dresser where a bowl and pitcher of water were situated on top, under a large wall mirror. I washed the blood off my face and hands, then moved to the desk, setting the shotgun on the flat top.

"Bastard," the bird squawked as he jumped at the noise and flew over to a brass perch next to the desk.

I sat down behind the desk, setting my Tec-9 and Thompson next to Jake's shotgun. I placed the three guns so that they were not only in hand's reach but pointed towards the door. Just in case the crew changed their minds and wanted another alteration in command.

A few minutes later, a knock came at the door. My head popped up as I had been searching Captain Smith's desk.

"Enter!" I yelled after grabbing my Tec-9 with my right hand and aiming it at the door.

The doorknob turned slowly, and the door pushed open with a creak from the huge, sea-worn hinges. Mr. Task peeked his head through the door, sensing the dangers of coming in the room too fast.

"Come in, Mr. Task," I said, lowering my pistol and setting it back on the desk.

Task entered the room, opening the door only as wide as was necessary to fit through the doorway. He was a thin man, so he didn't need to open it very wide. Once inside, he secured the door behind himself and stared at me, waiting for something. He carried a bundle in his hands.

"Leave or die," the bird cawed again. "Leave or die."

"Please sit, Mr. Task," I told him, motioning to one of the two chairs in front of the desk, my desk. "It's good to see you again. It's been a long time since we sailed together."

"Aye, Captain." Task squirmed in the chair as he spoke. "It's been at least thirty years."

I flapped my fingers at him. "You have questions?"

"Yes, sir," Task responded. "Questions. A lot of them. Why are you here?"

"I need to take care of a quick chore in Pensacola," I answered. "Then I need to locate a friend who was last seen in New Orleans."

"Oh, thank the Lord," Task said, releasing a lung full of air in a long breath. "When I first saw you walk on board the ship, I thought you were here for me."

"You?" I asked, frowning at him. "Why would I be here for you?"

"Well, sir," Task said, shifting his gaze around the room uncomfortably again. "When we last sailed together, I was living an honest and honorable life. I was a Lieutenant in the American navy and now . . . you understand."

"And now you're a pirate?" I finished for him. I nodded my head in understanding. "Sailing with other pirates?"

"Aye, sir," he said and dropped his gaze to his lap.

"I'm the Pale Rider, Mr. Task," I told him. "Not the Pope. I'm not here to judge or punish you. If anything, it's nice to see a friendly face."

"Very good, sir," Task said as his lips curled up at my comment.

"Did you set course for Pensacola like I ordered?"

"Aye, Captain," Task said. He lifted his hands and dropped my satchel, coat, and knives onto my desk for me. "We do have some problems to talk about."

"Bastard!" the bird cawed from his perch.

"The men aren't happy about their new captain?" I looked over at the bird who was bobbing up and down on his perch.

"No, sir," Task answered, confirming what I already knew. "They're already starting to talk."

"Can you buy me a few days before they mutiny?" I asked, turning back to Task.

"Aye," Task answered. "Two maybe three days. But if you don't do something to earn the crew some coin soon, they'll be taking a vote for a new captain."

I pointed to Jake. "What did Smith give my friend?"

"Nightshade and poppy," he answered dismissingly, waving a hand. "Mixed with wine, you can't taste it. He'll sleep hard tonight but will be fine come sunup. I take it myself some nights."

"Bastard," the bird called out as Task sat down.

"I see you met Rooster," Mr. Task laughed.

"Rooster?"

"Aye, Captain," Task answered. "He crows at first sunlight, like a rooster. He also barks like a dog when he's scared, yells bastard to anyone that comes near the desk, and tells people to get out. He was like a watchdog for Captain Smith. No one will sneak up on you in here so long as he's awake."

"I'll remember that," I said, eyeing the bird in a new light.

"Captain," Task broke in. "May I ask why we are heading for Pensacola? The men are not happy about this. I can tell you that the town is controlled by the British, and they have five warships there. Or at least they did last time we sailed near the harbor."

"What's today's date Mr. Task?" I asked.

"November sixth," Task answered.

I ran my fingers through my hair. "We may already be

too late."

"Too late for what, Captain?"

"Do you know who General Jackson is?" I asked.

"Aye, sir," Task answered. "Old Hawk Face."

My eyebrows raised at his assessment. "He'll be fighting the British there on his way to New Orleans. And you know how I like to fight the British."

"Aye, Captain. I remember quite well how you like to fight redcoats. These men, on the other hand, don't have any disputes with the British or anyone else. When you live the life of a pirate, one country is as bad as the others for you."

"How will they feel when the British take New Orleans and push them out of their homes and sink their ships?"

Task rubbed his chin. "Aye, sir. But the British haven't kicked them out of their homes yet. Indeed sir, the British are not even in New Orleans right now."

I nodded my head, letting him know that I was listening. Every word he spoke was the truth. I was only captain if and as long as the crew allowed it, and if I asked them to fight the British now, this would backfire on me.

"Let the men know that we'll not be going directly to Pensacola," I said. "The ship will anchor a mile away out of sight, and I'll go ashore by myself. I'll be gone one or two days, then we sail for New Orleans."

"And if you're not back in two days?" Task asked.

"That will be for you and the men to decide," I told him. "Wait longer or sail away. But let the men know that if you sail away before giving me two days, I'll hunt every one of them down."

"Aye, Captain," Task said. He raised a hand towards me, then stopped himself, bringing his hand back down. His eyes shifted downward. "I'll pass those words to the crew."

"Go ahead and ask, Mr. Task," I told him as I stood. "Do it and get it out of your system."

Mr. Task raised his eyes, then his hand, and poked me in the chest.

"Is it really you, sir?" he asked.

"Aye Mr. Task. It's me."

He was quiet for several heartbeats, allowing the confirmation of my presence to sink in. He finally shook his head to collect his thoughts. "Will there be anything else, sir?" he asked.

"What do you know about Jean and Pierre Lafitte?" I inquired.

...aerwirici and joint bookbinders...

Chapter Seven It's a Trap

November 07, 1814

The next morning, Mr. Task was good to his word when the sun's rays glimmered through the window, and the crowing of a rooster broke the quiet of my room. That crazy ass bird really did crow like a rooster. The parrot kept going, no matter how much I yelled at him. It wasn't until I sat upright in the chair I had slept in and gave the little bastard a cracker that he stopped. At least I wouldn't sleep the day away.

"What the hell is that?" Jake asked from the bed. His clothes and hair were rumpled as he sat up and squinted.

"That's Rooster," I said as I rose and moved towards the door. "Mr. Task said he does this every morning. Hence the name."

"Are we nearing New Orleans?" Jake asked in a croaking voice. He struggled to his feet unsteadily and peered around the room.

Cannon fire exploded in the far distance and was

constant, with no discernable break in the repetition.

"No," I said, opening and walking out the door.

Jake stumbled like a drunk but followed me to the bow of the ship. Mr. Task was already awake and strode over to us.

"Where are we?" Jake asked as he shaded his eyes from the sun and took in the scene.

Task pointed to the harbor ahead of us. "Pensacola."

Five British warships sat in the harbor, firing their cannons high into the air so that the cannonballs arched and plunged into the Spanish establishment, recently taken by the British and currently being attacked by the Americans.

Jake leaned dangerously far over the railing, staring off at the harbor. "Pensacola?" he repeated.

"We can't go near that harbor," Mr. Task explained. "Any one of those ships might sink us. If we had the element of surprise, maybe we'd have a chance against one or two, but there are five and their crew are at battle stations, already engaged. We wouldn't last five minutes."

I studied the scene between the boats and the town. "Pick a spot around the bend, out of sight of those ships but close enough for me to walk, if you please, Mr. Task," I ordered.

"Aye, sir," Task answered without question and walked to the wheel of the ship.

"Why are we going to Pensacola?" Jake asked.

"Not we, Jake," I told him. "Just me. You're not yourself yet. You're staying on the ship and making sure it doesn't sail away, no matter what."

"But why are we here and not New Orleans?"

"Because Jackson needs our help," I told him.

"Aden needs us more," Jake said in an accusing tone. "This isn't the plan, Thomas."

I leveled my eyes and glared at him. "It is now. If we can

prevent Jackson from losing half his men, it will mean less men we need to recruit. And if Jackson doesn't have to spend weeks caring for his wounded, we can get him and his army to New Orleans faster. It'll be easier for him to defend New Orleans from the British rather than attack and capture it."

"I think we should stick to Aden's plan," Jake protested again, but his voice was lower, sullen, knowing he'd lost the argument. "We have a good plan, Thomas. Let's go with that."

"Aden's plan didn't work," I said in a tight tone. "We're going with mine now."

"Why do you think your plan is better than the one Aden and I came up with?" Jake asked.

"Aden got himself captured," I answered harshly. "The Pale Rider never got himself captured. And the one time I was almost captured doesn't count because I rescued myself."

"Almost captured?" Jake asked.

I ignored his question. "The point is Aden's plan sucked. Neither of you were trained to recognize the inherent problems of the plan. We're going with my plan now. I'll contact this Jackson, show him my letter of introduction, and warn him of the trap at the fort. Then make my way back to the ship, and we'll sail for New Orleans, and Bob's your uncle. We'll lose a day at most. We can save Aden, and then the three of us will wait and meet General Jackson when he arrives in New Orleans. It will take him a month to march there, but only a day or two for us to sail there."

"And I'm supposed to wait here for you?" Jake whined. Did he always whine like this? Or was it part of his hangover?

"No. Like I said, you need to make sure the ship doesn't leave me. The crew will want to sail away as soon as I'm ashore. Convince them to stay. When that doesn't work, and it won't, offer them coin. When that fails, and it will, threaten them that

I'll kill them in their sleep. And when all else fails, kill one of them and retake the ship."

"Kill one?" Jake asked, his forehead lined in confusion. "Which one? How do I choose something like that?"

"Doesn't matter," I said solemnly. "Anyone but Task. We need him. The first one to mention leaving would be the one I'd pick."

Jake stood silent and looked past the railing and out over the ocean towards Pensacola and the warships attacking it. He was trying to absorb his instructions, with extreme difficulty.

"I'm sorry to ask this of you Jake," I said, finally having a moment of compassion for the man. When he came with Aden, he surely didn't sign up for all this.

"The ship will be here for you when you return," Jake sighed and offered his hand in a handshake.

"Good," I said. "And tell Mr. Task to have the men hang a hammock in the captain's quarters. I'm not sleeping in the same bed as you or in that chair again."

The long boat had rowed me from the ship to shore, about a half mile down the coastline west of the British ships. I leapt over the side of the long boat and into the cold, white surf of the knee-high churning water. The sailors didn't wait for my boots to reach the beach before turning the boat around. They seemed to row back to the ship faster than they'd rowed me to shore, as if they were afraid the ship might sail away before they made it back. It better still be there – I didn't relish the idea of marching to New Orleans with General Jackson.

Taking a deep breath, I started walking up the beach, heading to Pensacola. Climbing a short hill on the outskirts of the town, I viewed the destruction below. The five ships were having a field day firing freely into Pensacola, which had no cannons firing back at them. I was going to have to enter a town being fired upon by five warships, where two opposing forces fought for land, while I searched for a single man in command of one of those forces.

I made my way to the west side of town where the battle had already been fought and won by Jackson's men. Musket fire boomed farther east into the city. I located a large, white canvas tent with soldiers standing guard around it. I stomped up to the tent in the open so as to not surprise anyone and get myself shot. The soldiers spotted me and pointed their bayonet-tipped muskets at me.

"Easy," I yelled, holding my hands up in surrender. "I'm from Washington City. I have letters from Congress for General Jackson. I've come all this way by ship."

"Advance," one of the soldiers ordered, still aiming his musket at me.

I continued up to the tent keeping my hands up, stopping a few feet short of them.

"And who would you be, sir?" an older, more experienced-looking soldier with dirt on his face asked.

"Thomas Nelson," I answered. "As I said, I'm from Washington City. I carry dispatches from Congress for General Jackson."

"The General's not here," the soldier said. "He's a might busy right now."

"Where is General Jackson?" I asked, trying to peer around him into the tent.

"In the city." The soldier pointed towards the sound of gunfire. "Leading the charge against a fortified position. The British jammed up a few of the streets with overturned wagons and rubble. You'll most likely find him where the fighting is thickest."

Looking in the direction that the soldier was pointing, I

116

watch as cannonballs flew high over and down into the heart of Pensacola.

"Where are your cannons?" I asked.

"They're still being moved into place," the soldier said. "We're going to return firing on the other side of the city as soon as they are in position."

"No!" I yelled at him. "Are you men blind? Have them moved to the beach and focus on the ships. We need to drive them out of cannon range so you can take the city. Stop the cannons and you'll win the battle."

The soldier stared at me, and I took the moment to wonder if I overstepped. Who was I to command him to do anything?

Something in my tone or my demeanor, or the sagacity of my words must have convinced him. "I'll order it, sir," the soldier said and dipped his head in understanding.

I nodded my head in thanks and raced down the street towards the sound of gun fire. As I got closer, I could hear men yelling, swords clashing, and the high pitch whistle that the imperfectly round cannonballs made as they tumbled through the air and down to the earth. I hadn't heard that whistle sound since the war. I remembered that sound all too well.

The street was blocked off by the backs of Americans who clashed with British in hand-to-hand combat. Men were stabbing with swords and bayonets or swinging empty muskets like clubs. Several British soldiers stood on roof tops high above, firing down at the Americans who were easy targets in the streets below.

Cannonballs plunged down from the sky like large birds of prey, landing exactly where the fighting was thickest, colliding with and ripping through the walls of a buildings to explode inside. Others crashed down into the earth amongst the men, killing groups of American soldiers and British alike. Bodies were thrown in all directions. I backed away – I was never going to get through that tight-packed mob, nor did I want to be among them as death rained down in the form of giant steel hail.

The cannon fire was amazingly accurate and seemed focused on the thickest parts of the battle. I seemed relatively safe where I was as long as I didn't go any closer.

I took the time to fire off my Thompson and with three quick shots I killed the three British soldiers on the roofs. The first shot was easy, but then it was a race to shoot the two still standing, as they saw me and were reloading their muskets to shoot me first. Killing them gave me the idea of moving through the city by rooftop instead of the clogged streets. The two-story building off to my left side had crates stacked up next to it. I climbed up the crates, which got me close enough to the roof that I could jump and grab the edge and pull myself up to the top.

I leapt from rooftop to rooftop, searching for General Jackson in the streets below that were filled with fighting men. A few buildings over and across the street, a man in brown pants and a stained white shirt stood on a church steeple with a white flag in his left hand pointing up and a red flag in his right pointing to the west. I wasn't sure what he was doing but he held the flags high in the air, signaling someone.

I swiveled my head around, trying to figure out who he was signaling, when I spotted a man who had to be General Andrew Jackson on his horse. The image of him online was close but didn't do him justice. Jackson was an older man but still fit. He was tall and a lion's main of shocking steel gray hair flowed wildly from his head. He wore black pants and a sweat-stained white shirt, but no coat or hat. Jackson gripped a sword in his right hand and what had to be an empty flintlock in the left hand. I say *had to be empty* because he held it by the barrel and was using it as a club.

The General stood in front of his men alone, trying to blaze a trail and lead the way through the fighting. He was on the other side of the killing zone but surrounded by a dozen British soldiers on the ground who were trying to pull the General off his horse. The General slashed down on his right with his sword and then down on his left with his musket-club, killing or knocking away the soldiers who grabbed at him. The soldiers had muskets with bayonets at the ends but seemed content with using them to block the General's sword strikes. None of them jabbed their bayonets at the General. They knew who he was and were trying to capture Jackson alive, not kill him – capturing a general was a valuable wartime asset. Jackson's men fought hard trying to get to their leader but were held off by the British soldiers between them and Jackson.

I jumped over and down to the next roof, which was a single-story building, which brought me closer to the General and the group of men trying to capture him. Cannonballs still landed in this section of town, destroying buildings and slaughtering men on both sides with no discretion or prejudice. I pulled my Tec-9 in hopes of killing the men around the General and giving him the opportunity to escape the hoard.

Just as I aimed at the first of the soldiers, one of his comrades scrambled through, close enough to jump up, grab ahold of the back of the General's shirt, and pull him off his mount. The General plunged to the dirt hard, landing on his left side in a plume of dust, and lost his flintlock. The rest of the soldiers dropped their muskets and descended upon him like a pack of hungry wolves, snatching at his arms and legs. One of the soldiers kicked Jackson in the face, dazing him, while another yanked the sword out of his now-opened hand.

Only six of the soldiers had the space to fall upon and grab the General. The four who still held their muskets stood around in a loose circle facing outward, making sure none of the American soldiers could try to liberate the General from their grasp. I fired two quick shots at the two closest soldiers facing outward. My rounds exploded their chests, and blood splattered the ground as they collapsed onto their backs. I took aim at the farther two soldiers still standing with muskets. Two rounds into the back on one and then into his friend, and they too were dead and bloodied, face down in the dirt. The rest of the soldiers were too close to the General for me to risk shooting.

Holstering my now empty pistol, I ran three quick steps and dove off the single-story building, arms out wide, landing on top of the soldiers as they lifted the General to his feet. The whole group, British soldiers, the General and I, went down in a heap. I came up in a roll and managed to grab the General's arm before any of the soldiers did, pulling Jackson backwards as he shook his head to clear the cobwebs.

I withdrew my sword as the British soldiers rose to their feet, snatching their muskets off the ground. They formed a line in front of us like professional soldiers, muskets up and bayonets targeted at us. They'd no longer be content to use their muskets to block our attacks – now they were intent on killing us. Yet, none of the muskets fired so they must have been discharged already. The American soldiers yelled the General's name as they tried to surge forward to his aid, only to be blocked again by the clog of British soldiers.

I handed my sword off to Jackson as I clutched both my hunting knives, blades down in my usual fighting style. My feet were shoulder length apart, with my left foot forward, so my weak hand could jab, block or slice, reserving my right and more powerful hand for the real punches or death blows.

"They'll charge at us as one," Jackson panted as he raised my sword and readied himself. "Stay together and if they circle us, go back-to-back with me. By God if they want a fight, I'll give them one."

It was sound advice, and I grunted to acknowledge his words. He possessed a warrior spirit, and I had no doubt he would give a good showing.

The six soldiers screamed as one and rushed at us. The first to reach us went down under Jackson's blade. He had swung the sword twice, deflecting the soldier's musket out of the way, then back to rip open his throat. He had mean fighting skills, of that there was no doubt.

I hooked one of the bayonets with the knife in my left hand and yanked it to my left, causing the other soldiers to pause or risk being bayoneted by their comrade. I had also moved the musket out of my way, so I could plunge the knife in my right hand down into the man's chest. Ripping my blade free, I brought my left foot back and around as the man fell, so I was back-to-back with Jackson as he had instructed. With two soldiers now in front of me and two in front of Jackson, I couldn't see what Jackson was doing, but I spun the knife in my right hand so that it was now blade up, ready for a fight.

One of the soldiers thrust his musket forward, and I blocked the bayonet with my left knife and shoved his musket to my right, as I chopped down with my right knife to block the second bayonet. The two soldiers were now at a momentary disadvantage, as their muskets were crossed over each other, forming an X. I lunged forward between the two bayonets, forcing their muskets forward with my body as I brought my right knife up into the stomach of the soldier on my right and my left knife down into the right shoulder of the soldier on my left. The first soldier sank to his knees as I pulled my knife free while the second soldier dropped his musket with a scream of agony, running off in a bloody mess as I ripped my left knife up and out of his flesh.

Then I spun around; Jackson faced off with only one soldier as the other laid on the ground, dead. The last soldier sliced down with his bayonet, and as Jackson deflected the attack with his sword, the soldier followed up by bringing his butt stock up for the General's face. The General stepped back and away from the butt stroke, then leaped forward, driving the tip of the blade into the man's chest.

As the last man collapsed, Jackson strode over and retrieved his own sword and handed mine back to me.

"By God man! You've got good timing," Jackson complimented breathlessly as he looked me over. "Who are you? I've not seen you before. You're not one of my Kentucky riflemen, that's for certain. I know all of them. You don't sound like you're from Tennessee. Are you with the Mississippi militia?"

I sheathed my knives and sword. "No, sir. Name's Thomas Nelson. I come from Washington City with letters for you from Congress."

"You can show them to me later," he said as he waved me off. "In the meantime, tell me what they say."

"I was sent to assist you, General," I told him. "I'm to act as Congress's eyes and ears."

He barked out a guttural laugh. "Assist me? Very well, sir. Find a musket and join in the fight."

"We need to move, sir," I told him. "Get your men out of here. The British Navy is focusing their cannons on this part of the city."

"Running won't help, son," Jackson responded. "They must have a damn spotter directing their blasted aim."

The man with the two flags. *He* must have been directing the naval fire. That's what he was doing.

"I'll take care of the spotter. Maybe I can even trick them into turning their cannons on their own soldiers. Can you get some of your cannons in position to return fire on the ships?"

"If you can give us a respite from those blasted cannons, by God, I'll get my own six pounders in position," Jackson boasted. "Then we'll give them what for. My Kentucky militia will throw hell itself at them."

"I'll do my part, sir," I yelled over the sounds of battle and ran off to the church where I had seen the man standing.

I reloaded my Tec-9 before entering the double doors. The main hall of the church was empty, and I ran up the stairs and around to the ladder leading to the roof. The hatch to the roof was open, and I climbed up and through it. I guess the man had seen me run into the church, because as I was climbing through the hatch, he came out of nowhere and kicked me square in the face.

Pain exploded in my face and stars filled my vision as I dropped my Tec-9 onto the roof, lifting my right arm to protect myself from any follow up kicks. I rolled out of the hatch and onto the roof. The man dropped his flags and picked up my Tec-9, studying it.

The man turned to me in time to see my Thompson out and my thumb pull back the hammer. I pulled the trigger and he snapped back off his feet. His hand opened, releasing my Tec-9 as his eyes squeezed shut, and he blew out his last breath.

I retrieved my pistol and then the two flags. Glancing around, I realized that I might have made a mistake. I was not able to see the harbor from this position – there were too many roof tops between me and the ships for the flags to be a signal. I scanned the roof tops and through the smoke and debris in the air, noticed another male at the edge of the city with matching red and white flags. He was too far to see clearly but the flags were large enough to identify. I held the white flag straight up like I had seen the dead man do, but instead of pointing the red flag westward, I pointed it eastward to see what would happen.

The man on the rooftop at the edge of the city had the same difficulties seeing me as I had seeing him, but I could see his flags and he was able to see mine. He copied my movements and relayed the signals to the ships in the harbor.

The British readjusted their aim eastward and cannonballs started falling into the British ranks instead of the American's. The British soldiers, who were only minutes ago fortifying blockades in the streets of Pensacola, were now breaking ranks and running for the huge stone Spanish-constructed Fort Barrancas.

The troops that were already locked in combat with the Americans found themselves at a severe disadvantage, no longer receiving reinforcements. A group of about fifty Americans dressed in buck skins came running down the street on the British soldiers' left flank, forming up on the run. They suddenly stopped fifty feet away, with twenty-five men in the first rank and a few more than that in the second rank. The men in the first rank dropped on one knee, with the muskets of the soldiers in the second rank leveled towards the British above the heads of the men in first rank.

An officer standing behind them holding a curved sword, swiped downward with the blade and screamed *"Fire!"* The entire American detachment disappeared with a deafening, continuous boom, and a cloud of black and gray smoke appeared as fifty muskets fired as one.

Most of the British troops still fighting were thrown to

the dirt screaming in the barrage of lead round shots that ripped through their flesh. Those who didn't crumple to the ground were quickly killed in the wave of blue-jacketed and buckskin-clothed Americans they'd been fighting but were suddenly outnumbered by.

Cannon fire from the five ships in the harbor continued to readjust eastward in my direction, landing among the British soldiers who now ran for their lives, heading toward the fort. The flags were a genius and easy way to redirect the cannon fire.

By the time the British soldiers had made it to the fort where they were safe and secure, General Jackson had relocated his cannons to the beach and fired at the ships in the harbor. It only took the first round of cannon fire for the British to realize that they were sitting ducks, anchored in the water. Their cannons stopped as their anchors came up and the sails went down. They sailed east along the coastline and out of sight as fast as they were able.

Walking out of the church I blinked into the dusty light, searching for General Jackson. I figured the command tent was the best place to start and made my way back there. I found the general leaning forward with both hands flat on his table, staring down at a large map.

"General," I called out, announcing myself to the tent as I ducked past the flap.

"Mr. . . " the General said slowly as he lifted his head and tried to remember my name.

"Nelson, sir. Thomas Nelson."

"Yes, Mr. Nelson," Jackson said. "I believe you mentioned earlier something about correspondence from Congress, after you saved my life. Thank you for that by the way. I may have been distracted before and forgotten to relay my appreciation for your timely extraction of myself from the enemy."

Wow, that was a mouthful. This man sounded more like a lawyer then a general.

I recovered from my moment of thunderstruck at his speech, then reached into my vest and withdrew the letters that Benjamin Tallmadge had written for me. I handed him the letter of introduction. He read the letter quickly without saying a word. His eyes smoothly scanned the paper from left to right.

"Benjamin Tallmadge says that I'm to afford you every courtesy," Jackson comments, lifting his eyes from the letter. "Unfortunately, I don't have much use for men like Benjamin Tallmadge, and I don't take orders from him. You see, I know about Mr. Tallmadge and his work for General Washington. The fact that he wrote this letter of introduction for you leads me to believe that perhaps you're some kind of spy. I don't care for spies Mr. Nelson. I don't care for them not one little bit."

That response was *not* what I'd expected. "I can appreciate that, General. I've had a few bad run-ins with them myself. Ask yourself, would a spy leap from a building to crash into a platoon of soldiers to save someone they are supposed to be spying on? I'm here to help, sir, in any way I can."

"It was only a single-story building," Jackson said, waving a hand dismissively. "And a British platoon is thirty men, Mr. Nelson, not ten. Yes, you help when I may have needed it, but you certainly have a flare for the dramatic. Let's not exaggerate. A whole platoon indeed."

I shrugged and ignored his attempt to lesson my saving his life. "Please call me Thomas, sir."

"Very well, Mr. Nelson," Jackson said, evidently not willing to call me Thomas. He narrowed his eyes at me. "Why are you *really* here? How do you intend to help? Did you bring men with you? Cannons and wagons maybe?"

Here was my window. I handed him the second letter authorizing pardons for pirates who assisted Jackson in the fight to protect the city of New Orleans. He read the letter, nodding his head, then folded it back up before setting it on the corner of his desk.

"We could use the men," he said to himself, running his right hand through his wild hair. "They know how to fight, but why would I want men like them under my command? They're unpredictable, to say the least."

"Two reasons, sir," I said. "First, as you say, these are the kind of men who know how to fight. And second, rumor has it that you plan on hanging all pirates upon your arrival to New Orleans. There are over a thousand pirates there. That would be a hard and bloody task. How many of your men will you lose trying to hang all those pirates? By giving them pardons, you don't lose men fighting them and you increase your numbers."

"A thousand pirates?" Jackson asked. His hand stopped, lost in his mane of hair. "Are you sure there are that many?"

"Yes, General," I repeated. "A thousand."

Jackson's jaw shifted as he took in that large number. "That's all very well. I'll decide what to do when I get to New Orleans. Right now, I have a fort to capture."

"About that, sir," I interrupted, holding up one finger. "Fort Barrancas is a trap. You can't attack it without losing half your men."

"Who told you this?" Jackson asked as he turned his back to me to pick up what looked like a glass of milk. He didn't appear overly concerned with anything I was telling him. "Benjamin Tallmadge, I'm guessing?"

"It's not important how I obtained the information, sir," I told him. "What is important is that the information is reliable. You should leave the British sealed up in the fort while you make your way to New Orleans. It will take you a month to get there, and the British are closing in on New Orleans as we speak."

Jackson spun around to face me and pointed his arm out to what I guessed was the direction of the fort. "By God man! Be that as it may, I'll not be leaving that many enemy troops at my back to attack me at a time and location of their choice."

Now the man sounded more like a general and less like a lawyer.

"General," one of his younger officers interrupted us from the entrance of the open tent. "Governor Manrique is here to see you, sir. He came here under the white flag. He wishes to discuss the surrender of Fort San Carlos with you."

"San Carlos?" Jackson asked, motioning his empty hand in a small circle to indicate he needed more information, while taking a drink of mystery milk with the hand holding the glass.

"Yes, sir," the lieutenant answered. "It's the Spanish held fort. About fourteen miles from here.

The General set the milk down on the table and grimaced, rubbing at his chest. "Oh, yes. Didn't we ask Governor Manrique to surrender the lands held by his forces so that we could attack the British without invading Spanish held lands? Didn't he refuse my offer?"

"Yes, sir," the Lieutenant said, bobbing his head. "That he did, General."

"So why would I want to entertain meeting with him today?" Jackson asked, pacing back and forth with his hands clasped behind his back, as he thought about his next move. His hair brushed against the top of the tent as he paced. "When I have a British-held fort to attack right here?"

I took this as my opportunity to save half the General's men.

"Sir," I broke in and stepped closer to his table. "If you gave me until morning to prove to you that attacking Fort Barrancas is a bad idea, you could meet with this Governor Manrique today to prevent the news of American forces attacking Spanish lands. Your actions here could have dire consequences between our two nations. A few signed documents from the governor could make this action legal and not an act of war."

"Act of war?" Jackson hollered and threw his well-muscled arms in the air. "I'm expelling the British from Spanish lands. Something they were unable or unwilling to do themselves. They should be *thanking* me."

"I understand that, General," I agreed, trying to calm the man. "But you know how politicians will twist this event. This is a way for no one to protest your actions. You can always attack Fort Barrancas at first light."

Jackson cut his eyes to me. "How do you plan on proving to me that attacking the fort is a bad idea in one night?" he asked.

"By walking into the trap meant for you and your men," I answered.

"It would look bad for you, sir, if word got out that you invaded Spanish lands without permission or orders," the Lieutenant added.

Jackson rubbed his right hand against his chest again, as if something itched under his uniform, coming to a decision but obviously aggravated by the whole conversation and the politics behind it. "Very well, Mr. Nelson. I'll meet with the Governor and give you this night to prove to me that the British have somehow set up this trap you talk about. Otherwise, I attack come morning. First light, mind you."

"Very good, sir," I said with a half-bow. "May I impose

on you to ask a small but important favor before you meet with this Governor Manrique? He will expect demands from you. You could make a small one on my behalf."

"I'm already granting you a favor against my better judgement by putting off my attack," Jackson said flatly. "But you did save my life, so ask this favor."

Jewriter and joint bookrunners.

Chapter Eight Through the Surf

November 07, 1814

I stood in the dimming light at the end of the tree line, about two hundred yards from the front of the fort, trying to come up with a plan that didn't involve me dying. So far, I hadn't come up with one. The killing field between where I hid and the fort was one that I could not cross without getting shot. It was getting dark, but the British had lit several bonfires in the expanse between us, obviously expecting Jackson to attack tonight.

I pursed my lips as I studied the landscape. I had planned on being back to the ship before sunset and pondered if the *Shining Star* would be there come morning or if I would be walking to New Orleans with Jackson and his men. I had to question my decision of relying on Jake to keep the men in line. This was too much to ask of him. But that was a problem for tomorrow. I needed to focus on what I was doing now or there would be no tomorrow. At least not for me.

Two separate parts comprised the Spanish stronghold of Fort Barrancas. The main and larger structure that faced me and a smaller structure between the main building and the beach. The smaller building was like a back door where the men manned the cannons that faced the harbor. I presumed there had to be a tunnel that led from the larger building to the smaller one which allowed the soldiers to go from one building to the other without exposing themselves to attack.

Six cannons sat out around the smaller structure on the highest part of the hill between the structure and the beach, pointing out to sea to defend the fort from attacking ships. Stacks of cannonballs formed small pyramids with barrels of powder and fuses sitting behind the cannons. The fort was well designed and finely constructed.

The Spanish had wisely cut down the trees surrounding the area, so no one could get near the main structure of the fort without being seen. Nothing but open field and open beach extended from the smaller structure and the water.

The smell of salty air blew in from the ocean as the sun touched the earth to set in the west behind the hills. The cover of darkness would be my only hope of getting close to the stone fortress. If I made it across the vast opening in the dark of night, I still had no way of getting into the fort. The large front door of the main structure was designed like a draw bridge over a dry moat. The bridge was up with the entrance sealed shut. To make matters worse, a large drop circled the entire fort that the draw bridge allowed a person to cross over when it was down. The only thing I had going for me right now is that it was a *dry* moat, more of a dugout. At least no alligators.

Instead of water below, the British had installed shooting ports to shoot out of from the safety of inside the stronghold, killing anyone in the channel-like area. My memory of the

Spanish fort that Jake and I explored came to me. Those shooting ports had looked very effective. I had no idea how many British soldiers were still in the fort, but it would only take one to end me.

How were the British planning on blowing up the fort with the General's men inside? If the history books that Jake and Aden had read had documented the event better, I would be going in with a plan of action. Instead, I would need to figure out how they planned on blowing it up and then stop them.

They would need to evacuate the fort before blowing it up. I mean that only made sense, right? The men inside wouldn't blow themselves up, not even for king and country. That meant leaving from the rear and smaller structure, like thieves in the dark sneaking out the backdoor of a house they didn't belong in. And like a thief, they needed a getaway car, and that was where the ships I had seen earlier undoubtingly came into play. The captains of those ships sailed away under cannon fire, but they didn't intend to abandon the soldiers in the fort. I was betting they'd return and were now sitting in the harbor close to the fort.

The fort was about a hundred yards from where the beach began and another hundred yards after that before reaching the water. The tide was coming in and that shortened the distance from the water line to the end of the beach. Maybe by half. So, one hundred and fifty yards from the waterline to the fort when the tide was at its highest.

Footsteps of an army shuffled behind me. Jackson's army was moving up to my back. I turned my head to look and saw General Jackson leading his men towards me, as his officers yelled orders. I needed them to stay in the tree line so as to not alert the enemy of our arrival.

"Mr. Nelson," Jackson yelled down to me from his horse

as   he   drew   near.

"General," I responded, looking up at his shadowed face. The sunlight was nearly gone.

Jackson flicked his gaze across the open field to the fort. "What is your plan?"

"I'm still working that out, sir."

"You have until the first rays of the morning sunrise," Jackson reiterated. "Not a minute more. By God, one way or another, I will have possession of that fort."

I looked away from him and rolled my eyes. "Aye, sir."

After the sky turned full dark and the yellowish quarter moon had risen in the sky, I made my way along the right side of the fort and into the waters of the cold surf. As my balls climbed up into my stomach for warmth, I cringed and went far enough out into the surf that the waves broke over my head. As I closed in on the fort, torches brightened, twinkling on the beach, held by British sentries standing guard and on the lookout for advancing Americans.

Between my limbs going numb from the cold and having to fight the waves, it took longer than I thought it would to travel through the surf and along the beach to the backside of the fort. Over a dozen long boats rowed men from the shore to the five ships farther out in the water. Several hundred men on shore waited to get into one of the long boats. They were already starting to evacuate the soldiers from the fort.

There was no way for me to get to shore with so many men standing around waiting for their turn to get in one of the boats. I stayed far enough out in the surf to not be seen, not that they were looking for anyone stupid enough to be treading water in the freezing cold waves.

After another hour of shivering and watching boats pull away from shore filled with men to return empty and pick up more soldiers, I noticed the number of soldiers dwindle down until only a few remained. Three long boats were tied to the beach, awaiting the last of the soldiers. If I was right, then the British had left a skeleton crew behind to prepare whatever trap they had planned. The three boats each had a sailor sitting at the oars, waiting and ready to row. An additional three soldiers with torches stood farther up the beach, closer to the fort. I counted quickly in my head – three long boats meant thirty soldiers at most.

I paddled through the bone-chilling water to the beach, coming out of the water with the surf breaking around me and against the shore. My teeth chattered uncontrollably, and my limbs shook so painfully I was afraid I wouldn't be able to use them. My legs had gone numb and although I managed to command them to move, I could not feel them.

The smashing waves and blowing winds covered any noise that I may have made. Water poured out of my satchel as I slogged over the sand. I moved up to the three guards from behind. They were looking outward towards the fort, waiting for the remaining soldiers to come running out, and never saw me walk up to them.

The three sailors on the boats, however, saw me and cupped their hands over their mouths to yell warnings to the unsuspecting soldiers. The waves smashing against the rocks and sand, combined with the whistle of the wind, drowned out the warning shouts from the sailors. To my relief, none of the sailors in the boats had muskets. Most likely they had knives on them.

The sailors jumped out of their boats and sloshed through knee-high water, pulling out their blades as I turned to the three soldiers and raised my Tec-9. My hands trembled badly from what I feared might be hyperthermia. I had been in the cold water longer than I had planned on, and it was taking a toll on my body, sapping my strength and muscle control. I had to hold my pistol with both hands and even then, I could not stop my hands from shaking.

I was afraid of missing and had to move closer to the men for better aim. When I was only ten or twelve feet away from the three unsuspecting soldiers, I raised my pistol again. Starting with the man on the left and working to my right, I fired one round into each of their backs. The *thunk thunk thunk* of my pistol couldn't be heard over the noise that the elements put out. I had a hard time holding up my pistol and my aim was off. All my shots were low, hitting the men in the lower half of their backs, but the men were just as dead.

Then I turned to face the three sailors who just witnessed the soldiers fall face first in the sand for no discernible reason. They'd been running toward me to stop me, but abruptly decided that they wanted no part of the man who came out of the ocean like a haunted soul from Davy Jones's locker and killed without making any noise. They splashed back to their boats and untied the rope holding one of the three boats in place and pushed it into the surf, then jumped in and rowed away as fast as they could.

I didn't see any advantage to killing the sailors or wasting my short supply of ammo, so I let them row away without stopping them. In truth, I didn't think I could have shot them if I'd tried. It would take them ten minutes to row back to the ship and report what they saw. Turning back towards the fort, I trudged up the beach, shaking my hands and arms, trying to get my blood flowing again. My skin was deathly white, and sand stuck to my boots and pant legs, slowing me down.

Another three soldiers acted as lookouts on top of the main structure but none on top of the smaller one. The soldiers on the main structure focused on the road by which the

Americans would have to come. It made sense; they had no reason to watch the harbor when their ships were out there. Stepping from the sand to the dirt, I crouched low and ran the last hundred yards up the steep hill to where the cannons laid. My legs didn't want to function but running helped the blood pump through my body and gain the feeling back in my limbs. Diving to the ground behind one of the cannons, I took a second to catch my breath and rub my hands together.

Crawling the last ten feet on my stomach to the edge of the trench, I discovered two guards standing eight feet below and twenty feet away at the open wooden door that led into the fort. Torches hung in brackets mounted on either side of the door.

My hands were still shaking, and I didn't think I could hit the broad side of a barn at this distance. I slowed my movements and holstered my pistol. I rolled over the side, hanging onto the edge. The two guards divided their attention between talking in conversation and looking into the tunnel, as if they were waiting for something or someone.

I let go of the edge and dropped the last three feet to the ground. As soon as my feet hit the ground, I allowed my body to continue downward so that I laid prone on the grass while the two guards searched around for the source of the noise they heard.

Since they didn't see me in the dark shadows against the wall, they returned to their conversation. I crawled half the distance to them, stopping outside of the ring of light that their torches put out. With a slow roll onto my left side, I pulled out my Tec-9 and then pushed myself up onto my knees. I took a step forward with my right leg, stumbled, and almost tripped as my leg briefly gave out on me. Taking a breath, I tried again, this time bringing myself up to my feet, a mere eight feet away. I fired my first shot at the guard on the right, aiming for his head. I missed and my bullet smacked into the thick wooded door with a loud whack. The two guards jumped at the sound and studied the door where my bullet had made a shallow hole. The bullet impacting with the door had been louder than the quiet *thunk* of my pistol firing and they had no idea what was going on.

As they stared at the door, I continued moving forward and fired again at the same soldier, hitting him in his back and knocking him forward into the door, where he crumpled into the dirt at his friend's feet. When his friend bent down to see what had happened to his comrade, I fired one more quick shot, striking him in the side of his rib cage and knocking him sideways into the same door.

I reloaded my Tec-9 with a new, fully loaded magazine and scanned the area for any new targets. The three boats were designed to hold about ten men each. The three sailors, three lookouts, and five soldiers I had killed in total meant that nineteen soldiers at most remained in the fort.

Closing the door behind me, I made my way through the brick walls of the tunnel. Muffled voices of men talking came from the far end. The sounds of the wind and waves were now blocked out by the thick walls, but the sound of water dripping off my still wet pants and shirt onto the stone floor, as well as my footsteps, seemed amplified as they echoed in the empty stone tunnel. I pulled my night vision goggles out of the waterproof case and slipped them on.

I had assumed that the British had taken a move out of my playbook and were going to use a long fuse, lighting it as the Americans entered the fort. I searched the ground, but I didn't see any fuse or line of black powder. I still had no idea what they were planning.

In the green haze of my night vision, the tunnel

continued straight for about twenty feet, then ended at another closed door. Moving to the door, the voices on the other side grew louder. I pulled the door open an inch and found British soldiers stacking barrels of black powder. They had their coats off and sleeves rolled up. Muskets were stacked together against the wall. The soldiers worked to bring the barrels of gunpowder from different parts of the main structure to stack them together in one large pile.

Only one lantern illuminated the room, and it was well away from the men and gunpowder. They stacked the barrels in neat rows, uniformed and aligned in proper British fashion. Four rows of barrels, five barrels in each row, stacked two high with a total of forty barrels so far and they were still bringing in more. I didn't know how many barrels of gunpowder this place had, but it was a heavily fortified stronghold, so I was sure it was a lot. The Spanish would have kept all their gunpowder in different areas for easy to retrieve reasons and so that the whole fort didn't explode if a bullet happened to hit one of the barrels. Sure, there would be an explosion but not one big enough to kill everyone in the fort.

"Hurry up, you fucks," one of the men who seemed to be in charge yelled. "I want to be on one of those ships before the Americans get here. The major won't hesitate to fire on this building whether we're back or not."

"Why are we piling the barrels inside here and not outside?" one of the others asked, rolling a barrel closer to the first man.

They tipped the barrel onto its side, starting a fifth row.

"These walls are thick," the first man in charge said. "They can take a real beating. But if only one cannonball makes it through, it'll set all these barrels off. Every cannon from our five ships will be aimed at this spot. It won't take long for the might of the English fleet to knock one hole in a Spanish fort. Once the Americans are in the fort, they'll all die, trapped in a hellfire explosion."

I had to admit, it was a good solid strategy. The British must have planned this out as a fallback plan when the fight for Pensacola first began. Between the five ships, they might bring over a hundred cannons to bear on this one spot. It would not take long for them to chip away at the fortress so one of the cannonballs could make it through.

Now that I knew what the plan was, how could I stop it? The answer was simple. I *couldn't* stop it. My only option was to set the explosives off before Jackson got here. The sailors in the long boat would reach the ships any minute now, telling their captain that the fort was under attack. I didn't want to be here when the ships started firing.

Slowly and quietly shutting the door, I ran back out the way I had come in. I rushed out the door, pulled my night vision off my head and was hit by the cold, fresh salt air.

As I ran to the wall I had dropped from, I grabbed one of the dead soldier's muskets. I lacked enough strength to jump up to grab the ledge and pull myself up, so I stabbed the bayonet from a musket into the ground right next to the wall. I managed to get my foot onto the top of the buttstock of the musket and stepping up I stretched high, grabbing the ledge. With a solid jump and using what little arm strength I had left, I was able to get enough of my body over the ledge and let my center of gravity do the rest.

I took sever steps then stopped as the six flat black cannons caught my eye. I didn't bother moving or aiming the cannons, I just needed to fire them. An unlit torch laid on the ground near the first cannon. I grabbed it, withdrew my pack of waterproof strikers, then tried to lite the torch. The first three matches broke when I couldn't use my fingers correctly. I pushed too hard and broke the stick parts in half. Each time a match broke, I cussed under my breath. The next two wouldn't light. The heads were waterproof, covered with wax, but the sticks were not. I had been in the surf too long and water had seeped through the wooden sticks and ruined the chemicals that made up the striker. I cussed again.

My sixth match worked, and I was able to light the torch.

Touching the yellow flame of the torch to the fuse of the first cannon, the weapon fired, rocking back four feet from the detonation as the cannonball exploded from the tube, heading out to sea somewhere. I ran to the next and then next, setting off the six cannons. When the sixth cannon fired and rolled back to a stop, I dropped the torch and ran as far away from the fort as possible.

The five captains of the five ships answered my call by firing their own cannons as one. They assumed that Jackson had taken the garrison in the dark of night and were now firing on it. Cannonballs rained down, hitting the small and large structure alike. Unlike in the daytime, the six, twelve and eighteen-pound black cannonballs could not be seen in the sky at night as they plunged heavily upon the fortress, colliding into the thick stone walls. Every single cannonball that plummeted from the sky seemed determined to be the one to destroy the proud Spanish fort. Brick and stone chipped off the fort and rained down on me as the thunderous impacts of steel cannonballs smacked into the fortress, whittling away at the impenetrable walls.

I collapsed onto all fours as I was hit by what might have been a brick. I struggled to get up and run, then tumbled again off balance. A cannonball exploded near me, and I rolled away from the fort to avoid the stone shrapnel. Regaining my feet to run out of danger, I was unsure which way I was running. But it was away from the fort and explosions and that was what I cared about. Explosions increased behind me as cannonballs exploded after hitting the walls of the fort. I ran blindly, pushing my hands over my ears, hoping to keep my hearing. My mind briefly wondered about the British soldiers still in the fort who were going to die by their own trap.

Then my feet were running in sand and not dirt, and I knew I had made it to the beach. I turned to my left and ran down the beach, thankfully farther and farther away from the fortress. When the fort exploded in a deafening eruption, I careened through the air. One of the cannonballs had finally made it through the walls of the impressive stronghold and set off the stockpile of consolidated black powder.

I landed flat in the water, not sure which way was up. I twirled around as a wave tumbled me back one way then the other, and I finally tumbled in the sand on shore. As the water swept against me to pull me back out to sea, I clawed at the sand to drag myself out of the water until I was back firmly on shore. The salt water I had swallowed violently came back up, and I vomited in the sand. I remained on my hands and knees gasping for air, and the cannons from the ships stopped firing.

Rolling over and falling to my butt, I saw the white sails of the ships sailing into the distance, having destroyed their target. I stood on shaky feet, and putting in all my effort, I ran again, this time away from the beach and towards the road that led to Pensacola. I tired quickly trying to run in the sand and dirt in clothes weighed down with water. I forced myself to keep going until I collapsed where the tree line began. The whole world went gray before my eyes.

Men yelling in different directions drew me back to full consciousness, and I sat up on my knees. I raised my empty hands high to avoid getting shot. Dark forms closed in on me, surrounding me, and one of them approached with a lantern.

"Is he British?" a voice called out.

"Not sure," came the answer. "He's not in uniform."

"You men, straighten up the line," the first voice hollered back at the troops. "Two of you take him to the General."

Rough hands grabbed me and dragged me to my feet. I hadn't caught my breath enough to speak yet and felt hands snatching at my weapons, disarming me. They took my pistols, hunting knives, and sword, but like most people, didn't notice my smaller black throwing knives.

I was shoved down the road to the same large white tent I had been in before, but it had been relocated to oversee the battle that was to come in the morning. I stumbled to my knees as I was thrust forward into the tent. Several lanterns lit the large tent and I squinted at the brightness.

"We found this man on the road, General," one of the men who'd pushed me announced. "He was running from the fort but is soaking wet, as if he came from the ocean."

"I can see that he's wet, Sergeant," the familiar voice of General Andrew Jackson deadpanned as shiny black leather boots entered my downward view. "Set his weapons on the table and get the man a blanket."

I had finally caught my breath enough to talk and looked up, straightening my upper body and falling back onto my ankles.

"Evening, General," I said.

Unlike before, this time he did have his coat and hat on. His sword hung at his side and his flintlock was tucked into his belt. He appeared the full general he was.

"Mr. Nelson," Jackson answered with a wry smile. "It seems you were right about the British setting a trap for us."

I wanted to say, *You think?* but instead I kept my mouth shut for once and shrugged my shoulders, as if to say, *looks like it.*

He stuck his hand out to me, and as I grasped it, he hauled me to my feet with more strength than a man his age should have had. He stepped to his table and to his military-issued tin cup filled with water and handed it to me.

"Drink this," Jackson instructed, his arm outstretched.

Taking the water, I poured the metallic-tasting water down my throat in one long drink, then handed the empty cup back to him. One of his men marched in and handed me a brown woolen blanket. I really didn't want to smell like wet wool, but I was still shivering so I took it.

"I was a much younger man back in the Revolutionary War," Jackson said out of nowhere, getting my attention. "My hair was darker back then, not so much gray. General Washington had a man with him who had his absolute trust. A man he called upon to do . . . well, truly difficult jobs. Impossibly difficult. His name was Thomas Nelson, if I remember correctly. Your father maybe?" One bushy gray eyebrow raised with the question.

"No, sir," I answered. "No relation."

Better to keep it simple.

Jackson refilled the tin cup from a pitcher that was also on the table and tried to hand it to me, but I held up my hand.

"I'm good, sir," I said.

He didn't get what I was saying and seemed to think I was boasting.

"Yes," Jackson said, still holding out the water. "I must admit, you're very good at what you do. I may not like the man, but I can see why Benjamin Tallmadge sent you."

I licked my lips, trying not to smile. "I mean the one cup

of water was enough, General."

Without pause, he set the cup and pitcher back onto the table, then turned to face me again. He placed a hand on the table and leaned back onto it.

"The British?"

"They're on the ships you fired on earlier today," I told him. "Now that the fort is destroyed, I think they'll be sailing away. To where, I don't know."

"Hmmm," he mumbled. "What would you and Benjamin Tallmadge suggest I do now, Mr. Nelson?"

"March to New Orleans. Your orders haven't changed, sir. The British will still want to take the town as a starting point. If they hold New Orleans, the war will continue. If we can stop them from getting a foothold, you can end the war. But it'll be a race between you and them. The first army to get there will have the advantage of defending the city and not attacking it."

The General crossed his arms over his chest. "And what of you? What will you be doing?"

"I'll be sailing to New Orleans tonight. I'll prepare the city for you as best I can."

"Very well, Mr. Nelson," Jackson said and reached into his coat to withdraw the two letters and handed them back to me. "Take your pardons and speak with these pirates before I arrive. But by God, you let them know that they'll either be taking the offer and fight the British with me or they'll hang for their crimes."

"Yes, sir," I responded as I accepted the letters. "I'll pass on the word. And sir, please call me Thomas."

"Let the leaders of New Orleans know that if the British attack with more men than I can handle alone, I'll be expecting every man from New Orleans over the age of fourteen to pick up a musket and stand on the line with my men. If my men must die to protect them from the British, then so must they. Is that clear, Mr. Nelson?"

"Crystal clear, sir," I said. "I'll let the leaders know."

Jackson turned around to face his desk, searching for something. Finding what he was looking for, he plucked it with his right hand and handed it to me.

"This is what you asked for," Jackson said. "The Governor wasn't pleased about it. But since it was my only demand, he agreed to it."

"Thank you, sir," I said, taking the item.

As I picked up my weapons from the table, I asked the General for a horse to ride back to where the *Shining Star* waited for me. If they were still waiting for me that was.

The same sergeant who had brought me to the General's tent rounded up two horses and escorted me back to where I had been set ashore. After gathering wood and lighting a fire for a signal, I did the only thing I could do. I waited, hoped, and kept throwing more wood onto the fire. My sodden garments hung on a log that I dragged over to the fire, drying while I stood on the beach naked with only a smelly wool blanket around me and watched steam rise from my clothes.

No longboat came for me that night, and no ship could be seen offshore in the morning as the sun came up. The sergeant had taken both horses with him, so if I was stuck here, I was going to be racing to catch up to General Jackson's men. Seagulls flew overhead, laughing at me, as I continued to wait for Jake and Mr. Task to rescue me.

Two hours after sunup, the white sails of the *Shining Star* sailing appeared down the coastline, coming my way. She came as close to the shore as she dared, and they lowered her longboat into the water. Two sailors rowed the boat and picked me up. A wave of relief washed over me as I waded out into the chilly water and climbed into the boat.

Back on the *Shining Star*, Jake and Mr. Task met me on deck.

"It's good to see you, Captain. We were worried after the British destroyed the Spanish fort," Task said stepping up to me

"You and me both, Mr. Task," I responded, slapping him on the arm.

Jake greeted me with a bear hug and pat on the back.

"How'd it go?" he asked, setting me on my feet and stepping back.

"I'll tell you all about it, in private. What's the status of the ship?"

Jake lowered his gaze. "We need to talk about the crew."

"What about them?" I glanced around the deck, as though I'd find trouble right then, and I did.

A dead man laid face down on the main deck. He wasn't merely on the main deck; he was in the center of the main deck as if he'd been dragged there as a reminder or a showpiece. I couldn't see his face but I recognized him as the man who I had sliced across the face.

"You?" I asked Jake as I waved to the dead man.

"You were right," Jake said. "Coin and threats didn't work. He was still holding a grudge about the mark you put on him and calling for a mutiny. He wanted to sail for New Orleans without you. I gave him a chance. I told him we weren't going anywhere until you got back. He grabbed his knife and I shot him. I had no choice at that point. I had him placed there until you got back to stop anyone else from making the same demands."

His voice rose as he spoke, justifying his actions.

"Well done, Jake," I told him. "I'm sure you didn't have any other option, short of leaving me behind."

147

"After the killing, I had to make certain promises on your behalf," Jake continued, his voice lowering. "The crew and I came to an agreement that I thought was fair for all parties concerned. The crew agreed to give you two more whole days before taking a vote on whether to pick a new captain. For my part, I agreed that if the crew wanted a new captain, you and I would leave the ship without you killing anyone else."

"Sounds fair," I said, turning back to Task. "But for now, make sail for New Orleans, Mr. Task. Then introduce me to the crew. I need to get to know these men."

Mr. Task led me around on deck to speak to the crew. He introduced me to the men, whose names I knew I likely wouldn't remember at the end of the day.

ervriter and joint bookrunes.

Chapter Nine Riverboat Ride

November 09, 1814

We sailed all day and through the night for New Orleans as the *Shining Star* sliced through the water like a razor through silk. She wasn't as fast as *The Lucy* was, trading speed for cannons, but she was fast. The next morning, we navigated into Lake Borgne. Sails were dropped, and the crew managed to glide the *Shining Star* up to the docks of New Orleans with little effort. The crew was experienced, and it was obvious that they'd been here many times, by the way they let the ship's momentum carry the vessel to the docks. Men on the *Shining Star* waved to men on the docks.

The wharf had been built up upon thick, wooden support beams high above the water, so the main deck of the ship was level with the docks where they were moored. The dock itself was constructed of wooden planks over the scummy green water, and then beyond that, a hundred yards of packed down dirt, which expanded the work area. The whole expanse was busy with ships not only coming and going but with men running around on the wooden planks of the docks.

Ships used ropes, nets, hoists, and pullies to off-load cargo to the men waiting on the docks. Other ships used the same method to on-load cotton, tobacco, and lumber, while the scene on the docks was crazed. Men raced to move barrels from the ships to the docks, then dock workers with wooden wheelbarrows moved those same barrels to different destinations. Bolts of cloths or items of large equipment were stacked high in carts, pulled by horses, oxen, or mules. One area of the docks was designated to moor damaged ships, where a dozen anchors sat in the dirt, and piles of ropes waiting to be used were coiled next to stacks of spare masts and a small lumber yard-worth pile of boards. Men on the ground were yelling at the men on the ships. Men on the ships yelled back to the men on the docks. Seagulls in the air were cawing at everyone below in hopes of finding food thrown their way.

"Mr. Task," I called out as I approached the man. "Who runs this city?"

A sweaty Task paused in his work of winding his arm-thick rope into a neat pile. "Mr. Nicolas Girod is the mayor and leader of the upper class and business district. He's in charge of the whole city in name, but not in reality. There's also a city council, more of a committee. They help write and pass laws. Jean and Pierre Lafitte have more say in the growth of the city. Unlike Mayor Girod they have no titles or appointments but control the city with their influence."

"Send two of the crew to this Mayor Nicolas Girod and city council," I instructed Mr. Task. "Request a meeting with them. Separately or together, whatever the mayor thinks best.

Inform them that I wish to meet as soon as possible. Let him know that I speak for Congress and for General Jackson."

I pulled my letter of introduction from my vest and handed it to Task. "Have the crewmen give the mayor this. Tell him that the British and General Jackson are both on their way here, and they should plan on supporting Jackson in the defense of the city. He will need to form a militia as soon as possible, if they don't have one already."

"Aye, sir," Task said, bobbing his head and tucking the letter into his pocket. "But I can take you there myself right now."

I turned back to face the harbor. "No. Right now, I want to talk to this Pierre person about my missing friend."

Task, Jake, and I left the ship in the hands of the crew while Mr. Task led us through the city of New Orleans. The city was not the red brick buildings and clean cobblestone streets of Philadelphia but more resembled a large village, packed tight with people living in wooden houses and buildings. Not all the buildings were made of wood – many houses and buildings had some masonry work covered in what looked like a type of off-white plaster. The whole city bustled with movement and noise from people working.

Task led us to Pierre Lafitte's two-story blacksmith shop. The shop was one of the few buildings made of brick and covered with plaster, built with an A-frame style shingle roof. Three doors stood ajar on one side and two more on another to allow heat out and fresh air in.

As we strolled into the shop, the air was thick with heat and the first thing we saw was the giant blacksmith. He had to be a good four inches taller and a hundred pounds heavier than I. He boasted huge arms from swinging a hammer and bending metal every day. A brown leather apron covered his brown cotton pants, and he had rolled up the sleeves of his white shirt. He appeared to be setting the shop up, getting ready for the day's work. The forge blazed hot already and he stoked the coals, making it hotter.

"Granger," Mr. Task called out with a friendly wave of his hand.

The big man stopped what he was doing and twisted his square head to look at us. He didn't say a word but gave a neutral nod to Mr. Task as if he was acquainted with him. His hard eyes then drifted to Jake and I, weighing us to the pound in ounce, deciding if we were a threat or not. I was not sure how smart the man was, but I marked him in my mind as a potential hazard. He may not have any conventional weapons on him, but he did carry two different size hammers on his belt. With his bulky arms swinging them, either hammer would kill a man.

"Is Mr. Lafitte in?" Mr. Task asked, pointing to a door in the back.

Granger motioned his head to the back of the shop in answer. I had a feeling that if Granger thought we were a threat to him or his boss, we would have a hard time going any farther. I was a little offended that this Granger didn't see us as a threat, while grateful he didn't at the same time. We didn't need more complications.

Jake and I followed Mr. Task through the shop, skirting barrels of water and crates of scrap metal, to an office with a closed door. Task knocked on the door, and a male voice with a French accent yelled *"Oui."* Mr. Task opened the door, and Jake and I followed him into the office.

Four men were in the room, three leaning against the far wall and one sitting at a large desk covered with papers. One of the three against the wall wore a bright yellow shirt and like a peacock, he stood out in a crowd. Two flintlocks and a sword rested on the desk, lethal paperweights on top of some papers.

The man behind the desk was older than me by maybe ten years, dressed in a fine black suit, rather surprising given the heat. He stared at us down a large, sharp nose, and his lips made more of a straight line across his humorless face than a smile or frown. His thick black hair was slicked-back from a high forehead that made his intense, dark eyes stand out all the more. When I looked into his eyes to measure the man, I saw no humor or tolerance. If the eyes were the windows to our souls, his soul was shadowy, cold, and emotionless.

His three men were rough-looking men, accustomed to violence and, if Task was right, they were Pierre's three lieutenants. But in no singular way were they remarkable. According to Task, no criminal activity occurred in New Orleans without these men knowing about it.

"What do you want, Task?" the man behind the desk asked with an air of impatience, but clearly recognizing Mr. Task. "Where is Captain Smith?"

"There's been a change in the leadership of the *Shining Star*." Task wrung his hands as he spoke to Pierre. "A new captain."

Task kept a respectful tone of voice as he introduced Jake and me, and then introduced the man behind the desk to us as Pierre Lafitte. Task didn't bother introducing Pierre's three men in the room.

"*The Star* has a new captain, huh?" Pierre asked, his dark eyes skipping back and forth between us. He was a man who missed little. "That's nice for you, but I'm not sure how I feel about that. My brother and I had a nice, profitable arrangement with Smith. A new captain that I didn't have a say in doesn't please me. *Pas du tout*. But I asked you what you wanted?"

That's when I spoke up, saving Task. "We're looking for

an acquaintance of ours. I was told that you were the man to talk to in New Orleans."

"*Oui*, that much is true." Pierre focused his gaze on me. "Who is this acquaintance of yours?"

"His name is Aden," I said, taking a slight step forward. "Somewhat pompous, but a powerful and influential man. A rich landowner and of some nobility. My age, same height, and would have been wearing a brown cloak, nice boots, and a vest like mine. He was snatched from your docks."

"When was this to have happened?" Pierre asked and waved a hand, as if my inquiry was of no importance to him.

"About two months ago," Jake answered quickly, also stepping closer to the desk.

"I've never heard of him and don't know anything about it," Pierre answered, returning his attention back down at the paper on his desk.

As a police officer, I had interrogated a lot of suspects and that had often come in handy in the 18th century, as it did now. Pierre didn't display any lying tells or signs that he knew what we were talking about. He wasn't defensive, didn't skip a beat in denying any involvement, and didn't act guilty of anything. He didn't even care if we believed him or not.

He was good.

"He would have had a fancy sword like Thomas," Jake quickly added. "And a knife. Both made from a finer steel than you might be used to seeing."

Pierre's head didn't move but his eyes shot upward to Jake in recognition. *Oh, he did know something.* That was something, and I kept my face perfectly still. He knew what we were talking about. The mention of the sword or knife meant something to the pirate boss. He looked back down at the paper in his hands, trying to cover the misstep of his reaction.

"I said I never heard of him," Pierre responded, his tone rising a bit.

I stuck out my hand to Jake, and he pulled his leather purse off his belt and handed it to me. I dropped a whole purse of gold and silver coins onto the desk in front of Pierre. The weighted thunk against the wood and the sound of coins clinking against each other louder than any of his protestations.

"Have you heard of him now?" I asked. "As I said, our friend is rich and influential. There is more for you if you can help us find him."

With a slow, calloused hand, Pierre reached over and dragged the leather purse closer, opening the strings and peering inside. He gave a low whistle as he looked over the contents. Pierre tugged the strings, closing the purse, and tossed the purse back to Jake, who caught it.

"*Non*," the pirate boss said. "I have no idea what you're talking about. I don't know of your friend. It's time for you to leave."

He had tossed the purse to Jake, but he was eyeing me. We had locked eyes and neither of us was going to look away. He had answers that I wanted and would have, one way or another. My breathing increased, and my chest started to rise a little fast and higher as I started pumping oxygen to my muscles in anticipation of needing to move quickly and violently. Pierre's right hand opened up as if he was ready to snatch one of the weapons on his desk. We stared at each other, both knowing what the other was thinking.

After a few seconds the overly hot room vibrated with the violence that was about to explode. He didn't even glance at his flintlocks on his desk, but then, he didn't need to. He knew right where they were, as did I, well within hand's reach. My right hand rested on my belt, equal distance from both my knife

155

and Tec-9. Neither of us moved since we both knew that if one of us did, we would both most likely die.

"What about your brother, Jean?" I asked in a level tone. "Maybe he knows. Any idea where I can find him?"

"*Oui*. He's out at sea somewhere on his ship, increasing our wealth. But I'll be sure to tell him that you desire to speak with him. He'll find you when he's done with business dealings, I'm sure."

His words were meant as a threat, and they might have been more frightening if I knew more about this Jean Lafitte. The three men leaning against the wall stood up straight, their hands slowly moving towards flintlocks tucked in their belts. The giant blacksmith with the two hammers came to the doorway, waiting like a dog that somehow sensed his master's need for him. His immense frame took up the whole doorway.

Jake stepped up and gently touched my elbow, saying that we should leave directly into my ear. He sensed the trouble that was brewing and was ready to explode. Seeing how we had one man to our back, one to our front, and several to our side, it wasn't looking good for the home team.

I could pull my Tec-9 and try to kill them before Pierre reached his flintlocks, or before the big guy behind me got his hand on me, but that wouldn't get me the answers I wanted. Task didn't have a flintlock or sword on him. Jake's shotgun was in his satchel, but he was not reaching in for it, so I couldn't count on either to do much more than get in the way.

Jake squeezed my elbow again. "Thomas, may I speak to you outside?"

Pierre and I kept eye contact like two wild dogs ready to jump at the other's throat.

"Thomas, really, I need to talk to you outside now," Jake repeated with urgency in his voice.

Mr. Task pulled on my right arm as Jake pushed my left, forcing me toward the door. The giant remained unmoving in the doorway until Pierre nodded his head. The giant took a step back and to the side, out of the doorway, so Task and Jake could guide me out of the office.

As I was being pushed and pulled past the blacksmith, he glared down at me with a challenge in his eyes. I knew then that this man and I would lock horns sooner or later.

My bones groaned at the prospect, but I couldn't let him know that.

"I'll be back, princess," I taunted to the oversized blacksmith as Jake and Task pushed and pulled me out of the shop. The oversized blacksmith let out a deep growl, and his right hand moved to one of his hammers on his belt. He continued giving me the stink eye until we were out of his shop.

As we stepped outside, the smell of piss struck my nose like a punch to the face. The streets were cluttered with people standing around talking or walking in and out of different shops. It was loud and crowded.

Jake took his hands off me. "There's a better way, Thomas, besides getting everybody in that room killed."

I spun on Jake, shoving my finger into his chest. "Jake, I told you before, if you're not willing to do what needs to be done, you should go home. That man knows something about Aden. I saw it in his eyes. He's not going to give it up freely, and he didn't think twice about the coins. There's only one way we are going to learn what he knows."

"And if you hadn't been so busy with your staring contest with Lafitte, you would have noticed that one of his men had Aden's powder horn on his side," Jake countered, raising his voice to be heard over the crowd.

"What?" I asked, turning to look back at the shop. "Are

you sure?"

Jake gave me a tight smile. "Yes, the one in the middle."

"That was Oliver," Task added.

"Maybe he can lead us to Aden," Jake said.

"That's good thinking, Jake," I told him and clapped my hand on the man's back. "I'm sorry for what I said. You did good. Better than I did, in fact."

Jake shrugged as we loitered near the shop. In my old world as a cop, it was common for us to push hard on someone and then let them go. When they ran, they ran fast and hard, and more times than not, whether they sold drugs or weapons or people, they would go straight to their stash to make sure their product was still safe. I hoped that would happen here. If I was right, then Pierre and his men would lead us straight to Aden.

It didn't take long for the three lieutenants to push out of the blacksmith shop. Two of them rushed north on the street, while the one with the bright yellow shirt scrambled to head south. Pierre was not among them.

"Those two are Oliver and Pete." Task pointed to the two men. "The other was Henry."

I didn't want to split up, and since we were able to track Oliver with the powder horn, we followed him and his friend. His friend was about forty years old, with black hair in a messy ponytail, a thick black matching beard and mustache, and dirt coating his face and hands.

We let Pierre's two lieutenants get far ahead of us so they would not see us following them. Jake switched on his cell phone and pulled up the tracking app, while Task looked on wide-eyed. I'm sure he craved an explanation, but it wasn't forthcoming. I stayed between Jake and Task so that Task couldn't see exactly what Jake was doing.

The tracking app worked perfectly. Like a compass, an

arrow turned as we moved, always pointing in the direction of the tracker. Next to the arrow was the reading in yards indicating how far we were. We stayed about a hundred yards behind the two men. We never saw them in the crowd, but that meant that they didn't see us either. They headed in the opposite direction of the harbor. We followed them through the city, eventually coming out by the Mississippi river.

I didn't cover my surprise when Oliver and his buddy boarded a steamboat tied to the docks.

"Wow," Jake said, his mouth an open O. Evidently, he was surprised as well.

"Yeah," I replied.

An actual riverboat. More than that, a real-life, Mississippi steam-power paddleboat, like an image from a painting. The boat was long, with the waterline only a few feet below the main deck. This was new to me, as I was used to ships designed to sail the open oceans. This boat would never leave the river and face oceanic, storms, or twenty-foot swells. Rather, it was made for shallow, smooth sailing. She paddled up and down the swift-moving but calm current with the option to stop and tie off anywhere she wanted along the riverbank.

I had seen pictures of these boats and in a few movies about gamblers playing poker on them, but this boat was far larger than I had imagined.

The steamboat I was looking at was named the *New Orleans*, and she was getting ready to pull away from her namesake city and head north. She bore three high and distinct decks. The head room of each deck was elevated several feet higher than I had seen on open water ships. In the lower decks of a ship, you had to bend your head to walk around with their low ceilings. On these boats, the tallest of men could walk around standing upright. Two giant steam stacks were to the front of the boat and two smaller ones in the middle. She had a fresh coat of bright white paint, while her smokestacks were painted flat black and the paddle wheel in the back of the boat painted bright red. The ship was enormous.

"First time seeing one?" an older man walking by asked, interrupting our gaping.

I guess our mouths hung open enough for him to notice. He appeared to be a captain of one of the steamboats, sharply dressed in black pants and a large, uncomfortable-looking black coat with a matching black hat. Hidden in his thick gray beard, a pipe poked out of his mouth and it had a line of smoke curling out the end which left a sweet smell of burned tobacco behind him.

"The wave of the future," the old man said as he plucked his pipe from his lips. "Mark my words, son. There are over twenty-five steamboats paddling up and down the Mississippi River at any given time. The number of steamboats is increasing with the demand for travel. At least two a day arrived in New Orleans while another two leave the city heading north. They are going to connect New Orleans with the rest of the country. Mark my words, the riverboat will be around for the next hundred years."

The old man spat on the ground, set the pipe back in his mouth, and ambled off.

As the old man continued on his way, I brought my attention back to our prey. I found the villainous men walking up the stairs to the boat's second level. I didn't know how long we would be gone on this steamboat excursion, so I sent Mr. Task back to the ship to keep the crew under control and make sure they didn't decide to take any type of mutinous vote early.

"Ask around the city," I instructed Mr. Task. "See if anyone knows where Jean Lafitte is or what he's doing. I want to know as much as I can about him."

"Yes, sir," Task answered. "Anything else?"

"Feed Rooster for me," I requested. I didn't want the poor bird to starve.

It was only ten in the morning, but I had Jake give Task a hand full of coins to divide up among the men so they could go out and blow off some steam with whiskey and women tonight, in case we were not back before sundown.

Jake made a point of telling me that our coin reserves were starting to get low as he paid the first mate two silver pieces for our passage. We stayed on the main deck, finding a spot out of the way behind a stack of wood which had been cut and stacked for the main steam boiler, and where we were not overly visible. The steamboat emitted a horribly loud bellow as the steam horn notified people the boat was pulling away from shore. We made ourselves comfortable since we had no idea where we were going or how long it would take to get there.

After about forty minutes, the sound of the paddles slowed and the boat drifted to a dock in the middle of a clearing. There was nothing else around this dock. The steamboat never stopped, it just slowed down enough for Clancy to leap off the boat and onto the dock as we passed by. His friend had stayed on the boat but watched Clancy as he strolled down the dock.

I didn't know where his land-bound friend was going, but the man still on the boat made himself comfortable, so he was planning on being on the boat for a while. We stayed on the boat until it paddled around a bend in the river. Jake and I made our way to the middle of the boat, where the waterline seemed to be the highest. Jake made sure his phone was secured in its waterproof case, and I did the same to my night vision goggles. To avoid making too much of a splash and bringing attention to ourselves, we perched on the railing and swung our legs over the side, then slowly lowered ourselves into the water.

We were only twenty feet from the shoreline, but the water was deep and the current strong. My bullet-proof black vest was weighing me down. Jake didn't have a vest, but he had to swim with only his right arm as his left arm was busy holding his satchel, which held his gun and ammo, over his head. His shotgun ammo wasn't as waterproof as my nine-millimeter and 30-30 ammo was, so he needed to keep them out of the river as best he could. For every foot we swam towards the shore, the current took us five feet down river. Eight feet from shore, our feet finally touch bottom. We were able to walk the rest of the way out, water pouring out of my satchel as if I had been trying to net me a fish with it.

"Think there are any alligators in there?" Jake asked, pointing to the river we just climbed out of.

The image of alligators swimming around in the river sent a hard shiver down my back. Thank God, he hadn't asked me that *before* we got into the water, otherwise I don't think I would have done it.

We took a few minutes to rest from our swim and wring out our clothes as best we could. Jake pulled out his cell phone, making sure it was still dry and in working order. After powering it on, he selected the tracking app and located Oliver.

"He's about a half mile that way," Jake said, pointing down river. "We need to hurry before he's out of range."

We strode down the river along the bank where we could, breaking into the trees when the bank ended and the waterline rose to the vegetation. Shifting around a group of weeping willows, we came to a clearing, where a long two-story brick building with a wooded roof sat by itself in the middle of nowhere. It looked to be in good shape and didn't appear old. Someone had this building constructed here only a few years ago.

"He's in there," Jake said. He stared down at his phone and pointed to the building. "You think Aden's in there, too?"

"That's my guess," I said, withdrawing my Tec-9 and moving out from the cover of the trees.

Two saddled horses stood tied to a picket post next to a wagon hitched to a third horse. Windows extended along the sides of the building, so we crept up from the front so as not to be seen. Two large double doors welcomed us in the front. We crept up to the building on the side of the two large barn-like doors.

The doors were open two feet apart, as if someone had recently entered and didn't shut the doors behind them. From outside, I could see that the building was really a warehouse. The only light inside came from the windows, which let in more than enough so we could see. Four nice tables were set up front, laden with about twenty silver and brass candleholders atop them. Under the tables were a cluster of wooden chests. Behind the tables, a wall of crates was stacked high. Standing next to the opening, I leaned in, listening for movement or voices. Not hearing any, I silently stepped inside the warehouse. The farther I entered, the thicker and mustier the air became. Dust flew in the air, dancing in the rays of light pouring through the window, tinged with the scent of fresh wood.

As we snuck around the tables and crates, voices sounded in the rear. We snuck through and around expensive furniture and what had to be a fortune's worth of paintings and stolen goods, when we came upon a group of cannons, barrels of gunpowder, open crates of cannonballs, boxes of fuses, stacks of muskets, containers of musket flints, and barrels of musket shot. My chest clenched at the sight of this much artillery. These guys had enough weapons and paraphernalia to equip a small army.

Just beyond that were barrels of whiskey and canvas bags filled with coffee beans. The coffee bags were stacked high to form another wall that we had to walk around to go deeper into the warehouse. I wondered if these were the stolen bags of coffee from the Spanish sailor we had spoken to.

"Don't move," a voice behind us commanded.

My body froze but I turned my head slowly to see Clancy's partner standing behind us. His pants were wet up to his knees, and he leveled a pair of flintlocks at us.

"I said don't move," he said again, aiming the weapon closer to my head.

One flintlock pointed at me and one pointed at Jake. I had no idea where he had come from to surprise us like this.

He gave us an eerie grin. "Drop the matchlocks."

Bending over, I dropped my Tec-9 onto the straw-covered floor. Jake followed my lead and lowered his shotgun.

"Now the sword belt," the man said.

I lifted my belt over my head and let it drop with my Tec-9.

"And the other. Slowly."

I complied and pulled out my Thompson, dropping it to the floor. A jerk snapped at the back of my belt as he yanked the knife in the small of my back from its sheath. The thunk on the wooded floor told me that he had thrown my knife somewhere behind me. A second knife hit the floor, so I knew he had taken Jake's knife from him as well. He was behind me so there was a chance that he hadn't seen the knife on the front of my belt.

"Now the knife on the front," he said, as if he'd read my mind.

At that point I didn't see any choice I had so I pulled my knife out and opened my hand letting the blade drop to the ground.

"Now walk," the man said.

He didn't say which way, but I thought it was a safe guess he meant towards his friends. We filed along another twenty feet, skirting more stolen valuables, and there stood Oliver and three more men. Criminals, I assumed. My father always told me not to make assumptions, but I thought this assumption was a safe bet. The four men jumped and went for their knives when they saw Jake and I walk into view. They relaxed when they saw their friend behind us with his flintlocks on us.

They were standing in an alcove between the merchandise, and without moving my head I surveyed the scene. Oliver was straight in front of me, holding a knife and sword in his left hand. The weapons matched my own, so I knew they belonged to Aden. Oliver still had the powder horn over his shoulder, sitting on his left hip. To Oliver's right, my left was one criminal and to Oliver's left were two more. Oliver had a knife and flintlock in his belt, but his three friends carried only knives, no flintlocks. The four men relaxed a little with their friend behind us, pointing flintlocks at our heads. They stepped towards us, forming a tight half circle, stopping three feet in front of us.

"What are you doing here, Pete?" Oliver asked his comrade behind me.

"After you got off the ship, I stood up to piss off the side of the boat," Pete said. "These two were in the water, swimming for shore. I figured they were following you, so I had the captain pull up to a sandbar and jumped off. Found their tracks and followed them. Lucky for you that I did."

"Why didn't you take his knives?" Oliver asked.

"I did," Pete answered confused, as I tilted my head to

judge the distance from him to me.

Right as I turned my head, my hand shot back, hurling one throwing knife I had already palmed from my vest in a backhanded throw. At six feet, I couldn't miss, not even throwing backhanded. The knife handle appeared like magic in what used to be his left eye socket, slicing through his round orb like butter, and he dropped his flintlocks to grab his face. The knife didn't go deep enough to pierce his brain and kill him, but I was sure he was out of the fight, as he crumpled to his knees, screaming in terror and pain.

I was already in motion, stepping forward, and as Oliver seized his flintlock, I kicked him in the balls. He squeaked and doubled over as Jake launched himself at one of the other men.

The men on both sides of Oliver attacked at the same time, rushing forward and throwing punches. I threw a quick one-two, jab-punch combo at the man on my right as the one on my left nailed me with a solid right-handed punch to the face. The one I had struck flung backward, tripping on some boxes before crashing into a large mirror, shattering it with a crash and a tinkling rain of glass.

The man who had landed a good punch to my face drew back for another. As he swung again, I stepped into his swing, turning my body so that my shoulder collided into and up against his chest. I grasped his extended wrist with my left hand and his elbow with my right. With his arm fully extended and his weight off balance, I rotated my body to my left, bent at the waist, and whipped the man over my hips and shoulder, throwing him to the ground. He landed hard, flat on his back with the wind knocked out of him. I held onto his arm, and tucked his wrist into my armpit, then slid my left hand up to his elbow, locking it with my right hand.

With a grunt of effort and a hard violent jerk, I heaved

upward, snapping the man's elbow and yanking his arm out of its socket. His elbow gave out a loud bone-snapping pop, as a jagged piece of his lower arm bone exploded out of the skin. He screamed until my boot came down hard on his head, knocking him out when his head collided with the wooden floor. Probably better for the poor fool that way.

The man with the missing eye covered his eye socket with his left hand. My knife handle stuck out gruesomely between his fingers, as his right hand picked up one of the two fallen flintlocks in front of him. Before he could get a decent grip on it, my second knife spun in the air and sunk deep into his chest. He released the flintlock again, his hand flexing open as he crumpled over onto his side.

As I swiveled around, the man I had punched had regained his feet and was charging at me. He bled from his hands and forearms from rolling over the broken glass of the destroyed mirror. I bent at the waist as he collided over me. I grabbed his legs and stood quickly, tossing him into the air to land on his back.

Oliver was still on the ground but had managed to pull out his flintlock. He was drawing the hammer back as I shifted and kicked the flintlock out of his hand. The flintlock flew in the air to land clattering among the ill-gotten merchandise.

I didn't know how Jake was doing, and when I paused to look, the man I had flipped in the air had rolled over and shot forward, crashing his shoulder into my waist. I collided face first into more wooden boxes, then onto the floor with him still driving me forward. My mouth filled with the metallic taste of my own blood – I had bitten my tongue.

Reaching back with my left hand, I got my arm around his head in a headlock. Jerking on his head and moving my shoulders, I managed to roll to my side and jam two fingers into the man's eyes. He howled and recoiled, trying to free his head and save his eyes from being pushed into his skull. His head snapped back and I punched him hard in his exposed throat to crush his windpipe. I couldn't produce enough force to crush the windpipe, lying on my back the way I was, but getting punched in the throat was never a good thing. He rolled off me and away, clutching his damaged gullet.

When I finally took my gaze off the man, I found Oliver standing over me, his right leg pulled back. He kicked me in the ribs hard enough to lift my body off the ground. Air exploded out of my lungs in a breathy grunt, and he might have broken a rib if my new vest hadn't had a thick layer of gel inside, designed to disperse kinetic energy. He roared in anger as he kicked me again. I took the blow to my ribs a second time, but this time, I was ready for it and tightened my core and upper body. When his foot sunk into my side, I grabbed his leg with my right hand, locking his foot into my armpit. I withdrew my last throwing knife with my left hand and stabbed him, sinking the knife deep into his right thigh. His roars became screams as Oliver hopped backwards on his left leg and tumbled to the ground. He rolled over and limped away.

The man who I had punched in the throat managed to regain himself and came at me again, but this time he clutched a sword in his hand that he had picked up off the ground. I reached for a throwing knife and dismally realized I had used all three. His sword came down for my head, and I quickly snatched a piece of broken wood from the mirror and blocked his strike. The wood stopped the first swing, but the blade bit deep into the wood.

As he raised his arms for another chop at my head, the sword didn't free itself and he ripped the mirror frame out of my hands. I braced myself for his next attack, but before he swung down again, a shot rang out. We both froze and turned to see that Jake had gotten a hold of one of the fallen flintlocks and shot his opponent who had been reaching for the other flintlock.

I took the moment of distraction and kicked out, so the heels of my feet smashed into the bottoms of his kneecaps. The vibration of his knees snapping shot up my legs, forcing a shiver across my back with it. With a scream of pain and flaying arms, he fell atop me, face down. He tried to wrench his arm back to stab me with the sword still held. I grabbed his head with both my hands, rotating his head to his right to drive his whole body to follow. Now that his back was to me, I pulled harder to his right. He resisted and his neck muscles bulged as he tried to turn his head to the left for all he was worth. He strained his neck muscles to resist me as his body tried to roll off me. I wrapped my legs around his waist and locked my feet together, both pulling him into me and squeezing him as tight as I could. He swung the sword over his head, trying blindly to slash me in the face. I tipped my head to the left and his blade scraped the floor next to my ear. With a sudden and forceful quick jerk, I reversed direction with my hands and snapped his head hard to his left. The hard snap of his neck breaking filled the warehouse as his lifeless weight collapsed onto me, no longer moving.

I laid under him for a moment, panting to catch my breath, when Jake stepped up and shoved the dead man off me with his foot.

"You, okay?" Jake asked between breaths.

Not yet ready to talk, I spat a mouth full of blood off to the side and nodded my head *yes*. Jake stuck out a hand and when I grasped it, he hauled me to my feet. He sported a fat lip and a purplish bruise on his cheek. I looked around at the carnage at our feet. Panic shot up my body when I realized Oliver was gone. The sound of the warehouse doors closing echoed in the dust-filled air.

"Fuck," was the only thing I could say as I lunged forward, leaving Jake behind.

I opened one of the doors to see Oliver mounting a horse, kicking the animal in the sides and sprinting away. Moving forward, I grabbed the reins of the remaining horse and swung into the saddle. I reined the beast's head around and spun my horse in the direction Oliver had gone and leaned forward to urge the horse into a gallop.

Oliver and his horse sprinted towards the river, and I was riding fast in his dust, my horse's hooves pounding hard in the dirt. Oliver made it to the river, then turned to run parallel it. Oliver may have been born to this world, but he was a sailor, where I had been born in a world traveled by cars but had spent the last five years riding Little Joe for speed and for fun, honing my horsemanship skills. As a result, I was the better horseman. I veered to the left and away from Oliver. I urged my horse to go faster, his muscles shifting and thrusting between my legs that kept the horse under my control, and we rode out of the dust cloud. Oliver was to my right glancing over his shoulder as he tried to locate me. I got far enough ahead of him to rein my horse back towards the river.

I rode at him at a steady pace, then pulled my horse up at the last second. Our horses collided in a sharp retort, and I flew in the air, ramming into Oliver and taking him out of the saddle. We sailed through the air, and I landed headfirst in the dark, muddy water of the mighty Mississippi. I released Oliver and lost track of him when I slipped under the surface of the swift-moving river as the current sucked me down. I swallowed what must have been half the river, the sentiment-filled water scratching my throat.

Twisting upward and kicking off the bottom, I broke the

surface of the river coughing and gasping in lungs full of air. Though my dripping, sodden hair, I looked around to reorient myself. The shore was behind me, and Oliver was nowhere in sight. I began swimming for the riverbank when Oliver popped out of the water behind me, jumping on my back and shoving me back under the murky surface. His hands gripped on my shoulders, forcing me down as he was directly above me. He also used me like a floating device to keep himself above the water.

In the dark, cloudy water, my feet hit bottom, digging into the loose muck. I grabbed Oliver's wrist and yanked him forward, while shifting my shoulders back, causing him to lose his grip on me. Kicking off the bottom, I shot up, breaking the surface again, sputtering. This time, Oliver was directly in front of me. Turnabout is fair play, so I lunged forward and grabbed his shirt, climbed on top of him, and shoved him under the water. His body twisted under my weight and his right hand came up with a knife in it.

I had forgotten about the knife on his belt.

I grabbed his hand holding the knife, and we sunk under together twisting around one another while fighting for the knife. My shoulders struck the mud as he drove me down, and I lost my grip on his knife hand. He had a free shot and could have stabbed at me, but his lungs needed oxygen, so he pushed off me to swim upward. I seized his legs to drag him back down and rolled over on top of him, driving him into the muck. My lungs burned as they screamed for oxygen. We both were breathing hard before we went into the water, and I'd only had two breaths of air since. I thought my chest might burst before Oliver would get to me.

His knife sliced across my ribs, not cutting me but cutting through the leather covering of my bulletproof vest. I grasped at his knife hand, but the water was too dark to see. I managed to grip his wrist several times, but each time he was able to break free. He kicked off my chest trying to get away from me, heading for the surface. His lungs must have burned for oxygen as mine did.

I grabbed his leg again to pull him back down, but my left hand accidentally grabbed my throwing knife that was still stuck in his leg muscles. I ripped the knife free, feeling the blade slice through more muscle. What I wanted to do was stab him with it, but I was afraid of passing out and disengaged from him, fighting the current to reach the surface. My head broke the surface, and I sucked in as much air as I could before going back under. I swam for the shore again, with Oliver off to my right, also swimming for the bank.

We reached the bank at the same time, both of us crawling over the mud on our hands and knees, gasping hard. It felt like a race to see who could stand first, both of us knowing that whoever managed to rise to their feet first would have the advantage. Neither of us won, as we managed to stand at the same time. I did have an advantage now that we were out of the water – his injured leg had to deal with the hardships of gravity and had trouble keeping him up right.

I would like to say we ran at one another as gladiators trying to please the crowd, but in truth, we moved slow and cautiously like two geriatric old men fighting over the last bowl of pudding. Neither of us were able to hold up our arms very high. My knife hung at my side, as I waited for the last second to raise it. I didn't have the energy for anything more.

He lunged for me, sweeping with his knife. With all the strength and speed he could muster, coupled with a scream, he slashed at my face. I jerked my upper body back and he missed. Taking a deep breath, I kicked out with my left foot, nailing his right leg where my knife had been a minute ago. I didn't have enough strength or energy to kick out with any real power, but he did collapse to the ground and rolled off the bank and into the water, dropping his blade as he went. My limbs quivered with exertion, but with a shaky step, I managed to step up and kick his knife off to the side and into the dark fast-moving Mississippi River with a *plunk* sound.

I was on land with my knife, exhausted, and half-drowned, but relatively uninjured. He was in the water, exhausted, injured, and weaponless. This was my chance to take him alive, so he could answer our questions before we decided what to do with him.

He crawled to the shallower water and tottered on his knees, trying to get to his feet. Again taking advantage, I waded into the water in front of him and drove my knife deep into the side of his neck. I ripped my knife out with a wet sucking sound, and blood sprayed out over the river. He collapsed backwards into the river, arms sprawled out. Then the current slowly dragged him away.

I sat down hard on the muddy riverbank. I didn't have the energy to take him alive, and I remembered we could still question the man whose elbow I broke.

...esWriter and Joint Bookbinders.

Chapter Ten Deals

September 19, 1814 – *Two months earlier*

Pierre looked up at Chauncey, who held up his left hand to display the sword and knife.

"Are those the property of the gentleman you sacked last night?" Pierre asked, his lips pressed into a slight moue of interest. "Is he dead? Can I even sell them, or do I need to put them in the warehouse for a few months? Your mates reported that he had a friend who got away from you."

"No, I didn't kill him," Chauncey said. "He's alive but not a problem. I don't know who his friend was so aye, the warehouse would be a good idea."

"Granger," Pierre yelled towards the open door.

The large smith was suddenly standing behind Chauncey. Chauncey didn't hear the man walk up behind him. How did a man of his size move that quickly or quietly?

"What do you make of those?" Pierre asked, pointing to the weapons. "They look French made. Are they of good steel or just fancy looking for some wealthy gentleman to show off?"

Granger reached out and took the sword from Chauncey. He unsheathed it and handed the scabbard back. Then he eyed the sword up and down, studying the handle and the blade. With an easy shift of his hands, he transferred the sword to his immense left hand and pulled the smaller of his two large hammers from its belt loop with his right.

"Not French," Granger said in his deep, rolling voice. "Not British, or German neither. I don't recognize the work."

Granger tapped the sword with the hammer, listening to the sound it made. Up until that moment, Chauncey had never heard Granger talk. In truth, he had thought the man mute. The sword made a dinner bell-like ping with an echoing vibration that lasted several seconds.

"Strong steel," Granger declared, handing the sword back to Chauncey. "Very fine work. Best I've seen."

Few words but high praise from a man who never spoke. Granger slid his hammer back on his belt and strolled out of the room, presumably to go back to his forge and beat on some more steel.

"Pay him, Henry," Pierre said, motioning his head towards Chauncey. "Oliver, you're going to the warehouse later today with a shipment of tobacco. Take the sword and knife with you. We'll keep them there until we know who his friend was. We'll sell them in two or three months. Take the wagon, not one of the boats."

Oliver pushed himself away from the wall and took the two blades from Chauncey.

"New powder horn?" Oliver asked, raising an eyebrow at the horn Chauncey lifted off the man who called himself Aden Steel.

For a powder horn, it was very fancy. Made from the

175

horn of a bull, it was exquisitely etched with animals and crowned with brass on the bottom end and silver on the top.

"Here," Chauncey said, pulling the horn off and handing it to Oliver. "I won't be needing it. You can have this too. Its empty and looks to have never been used. You'll need to fill it with powder."

Oliver smiled as he took the horn and walked out of the room. Henry withdrew about twenty gold pieces from a small chest on the desk the size of a loaf of bread, counted the coins, thought about it, and dropped two of the coins back into the chest and handed the remaining coins to Chauncey.

"The knife is made from the same steel as the sword," Chauncey said in protest, still holding out his hand.

Henry grumbled, then pulled five more coins out of the chest and dropped them in Chauncey's hand.

"Be happy with that," Henry said angrily, "you fucking ship rat."

Chauncey ignored Henry's insult. "Do you know where I can find Jacques?" Chauncey asked Pierre.

"Jacques?" Pierre asked, sitting up straight and seeming interested in Chauncey for the first time since he'd strode into the shop. "Why are you looking for Jacques? If you have something bigger going on, I want to know about it. Don't even think of cutting me and *mon frère* out of any deals."

"Nothing like that, Pierre," Chauncey responded with a laugh. "I swear. I owe the man some coin and want to pay him back before I spend it. Nothing more than that."

"Try looking down at the tavern," Pierre recommended, referring to Samuel's Tavern. "Jacques recently bought the tavern from Samuel. Now he spends most of his time sniffing around one of the new barmaids. The one with red hair and big teeth."

176

"Thank you," Chauncey said, dipping his head, then wandered out of the office, bouncing the coins in his hand.

Chauncey ambled into the tavern and waited for his eyes to adjust to the dim light from the lanterns and candles. The smell of the cheap lamp oil that Samuel was known for buying attacked Chauncey's nose, making his eyes water. Once his eyes adjusted, Chauncey peered into the gloomy interior. The tavern had about ten customers already, most drinking beer, but a few were also eating.

Chauncey spotted Jacques sitting in the back of the room at a table with the red-headed barmaid, who sat next to him, giggling at something. He was an unremarkably-sized man with hard eyes deep set in a soft face. He was a man who didn't miss much. His seat placement was not by chance. Rather, he sat at the table in the darkest corner of the room. Jacques and the female gazed into one another's eyes like lovers or like those who planned to be lovers in the near future. Her hand rested on his arm, so Jacques was making headway with his desires to seduce the young lady.

Jacques's faithful lap dog Big Jim hovered at the bar, cracking walnuts with his bare hands while his eyes lingered on Chauncey. Big Jim was the biggest man Chauncey had ever met, even slightly bigger than Granger. Two oversized flintlocks laid on the bar in easy hands' reach. Chauncey didn't understand why

Big Jim was so faithful to Jacques, but it was well known that if anyone wanted to get to Jacques, they had to go through Big Jim.

Jacques was a French born citizen raised in England by his father, a small-time merchant, after Jacques's mother had died. He possessed the ability to speak perfect French with a French accent as well as perfect English without the accent. He had traveled to the new world twenty years ago as a young man and had gone into business with the Lafitte brothers, making contacts in the French and British communities. He proved to be rather skilled at finding the right buyers from merchandise that may not have been obtained strictly legally. His cut was a one percent finder's fee that the buyers paid, mostly because Pierre Lafitte would have him killed if Jacques ever entertained the thought of taking money from the Lafitte brothers' profit.

Chauncey strode up to Jacques, who either didn't notice Chauncey or was pretending not to notice. The table in front of Jacques had a flintlock and a hatchet on it within hands' reach. Chauncey knew that that flintlock was French made – he'd seen it before, but the hatchet was new. The steel head appeared well made, and Chauncey wondered if Jacques had bought it or if the hatchet was part of some financial venture. Jacques was known for importing merchandise and reselling it at twice the market price.

Chauncey coughed into his hand to get Jacques's attention.

"I see you, Chauncey," Jacques said with his French accent strong, trying to impress the young lady. "I'm just ignoring you. What do you want?"

"To talk business," Chauncey answered.

"So, talk," Jacques demanded, still not looking up at Chauncey. His attention was on the barmaid.

"In private," Chauncey said, looking at the young lady with meaning.

"Come back later then." Jacques flicked his fingers as if shoeing away a fly. "Can you not see I'm busy right now?"

"Jacques," Chauncey called out. "This is big. Real big. Even at one percent, you'll make more money than you will working a whole year with the Lafitte brothers."

Jacques's head slowly turned to look at Chauncey for the first time. He glared into Chauncey's eyes, searching for the prank or swindle. Not seeing one, Jacques kissed the young lady's hand and whispered something in her ear. She smiled back, kissed his cheek, and stood up to leave, giving Chauncey a narrow-eyed, indignant look for disrupting her romantic interlude. Chauncey watched her walk up the stairs to the second floor.

"Captain Burlington is looking for you." Jacques leaned back and pointed his first finger at Chauncey.

Chauncey took a seat across from Jacques without waiting to be invited. Jacques took a drink from his chipped clay cup, never taking his eyes off Chauncey.

"What's with the hatchet?" Chauncey asked, gesturing to the weapon. "It's new, never seen you with it before."

Jacques lifted the weapon and smiled. "I bought and imported fifty of them from Canada. Sold forty-nine of them for three times what I paid. Kept this one for myself."

"Good deal for you," Chauncey said, nodding his head.

"What do you want, Chauncey?" Jacques asked with a sigh as he set the hatchet back onto the table. "You didn't come here to ask about hatchets."

Chauncey ignored Jacques' comment about Burlington looking for him. "Do you still have contacts in the different governments from your two mother countries?"

"If you're referring to my beloved France and my not so beloved England, then the answered is *oui*. I have contacts with men of importance from both those governments. They pay me from time to time for information about one another. Why do you ask this?"

"I need you to set up a meeting with both parties," Chauncey said and set his satchel on top of the table. "I have something to sell that they'll both want to buy. I'll sell it to the highest bidder. The British will no doubt end up with the item, but the French will help bring up the price."

"What information do you think you know?" Jacques asked, setting the cup down on the table and giving Chauncey a regretful look. "I most likely already know it and sold it."

Chauncey rested his hand on top of his satchel. "It's not information. It's a weapon. One that you've never seen before. One that will change warfare and decide the victor of any battle."

Jacques picked up his cup again and took another drink. He looked bored. "You think you're Ares, do you? Such delusions will get you killed."

"I don't know this Ares, but I have a new weapon to sell," Chauncey explained and leaned over the table towards Jacques. "Set up a meeting and let them know that the highest bidder wins."

"What kind of weapon do you think you have?" Jacques inquired, interested in the conversation for the first time since Chauncey had strolled into the tavern.

"Tell them that it's a flintlock that holds six preloaded containers," Chauncey leaned farther forward whispering, his eyes wide. "You load the containers, not the flintlock. The containers go into the flintlock. You can fire six times, as fast as you can pull the trigger. I think the design can be adapted for muskets, maybe even cannons. Whichever army has this weapon will be unstoppable."

"Fuck off," Jacques said angrily. He leaned away from Chauncey and crossed his legs, having dropped his French accent. "You're wasting my time and my chances with my new red-headed friend. Go back to Burlington and take your beating for whatever offense he wants you for."

Chauncey glanced around the room, then slipped his hand into his satchel and slowly pulled out the flintlock. He showed it to Jacques but didn't let him touch it. Jacques set his cup down on the table but didn't take his eyes off the weapon. Not that Chauncey worried he might grab it from him – he had beaten the man named Aden and forced him to show Chauncey how to reload the weapon. If Jacques tried to take the flintlock, Chauncey could kill him, his bodyguard Big Jim, and anyone else who tried to stop him from leaving. Chauncey pulled the hammer back several times, rotating the cylinder to show Jacques a sample of how the weapon functioned.

"Where did you get that?" Jacques asked, now more interested. His hand rose as if he intended to grab it.

"From a leprechaun," Chauncey intoned ominously, moving the flintlock back and away from Jacques. "One that has provided us with a rainbow. We just need to follow it to our pot of gold. He's still alive and he's part of the deal. Highest bidder gets the flintlock, all the preloaded cartridges that I have, and the man who can explain how the weapon functions and how to reproduce more."

Aden had told Chauncey how the weapon worked but sworn he had no idea how they were made. The British or French could beat that information out of him when he was theirs. Chauncey knew that whoever bought the weaponry would want Chauncey to go with them to explain the weapon to their gunsmiths so the flintlock could be reproduced. But Chauncey was no fool. If he got on a ship with either Navy, he would never be released. They would not only not pay Chauncey, but they would use torture to obtain any information that they could, then kill him so he couldn't sell the information to their enemies. At least, that's what Chauncey would do in their stead.

This was why it was important to keep his peculiar leprechaun alive. Let them have the stranger instead of Chauncey. Then Chauncey would take the gold, and the leprechaun would take the pain.

"It'll take me a few days to get the word out." Jacques spoke slowly, leaning back again. "Maybe weeks before they agree, then they'll need at least a month to settle on a time and place. They'll also need to be told how much they are authorized to bid. They'll pay more than a king's ransom for it, but that will take some time. They'll want to pay in gold and promissory notes. The British may offer lands and titles, thinking they have value to men like us. Where are you keeping this mysterious leprechaun now?"

"I'm going to take him to Baton Rouge," Chauncey said vaguely as he placed the flintlock back into the satchel. "I have a friend there who operates a tavern much like this one. He will hide me and keep my new friend safe. For the right amount of coin that is."

"Very well," Jacques said. "Take your leprechaun as you call him, and your new weapon to Baton Rouge. Keep him safe, you'll be with him for a while. I'll set up the meeting and come to you. But I warn you, neither party will want to meet there. Too far inland. They'll want to meet in a safer place. Most likely on one of the small islands in or south of Lake Borgne."

After Chauncey left the tavern, he tried to figure out the best way to get Aden on a riverboat without prompting any questions. He knew a captain who, for half the coin he had left in his possession, would let Chauncey board at night. Chauncey planned to hide the outsider in a room until they reached Baton Rouge and off load at night with no one around to see. His friend's establishment was close to the docks, so it would be easy to get him behind closed doors and out of the eyes of strangers. Maybe Chauncey would just drug the man and stuff him in a large clothing trunk. He wasn't a big man and would fit easy enough, which convinced Chauncey to buy some nightshade and some wine on his way back to his room. Chauncey grinned as he thought about the fact that he was finally going to get the big score that he deserved, his pot of gold.

...venturi and joint bookmarks.

Chapter Eleven Salt

November 09, 1814

I waded into the river and grabbed Oliver's dead body before it floated away too far. Cutting the powder horn strap from Oliver's body and throwing it in the river meant I had one less item from the future to keep track of. With any luck it would sink and be buried in the muck at the bottom of the river. I found the horse Oliver had ridden. As I rode back, I took it easy on the creature, riding him at an easy walk back to the warehouse.

By the time I arrived, Jake had the lone, living man tied to a chair with a tourniquet fastened around his right arm above the elbow, to prevent him from bleeding to death. The sleeve of his shirt was already wetly soaked with his blood. His head lolled forward, eyes closed, his chin laying against his chest. His slack face was blanched pale from blood loss. His right arm looked awful with the skin ripped open and red muscle and white fat protruding out and around the jagged white radius bone that stuck out.

"Thank goodness you thought to keep this one alive," I said, lifting my chin to the unconscious man in the chair. "He is alive, right?"

Jake handed me my weapons that he had set on a crate. "Well, I wasn't going to just stand here and watch him bleed to death. Plus, after spending the last few days with you, I thought there was more than a good chance you would be coming back alone. You killed Oliver, didn't you?"

"I had to," I lied, realizing my voice sounded a little too defensive. "Think this one will talk?"

"If we can keep him conscious. He keeps passing out from the pain," Jake answered with a doubtful look on his face.

"Let's load up that wagon while we wait to see if he lives or not," I said.

"Load up the wagon with what?" Jake glanced around at the stolen merchandise.

"You said that one of the reasons General Jackson lost the battle was because he needed cannon and cannonball fuses. You said General Jackson would need them when he gets here. There are dozens of boxes of them over there. We might as well take what we can now."

"What about Aden?" Jake asked. "You said we needed to stay focused on finding Aden."

"Focused not blind," I explained, waving my hand at the merchandise around us. "We are still looking for Aden. We can take the cannonball fuses now and give them to Jackson later. We can also look around for anything else he might need."

We spent the next hour loading up the wagon with the cannonball fuses. We also grabbed cannon fuses, muskets, flintlocks, and swords. We found several chests filled with jewelry that I loaded up onto the wagon to give to the crew.

They needed a reason to keep me as captain, and I thought this might be the answer.

I had my arms full of bolts of silk when Jake called for me. I thought our wounded prisoner had woken up, so I tossed the silk into the back of the wagon and ran back into the warehouse. Instead of the prisoner, I found Jake looking through a stack of upright paintings leaning against a pile of crates. He had thumbed through half of them, but one in particular caught his attention. I moved up to him, peering over his shoulder.

"I can't believe this," Jake said, sounding amazed. "It's here."

He was looking at the painting that he had showed me a picture of two weeks ago. General George Washington, Lafayette, and I were sitting on our horses while the British surrendered. The colors were brighter and really brought out the detail of the scene. The crimson British uniforms, dark mossy-green grass, and tattered blue uniforms of the colonists were so bright. I could see every brush stroke that the painter had laid down on the canvas. The picture I had seen earlier was two hundred years old, so the colors were not as vibrant as they were in front of me now.

In that moment, I made a decision. "Put it in the wagon."

"We can't," Jake said, sounding offended by the mere idea of taking it.

I now understood how General Washington felt when we first met and I'd told him he couldn't attack the British.

"Can't?" I asked, also quoting Washington. "I'm pretty sure I can."

"Who knows the history of this painting?" he explained, pointing at it. "How many different owners it belonged to; how many hands it went through before your grandkids bought it?"

"You said my grandkids paid a fortune for this painting," I countered. "I'm not only going to save them the money they spend, or will spend, but this way, Annie will get to see it."

I loaded the painting up into the wagon while Jake followed and continued to object. I grabbed a few of the less impressive paintings to put on top on mine. I didn't want the crew to see this painting, and I would later give the other paintings to the crew as payment.

"Drive the wagon back to the ship and load it up," I instructed Jake. "Have Mr. Task divide up the silk and jewelry among the crew to keep them happy. Make sure to tell them not to sell the stuff in New Orleans. Put the paintings and cannonball fuses in the captain's quarters. You can have them store the rest of the stuff in the hull in case Jackson needs any of it."

"What will you be doing?" Jake asked as he stepped up onto the wagon.

"Talking to our friend in there and hopefully finding out where Aden is," I answered, jerking my thumb over my shoulder toward the barn.

I could see that Jake wanted to argue about leaving me and about leaving me alone with the unconscious man, but he didn't say a word. He sadly nodded his head in resignation and lifted the reins. I turned back and marched into the building to the echoes of horseshoes as Jake rode away.

The man tied to the chair was awake. He was in a lot of pain, so I didn't think torture would work. I didn't know if I could have caused him any more pain than he was in right now.

Yes, I did. I knew I could.

It would involve me stepping over that line that I had been trying not to step over again, but I could. But I didn't think

I would need to resort to that.

I found a few barrels of different spices. The first two barrels had pepper in them, but the third barrel contained salt. In hindsight, we should have loaded the salt and pepper into the wagon with the weapons. The cook on the ship would have been grateful for the flavoring, and the crew would have been even more grateful for the spices than the cook.

I filled a cup with salt and pulled a chair up in front of my new friend.

He was sweating badly from the pain and clenching his jaw, trying not to scream. I picked up Aden's sword and held it lightly in my left hand, leaving the knife where it was. I sat in front of him for a minute, staring him down.

"What's your name?" I finally asked as I held the cup of salt in my right hand.

"Fuck off," he spat out and lifted his head to look up at the ceiling. He was panting hard.

I set the cup of salt down on the floor between us but didn't say a word. Pouring salt on an open wound is very painful. Beyond painful to a new plane of misery. I never *said* I would use the salt on him; I didn't have to. The implication hung in the air and he knew what it was for.

"Jacob," he mumbled after scowling at the salt for about three seconds.

"I'm looking for a friend, Jacob," I told him in a calm voice as I leaned forward, my elbows on my knees. I fiddled with the sword in my hand. "The owner of this sword. What can you tell me about him?"

"The man who sold Pierre that sword is named Chauncey," Jacob spat out again as he motioned his head towards the sword. "Ask him, that's all I know."

"Tell me how I can find this Chauncey fellow and we're

done here," I said.

Jacob's head rolled over his shoulders. "I haven't seen him in about six weeks. The last person to see him that I know of was a man named Jacques."

"Very well. Tell me where I can find this Jacques."

"That's easy," Jacob said. "Either Samuel's Tavern or his room above the tavern. He used to stay at Millie's Inn but moved into a room at the tavern last month after buying the place."

I bent over and retrieved Aden's knife. Jacob's eyes widened, probably thinking I was going to cut his throat. His expression turned to surprise when I cut the rope tying him to the chair.

"If you walk down to the river, one of the riverboats might pick you up and get you to a doctor," I told him, pointing in the direction of the river. "I'll be taking the horse."

"You're going to let me live?" Jacob asked, his face painted with incredulity. He presumed I would shoot him in the back as he stumbled away.

"You told me what I wanted to know," I said, nodding. "You should hurry, or you'll lose that arm. You should also relocate north. If I see you again, I'll kill you."

Thoughts about the last time I let someone go and lived to regret it crossed my mind. A sniper who later came after me again. He almost killed me, *twice*. A character flaw of mine? Perhaps. But this man was no John Brooks. I doubted I'd ever see him again.

I spent about thirty minutes digging through the warehouse for anything else I might want while I tried to plan my next move. I was getting weary of bouncing around, following random leads in hopes of finding Aden. In the mood I was in, I worried I might walk into Samuel's Tavern and kill anyone standing between me and this Jacques fellow.

Mounting the horse, I rode south with only about two hours of daylight left. The road Jake took to the docks was the same road I was taking now. It went south towards New Orleans and Pierre's men had obviously been using it, so where else would it go? Plus, it was the only road, so I didn't have any choice. I road for about thirty minutes and had made it to the outskirts of the city when Jake still on the wagon was riding back my way faster than he'd left.

Jake was waving his arms to get my attention. Why he was doing this was beyond me since we were the only two on the road at that moment. He drew the wagon to a stop when he reached me.

I yanked back on my reins to halt the horse. "What happened?"

"The ship," Jake answered, gasping. "The ship was taken."

I shook my head. "Damn. I was hoping Task could keep the crew in line for another day before they picked a new captain."

"No, Thomas," Jake said. "The ship isn't gone. They didn't sail away. It's still tied off right where we left it."

"Then what are you talking about?"

"It was taken," Jake said with heavy emphasis. "As in *captured*."

I ran my hand through my damp, silt-encrusted hair. "How can a ship get captured when it's docked?"

"I saw about twenty of Pierre Lafitte's men on the decks," Jake explained. "They were walking back and forth on guard, like they were waiting for someone. I didn't see any of our men. They must be locked below."

"How do you know they were Pierre Lafitte's men?"

190

Nothing he was saying made sense.

"I saw the man Task pointed out to us, named Henry," Jake answered. "I didn't see Pierre, but I couldn't miss that bright yellow shirt of Henry's."

No, he couldn't miss it. "You said it looked like they were waiting for someone?"

Jake nodded vigorously. "Yeah. I didn't want to get close enough for them to recognize me, but all they were doing was walking around on deck. You know, like they were waiting for something or someone. They were lighting the ship's lanterns when I turned away."

"Well, now we know where Henry went when he left the blacksmith shop," I said, running my fingers through my hair again. "He was gathering men to take the *Shining Star*. Pierre wasn't happy about me being captain and decided to do something about it. They are either waiting for you and me to return or for Pierre to get there and pick his own man to captain the ship. Did you see any dead men on the main deck?"

Jake's eyebrows lowered. "No. They must have taken the ship without a fight. Our men must have not wanted to fight with Pierre's men. Not their fight, after all."

"Okay, then. Let's go," I said.

"Go where?" Jake asked, raising both hands to his shoulders and looking around. "We lost the ship, and New Orleans can't be safe for us any longer."

How could I tell him none of this was *safe*? I leaned forward in the saddle. "Let's go get our ship back. We can't leave New Orleans yet anyways. I found out that Aden's sword was sold to Pierre by a man named Chauncey. This Chauncey guy was last seen by a man named Jacques, who stays at a tavern called Samuel's Tavern here in New Orleans. So, our business isn't done here until we talk to this Jacques, no matter what

Pierre thinks."

"Can't we let them keep the ship and go find this Jacques person?" Jake asked. "They'll be distracted. It's our best chance and a smart move."

"No. I'm afraid not. First off, if we don't take the ship back New Orleans won't be safe for us. I know men like this Pierre. He's a bully, Jake. My father used to say that if you let a bully push you once and get away with it, he'll keep pushing. We need to push back. We need to push back *hard*."

"And second?" Jake asked.

"Second," I continued, "it's *my* ship, no matter how I became captain. Pirates or not, those men are my responsibility, and I can't leave them to whatever fate Pierre decides for them. Nobody shits in my sandbox and walks away unscathed."

Jake's nervous face appeared doubtful, and I had to bring up his confidence. Big talk was just what he needed. It's natural to be scared in the face of danger, healthy even. Fear can heighten the senses, send adrenaline throughout the body to help hide pain or injury, increase strength and stamina, and it may be the difference between life and death. But if you let the fear control you instead of you controlling it, you can't operate or function effectively, and I needed Jake operating effectively, or we would both die.

"Jake," I told him in a calm voice as I tilted my head a little and lifted my eyebrows. "It's what the Pale Rider would do." I referred to myself in the third person for the second time in my life.

"Yeah," Jake said nodding, with a slight smile and some of his lost confidence returned. "It is, isn't it?"

The sun had burned itself out in the ocean, and only torches lit up the dark expanse of the docks. As our wagon passed each torch, we were bathed in yellow flickering light, only to disappear in darkness again until we reached the circle of light made by the flames of the next torch.

We rode the wagon down the dock together, with my horse tied to the back, and purposely stayed on the wooden planks and not the hard packed dirt. We kept the wagon at a slow pace, horseshoes clomping against the wood and wagon wheels squeaking as if demanding more grease. Like a bad horror movie, the sounds of our approach added to the darkness of the night and the shadows cast by the sporadic torches gave off an eerie vibe.

We made it to the ship before anyone really saw us. Several of Pierre's men had been looking our way as they'd heard us coming down the docks long before we came into sight. They seemed a little surprised to see that it was us. I guess they figured we were either dead or had left the city once they took our ship to announce their intentions of moving against us. It made some sense, seeing that if we didn't leave, the next logical step was for them to kill us. That meant that they were waiting for Pierre to show up eventually. Men on the ship hollered Henry's name, letting him know that someone was here.

I had a feeling that Mr. Task and my crew had informed

this Henry fellow and his men that I was the *real* Pale Rider. I didn't think Task was going to keep that to himself. He believed in the whole Pale Rider myth more than most and had no real reason to keep it a secret. In his defense, it appeared to him that I never aged. Why didn't that make me a ghost? I hoped that the stories he may have told caused some fear among these pirates. If they didn't believe that I was the real legend, the immortal Pale Rider before, then they would have after hearing how I took the ship almost single-handedly in the first place. Almost single-handedly, because Jake did take out the ship's former first mate right before the man shot me.

I climbed down from our stolen wagon on the near side nearest the ship with nothing between me and the *Shining Star* as Jake handed down a small redwood chest adorned with solid black hinges. Jake then climbed down on the far side, away from the ship. I had Jake stop the wagon between the torches so that we were half hidden in plain sight. They knew we were there; we just weren't lit up like they were. The five large, bright lanterns on the ship would also ruin their night vision, making it harder to see us. The two bigger lanterns hanging on their mounts near the hull bathed the whole main deck in the bright glow, the light of the fire magnified by the mirrors set onto the back part of the lanterns.

I gave Jake a slight nod from across the wagon bench, letting him know that we were ready and could do this. Jake nodded back, his shadowy face a mask of determination mixed with fear.

"I'm good," Jake whispered, knowing that I had some concerns about him. "I'll do my part. This is going to work. It's a great plan, Thomas."

He sounded more like he was trying to convince himself, not me.

I crept up to the ship alone, holding the small chest under my left arm. Since the dock was built up above the water level, I was able to see the whole main deck. In the light of the lanterns, a man was tied to the main mast of the ship. He was shirtless with his bare chest against the smooth wood of the ship's mast. His hands were tied together as he hugged the pole. As I got closer, I could tell that the bound man was Mr. Task. Thick, red stripes crisscrossed his back in different directions.

The man standing closest to the end of the gang plank held a brown rolled-up leather whip in his left hand. This was the man who had punished Mr. Task for helping me. I stared hard, marking his face in my mind, and made a silent promise to Mr. Task that this man would be the first to die tonight.

The man named Henry and his bright yellow shirt came into sight as he stepped out of my captain's quarters after his men called for him. Two men flanked him, walking towards the center of the ship as if they owned it – which they thought they did and would soon learn differently.

As I marched across the gang plank, I scanned the ship from bow to the aft, counting men and assessing their weapons. Four men stood at the bow at the ship with muskets, a dozen combatants on the main deck had swords and knives, one had an axe, three more stood at the aft with muskets and one man in the crow's nest who also had a musket. Henry and a few on the main deck had flintlocks. I walked up onto the ship next to the port side lantern.

"Mr. Task said you would come," Henry said as he strolled up to me smiling, as if he was looking at a dead man that didn't know he was dead yet. "He also said you would kill us all."

Henry, his two friends and the man with the whip stood in front of me just out of reach. No one else on the ship moved to get any closer but their eyes were on me now. Off to my right, the hatch to the stairs leading down into the ship was closed with a large roundish block lock securing it shut.

I stepped forward and threw the small chest into the hands of the man between Henry and the man with the whip.

He caught the box out of reflex and held it. The men under the large starboard side lantern flinched, believing I was attacking. Swords and knives were drawn until they realized I wasn't moving. The four men in front of me looked at me with confusion written on their faces. I half opened the unlocked wooden lid and stuck my hand into the box, pulling out a handful of jewelry. I tossed the rings, earrings, necklaces, and bracelets to the deck behind Henry for his men to see.

"I'm buying my ship back," I announced loudly as I reached back into the chest again for more jewelry. "I'll pay with the gold in this chest or with the lead in my flintlocks. It's your choice, but the ship is mine."

"I'll admit that greed is a good motivator," Henry said laughing, then lifted his arms wide to indicate the whole ship. "But fear is a better one. These men are more afraid of Pierre and his brother than they are of you."

"Well, that is about to change," I said as I pulled out Jake's shotgun that I'd hid atop the loose jewelry inside the box.

Before anyone could react, I pulled the first trigger of the Lewis and Sons shotgun, which was only a few inches away from the chest of the man holding the whip. The loud *boom* of the sawed-off twelve-gauge shotgun and the burst of flame that came out the end of the top barrel made everyone jump in surprise, except the man with the whip. He flew backwards in the air as eight pellets, each the size of a thirty-eight-caliber bullet, ripped through him.

The shotgun shells are designed to open up upon firing, causing the pellets to spread out, but at a mere five inches away from his chest, they not only didn't spread out but tore a gaping hole in his flesh the size of my fist, snatching him off his feet. He landed six feet away and rolled to his side, like a crumpled-up rag doll that had been mangled and thrown away by a pissed off dog.

Holding the powerful gun with one hand made controlling the recoil difficult, and my right arm flung into the air, following the large pistol size shotgun. The man holding the jewelry chest didn't know what to do since a fortune in gold and jewels was in his hands. Next to him, Henry grabbed for the flintlock on his belt. I swung the shotgun down onto Henry's head, connecting with both a thump and a crack sound before he could raise his flintlock. His eyes rolled into the back of his head as he dropped like a sack of potatoes, blood streaming down his face.

I pulled the second trigger and shot out the large lantern on the starboard side of the ship, and the glass sides exploded liquid fire in every direction. Three of the men near the lantern were ignited as the lamp drenched them in a molten inferno. They screamed in agony as they ran down the side of the ship, creating more confusion and panic for their stunned and shocked comrades.

A half-second later, Jake fired my Thompson from the docks, exploding the glass oil base of the lantern at the bow of the ship. Men near that lantern dove out of the way, hoping to avoid the same fate as the three I had set on fire. Their hopes lasted only a moment before the fiery lamp oil gushed over the deck, moving like a living, intelligent organism in search of victims, and finding them. Jake made a good shot with my Thompson and took out two of the four combatants with one bullet. The five sailors on fire continued to shriek for help as they ran around in circles, consumed by their panic and pain.

With the distraction, I kicked the man who still holding the valuable jewelry box against his own personally valuable family jewels. His face crumpled as he let out a whoosh of air and a moan of pain, then dropped the box and fell to his knees, holding his swollen and most certainly ruptured testicles.

The fourth man in front of me stepped up and landed a punch on the right side of my face. I stumbled sideways, doubled over with a ringing in my ear, and dropped the shotgun to the deck. Blinking to clear my vision, I drew one of my throwing knives and threw the knife in one fluid movement, impaling the fourth man in the right side of his chest as he was drawing his flintlock. He turned away running but tumbled and his flintlock clattered to the deck. In reflex and a sense of danger, I dove and rolled as several of Pierre's men fired their flintlocks and muskets at me. Two rounds pinged the railing where I had stood a moment ago, while the rest of the shots went wild into the night.

My men below deck yelled upward, wanting to know what was happening on deck. They beat on the closed hatch that prevented them from coming up. Men on the top deck shouted at one another to get me. The fires on the main deck and at the bow adding to the general confusion as burning oil caused black smoke to billow up and obscure the decking. The giant yellow flames not only added to the chaos but caused huge shadows from the running men, making the fight resemble an epic battle.

The distinct cracking sound of my Thompson firing from the wagon was followed by the man in the crow's nest careening to the deck, musket still in hand. He screamed the whole way down until he smacked the wooden deck with a loud wet thump.

The five men on fire must have realized that no one was coming to help them and one by one, jumped off the ship and into the black water below. Several of Pierre's men danced around the fire on the main deck, while the rest turned to charge at me. I drew my Tec-9 with my right hand, trying to assess the scene and determine which was my most immediate threat.

I ran to the hatch and fired my pistol, hitting the lock. The lock blew open with a loud ping and skidded across the deck. Shadows stretched across the ship, twisted by the light of the dancing flames of the fire, giving me warning as men ran towards me from behind. I flung open the hatch and spun as I raised my pistol and shot the closest man in the face. With his body still in a run, he collapsed hard and rolled my way, and I had to jump over his tumbling body.

The next two pirates came at me together from my left, their swords lifted high. One of the two men plummeted on his back, legs ripped out from him, a gaping hole where his nose used to be. The back of his head had exploded outward when my Thompson boomed in the dark from the wagon. I shot the second man charging me, clipping his side, and he dropped his sword as he spun around.

The three men to my right at the back of the ship finished reloading their muskets and brought their buttstocks into their shoulders. Their barrels dropped to point at me as the axe-wielding man to my left inched forward, around the flames, towards me.

Ignoring the man with the axe for now, I quickly shifted and grabbed the man who I shot in the side by the back of his shirt collar. I shoved him forward hard toward the back of the ship at a full run, keeping his body between me and the three with muskets. My pistol balanced over his shoulder but bounced around too much to shoot accurately. I was going to have to wait and fire when I was close enough not to miss. The pirates must not have had much love for the man in my grasp because they didn't let the fact that I was using him as a shield, or that he was waving his arms and screaming for them not to shoot, dissuade them from firing at me.

Three rounds smacked into the man's body as their guns fired. Black powder smoke billowed out of their barrels, temporarily hiding their upper bodies from my view. The man I was pushing jerked three times and then flopped to the deck hard in front of me, both pulling me down and tripping me at the same time. I rolled over him and came up fast, firing my Tec-9. Three rounds later, my pistol was empty and two of the three musket-holding pirates laid dead.

I swiftly holstered my pistol and drew my sword, ready to leap at the last man who was backing away from me. My Thompson fired again in the dark of night, and the loud, hard thump of a body striking the deck behind me made me turn around. The man I had seen earlier with the axe now laid face first on the deck a few feet behind me, unmoving with a hole in the back of his head. A pool of blood spread out from his downward face. His axe had landed mere inches from his outstretched hand, its blade sunk deep into the wooden deck of the ship.

The crew of the *Shining Star* finally came running up from below, screaming for blood and revenge, hoping to regain their dignity and self-respect after having their ship taken from them without a single shot fired. None of my men had any real weapons, but they wielded small knives, chains, and cudgels. Half of my crew attacked the remaining seven of Pierre's men still alive and on their feet, as the more experienced half of the crew tried to save the *Shining Star* by pouring buckets of sand on the fires that Jake and I caused. Most of the fire was not igniting wood yet, rather it burned the layer of lamp oil itself that spilled out across the deck.

Sword held high, I swung back around to attack the last of the men at the ship's aft. I wanted to finish him off before he had a chance to reload his musket. A dozen of my crewmen rushed my way, screaming to help me with this last man. As I ran toward the railing, the last man jumped from the back of the ship into the water below – a final last-ditch effort to save himself and survive the night.

My crew were not gentle or kind to Pierre's men. His men died fast, and without a single order from me, my crew threw Pierre's dead men over the side of the ship and into the water. This immediate action was my fault. I, or the Pale Rider I should say, had earned a reputation of tossing the dead overboard. But that was at sea and for sanitary reasons. Dead and decaying bodies spread diseases. This ship was presently tied to the pier, and it would have been just as easy to carry the dead men off the ship and to dry land for their families to claim their bodies.

Well, at least the sharks and alligators will eat well tonight, I thought morbidly.

I tried to stop several of my men from tossing Henry's limp body over the side before I had a chance to question the man. One man held his arms, and another had his legs. They were swinging him back and forth to work up enough momentum to clear the railing. I was sure the man was still alive, just knocked unconscious. I ran their way, yelling for them to hold on. I didn't make it to them in time, and over the side he went, high into the air and then down into the water with the rest of the men that he'd brought on board my ship. It was a shame I wouldn't get the chance to question the man, but then again, I wasn't going to lose any sleep over it.

In truth, more than anything else, I had been looking forward to asking him if his men were still more afraid of Pierre and his brother than they were of me.

Someone had cut Mr. Task free of his ropes, and two men held him upright as he was still too weak to stand on his own.

Mr. Task didn't miss his chance. "Pale Rider! Pale Rider!" he yelled, chant-like.

Jake raced up the gangplank and picked up his shotgun from the deck. He moved to me and grabbed me in a bear hug.

"I can't believe that insane plan worked," Jake said breathlessly as he set me back down on the deck.

"I thought you said it was a good plan," I said, a little hurt.

"I lied," Jake said with a barking laugh. "I thought for sure we'd both be dead by now. I didn't really think we had a snowball's chance in hell."

"Thanks, Jake."

The whole crew took up Mr. Task's chant and were yelling *Pale Rider* loud enough for the whole dock and the men on the ships nearby to hear. The chant probably wasn't a good idea but lifting the crew's morale and confidence was also important, so I let them have their moment.

Several men had collected up the discarded jewelry, put it all back into the wooden chest, and brought it to me. It sounded crazy even to me, but somehow, I knew in that moment that these thieving, murderous pirates had put every piece of gold and every jewel back into the small chest and not in their own pockets.

"Divide it up amongst the crew," I announced loudly. "They earned it."

This proclamation was met with more cheers and a few flintlocks fired into the air. As the crew finished smothering the last of the fires and checking the rest of the ship for damage, they then patted themselves on the back for the victory over their recent jailers.

"Here," Jake said, handing me my Thompson. "You were right. It shoots like a dream. So much more accurate and easier to control than my monster."

"Keep it," I said, holding up a hand. "You did great with it. Saved me several times tonight. And I really liked your monster here."

"Trade?" Jake asked, eyebrows raised while handing me the sawed-off shotgun.

"Yeah," I answered, taking the large shotgun-turned pistol from him.

One of the men called for me and pointed down the docks. The men stopped yelling and waited to see what was going to happen next. A clomping of horseshoes of a horse-drawn carriage came down the docks. I moved to the railing in time to see an open carriage turn around quickly and trudge back the way it had come. It was too dark to see who was in the carriage, but I figured we knew who it was.

"Are we going after him, Captain?" Mr. Task asked as the two men still supporting him brought him to stand next to me.

"No," I answered in a tight voice as I stared after the carriage. "I have someone else to visit tonight."

...written and joint bookbinders.

Chapter Twelve Prisoner

September 21, 1814

Aden lifted his aching head from the hard floor. Two itchy horse blankets, one under him shielded him from the cold coming up from the ground, and one rested over him, shielding him from the cold in the air. The blankets were thick, rough, and smelly, but Aden, a man who was used to silk sheets and the softest warmest bed coverings, was grateful for them. He'd froze at night until one of his guards took pity on him and brought the blankets yesterday. Aden smelled worse than his blankets did, so he no longer could smell them or anything else. He assumed they still stunk, which was a safe assumption.

He took the moment of not shivering to assess himself. His ribs and jaw were sore from being punched. His back and legs throbbed from the inflamed welts left by the beating with a thin bamboo switch. His right ankle had blisters from where the shackle rubbed his skin raw, and his whole body ached and was stiff from sleeping on the wooden boards.

The man named Chauncey had brought him here weeks ago and didn't seem to care about whether Aden was comfortable or not. Chauncey treated Aden no better than an animal. And like an animal, Aden didn't have any idea where *here* was. He had been in a different room when he first woke up after being knocked out. One that felt like it might have been in Chauncey's meager and poorly kept home.

Until his kidnapper had forced him to drink a cup of sour wine. Chauncey must have laced the wine with something that put Aden asleep, because Aden plunged into a deep sleep in one room and woke up groggy in another. Based on the laughter and different sounds that came from outside of his new room, it sounded like he was in a tavern.

A clanking chain led from the shackle around his right ankle to the recently mounted hook in the wall. The chain gave him free moment anywhere in the room so long as he didn't have to go more than five feet. He was forced to sleep with his feet next to the wall as he didn't have enough freedom to sleep any other way. Not that he slept much. His ankle had been rubbed raw, and he had difficulty standing after Chauncey had focused most of the beatings on his right knee.

Three different guards watched over him, none of whom were willing to talk or answer any of his questions. As best as Aden could tell, they were being paid to watch him by the man who had knocked him out and kidnapped him in the first place. The guards brought him food twice a day and took the piss and shit bucket away every night, replacing it with another. They basically ignored him and squatted in a chair outside of his room, unless he tried to escape or yelled for help. The one time he had yelled for help, the guard came in and struck him in the head with a wooden club.

Since this ordeal started, Chauncey had questioned him

non-stop about his equipment. At first, Chauncey only cared about the revolver. He beat Aden with a thin bamboo stick until Aden explained how the Webley 45-caliber six-revolver worked. When Aden managed to convince Chauncey that he wasn't an armorer and didn't know enough to answer most of Chauncey's questions, Chauncey focused on loading and firing the weapon. Aden did manage to convince Chauncey that the flintlock was designed and built by a genius armorer from Russia who had died after creating the weapon. At first, Chauncey kept referring to Aden as a *leprechaun,* which made no sense to him. Even now, Aden was still unsure if Chauncey thought he really *was* a leprechaun, which was entirely understandable seeing how the Webley might seem magical, or if it was meant as a metaphor.

Talking guards on the far side of the door, however, spoke too loudly, revealing that Chauncey was only keeping Aden to sell to the British or the French. Whoever paid Chauncey the most for the Webley, Chauncey was going to sell Aden with the Webley as a package deal. That damn Webley.

I never should have brought it.

How could he have been so stupid? The French or British, whoever ended up with the future weapon, would rule the world. Not over the course of the next two centuries, but within the next twenty years. The Webley would go down in history as the single biggest leap of technological advancement, and it was solely his fault.

Thomas had done such an amazing job saving the life of General Washington and then helping him and the colonists win the war. Thomas had unintentionally written himself into the history books as a legend and as a hero or villain, depending on how you looked at it. He'd made his mission seem easy.

Thomas and himself had been best friends, growing up together as kids. From Aden's point of view in his time, his friend had died at the hands of the British years ago. Aden had cried when he learned about the deaths of Thomas and his wife, even though he hadn't seen Thomas for years. When Jake, this *new* version of Jake that is, had come to him, he had also explained that there was another living version of Thomas stuck in the eighteenth and nineteenth century. Aden's first thought was to go to Thomas and see his old friend again, but Thomas had already suffered enough. Seeing Aden would only give rise to old, painful memories.

It had been arrogant for Aden to think he could do as good of a job as Thomas. Aden had spent two years preparing for this mission, studied the history of his world, and the history that was written on Jake's phone. He knew what needed to be done, but he was wrong to think he was the right man for the job.

Jake wanted to ask Thomas to help this General Jackson, but Aden had refused. Aden believed Thomas had done enough for the world, or at least that was what Aden told himself. In his time as a prisoner, Aden had reflected on how he had ended up in these present circumstances. He was fucked, and it was his own fault. His hubris brought him here to his downfall. Aden was not Thomas Cain, Thomson Nelson, or the Pale Rider. He was Aden Steel. Multi-millionaire yes, but he'd earned his fortune by his brains and his good business sense.

His father had taught him mathematics while Thomas's father taught him how to fight and throw knives. He had gone to college and earned a business degree, while the Royal Police had taught Thomas how to shoot pistols, rifles, and who knew how many different weapons. Aden, a man who had everything, saw this as an opportunity to really prove himself. To prove himself to whom, that was the question, but he had felt the need none-the-less.

Aden hadn't given up hope of being rescued, yet. Jake had escaped Aden's fate and was out there looking for him. Jake was a capable man. The only question was whether Jake was alone looking for Aden, or did he go back to get help?

Since coming to this new location, Chauncey had questioned Aden about the other items in the satchel. The compass was obvious, so Aden didn't bother lying about what it was. Chauncey now owned the best compass in the world. Aden didn't think a compass was going to damage the timeline much, so he wasn't worried about that.

The grenades Aden had lied about, but grenades had existed in the nineteenth century. Unreliable, crude, and poorly made, but an archaic type of grenade existed. Chauncey recognized them for what they were, or at least guessed at what they were. Aden didn't think anyone could reproduce them and would most likely blow themselves up trying, so after a beating, Aden broke down and confirmed that Chauncey was right about the grenades.

The cell phone was the worst item in the satchel. Chauncey had no idea what it truly was or what to make of it, so Aden convinced him that it was a religious relic. How else could he possibly explain it? Aden had judged that Chauncey didn't have any use for religion, and he was proven right when Chauncey had thrown the phone into the river. Thank God it wasn't in the waterproof case. Better it was destroyed than found and used.

Chauncey was curious about the night vision goggles. He recognized them as spectacles of some sort and tried them on. As they were turned off, they didn't work, and the mere idea of turning something on would not come about closer to the twentieth century. He'd thrown those in the river as well.

Aden had no idea what had happened to the bulletproof

vest he had been wearing when Chauncey had knocked him out and kidnapped him. Chauncey hadn't mentioned it or asked any questions, so maybe he'd thrown it away as well. Aden hoped it sat at the bottom of the Mississippi River, like the cell phone and goggles.

Aden's thoughts were pulled back to reality when he heard a key turning in the door lock. A click sounded as the bolt released, and the door opened slowly. Chauncey's head popped around the door, peering into the room. The smile on his face resembled that of a greedy, happy little parasite. Chauncey sauntered into the room and closed the door behind him. He held a folded piece of paper between two fingers.

The first time Aden had laid eyes on Chauncey, the weaselly man had been dressed in cheap, dirty cotton sailor's pants and shirt. Aden couldn't remember for sure but didn't think the man had worn shoes. Aden did, however, remember how badly the man smelled to Aden's twenty-first century nose. Now Aden was sure his stink would give Chauncey's a run for his money.

Today, Chauncey was dressed in clean, not rich but nicer, clothes and had a pair of shoes on his feet. Chauncey also smelled strongly of sweet flowers. He must have doused himself in some sort of flowery perfume. Aden had to rub his nose to prevent himself from sneezing.

Chauncey also had Aden's satchel slung around his neck, and it sat against his left hip. Aden considered diving for the satchel, hoping that his Webley was in there, but Chauncey was still out of Aden's limited five-foot range of his chain.

What did this mean? Chauncey and the others had taken Aden's purse and Chauncey had sold Aden's sword and knife, but still he was paying for Aden's guards, food, and lodgings. Aden knew how this worked. Chauncey must have had a shadow partner sharing in the expense of this business transaction. Someone who Aden had not yet seen or met. Someone who was paying Chauncey's expenses, bankrolling the operation. Or maybe Chauncey had money saved up, but another glance at Chauncey confirmed that Chauncey was not the sort of man to save his money. This guy spent his money faster than he made it. No, he had a partner somewhere, and he most likely was planning on double-crossing the man later. That would explain why Aden hadn't meet him – Chauncey didn't trust him.

Chauncey settled into one of the chairs in the room. The second chair sat within Aden's allowed movement, and though it hurt his ankle and knee to move, Aden managed to get up off the floor and sit in the chair.

"I have some good news, old chap," Chauncey said. "To be clear, it's good news for me, not you."

Aden didn't respond. He leveled a bored gaze at Chauncey, waiting for him to continue.

"We set up a meeting with the British and French," Chauncey told him with a grim smile and held up the paper for Aden to see. "In six weeks. We'll meet on neutral ground. You can understand why the British and French worry about the other being there. We'll meet both parties on a small island south of New Orleans. Both parties will bid on the flintlock and on you as well. Highest bidder wins. I insisted that all parties involved only bring a set number of soldiers with them. Don't want any sore losers killing everyone and taking the flintlock for themselves. They'll want a demonstration undoubtedly, so we'll have to use six more of the cartridges. That will leave only eighteen cartridges for them to figure out and reproduce. I promised them that you could help with that, so be a good fellow and keep the fact that you can't to yourself until I get paid and exit the area."

Aden painted a fake smile on his face. "Yes, certainly. Anything I can do to help."

In truth, Aden planned on telling the winner of the bidding war that Chauncey had lied to them in hopes that the winner might kill the little fuck before Aden was on a ship sailing for England or France. A ship? Aden's insides sank to his feet as he realized once he was on a naval ship sailing to Europe, it would be too late for Jake to do anything about it.

Chauncey had kept talking, but Aden was too deep in his own thoughts and self-pity, thinking about his own probable fate, and missed what Chauncey said. Chauncey laughed again and then stood up as if to leave.

...rawriter and joint bookrunners.

Chapter Thirteen Out of the Shadows

November 09, 1814

Earlier tonight, Mr. Task, Jake and I sat around what used to be the late Captain Smith's desk, in the late Captain Smith's quarters, going over our next move. We were deciding who was going to die tonight. As I stood over the desk with Rooster on my shoulder, bobbing his head while I fed him a cracker, Task and Jake tried to convince me that we should move against Pierre right away, before his brother Jean returned to New Orleans, or we'd have to deal with both of them. When Jean Lafitte returned, he would also have his entire crew with him, plus men from other ships under his control would come to his call. His own personal navy. The fact that they were not mobilized already meant they answered to Jean and not to Pierre.

Mr. Task had also learned about Jean Lafitte's business dealings. It had turned out he was in talks with the British. Negotiations as it was. I didn't understand why the British would be talking to Jean Lafitte until Mr. Task explained that Jean had a strong hold somewhere down in the Barrataria Bay – the fortress was between the bay and the Mississippi River. According to Mr. Task, Jean controlled that whole area. No one, not even the pirates of New Orleans, traveled those waters without Jean Lafitte knowing about it.

That meant that the British were trying to buy safe passage from the Gulf of Mexico to New Orleans through the waterways. British war ships could never go up the Mississippi River, but they could move men in longboats. Hell, they might pay Lafitte to provide paddleboats to transport them.

If Lafitte had already made a deal with the British, I would have to kill him. If he hadn't made a deal yet, maybe I could get him to side with General Jackson.

Either way, that was a problem for tomorrow. I had a different set of problems tonight.

Task assured me that after tonight, the crew was fully behind me and ready to take the fight to Pierre. Now that they believed that I was the *real* Pale Rider, either returned from the dead, straight from hell, or an immortal assassin, they wanted to march down the streets of New Orleans with torches, muskets, and swords, like villagers marching to the castle to kill Frankenstein's creature.

The part that surprised me was that I wasn't the monster in their eyes, Pierre Lafitte was. They wanted to hang Pierre from a rope tied to the beams of his own blacksmith's shop. The crew of the *Shining Star* had once been one of many ships that if not owned or captained by the Lafitte brothers, at least controlled by them. That was before they'd been captured, threatened, held against their will, and told they didn't have a say in who was to be their next captain. They had been insulted and wanted satisfaction for their mistreatment. In the mood they were in, blood was the only payment they were willing to accept for those recent insults.

I managed to calm the crew down, and after dividing up the jewelry and bolts of silk and explaining that their reward had been removed from the Lafitte brothers' warehouse, they cheered and agreed to let me seek revenge in their name, but in my time and by my methods. Unfortunately, Pierre would have to wait. Instead, this was the best time to go after this Jacques person, while everyone in the pirate community thought we might move against Pierre. They would never expect I might go after anyone else.

I wanted to stay focused tonight and not let this opportunity pass by unrecognized. Finding Aden was my first responsibility and mission, which meant I could not afford to allow myself to get distracted with petty revenge. I tried something new this time and was honest with my crew about what I was doing tonight and why Pierre would have to wait. I explained to them about my associate who had been apprehended and about the pardons I had for them if they wanted to be free of their past transgressions.

For the life of me, I couldn't figure out how they believed me or why they offered to help. They voted and I remained captain of the *Shining Star*. They had showed me more loyalty in going against Pierre than I ever expected from this crew of pirates, thieves, and murderers.

After all that, Jake and I now stood half a block away and across the street from Pierre's blacksmith shop. The night was warm, so no coat was needed. We weren't getting any closer to the shop, though. Rather, I wanted to see how many men were there. I counted ten loitering outside the shop and another dozen walking inside that I could see. Pierre was ready and waiting for us.

We turned around and skulked two streets down to

where Samuel's Tavern was located. My three volunteers from the ship met us a few buildings over from the tavern. I had sent them into the tavern first to get the lay of the land for me. As they were men known to New Orleans, they would not attract attention to themselves.

One of the volunteers was named Benny Egger. When I asked for volunteers, Mr. Task suggested I take Benny and his two mates. The two men with Benny were his younger brother James Egger and their cousin Robert Egger. They were in their thirties and claimed to be from Australia but had accents I couldn't place. Their accents didn't sound like the twenty-first century Australians I had known in my past life. They sounded Australian with some strong British influences mixed in. After hearing them talk, I recognized them as the men who had spoken up and initially threw their support behind me when I'd fought Captain Smith. They were skinnier than I but a few inches taller, with mussed blond hair and sun-darkened skin. Benny's long blond hair fell freely around his neck while his two companions preferred ponytails.

I liked these men from the minute Mr. Task introduced me to them. They hated the British King, and with their large, curved Kukris on their sides, they were the first people I'd met whose knives were bigger than mine own. The three men had come over from the land down under in search of fortune and fame.

Benny told me how the main room of the tavern was laid out and where Jacques was sitting. He also said that he saw a dozen men and recognized as being on Jacques's payroll.

"There's no way you're getting in there with a flintlock, mate," Benny said, pointing to my pistol. "Three of Jacques's men outside the tavern are collecting flintlocks and swords if you want to get in. I've never seen them do this before. They'll be losing customers tonight because of that, so there must be a powerful reason why. We had to give ours up to look around and get a drink. They gave them back when we left, without any problems."

"They let you keep your knives?" I asked, glancing down to Benny's blade.

Benny screwed up his face at me like I was crazy. "Aye, sir. They only took our weapons."

In the nineteenth century, knives weren't considered weapons as much as they were tools. Sure, you could kill someone with a knife, but you could also kill someone with a rock. The thought of asking someone to voluntarily give up a knife would never occur to someone here. Their flintlocks, muskets, or swords, those were recognized as weapons designed to kill, but never knives. Benny's Kukri was almost the size of a short sword, yet they allowed him to take it in. Anyone who didn't see the long-curved blade as a weapon was a fool.

"Well done, Benny," I told him. "Are you men up for going back in?"

"Aye, sir," the three men said at the same time, nodding their heads.

"Very well, then."

I laid out my plan and their part of it to them.

Three men were standing around outside smoking, as Benny had mentioned. Knives hung on their belts, and one of them had a flintlock. But that was nothing abnormal for anyone around here, and they looked more relaxed, more natural than the guards in front of Pierre's shop. A large barrel sat by the door, with several swords and muskets sticking out the top. They were collecting everything but knives it looked like. Benny had been right.

"There's no way you are getting in there with your guns,"

Jake said in a hushed tone. "You'll have to kill them first if you hope to get through the door."

"The front door is open," I pointed out. "If they go down outside, someone inside might see them fall, and that will make everything harder."

I took off my sword belt and Tec-9, handing them to Jake.

He held them like he held venomous snakes. "Are you fucking kidding me? You can't do this, Thomas. It's crazier than the plan you came up with to retake the ship. You can't go in there unarmed."

I took what I needed out of my satchel and handed him the man purse with the shotgun inside.

"I'm going in with you," Jake proclaimed.

"You can't. If I don't make it back, it'll be up to you to find Aden. Besides we can't leave our guns out here just laying around for anyone to find."

Jake's mouth worked as he thought about it, then nodded his head.

I wandered up to the tavern with the three guards. They stopped talking and stood up straight but didn't move to stop me. From under my hooded gaze, I saw them looking me up and down for any flintlocks. They let me pass without a word, so they were only being cautious men, and I kept my gaze down and continued walking. The large thick front door was on the left side of the tavern, not in the center, and I stepped inside.

The tavern resembled every tavern I had been in over the past four years, if not a little larger. The long bar was to my right against the front wall. The rest of the room was filled with tables and dirty men who talked, drank, and ate. Smoke and laughter filled the large room. A large fireplace sat unlit in the shadows against the far wall to my right. It was too warm out, and the added heat of a fireplace would have made the room uncomfortable.

The lack of light not being put out by the fireplace was easily made up by the four lanterns mounted to the walls, burning bright. The acrid smell of soot told me that the owner used cheap lamp oil. The lanterns did a good job of spreading light through the room. A lantern hung on each side of the fireplace and two more lanterns hung on the wall to my left. They'd been strategically placed so that their rings of light overlapped and filled almost the entire room. Small candles melted into clay bowls on the bar and on some of the larger tables. The small candles put out very little light but allowed the men to see what they were eating or drinking directly on their tabletops.

A back door was nearly hidden into the far wall on the left. Benny had said that three men stood on the outside of the door in the alley, but like the front door, the back door opened inward. Unlike the front door, the back door was closed, and athick beam slanted across the door, set in steel hooks mounted on the walls, barring the door shut. The door was flanked by an irritable looking man with thick gray hair and beard holding the only musket in the whole tavern that I saw. This was by design and not chance. Jacques had himself a bodyguard and he wanted his man to be the only one in the tavern holding a musket.

More than one conversation stopped when I stepped out of the shadows of the entrance and into the light of the room. I scanned the open space, counting men and scanning for threats. Shit, it only took a few seconds to count at least twenty men, and every one of them looked a threat, but thanks to Benny, I had expected this.

I located the man I was searching for in the back of the room, exactly where Benny said he would be. This man, who had to be Jacques, sat at the far table with a woman next to him. I was told she had red hair, but it was too dark to tell if her hair was red or brown. Jacques's face was in shadow, the small candle on his table not emitting enough light to reach his face, but his posture indicated that he was relaxed. Either he wasn't expecting me because Pierre hadn't bothered to warn him, or he, like everyone else, believed I was going after Pierre tonight. Since he had added security tonight, I assumed it was the later and not the former.

I learned a lot about this Jacques in the first few seconds as I stood at the front of the tavern. His table sat near the center of the room and against the far wall, so he was mindful of his security. Since this was the farthest spot from any of the lanterns, making it the darkest table in the whole room, he liked to keep secrets. Jacques was a thinker and liked to plan things out. He preferred to stack the deck in his favor. I was betting overconfidence was his biggest short coming.

The three tables adjacent to him sat empty of people or candles, as if to give him an added ring of protection from threats or light. Jacques was somewhat of a showman, too. He tried to pretend he was a boss, though he answered to the Lafitte brothers.

I took two more steps into the light and froze when the front door closed behind me. I slowly turned my head part way to see the three men who had been guarding outside were now standing inside, staring at me and blocking the door. Now I understood why Jacques seemed so relaxed. He definitely had all his bases covered. He appeared to leave little to chance, especially considering that everyone else presumed I would be moving against Pierre.

The three men outside hadn't let me pass by – they were letting me walk into a trap. I glanced around the room but viewed it in a new light. Half the room shifted, rising to their feet, openly staring at me. Everyone else in the tavern sensed the tension change and realized that this was the wrong tavern to be in tonight. Jacques's shadowy face peered my way; I couldn't see his eyes, but his chin had come up.

"Closing up for the night, lads," a large man behind the bar with a thick black beard and ponytail announced to the room but eyed me and the three behind me. "Get the fuck out."

I didn't move, nor did Jacques, nor did half the tavern that stood when I came in. Everyone else rose and moved for the door. They broke around me like water around a rock, heading for the exit. The three men blocking the door stepped aside to allow the throng of men to leave the tavern. After the last of the uninformed, but not totally ignorant of the danger looming, left the tavern, the door slammed again behind me. The loud thump and grind of wood scraping against wood told me that the door had been barred closed to match the back door. No one was coming in as long as the doors were barred shut.

One of the four lanterns was a few feet in front of me and to my left. I stepped up to it and cupping the top of the glass with my right hand, I blew hard, blowing out the wick. I sank more into darkness with this action, and my eyes adjusted to see better. The dozen or more men watching me didn't move but were trying to figure out what I was doing.

Since no one immediately attacked, they were waiting for the man paying them to give the word. I decided to press my luck and moved through the room towards the back. They assumed that if I made it through the front door, I was unarmed, so what did it matter if I talked to their boss?

To my relief, no one moved, and I made it to Jacques's table. He sat in the shadows, staring at me without saying a word. A hatchet sat on the table – its blade embedded into the wood as though he'd slammed it into the table to get someone's attention. I pulled out the chair across from him and took a seat without invitation, putting my back to the whole room. While I tried to do it in a way that made me look confident, the hairs on my neck stood up stiffly. The clicking of a hammer pulling back on a musket made me glance up at the man at the door, who had indeed thumbed back the hammer on the musket he was holding. He took a step forward, but Jacques raised a hand to halt the man from moving any farther. I figured he wanted to talk before he ordered his men to kill me.

"You must be the *Shining Star*'s new captain?" he asked in a French accent while looking at the top of my head, trying to assess what manner of hat I was wearing. "Or should I say you were? I heard Pierre took your ship from you."

"Yes," I answered slowly. "He did. Or rather, he tried. I took it back twenty minutes ago. His men are dead. At least, all the men that had boarded my ship. Did no one tell you of that?"

"*Non*," he said, his smile fading. "But it is unimportant. This is not your ship. Your crew is not here. This tavern is my ship. And it's filled with my crew. Tell me what you want before I order my man with the musket to kill you."

"Give that order and you'll be the first to die," I responded in a low tone, bringing my left hand above the table to display him the throwing knife I had pulled out. The blade was black and the table dark so I didn't think anyone but Jacques could see the knife.

Jacques peered down to the hatchet on the table.

"Go ahead and grab it," I offered, bringing my right hand up on the table near the lit candle. "If you're in that much of a rush to die."

His gaze left the hatchet and locked onto mine, weighing

221

my words and tone. Jacques broke eye contact, looked at his female companion, and motioned his head, not wanting her to see him threatened. She got up with a pout and sauntered away from the table without a word. Once she stood up, I could see that her hair was indeed red. We both watched her walk across the room and up the stairs.

"I wanted to know what you desired of me, if you were stupid enough to come here," Jacques said, looking around the room for help. "Maybe I should have given the order to kill you as soon as you entered the room."

"Could have, should have, would have, but you didn't. And now I sit here in front of you."

"What do you want?" Jacques said in perfect English, all hints of his French accent forgotten and gone.

"I'm looking for a companion of mine," I told him. "If you knew I might come here, then you already know who I'm looking for."

"*Oui,*" he said simply in French. "I do. Pierre's man from the warehouse lived. He told Pierre that he gave up my name. Why would you let him live? You had to know he would tell us about you."

I shrugged my shoulders. "I'm a man of my word. That's how you know I'll let you live if you tell me what I want to know."

Jacques made a temple of his fingers under his chin. "I see."

"And?"

"And I'm not going to tell you anything," Jacques said, dropping his hands to the table. "If you kill me, you'll die minutes later. Look around the room, sir. Be grateful if I let you leave here alive."

"Are you really going to make me kill all these men?" I

asked. "Just for a few questions that you're going to answer anyways after I kill them? Questions that you could freely give me answers to now?"

"I've heard a rumor that you think you are the *real* Pale Rider," Jacques said, leaning forward on his elbows to stare into my eyes. "Is this true? I think you are a man gone mad. You might kill three maybe four of my men if you are as good as you seem to think you are. But you will die from the onslaught of blades that come at you."

"Tell me what I want to know now, and I'll let you live," I said again.

"Leave now and maybe I'll let *you* live, eh?" Scorn was thick in his voice, emphasizing the word *you*, drawing it out.

I took a deep breath through my nose and blew it out the same. I was hoping to avoid confrontation but somehow it always came down to strength and violence with these men. I took a second to envision my next three moves. That's all I really had, three moves. After that, it would be chaos and butchery.

"Did you see the three men who came in before me?" I asked.

"I see everyone who comes in here," he answered impatiently. "There's very little I miss."

"Do you see them now?"

"*Non*," he answered without really looking around. "Only my men are left. Everyone else had the good sense to leave while they had the chance."

I tilted my head. "Are you sure? Look again."

His head didn't move but even covered in shadow, as close as I was, I could see the whites of his eyes moving, scanning the room until he found my three men, one by one, since none of them were standing together.

"*Oui*," he answered, sounding confused. "Three men

with knives will make no difference. They'll only die with you."

"Describe for me where they are standing," I asked of him.

His eyebrows furled with annoyance as he quickly glanced at them again. "Next to the three lit lanterns on the walls."

With that said, I reached over with my right hand and pinched the wick of his small cream color candle, snuffing out the flame and signaling my men. At the same time, my three men brought up their cupped hands and blew out the lanterns nearest them.

The entire room that had already been shut out from the outside world now plunged into darkness, with only a dozen tiny candles in their little brown ceramic bowls giving off the minutest amount of illumination, like stars in the night's sky. The whole back half of the room with me and Jacques was noticeably darker than the half with his men.

In that moment, I jumped up and violently grabbed the hatchet with my right hand as I threw the table over and away from myself to land on top of Jacques. He was knocked backwards in his chair, hitting the floor with the table crashing on top of him.

Before the back of Jacques's head hit the floor, the hatchet flew in the air. I threw it blindly in the dark at the spot where the grizzly man had been standing a second ago. If he moved one foot to the left or right, I would have missed him.

The thunk of the blade sinking itself into meat, and the sound of something heavy falling to the floor told me he hadn't moved.

As the room erupted in confusion, yelling, motion, and every hand grabbing at a weapon, I yanked my night vision goggles down my forehead and over my eyes, flicking them on. I had enough foresight to slip them on before entering the tavern, not caring how they looked. I spun around to face the room, and the sound clicking of flintlock hammers being pulled back echoed in the dark. With a shove of my hands, I flipped over the table between them and me as I crouched down behind it.

Several deafening booms exploded in the dark, and I could feel impacts smacking against the table I hid behind and the wall behind me. I was surprised they took the chance of firing in the dark since the chances of them hitting Jacques was as good as them hitting me.

Some of those impacts against the wall must have been close enough to Jacques for him to realize the danger he was in from his own men.

"No flintlocks, you fools!" Jacques screamed from the floor. He was still on his back, trying to get the heavy thick wooden table off himself. "Use your knives and kill him!"

The clunking sounds of heavy wooden and steel flintlocks dropping to the floor made me feel a little better. Then the sound of fists banging against thick wood came from the back door.

A flickering glow of dancing light on the floor to my left caught my attention. I popped up and saw two of Jacques's men moving towards me. The first held a candle and his partner was one step behind him. They used their knives to probe the darkness for me, arms outstretched at chest level, swinging their blades left and right. I threw my first knife hard and fast at the man holding the small candle. There was a *thunk* as my knife sunk deep into his flesh, and he and the candle dropped to the floor, spilling melted wax on top of the wick and extinguishing the already small flame. My second knife was in the air before the candlelight was extinguished. With a deep moan of pain, the second man landed on top of the first man.

Five of the men walked together on my right. They were bumping into one another in the dark, trying to stay in a tight group. Like a group of bison that sensed a wolf was among them in the dark, they needed to attack, but none of them were willing to leave the safety of the herd.

I withdrew my two hunting knives and waited for them to get a little closer and deeper into the dark. They charged around the table, stabbing with their knives, but I had already moved back to the wall and was not there. Jacques got everyone's attention when the sound of a table slamming the floor came from my right. It was too dark for anyone else to make out but in the green haze of my night vision, Jacques rose shakily to his feet, his hands on his knees as he shook the cobwebs from his head.

The banging at the backdoor now sounded like men throwing their own bodies against the wood, trying to get it open.

Jacques' men were looking in their boss's direction, or at least the direction of the noise he was making. Jacques finally stood up straight and pulled his own weapons out. His flintlock was in his right outstretched hand, that he blindly pointed at the sounds of his own moving men, while his left hand held a cudgel that he pulled from behind his back.

With the tunnel vision my goggles caused, I had to turn my head to take in the whole room again and see what had changed. Three men came around my left side, while the bartender and the three that had been at the door moved slowly in the candlelight, past the tables, trying to see who was who, before they rushed into the darker half of the room like the rest of their friends foolishly had.

Standing up, I shot forward and kicked Jacques in the butt with a forward kick, shoving him forward into the first two of his men. One of the two slashed out, believing Jacques was me, since he saw only a dark form at the last moment. He sliced across Jacques's chest, cutting through coat and skin. I didn't know if Jacques realized it was one of his own men who slashed him or thought it was me, but a flash of light disrupted my night vision goggles for a moment and my ears rang from the boom Jacques's flintlock let out. The man who had slashed Jacques was thrown to the floor.

"*C'est moi*, you idiots!" Jacques shouted into the dark as he swung his cudgel at the next man who stepped into range, striking the man in the head and dropping him at Jacques's own feet.

I crouched low next to a table that hadn't been knocked over yet, and the three cautious fellows who had come around from my left were moving slowly in the dark after having to step over the two dead men. They moved past me to the sounds of the struggle. As soon as they passed me and their backsides were in my view, I struck out, still crouched.

My left arm swung in a fiercely fast slash, slicing deeply through the hamstring in the back of the man's right leg. My right arm struck one second later and cut clean through the other man's hamstrings on the back of his left leg. They tumbled to the ground in unison, screaming and dropping their weapons. They grabbed at the vicious and large gaping lacerations, and red blood that my goggles showed as green fluid puddled on the floor under their legs.

The third man spun around in the direction of his screaming comrades, swinging his knife wildly back and forth while shuffling forward. On his second step, I leaped up and forward and brutally drove my knife down into his neck where it met his left shoulder. I ripped it out and shoved the man away from me while his hot blood sprayed into the air. A spray of blood hit my right hand right before he crashed down between me and Jacques.

Jacques and the three men turned to face the horrific screaming they heard coming from the two I had put on the floor. I had instructed my three men to blow out the lanterns and remain still until the fighting was done. I did not want them attacking me in the dark on accident.

Benny decided to disobey my orders and struck out, attacking the three doormen from behind. Benny's brother and cousin were inspired by his defiance and joined in the attack. Two of the door men went down quickly in the surprised attack, but the third had heard the footsteps and managed to spin around, slashing out with his blade and cutting one of my Australian companions. My man stumbled back, trying to lift his knife, but the doorman stepped into him and drove is knife deep into the Aussie's stomach. My man was not only forced to bend over but was driven upward with the force of the blow. The doorman ripped the knife free, and the Australian sank to the floor. The man who had fallen sported a ponytail, so it was either Benny's brother or cousin.

The bartender, finally having seen enough, turned and ran to escape the arena of butchery. If he removed the beam securing the door, then others rushed in to join the fight. I doubted they would be on our side in the battle, so I could not allow that door to be opened.

The bartender made it halfway to the front door when my hunting knife hurtled through the air, impaling him in his back between his shoulder blades. He dropped heavily on his face into one of the tables. He chose to be here and fight for Jacques, so fuck him, too.

The noise of the bartender colliding into the table got Jacques and his men's attention. I grabbed a knocked-over chair and flung it at Jacques, missing him and hitting the man next to him square in the face. The man never saw it coming and took the chair without trying to block it or duck. He didn't crumple down to the floor, but blood seeped through his fingers as he dropped his knife to cover his broken nose.

My two men were attacking the lone doorman left alive. The door man lunged for one of my men, but that was his mistake, because he gave Benny the opening he needed to slice down across the doorman's back with his Kukri. The doorman squealed and arched his back, and Benny brought the wicked blade back around and up into the man's stomach, like he'd been swinging an axe. The doorman and Benny froze in place for just a moment, as if both prepared for what was to come next, Then Benny ripped the Kukri through and out the doorman's body. The razor-sharp blade had driven deep and opened the doorman's stomach wide.

The doorman collapsed to his knees while struggling to hold his insides in place. He lost the battle and fell over onto his face with a squelch.

I made a mental note not to get into a knife fight with Benny and his Kukri. Everything in the room was green but clear with my night vision goggles, but I was disappointed that it had been too dark for Jacques and his men to have seen the horrific death.

As one of Jacques's men held his broken nose, the other two men moved towards me, and Jacques dropped his weapons and ran for the backdoor. Lifting the beam up and out of the hooks, he then threw the wooden bolt into the dark, hoping to strike me. Jacques shoved the back door open, allowing moonlight to enter the room with a fresh breeze of air, followed by the dim glow of a torch.

The three men who had been waiting in the alley rushed

into the tavern. The first held his torch high and a knife in his free hand, while the two behind him carried flintlocks and pointed them deep into the dark room, searching for who needed to be shot. The room wasn't flooded with light, but the torch did give off enough dancing flame to allow the men to see me.

I ripped the night vision goggles off my head and dropped them to the floor near the wall in hopes that they would not get stepped on. Jacques grabbed the flintlock out of the second man's hands and ordered them to kill me as he himself ran out the door and down the alley.

The man to my far right made it to me first, swinging a long knife, and I was forced to jump back and let my eyes readjust to the darkness after losing my advantage of the night vision. My eyes adjusted as the third man entered the tavern and raised his flintlock in Benny's direction. I pitched my third throwing knife and struck the man in the side of the neck. He squeezed the trigger of his flintlock as he went down in the doorway, shooting the floor.

Taking up a fighting stance, I transitioned my hunting knife from my left hand to my right, blade up this time, and kept my left hand empty. My two companions ran at the two men who had entered the tavern. The man who had his flintlock snatched from him was unsheathing a sword.

The two coming in at me separated as I rotated around a table. One went to the left and one went right, trying to trap me. The third man, still holding his bloody, abused nose, bent over in search of his knife. I side-stepped towards the man on my right. A glint of metal moved my way, and I grabbed at the wrist holding the steel.

With a vise like grip on the man's outstretched arm, I yanked the man forward so his stomach collided with the tip of my knife. My knife slid deep, to the hilt, as I spun the man's body to use him as a shield between me and my final attacker.

The two men on the floor continued screaming, which only added to the pandemonium and terror of the darkness. The final attacker came in fast and hard, driving his knife down and into the back of his friend, who I held in front of me. Ripping my knife from my captive, I pushed his limp body forward into the last attacker. The dead man slunk to the floor while the attacker stood frozen in horror as he realized that he had killed the wrong man.

The boom of a flintlock followed by the distinct crack of my Thompson came from the alleyway. Jake and Jacques had evidently crossed paths in the night.

Feeling the need to hurry, I leaped forward and punched the man in the face with a quick left jab. He stumbled back a step and then regained himself and jumped at me, swinging his knife high. I ducked low and under his blade, twisting my body around and driving my own blade deep into his leg right above his kneecap.

The sick sound of bone separating as I twisted my blade sent a shiver down my spine as the man tumbled to the floor, screaming and jerking my knife out of my hand in the process.

Another of my men were down on the floor with only Benny still standing, facing off against the man with the torch and knife. The man from the alley swung the torch like it was a sword, and Benny was blocking and parrying with his Kukri. The last of my three opponents, blood still pouring from his nose, stood up after finding his knife and look for me. He was too late, as I was already coming at him fast. My first punch was a quick and powerful right-hand side punch to his kidneys. He doubled over, and I maneuvered his knife out of his hand, flipping it around in the air and throwing it at the man with the torch.

My knife went deep in the back of his right shoulder, causing him to drop the torch. As he turned to see who had thrown the knife, Benny rushed in, grabbed the man's hair with one hand, and reached around to drag his curved blade across the man's throat.

I kicked the side of my man's knee with a heavy stomp, and I was rewarded with the sound of his knee snapping and a shriek. Grabbing the back of his head as he started to fall, I drove his face down into a table with a solid, bone-crunching *thump*. Not yet finished, his hands gripped the table in hopes of pushing off. I let his head lift up and away from the table, but only so I could drive it down harder this time.

His body went limp, and I was content with knocking him out. Well, breaking his kneecap first and *then* knocking him out.

Men were banging on the front door now. By the sounds of the shouting and banging, there were more than a few men out front.

Taking a quick scan of the room and finding Benny as the only person still standing beside myself, I ran out the back door, but the alley was eerily deserted. Then in the mouth of the alleyway I saw a figure on the ground, crawling.

"Jake!" I yelled and ran for him.

Jewriter and joint bookbinders.

Chapter Fourteen   Change of Plans

November 10, 1814

Aden sat at the table that had been dragged over to him and picked at the overcooked bacon, undercooked fish and stale bread on his plate. Chauncey sat across from him, also eating breakfast, although Aden noticed that Chauncey also had two fried eggs and several slices of cheese. Aden had been momentarily surprised when Chauncey arrived this morning with food and beer for both of them. In the almost two months that he'd sat prisoner in this room, Chauncey had never been the one to be generous with food, and no one had brought him beer. In fact, this breakfast was the most food he'd had anyone bring thus far. Aden would not be allowed to starve to death, but his ribs were showing more than they had ever shown in his life. He was not that muscular to begin with, but what muscle he had was lost in the past two months of being malnourished.

This was also not Chauncey's first mug of beer this

morning – in fact, the man reeked of it, reminding Aden of the carpet of a seedy bar, the result being Chauncey was in a good mood and so talkative.

"There's a large chain of small islands called the Free Mason Islands," Chauncey chatted and smiled as he took another swig of beer. "We'll be meeting our buyers on one that used to have a small trading post there. The old man who ran it died years ago. It's abandoned but the trading post is still standing. It should work fine for our needs."

The *buyers* he referred to meant the two delegations from the French and British governments who were going to enter into a bidding war over the Webley. And Aden.

"Our needs?" Aden asked as he shoved the undercooked fish around. He did not relish getting Salmonella along with his breakfast.

"My needs," Chauncey said with a laugh. "Right now, my needs are our needs. Just you remember that."

"When do we meet your new friends?" Aden asked, hoping to gather whatever information he might obtain.

"Five nights after tonight."

"Who all will be there?" Aden ventured. As long as it kept Chauncey talking.

"You, me, Jacques, and the Webley," Chauncey said, patting his pocket.

Chauncey never set the pistol down now that he knew how to use it. He seemed to have found a new well of confidence and bravery to draw upon with the revolutionary weapon on his person.

"How do you know they won't just take the flintlock from you?" Aden asked, hoping to plant the seed of doubt and distrust. "It's what I would do. And I think it's what you'd do, too."

Chauncey tapped the side of his own head with the first finger of his right hand as if to say, *I'm smart*. "Each delegation can only have eight men with them. But Jacques will have a dozen men or more with him. We both know I'm worth six men alone with this flintlock in my hands."

"Still…" Aden started to say.

Chauncey held up a hand to interrupt Aden. "Yes, yes. They'll try. I'm not stupid, I know they'll try. But they'll anchor their ships on one side of the tiny island, and we'll be anchored on the other side. If more than one long boat rows ashore from either ship, we'll sail away. They'll only see the three of us in plain sight and think they have enough men to do the job, but once Jacques's men step out from the trading post, they'll see that it's us who has the advantage and have to deal with us in good faith."

"You've thought of everything," Aden said, when a knock came at the door.

Chauncey jumped up and grabbed at the Webley in his coat pocket. The front sight of the pistol caught on the inner lining of the pocket, and he ripped the pocket as he jerked the pistol free.

"Who's there?" Chauncey yelled, pointing the pistol at the door.

"It's Jim," a very deep voice yelled back from the hallway.

Chauncey lowered the Webley. "Big Jim?"

"Aye, Big Jim," the man yelled back. "Jacques sent me here with a letter for you."

Chauncey quickly shoved the pistol back into his torn pocket and moved to the door, opening it. A large man who had to bend his neck to enter the room came in and handed an envelope to Chauncey. Chauncey quickly opened the envelope and read the letter inside.

"This was dated two days ago," Chauncey said with anger in his voice.

"Aye," Big Jim said, cocking his head to the right. "What of it?"

"Why didn't you bring this to me yesterday?" Chauncey asked, waving the paper at Jim's chest.

"You should be more grateful that Jacques sent you a warning at all," Big Jim commented, glaring down at Chauncey.

"I'm grateful that he thought to send the warning," Chauncey almost yelled. "I'm not grateful that you stopped off at whatever whorehouse you mother works at to visit with her, before delivering the message."

"Watch your tongue, Chauncey," Big Jim said as his very large paw of a hand came up to rest on Chauncey's shoulder. "Jacques may think you have some value, but I don't. You're a pissant. You've always been a pissant, and you'll always be a pissant. Jacques told me to help you so I am, but he never said I couldn't break one of your limbs."

Chauncey's coat scrunched up under the squeeze of Big Jim's hand, and Chauncey grimaced as his right hand moved to his pocket. His fingers stopped at the opening – he must have decided not to try and pull out the Webley. He was too close to earning his fortune to ruin it now.

"This letter says that Captain Burlington is looking for me," Chauncey said in a pain-tinged, tight voice. "He may be on his way here now. If he knows about our arrangement, he'll want in on it. He'll try to take over the whole damn thing."

"Not Burlington," Big Jim argued and released Chauncey, satisfied he'd made his point.

Chauncey held up the letter again. "What are you talking about? Jacques writes that someone calling himself the Pale

Rider is looking for me and my prisoner. If not Burlington, then who?"

Aden's eyelids flicked up at the mention of the Pale Rider. It was too much to hope for, and he couldn't let his hopes get the better of him. Was Jake here, pretending to be the Pale Rider, or did he take the ship and get Thomas?

Big Jim brought his paw-like hand back to his side. "He killed Captain Smith and took over as captain of the *Shining Star* single-handedly. The pirates all believe he's the *real* Pale Rider. Pierre has sent word for Jean to return to New Orleans and deal with this man himself. Jacques thinks that Pierre fears this man. Jacques has a dozen men at the tavern with him in case this man shows up there. He already killed all but one of Pierre's men at the warehouse."

"And yet you took your time coming here to tell me?" Chauncey asked, then took a step backwards as Big Jim moved to raise his arm again.

"What's the rush?" Big Jim asked, grinning a mouthful of gray, partially broken teeth at Chauncey's fear. "Pierre's man at the warehouse didn't know where you were, so this Pale Rider, or whoever he really is, can't know."

Aden couldn't imagine Jake killing this Captain Smith person or taking command of any ship by himself. Aden slipped and let a small smile curl up his lips. He knew the truth of it now.

Chauncey noticed the smile and in a flash of anger, slapped Aden so hard that Aden was knocked out of his chair to his side on the floor, the metallic taste of blood filling his mouth.

"It's your companion," Chauncey said, stabbing a finger at Aden's face. "The fat one that got away from us on the docks."

"No," Aden said as he wiped the blood from his lower

lip with the sleeve of his shirt. "It's him."

"Him?" Chauncey asked. "Him who?"

"The Pale Rider. The real Pale Rider. He's back," Aden answered.

"Back from where?" Big Jim bent at the waist to hear Aden better.

"From where he was," Aden said somewhat cryptically.

Big Jim straightened back up. "He's a myth. Maybe he was real thirty years ago. Maybe Washington had an assassin. Maybe he did all the things people say. But that's a lot of maybes, and he would be sixty or seventy years old today."

"He's not a day over thirty-four," Aden said honestly, a slight smirk returning to his bloodied lips. "Not then and not now."

"Doesn't matter who he is, or isn't," Chauncey responded angrily, snatching Aden's satchel off the floor and turning to walk out the door. He flicked his gaze to Big Jim. "Watch him while I wake up the rest of the men."

"What are you planning?" Big Jim asked.

Chauncey paused in the doorway after slipping the Webley into the satchel and slowly turned back to face Aden as he slipped the satchel over his head.

"I hope you enjoyed your breakfast," Chauncey said as he adjusted his coat. "We're leaving right now. If your friend comes, he won't find you. We'll be on a riverboat, making our way to the island."

Handwritten and Joint bookmark

Chapter Fifteen The Anchor

November 09, 1814
One day earlier

I ran down the alley but as I got close, I realize with a sigh of relief that the man on the ground in the alley was Jacques and not Jake. Jake walked around the corner, Thompson still in hand.

"I had to shoot him," Jake said defensively. "He shot at me first and was getting away."

Jacques's right pants leg was covered in blood and Jacques was writhing in pain in the dirty alley. Jake holstered his Thompson and handed me my sword belt with Tec-9 and satchel, while glancing over his shoulder.

"You did the right thing," I said, trying to reassure Jake. "We still need answers and can't afford for him to get away. Help me with him."

Jake looked over his shoulder once more. "Yeah, well there is about twenty men in front of the tavern banging on the front door. We need to get out of here fast."

I bent over and grabbed Jacques by the arm and lifted him to his one good leg. He tried pulling away, but Jake quickly grabbed his other arm. Jake and I dragged Jacques backwards back to the tavern to find Benny tending to his brother's injury.

Benny's cousin Robert had been killed, but his brother James, who had been stabbed in the side, was still alive and groaning miserably. Benny had already collected our weapons that I spotted in a pile on one of the upright tables. The men on the floor had stopped screaming and were trying to stop their own bleeding. I grabbed my goggles off the floor by the wall and moved to the table.

"We need to stop the bleeding," Benny said as he pressed a bar rag against his brother's side.

"How bad?" I shouted over to Benny. I grabbed my knives and placed them back into their sheaths.

"I don't think they hit anything vital," Benny answered, pushing the rag into James's wound. "But I can't stop the bleeding."

Pulling one of the lanterns off the wall, I pulled the glass off the top and tossed it away where it shattered across the floor. I lit the lantern with one of my strikers, and then set it down on the floor next to Benny's brother so we could get a better look at the deep cut. I pulled out my hunting knife and set the blade into the fire.

The banging on the front door grew louder. Someone had an axe and was chopping at on the door. The tip of the wide axe blade pierced the wood and glinted on this side of the door. They might not be able to cut through that thick beam, but they could cut through the door around the hinges and climb on over.

I motioned to Jake with my hand. "Drag Jacques over

here, next to James. Open his pants leg so I can see the bullet hole."

I grabbed a fallen tablecloth and folded it up, then handed it to James.

"Bite down on this," I told James as Jake ripped Jacques's pants leg open, exposing the bullet hole. "This is going to hurt."

My blade was red hot and sparkled with white.

"Are you ready?" I asked James, leaning close to him.

He didn't say a word, but in answer he bit down hard on the cloth, jaw muscles clenched, and nodded his head quickly. Without hesitation, I slapped the red-hot flat of my blade against James's stomach where it made a loud hissing sound, followed by smoke and the odor of burning flesh, all emanating from the man's wound. He screamed through the tablecloth, and his body jerked as his legs kicked out.

I pulled the knife away from James' bloody stomach, his skin now sealed closed with an ugly burn scar for a weld. I quickly turned the blade over, slapping the still red-hot side against the front of Jacques's leg without giving him any warning or something to bite down on. He screamed ear-shattering loud, and his body spasmed as the red glowing blade seared his skin together in a massive red blister.

The axe blade chopped down through the door, knocking the top hinge off the wood. Men outside yelled, encouraging the axe-wielder.

"You and Benny get these two back to the ship," I said to Jake as I pointed to James and Jacques. "I'll hold them off and give you time."

As I stood up, I watched Benny glance over at his dead cousin Robert, who was face down on the floor. A pool of blood formed around his stomach.

"I'm sorry Benny," I said softly. "He's gone and you can't take him with you. We'll have to come back for him later."

"I can't just leave his body here," Benny protested, starting to move forward.

"You have to," I remarked and grabbed his arm. "You can't carry him and your brother. We'll come back and get his body, I promise."

Jake lifted a complaining Jacques up to his good leg while Benny lifted James, still as pallid and stricken as the moon, and pulled James's arm over and around his neck. Benny took a second to look around the room at the bodies, some still alive, but most very dead.

"What're your orders, Captain?" Benny asked, as he hauled his brother towards the back door.

"Get to the ship," I told him. "Get all hands on deck and make ready to sail at a minute's notice. Point the cannons at the docks and be ready to repel boarders. Tie Jacques to the anchor. If he gives you any trouble on the way to the ship, kill him and leave him."

I had Jacques's attention now, who sagged against Jake and stared at me with horror on his face.

Benny stopped in his tracks. "Did I hear you correctly, Captain? Did you say tie him to… the anchor?"

I grabbed a half-empty mug of beer and poured in on my knife to cool it off. "Yes. Is that a problem?"

"No, Captain," Benny answered, shaking his head as he moved towards the door again with what I thought was a smile on his face.

The axe slammed against the door again, and Jake and Benny rushed Jacques and James out to the alley, then left towards the harbor. It wasn't a far walk to the ship, maybe ten minutes, but with Jacques and James's injuries, it was going to take at least twice long that for them to get there. I was going to have to stall at least fifteen minutes to ensure they made it aboard. Twenty minutes if I wanted to give them time to wake the men and rotate the cannons.

I didn't want to get trapped in the tavern, so I made my way to the back door. I thought about setting fire to the place with the lanterns, but if Pierre's men were in the alley or came around before I got out, then I would be stuck in a burning building. Plus, I didn't think I would win man of the year award in New Orleans if I accidently set half the city on fire. I had yet to recruit all the able-bodied men I could to help General Jackson.

I made it to the back door when my eyes settled on Robert lying in a pool of his own blood. I forced myself to turn around and took two steps into the alley. I needed to go. I needed to get out of here before it was too late. Stopping mid-step, I spun around again and looked back at Robert. He died helping me, and I owed him better than this. I had lied to Benny to get him to safety. I was telling the truth when I told him they could not carry three men and make it to the ship, but I think Benny knew I was still lying. With everything going on, we wouldn't come back for Robert's body anytime soon, if at all.

"Fuck," I cursed to myself, running to Robert's body.

Lifting him up with the fireman's carry technique, I laid his body across my shoulders and around the back of my neck.

The axe came down again with another thunk, and the wood around the bottom hinge splintered. The door was giving way. I considered leaving a booby trap behind, but the door wasn't going to hold any longer and I didn't have time for that. I did, however, have time to throw a grenade, so one-handed, I withdrew one out of my satchel. At the open doorway of the backdoor, I looked down the alley both ways. Then I pulled the pin and waited.

The axe landed again, and the door broke away from the bottom hinge and the whole door crashed to the ground with the beam still holding strong across the open doorway. I threw the grenade at the open door crammed with oncoming bodies and ran to the right down the alley, the opposite way that the guys had gone. With the ping of the spoon flying off the grenade and flintlocks firing into the door frame behind me, I ran fast and hard, my heart pounding and Robert's body bouncing on my shoulders the whole time.

I made it halfway down the alley when the grenade exploded inside the tavern. I turned my head partway to glance back the way I had come. Dirt, dust, and debris propelled out the backdoor in a violent, thick cloud that filled the alleyway. I made it to the mouth of the alley and cut around the corner to the street with the front entrance of the tavern.

Four men stumbled around in circles in the middle of the street like drunks incapable of walking a straight line, their hands squeezing their ears. Their weapons and a few torches had been discarded in the dirt. Half a dozen more men laid sprawled out on the wooden walkway in front of where the door used to be, stuck in odd positions, dark stains soaking their shirts. One of the downed men still held a tree axe in his dead hands. A dozen more men who weren't concussed ran into the smoldering tavern with flintlocks, muskets, and torches.

I crept back to the alley, pulling my Tec-9, in hopes of picking off a few more men as they ran out the backdoor. The first man stepped out and I fired two rounds, dropping him in the doorway. The next man stepped out to see what happened to the first, since my pistol didn't make more than a thunk when I fired it. The second man out the door dropped on top of the first after I fired two more rounds, taking him high in the chest.

The third man peeked his head out and scanned the alley both ways but didn't step out into the open. He spotted me and ducked back inside. I figured they were sending men out the front door to come around behind me, so I ran across the alley to the next street. A flintlock fired in the night, and the smack of the large lead ball hitting the alley wall as I ran chased me in the darkness. From there I made my way back to the ship. I had to stop several times and set down Robert's body to rest. I used my time to ensure no one was following me. It was a good bet that they were licking their wounds, regrouping at the blacksmith shop, and trying to figure out what to do next. My guess was that Pierre would wait for his brother before making any more decisions.

He had expected me to come to him tonight – instead I sacked Jacques, and as a result, his men came to me at the tavern, and I had killed nine or ten of them.

By the time I reached the docks, the ship's bell was clanging as men were called to station. I strode across the gang plank carefully, still holding Robert's body on my shoulders. I saw that Jacques was not on the side of the ship tied to the front anchor like I had ordered. Mr. Task met me on ship.

"Ready to cast off, Captain," Task announced, holding a sword in his hand and waiting for me to give the order.

I was panting hard, and my throat was dry. Two crewmen ran up to me, taking Robert off my shoulders and setting him down on the deck. I collapsed to my hands and knees, my stomach clenching enough to make me puke. I didn't look up, but someone held a tin cup near my face. I snatched it and drank deeply, emptying the cup. My stomach clenched again. The cup was removed from my shaking hand and refilled. Taking the cup again, I drank slower but emptied it all the same. I handed the cup back up and waved off the crewman, as two hands grabbed my arms and helped me to my feet.

"He's dead, Captain," one of the men kneeling down next to Robert said after checking to see if Robert was breathing.

"I know," I answered with a brief nod. "He was already dead when I picked him up. I just couldn't leave him there."

"Should I order the sails dropped, Captain?" Task asked again.

"We aren't going anywhere yet." I walked past Mr. Task toward the center of the deck. "I have questions for this Jacques fellow. Where is he and why is he not tied to the blasted anchor?"

"Benny told me you had ordered that," Task said, scratching at his head. "I thought it was a joke. Either way, he's below with James, being stitched up by the closest person we have to a doctor. Mr. Mendoza was afraid Jacques was going to bleed to death as he was."

"I already stopped the bleeding," I snapped as I turned to face him. "He was in no danger of dying."

"He ripped open his wound on our way back here," Jake explained as he came up behind me. "Slapping a hot knife on a gunshot wound is not a cure-all."

I pinched the bridge of my nose. "Fine. But he'll be answering my questions now. We may not have much time, and I need to know if we're casting off or staying."

When I made it down to the next deck, James was laying on a table with Benny standing next to him. A worried look covered Benny's face as he stared at his brother. Jacques laid on another table with an older crewman I didn't yet know, who was probing the bullet hole in Jacques's leg with his fingers. Jacques's pants were on the floor, rolled up in a ball and soaked in blood.

"Treat James first," I instructed the crewman who was working on Jacques.

"You did a decent job cauterizing the front hole, Captain," the crewman commented, pointing to Jacques's leg. "But the exit hole is still bleeding. The laceration on his chest isn't deep but could use a few stiches as well."

"That's sad," I said sarcastically. "Next time, I'll check for an exit hole. In the meantime, treat James first. I will not lose one of our crew because you were treating the guy who caused the wound. I already have one dead crewman up on deck because of him. I won't have another."

I was being sarcastic, but he had a point. I should have checked for an exit wound. The crewman placed a rag against the exit wound on the back of Jacques's thigh and told him to hold it there until he returned. He moved to James's table and investigated James's stomach.

Benny jumped to his feet and stepped towards me "Up on deck? Robert?"

"I couldn't leave him there," I admitted. "He's here on the ship with us where he belongs. We'll have a proper service for him as soon as we can. I'll have Mr. Task see to his body, so you stay with your brother."

"You can't keep me here," Jacques interrupted, clinching his teeth to fight back the pain. "Pierre won't allow it. He'll come get me with all the pirates in port. His brother Jean is sailing back to New Orleans right now. You'll have to face him and however many men he brings with him."

I stepped away from Benny and moved up to Jacques, a smirk tugging at my face. "We both know that Pierre doesn't give a shit about you or anyone else, and I doubt his brother does, either. Second, you'll be tied to the anchor, and if Pierre or Jean comes for you, that anchor will drop into the water, the rope will be cut away from the ship, and we'll sail away with you sitting on the bottom of the ocean. And third, I won't care if you're dropped into the water because you're going to answer my questions here and now."

"And if I don't?" he challenged.

"Then I'll close up the hole on the back of your leg the same way I closed up the front hole. Then I'll give you to Benny to talk about his dead cousin."

I pulled out my knife and pointed to Benny with it. "I could always allow him to question you. It's his cousin up on deck after all."

Hearing his name, Benny flicked his eyes over at us. He grinned at the thought of being the one to ask the questions. Benny was a good-looking man with a boyish smile that I'm sure all the girls loved. But this smile was different. It was the smile of a wolf as he strode out of the hen house, feathers still falling from his teeth.

"My companion?" I continued. "Where is he?"

Jacques kept his narrowed gaze on Benny. "Chauncey has your mate."

"I knew that already. Where?"

"Baton Rouge," he answered, finally breaking eye contact with Benny and looking at me. "He said that he had a friend who owned a tavern there."

I huffed out a sigh. "Great. Another fucking tavern."

"Chauncey doesn't have friends," Jacques added casually. "Only people he pays and people who pay him. His mother was a whore in Baton Rouge. I know him, and he'll be at her old employer's establishment, the whorehouse. It's where he feels safe. I don't know which whorehouse his mother worked at, but there are only three or four up there."

I could tell he was speaking the truth. His eyes leveled on me. He didn't look away or off to the side. He seemed to be blaming Chauncey for me being in his life right now – I did have that effect on people – and probably wanted Chauncey to share in his misery.

"What does this Chauncey want with my colleague?" I asked.

"If you're here, you already know the truth of it," Jacques said as he shifted to hold the rag to his leg with his other hand. "The flintlock that shoots repeatedly. Marvelous weapon."

"Yes," I agreed. "But he already has that marvelous weapon. Why is he keeping my friend?"

"He's going to sell your mate with the flintlock to the British. A paired set as it was."

Any sense of calm on my face fled, and I clenched my hands. "The hell he is."

"The French will offer a price as well, but the British have been sailing in these waters recently," Jacques clarified. "Rumor has it they plan on taking New Orleans. Half the city is ready to surrender to them already. The British will want that flintlock, and they have a deeper purse."

And that's when Jacques looked away. He was hiding something – a part of this plan I didn't know about. Something I didn't know *to* ask about. I pressed my knife on his leg, tip down under his torn pantleg. A drop of blood blossomed on his skin.

"What aren't you telling me?" I asked slowly.

"I sent..." he started then stopped.

"You sent what?" I asked raising my voice and pressing harder.

"Yesterday I sent a man with a letter, warning him about you," Jacques answered with a hiss. "My best man in fact. Lucky you for it. If I had sent someone else in his stead, he'd been there tonight and you'd be dead."

Anger boiled inside me. I thought about jamming the knife deep into his leg. But I knew that wasn't going to help

249

Aden.

"Like I told you earlier," I said. "Could of, would of, should of, but you didn't."

The ship's doctor coughed into his hand to get my attention. "James is going to be fine with a few weeks of rest. I should look at your prisoner's leg before he bleeds to death."

"Very well," I said, turning to go. "Stitch him up. Then have him tied to the anchor like I ordered in the first place."

Jacques's mouth fell open. "I told you everything."

"Yes, you did," I answered him, as I paused to turn back around and face him. "But you also took part in my friend's abduction. As long as we are secured to the docks, you'll be safe, tied to the anchor, but safe. If we are forced to make sail...well, you'll be getting wet."

I stepped out of the way of the so-called doctor so that he could work on Jacques. I told Benny to have his brother moved to my quarters, where he would be more comfortable, and then for Benny to meet me on deck.

Task and Jake marched up to me, curious to know our next move. Robert's body was no longer on deck. It had already been removed.

"I need to travel to Baton Rouge," I said more to myself than to anyone else. "Tonight. No time to waste. Do any of those riverboats leave to go upriver at night?"

Task shook his head. "No. They can paddle at night, but they leave in the morning so that people can pay for passage and board them. No one buys passage at night."

"Then I'll need to steal one tonight," I said.

"Steal one what, Captain?" Task asked with a confused look on his face.

"A riverboat, Mr. Task," I answered with my back to him as I gazed out to the city. "I'll need to steal a riverboat.

Tonight."

Jake stepped toward me. "And me?"

"You'll have to stay and meet with General Jackson when he gets here," I told him. "If I don't come back, he'll need help recruiting men, and you'll need to give him the cannon fuses."

"If you don't come back?" Jake asked as he grabbed my arm.

"I'll be coming back," I reassured him. "And Aden will be with me. It's just good to have a backup plan."

Jake nodded his head, understanding what I was saying and why. A backup plan was merely an excuse.

I flapped my hand at the captain's cabin. "You'll have to share our cabin with James. It'll be easier for Benny to take care of him if he's there."

"You can't go alone," Jake protested. I knew he would.

"He won't," Benny answered as he held James up and led him to my quarters. "Let me get James comfortable and I'll be ready."

"Thank you, Benny," I said, watching him walk his brother to my quarters.

"How do you plan on getting a riverboat?" Jake asked. "You aren't really going to steal one. Have you ever operated one?"

"No. But I don't need to. Give me a handful of coins from your purse."

Jake sighed but reached for his belt and pulled off the purse. "Why?"

"Plan A is for me to offer one of the captains enough coins to take us tonight," I explained. "Plan B will involve me sticking the barrel of my pistol into his stomach and asking nicely. I'm hoping the coin works. But I'll do whatever is

251

necessary."

Jake opened his purse and dumped half of the contents into my hands. He counted the twenty or so coins and then shook out six more. I could tell from the amount of coin he gave me that he was hoping I didn't hurt anyone. I shoved the coins in my vest pocket as Jake put away his purse. As I walked away, Jake reached out and gripped my arm, stopping me. He looked around to make sure no one was close enough to hear us, then leaned in close to me.

"I can see what you're doing, Thomas," Jake whispered. "And I don't like it. If Benny is going with you, it should be of his own free will and not through manipulation."

I flicked my gaze at Benny then back to Jake "What are you talking about? It is of his own free will. I didn't even ask him to go with me."

"No." Jake frowned. "I know you. You're as loyal as they come, so I'm sure you brought his cousin's body back for all the right reasons. But you did tell him to put his wounded brother in your quarters where he could rest easier, right before announcing that you were going off on your own. He's a pirate, but you can see there's loyalty in that man as well. You knew he'd feel obligated to go with you after taking a personal interest in his brother's well-being. You even made the doctor treat his brother before Jacques."

I paused at his words. Was Jake right? I had thought I was being faithful to my crew. Was I manipulating Benny to go with me? In the back of my mind, I was hoping he'd offer. He was a very capable man in a fight, and his wicked curved blade was almost as long as a sword. If I was going to be honest with myself, I put the mission first, no matter the cost. Annie could speak on that character flaw for hours. But then, that was why I was *here*, because men like Aden and Jake couldn't do what I

252

could do. Sure, I was a trained boxer, marksman, knife fighter, but men with these skills were easy to find, a dime a dozen. It was my ability to take direct action, make harsh, difficult decisions, and follow through with perseverance and relentlessness to the mission that made the real difference.

Shit! I *had* manipulated Benny into offering to go with me, even if I hadn't intended it. Somewhere in the recesses of my dark, amoral mind, I knew Benny would offer to accompany me if he felt he owed me, and I gave cause for him to think that he did.

But did that change anything? I needed to find and save Aden. And I needed Benny's help. I was doing what was required of me. But did that justify it? Before meeting Annie, I would have said yes without question. I didn't think I was the same man as I had been when I first came back in time, yet now, I feared I might be. Annie told me to *become* that man. I had promised her that I would be that man if that was what it took to return to her.

But was it?

Benny stepped out of my quarters and placed his flintlock between his coat and belt. He quick-stepped over to me with a slim smile on his face.

"James is resting," Benny said to me. "Robert's body has been taken care of, for now. I'm ready to go when you are, sir."

Jake still wore a disappointed look on his face as he turned away, not wanting to look Benny in the eyes.

"Change of plans, Benny," I said with a fake smile. "I'm going alone tonight. You stay here with your brother. He'll need you more than I do," I lied. I had to assuage my guilt somehow.

"No, sir," Benny answered quickly with a hurt look on his face. "James is comfortable and I'm ready to go now."

My fingers fiddled with my vest. "I'll be fine. Stay here

and assist Mr. Task in keeping Jake out of trouble. Ready the men. If the ship is attacked, don't hesitate to make sail and leave port. I don't know what Pierre will do when he learns we have Jacques."

Ignoring Benny's pout, I moved to Jake, slid my sword scabbard out of the belt and took off my coat and satchel, handing them over to my friend.

"I don't know what to expect, but I want to be able to move fast," I said. "I'm better with the knives than the sword, anyways. Hang onto these for me until I get back. If Pierre's men try to board the ship before I return, use the shotgun first, then the Thompson."

"Thomas," Jake called to me as I made my way across the deck. "I know what I said, but I don't want you going alone. Maybe you should take Benny."

I shook my head with an air of disappointment, then rubbed the skin between my eyes. I had a headache coming on and it wasn't from all the fighting.

"What do you want from me? Indecision kills, Jake. You need to learn that. First you don't want me to take him, then you do. The decision is made. It's final, and it's the right one. I'm going alone."

I stayed long enough to grab a water bag and made sure the men really had tied Jacques to the anchor. The whole crew gathered around and watched that. I don't think any of them had ever seen someone tied to an anchor before now. Another Pale Rider rumor for the rumor mill.

I then headed down the dock towards the Mississippi River. When I got near, torches lined the bank of the river to help guide people, and lanterns lit up the docks to help the different drunken boat crews not fall in the churning brown water and drown. Light splashing meant the fish were jumping out of the water to chase the stars, thinking them fireflies or other bugs. On the docks, young boys with bamboo poles stood or sat on boxes, fishing most likely for food and not sport this late at night. The moon's reflection stood in the middle of the fast-running river, clear and bright as if it were a mirror.

Most of the docked riverboats were dark and quiet, with lanterns extinguished and the crew presumably asleep or out in town drinking and whoring. One boat caught my attention, since it was the only boat with lanterns lit inside and out. She was smaller than the one I had been on earlier and appeared much older. The paddle wheel was painted back, not bright red, and the black paint was peeling off. She boasted only two decks, not three like many of the newer boats. The wheelhouse was on the second deck and to the front, not on top of the second or third deck standing alone. From where I stood, it looked like the main deck was a large, open compartment while the second deck held individual cabins or staterooms. Unlike the other boats tethered to the dock, this boat had people boarding her. Several well-dressed men and one lady were laughing and walking down the bank towards the boat. Maybe she was getting ready to paddle upriver. I might not need to bribe or threaten the captain if I could buy passage.

"That's the *Lucky Lady*," Benny said from behind me.

I jerked and spun around, pulling my Tec-9 before I realized who it was. Whether it was because he was that quiet or I was that caught up in my thoughts, I never heard him walk up behind me.

"What are you doing here?" I asked, trying to slow my racing heart. "I gave you orders to stay behind."

"Jake told me the truth of it," Benny told me. "He said that you thought I was only going out of obligation. I'm not captain. I'm going because Jake said finding your mate will hurt the English. That's enough reason for me."

"Why is that reason enough?" I asked.

"My parents are from Australia. I'm from Hobart myself. My father was born in England, but he killed a man in a fair fight and was sent to prison. The king had my father and mother along with many others sent to Australia instead of a prison. They were undesirables, aye? He and many others were forced into hardship that the land threw at them. They were expected to die but they survived. We'll be a full nation one day, independent of the English like these states, and the English will regret losing us."

"Very well," I said after a minute of thought. "But that's the second and last of my orders you disregard."

Slipping my Tec-9 back into its holster, I turned back towards the riverboat.

I pointed to the steam powered paddle boat. "Does she travel upriver at night?"

"No," Benny answered. "She's one of the oldest riverboats on the water. Pierre and Jean own her now. She's used strictly for gambling."

A real riverboat with real gamblers playing poker. This was a piece of history I didn't want to miss out on.

"Great," I said. "Let's go buy two tickets. Why didn't you tell me we could buy tickets?"

"We can't," Benny said. "She never pulls away from the dock. She's used as a floating gambling hall. The Lafitte Brothers thought it was a good idea, instead of buying or building a gambling establishment. I heard that someone had done the same up north. Some cities have made gambling illegal, so someone came up with the idea of doing it on the boat. No one has jurisdiction over the river, after all."

"Not yet," I commented. "But they will one day."

"Where are you going?" Benny asked as I strode down the bank towards the boat.

"If I'm going to take a boat, I might as well take Pierre's boat," I answered without turning around. "After all, he tried to take my ship."

Benny trotted up on my side. There was no gangplank. Instead, the ship was secured right next to the dock so that people could step onto it. A small platform with a set of two steps connected to the boat, so a person didn't trip stepping over the railing and down onto the deck.

As we strolled down the dock, a piano played inside the large main deck's only compartment. It sounded like the piano player was banging on the keys, trying to play over the din of people that apparently were not paying much attention to him. Cheap, opaque, square windows lined the side wall, the bulkhead, of the main deck's large single room.

Blurry upper torsos of people walking around having a good time appeared through cloudy windows. I could make out some objects, like hats on their heads or bottles of booze in their hands. Dozens of voices spoke loudly, as if yelling to be heard over the excessively loud piano – each was in competition to be louder than the other. From out on the dock the voices were merged with those into one loud buzz.

Now that we were closer to the boat, the white paint, old, faded, and peeling off the wooden boards was noticeable. Two staircases led to the second deck, one at the front and one at the back, near the paddle wheel. Under the stairs were several cords of firewood, ready to be thrown into the boiler. Two men stood at the platform, greeting those who wished to come on board. They didn't seem to be looking for threats or enemies, rather they were making sure that everyone that came aboard had coin to spend. After pulling a few coins from my vest pocket and bouncing them on my palm, the men seemed content and allowed us on the boat without a word.

The main compartment was a huge, long room. Lanterns lined the walls of the room and two large candlelit chandeliers hung from the ceiling, giving off plenty of light. A faded worn red carpet with more stains than not, laid on the floor and covered the wooden deck. A redwood bar with brass foot railing was set up near the door. The dry, unpolished redwood and rust covered brass had seen better days. Cigar and pipe smoke filled the room in a smelly, hazy cloud. Five tables were spread out, filling the room. Two of the tables were longer and deeper in the middle than the other three. I scanned the tables one at a time, weighing the people for threats and seeing what games they were playing, not that I would be joining them.

Other than employees who were armed with knives and flintlocks, I didn't notice any threats among the guests. Men and women hovered around the tables, drinking alcohol from short brass cups or straight from the bottle. Some were hugging or kissing each other when they won, or slammed fists on the tables if they lost. The two longer tables were crap tables. I didn't know if they called the game *craps* or not in this century, but that's what they were playing. Men threw dice and money changed hands. The three smaller tables were roulette tables. Men and women were placing bets on numbered squares and the employee spun a small ball with a snap of his fingers on the spinning dial.

"No poker tables?" I asked out loud, mostly to myself.

"What tables?" Benny asked, raising his voice so I could hear him over the voices and piano music.

"Card games," I said, leaning closer to his ear. "No card games."

"No," Benny answered with a shrug. "But that's not a

bad idea."

Benny pointed to the far side of the room where the captain, who I later learned was named Captain Mattson, walked around making sure people were having a good time. He was the older captain in the same uncomfortable black coat, who had spoken to me earlier. He wore the same captain's hat and his lips barely hung onto a pipe. Benny pushed his way through the crowd, and I was happy to follow in his wake as the cheers and music accompanied us. Benny tapped the captain on the shoulder to get his attention and leaned in to say something in the older man's ear while pointing to the door on that side of the room. The captain made for the door, and we followed. Once outside, I closed the door, cutting off half the volume of cacophony. The captain kept walking to the end of the ship, moving as far from the gambling tables as possible.

"What's this all about?" Captain Mattson asked and pulled out a small bag of tobacco from his coat pocket.

"We need to go to Baton Rouge," I said simply.

Without looking at me, the captain packed his pipe with tobacco and took his time adjusting the pipe back into his mouth. Still ignoring me, he reached into his coat pocket again and withdrew a small, narrow wooden box and removed a match. He lit the match and placed the small flame into the bowl of the pipe, puffing on the pipe to light the tobacco.

I noticed that the little box of matches read *Cain's Strikers* on the side. My lips curled into a slight smile – he was using one of *my* matches. My business must be doing well if they were selling down here in New Orleans.

Satisfied that his pipe was well lit, the captain shook the match and threw it over the side and into the water. He pulled the pipe out of his mouth and finally turned his attention to me.

"Sorry, son," Captain Mattson said. "This boat no longer

travels the Mississippi. She just sits here tied to the dock so these damn fools can give away their money."

I pulled out the coins from my pocket and poured them into the captain's hands. I poured them a little slower than I needed to, hoping that it would seem to be more coins than there really was.

The captain glanced down at the coins in his hand. "Again, I'm sorry, son. It's not a matter of payment. If it was, this would be more than enough to get me to take you. Like I said, this boat no longer journeys up and down the Mississippi."

"She doesn't or she can't?" I asked.

He moved his hands to pour the money from his hands to mine. "In this particular case, son, it's the same difference. I don't own this boat. Jean and Pierre Lafitte own this vessel. Unless and until they give the order, the boat stays tied to the dock."

My earlier smile left, and I looked him directly in his eyes. "I know who owns the boat. That's why I'm taking her. I'm paying you for the inconvenience. Make ready to pull away right now."

"Son," the captain said, taking a puff of his pipe as if he didn't think I was serious. "I don't think you understand. I said the Lafitte brothers own this vessel. If I pull away from this dock and hurt their business, my life wouldn't be worth the coins in your hands. And your life wouldn't be worth the coin in my empty pockets."

"If they get upset, you can blame me," I answered with a smile, dropping the coins in my purse. "In fact, I hope it upsets them, and I *insist* you blame me. They know where to find me."

"And who would you be, son?" the captain asked. Another puff of the pipe.

"He's the Pale Rider," Benny interrupted, pride thick in

his voice. "The *real* Pale Rider, not like Captain Burlington."

"Just tell them it was the captain of the *Shining Star*," I told the captain. "They'll know who I am. They already visited my ship earlier. I'm now returning the favor."

His pipe drooped as his mouth parted open. "I believe I heard something about that incident," the older man said as he removed the pipe from his mouth. "The whole town is talking about it. Word is Jean is on his way back to New Orleans because of you. He's not a man I would want after me."

I disregarded his warning. "How long will the trip take?"

"One of those newer boats could get you there in eighteen to twenty hours," the captain said, then gestured with his pipe towards his own feet. "This old girl will take about twenty-four to twenty-six hours."

"I'm taking the boat with or without you, Captain," I said. "Make ready or get off."

The captain pursed his lips, considering, then his voice boomed as he ordered his crew to get the boat ready before he returned to the gaming area of the vessel. The piano music stopped, and the captain got everyone's attention. He informed the patrons that the ship would be pulling away from shore. He told them that the *Lucky Lady* would be paddling to Baton Rouge and back. He gave them the option of getting off now or to keep gambling while the boat traversed the Mississippi. Only a few people chose to leave while most stayed on to keep winning or giving away their coin.

Activities and joint bookmarks.

Chapter Sixteen Who is this Man?

November 11, 1814
Chauncey

Chauncey had rounded up six desperate men who were considered unsavory by most influential people in the city, but he knew they would do anything for money. Kidnapping or murder was not beyond them for the right amount of coin – an amount that most would say was lower than it should be for such acts, but the better for Chauncey. Only one of the men owned a flintlock. The rest only carried knives, but that wouldn't matter. With the Webley in his satchel, Chauncey had flintlocks enough for six of them. These were also the same men he paid to sit outside Aden's door and make sure he didn't escape or call out for help.

These six men, along with Big Jim, Chauncey, and Aden, had made their way down to the docks. Aden had slowed them down with his limping, and Big Jim allowed the man to lean on him. Chauncey knew one of the captains who, if the right amount of coin passed across his palm, would turn a blind eye to a bound man brought on board his boat against his will. The boat was not set to sail until nine in the morning, but Chauncey intended to move Aden from the whorehouse to the boat under the cover of darkness. Once in the stateroom, they would be safe from prying eyes.

Aden had appeared surprised when they exited the room and learned that they were in a house of ill repute and not a tavern or inn. Chauncey had gripped a flintlock, its barrel pressed hard enough into Aden's back to leave marks and threatened if Aden dared yell out for help, Chauncey would kill him. Chauncey needed the man but if he drew attention to himself, he would have killed Aden without a second thought.

Aden walked barefooted in the dirt and then in the mud of the riverbank, grime and muck staining his tender white feet. Based on the look on the man's face, Chauncey was willing to bet this man had never walked shoeless a day in his life. Having grown up on the street and stealing food, Chauncey found himself despising this rich man named Aden. Not that Aden had done anything purposely to Chauncey, but the man was unable to hide the fact that he'd grown up privileged. That was enough to draw Chauncey's ire.

The sun had broken the horizon twenty minutes ago, and Chauncey craved a cup of coffee. He stepped out onto the walkway of the third deck, leaving Aden in the competent hands of Big Jim with the six newly hired men in the room next door. The ship was still empty of passengers, but the crew was up and moving about. Thick black smoke burped out of the smokestacks, meaning the boilers had already been lit.

Chauncey gazed back towards the city, knowing if everything went well, he'd sell the Webley, get rich, and never

263

see this city again. He took a moment to soak it in. He hated the city, but it was home.

Then his gaze landed on a man striding down the bank towards the docks, a man Chauncey had never seen before, and Chauncey prided himself on the fact he knew most of the criminals and derelicts in Baton Rouge. The man bore a serious expression and he wore a black vest, much like the one Aden had worn when Chauncey first sacked him – the one that Captain Burlington now wore. The man was too far away to tell, but the knife on the front of his belt might be the same knife as the one he'd taken off Aden. Chauncey squinted at the approaching man. Could he be the one who was calling himself Pale Rider? It was too coincidental otherwise, and Chauncey had long stopped believing in coincidences.

The man halted and stared straight at Chauncey. Not in Chauncey's direction but straight at him. Chauncey noticed the captain of the boat bounding down the steps from the wheelhouse and stepped towards him.

"Make way now, Captain," Chauncey ordered, still moving towards the man. He tried to hide the panic rising in his voice. But why should he be panicked?

"We'll not be leaving for another two hours," the captain explained and held up his hands to stop Chauncey. "The boiler is warming up."

"You'll pull away now, Captain, or I'll burn this boat down with you on it," Chauncey threatened, grabbing the captain's coat in both hands. "You know I'll do it."

The captain's lips thinned as he glared at Chauncey and tried to decide the best course of action.

"Mr. Pike!" Having come to a decision, the captain shouted up to the wheelhouse.

"Yes, sir," Mr. Pike yelled down after stepping out of the

wheelhouse.

"Blow the whistle, Mr. Pike," the captain said, tugging Chauncey's hands off his coat. "We're pulling away now."

"Now, Captain?" the crewman yelled back and leaned over the railing to make sure he heard correctly.

"Now, Mr. Pike," the captain repeated.

Chauncey headed back to the rooms as the captain sprinted down the steps and ordered his men to untie the boat from the mooring cleat and fill the boiler with wood. Chauncey knocked on the door to the room next to his, then opened it without waiting. A wave of body odor hit Chauncey's nose, and he wondered for a moment if these men ever bathed. Two of the men sat up on the two cots, while the other four reclined on the floor, having just woken up.

"The six of you, get down to the main deck now," Chauncey ordered, while waving his hand down to the deck. "Kill anyone other than the crew that tries to come on board. Keep a look out for anyone in a black vest."

One of the men yawned wide and scratched his balls. "Why? What's going on?"

"The man I hired you to protect me from is here," Chauncey hissed. "Now get out there and earn your pay!"

The boat jerked forward under Chauncey's feet, and he smirked. He might have seen the man in time to get away. His six men for hire strolled out of the room and made for the stairs. Chauncey returned to his room, again knocking and opening the door. Aden perched on one of the two cots, while Big Jim leaned against the wall, looking bored with his huge arms crossed in front of his burly chest.

"He's here," Chauncey announced to Big Jim who pushed himself off the wall in response. "Stay in the room but be ready to kill anyone other than me who comes through this door."

When Chauncey slammed the door and turned around, a boat that had been moored in front of his boat passed by six feet away. Chauncey's boat was moving, not the other boat. But this close together, it had the illusion that the other boat was going the opposite direction. Chauncey ran down the two flights of stairs and found his men standing on the main deck near the open area of the railing where people boarded.

"No one came on," one of the men said to Chauncey as he walked up. "No one even tried. You must not have seen the gentleman that you were worried about. Maybe it was someone else."

Chauncey scanned the dock, but like his men, he didn't see the black-vested man anywhere. "Very well. Let's get back up to the rooms. Keep your eyes open."

Chauncey climbed up the stairs to the second deck at the front of the boat, and as he turned to go up the next set of stairs to the third deck, he froze. The man was at the rear of the boat, striding up the catwalk towards Chauncey. All his blood turned to ice.

How had the man boarded the boat? He was up the hill the last time Chauncey had seen him. Chauncey had six men on the main deck watching to make sure he didn't get on board. How had this man managed to get to the second deck without anyone seeing him? Was he the real Pale Rider?

Chauncey finally gained his senses and pointed to the man walking his way as he bolted up the next set of stairs. "Get him!"

Chauncey needed to get to Big Jim and Aden, but they were all the way down by the stern. He was running down the walkway when he heard a scream from below. Chauncey peered down over the side of the boat in time to see one of his dim-

266

witted fools plunge into the water. Well, it was still one against five, and Chauncey liked those odds. At least until a shot exploded through the deck by his feet. The man somehow knew where he was and was shooting at him through the floorboards. How was this man able to see through the deck?

Chauncey burst into a run again when he heard another of his men scream out in pain. Chauncey stopped in his tracks but didn't look over the side. At least his good for nothing men were still fighting and, in all fairness, had a chance of killing the man. Then he heard another of his men scream, followed by another splash of water. Chauncey didn't need to look to know that he lost another one of his knives for hire. Four-on-one odds were still good gambling odds – odds that Chauncey would take any day of the week and twice on Sunday.

As he ran for his room, another splash broke the river. At least that one didn't scream the whole way down. Three-on-one was not as good of odds as six-on-one, but he'd take what he could get. His odds were dropping by the second, or in this case, dropping into the fast-running, muddy waters of the Mississippi River.

He made it to his cabin door with a fourth splash of water. *Damn it all to hell!* Who was this man?

He banged on the door then threw it open. Big Jim stood in the center of the room, two large brown flintlocks in his hands with their hammers cocked back and ready to fire.

"I heard a gunshot," Jim said. "Is he dead then?"

Chauncey shook his head. "No. But my men might be."

"What's your plan?" Jim asked.

"I'm taking this one with me," Chauncey said and pointed to Aden. "You kill the other. He'll have to come up the stairs. Wait for him and shoot him as he reaches the top."

Chauncey snatched Aden by the back of the shirt and

dragged him out of the room, rushing back the way he'd come and pulling Aden behind him. He glanced over his shoulder and down the catwalk and saw the man calmly walking up the stairs to the third level. First his head and face came into view, and then Chauncey saw the scar on his head. The rest of him came into sight, black vest and all.

He held a flintlock in his hand and was covered in blood, as if he had bathed in it. Chauncey knew it was his men's blood. If it had been this man's blood, he would be dead already.

"Thomas," Aden hollered as he twitched and struggled while being dragged backwards.

Chauncey didn't pause.

Big Jim stepped out of the room and onto the walkway, blocking Chauncey's view of the man. A wave of relief washed over him when Jim blocked his view. Chauncey had to admit that until he had seen the man up close, walking calmly towards him and coated in the blood of Chauncey's own men, he hadn't believed this man could possibly be the *real* Pale Rider. But now he didn't know *what* he believed.

Chauncey wasn't going to let this chance go to waste and moved faster to drag Aden down the catwalk. Aden yanked and squirmed, slowing Chauncey down, but Chauncey strained and pulled harder. When Chauncey finally made it down the length of the boat to the stairs, he spun around.

Aden's friend, this so-called Pale Rider person, was on the catwalk, walking towards Chauncey, glaring straight at him. The man didn't run or hurry, he was calm and focused and marched steadily, as if he had no fear that Chauncey could possibly escape his wrath. Chauncey saw retribution reflected in the man's hooded eyes, and he didn't like it.

Where was Big Jim? The man had disappeared. God knew the man was too big to be missed. Jim carried two flintlocks with him and hadn't fired either. Chauncey heard no shot, no scream of pain, and no splash of water. How could this man have killed Jim without making any noise? Chauncey knew Jim hadn't run away; Jim wasn't afraid of anyone. And Jim certainly hadn't let the man walk by. He had been directed by Jacques to help Chauncey, and Jim was loyal to Jacques to a fault.

Chauncey pulled his original flintlock from his belt and raised it at the bloody man as he thumbed back the hammer. Chauncey's hand shook, and he knew he was too far away to hit the man, but he had to try. He couldn't help himself; fear fevered him like a plague, and he needed this man to just *fucking die*. To die like any normal man would. How could that be so difficult?

Then the man surprised Chauncey when he stopped walking and stood in the center of the catwalk, as if he was holding still for Chauncey. He was giving Chauncey a free shot and once again, Chauncey's blood turned icy. This man had no fear of Chauncey or even of his weapon.

Who didn't fear a matchlock pointed at them? It was madness.

Firing the flintlock, Chauncey cursed under his breath as he of course missed and struck the wall next to the man. Ever since Chauncey began carrying the Webley, he'd stopped carrying extra shot and powder for his flintlock, so the weapon was useless to him now. He tossed the empty flintlock over the side. He didn't need it anyways. He still had Aden's flintlock in his satchel.

But his flintlock bought him a moment and Chauncey spun, yanking Aden down the set of stairs. He had to get off the boat somehow, and he wasn't going to swim.

Making it to the second-floor catwalk, Chauncey turned

to go down to the main deck when he saw the man standing on the catwalk, eyeing him. How had he gotten here? Who the hell was this man?

"Thomas," Aden yelled again, and Chauncey again tugged him down the stairs.

As he made it down to the main deck, Chauncey reached a weary hand into his satchel and pulled out one of the two grenades he'd found when he had sacked Aden. He had never used one of these devices, but after he had beaten Aden bloody with a stick, Aden had explained that you just pulled the thin little pin out of the top and threw the heavy metal ball.

Chauncey knew he'd find the man waiting for him on the main deck like some kind of hellhound commanded by Lucifer himself. The man had a bone between his teeth and refused to let go of it. Chauncey yanked the pin to the grenade, and when he reached the main deck, Chauncey punched Aden in the stomach with his free hand, doubling Aden over and watched him fall to the deck.

Bales of hay were stacked on both sides of the stairs, flanking what had to be tons of stacked cord wood under the stairways. Several large crates were tucked away at the very front between the stairs and the bow of the boat. Once Chauncey was sure that Aden wasn't getting up or running away, Chauncey slipped around the stacks of wood where the large boiler was on the main deck. Two crewmen were throwing cut logs into the boiler to raise the fire and increase the steam for more speed.

"Fuck off, you two," Chauncey yelled at the crewmen. "Now!"

The crewmen searched to find the source of the voice. They saw Chauncey and paused mid-throw. Their eyes locked on him and his sweaty face, then toward the stairs to see who was chasing him.

"Now!" Chauncey yelled again.

They knew Chauncey was trouble – if he was yelling for them to get out of there, then something bad was happening. They decided the captain could deal with him and whatever trouble this man was getting the boat into. They dropped the cordwood and ran up the stairs, heading for the wheelhouse.

With the crewman now out of the way, Chauncey stepped to the side of the main room to have a clear view of the catwalk, hauling Aden along with him.

There he was, right where Chauncey knew he would be. The man was now on the main deck, approaching Chauncey with murder burning in his eyes. Chauncey took a half-step back and then remembered his initial intention. He threw the grenade down the catwalk, right at the man. He saw the grenade hit the deck and roll right towards the relentless bastard's feet. Chauncey then shrank back to Aden, waiting to see what would happen next. The explosion thundered like a cannon, and Chauncey was so surprised he found himself knocked on his side, laying on the wooden deck.

"Shit," Chauncey cursed to himself.

Chauncey was in front of the main room and the stranger was on the side of it, so Chauncey didn't see the actual explosion. But the dust and debris that whipped in the air told him that no one could have survived it. The little rock-like weapon was far more powerful than he'd thought possible. He still had another one but now wished he had twenty more to sell to the French after the British bought the Webley. How could such a small device cause so much damage?

Chauncey slowly got to his feet and reached into the satchel again. This time he wrapped his fingers around the steel and wooden hand grip of the Webley flintlock. He pulled it out and thumbed the hammer back, watching the cylinder rotate around as the hammer made its clicking sound.

Aden half-rose next to Chauncey, who kicked him in the ribs. With a grunt, Aden ended up on his back, clutching his side. Chauncey brought the Webley up in front of him as he peeked around the corner and down the long catwalk. The man was gone. Did he go over the side and into the water? Most likely. There was no way he could have survived that horrendous explosion.

The boat's whistle sounded as men above on the upper decks shouted down, wanting to know what that explosion was. The crew also hollered something about the boiler blowing up from the pressure. Chauncey took a quick look but remarkably, the boiler seemed undamaged. Several men clamored down the stairs. Chauncey spun around to the sounds of the footsteps and fired the Webley into the stairs, right in front of four crewmen who promptly turned around and ran back up the way they'd come.

Someone coughed from inside the main boiler room.

Couldn't be.

It had to be one of the crew. Still, Chauncey had to check. He moved for the closed double doors and grabbed the doorknob, turning the handle slowly, more out of fear than any tactical reason. Chauncey pulled hard flinging the door open as he stepped through the doorway, flintlock up in front of him.

Impossible.

The man stood in the midst of swirling dirt. He was gray, covered in dust, and standing behind a turned-over table with both hands holding the top edge. The man reached for a flintlock on his belt and Chauncey, who already had the Webley out in front of him, pulled the trigger firing the flintlock.

Chauncey watched his shot strike the left side of the man's chest. A solid kill shot. The man spun around and hit the floor behind the same table he'd been using as a shield. Chauncey licked his lips, sure he had killed the man, and shifted closer to check. He wanted to make sure the man was dead. Chauncey took one step and froze. What if the man wasn't dead?

Instead of checking, Chauncey backed out of the doorway and turned towards Aden who was rising to his feet. Chauncey ran at him to stop him from getting away, then scanned the room, searching for the best direction to run. The captain wasn't in sight, or Chauncey would have ordered him to pull closer to the shore.

"He won't stop." Aden choked out the words between coughs. "Not until you're dead. You should let me go and jump off the boat while you can."

Chauncey realized that he'd forgotten to cock the hammer back again. As he pulled the hammer back, the *click click click* sound it made as the cylinder rotated seemed deafening to him. Chauncey shoved Aden to the railing and pistol whipped him in the back of his head, knocking Aden to the deck. Aden wasn't unconscious, but also not far from it. Chauncey sprinted to hide behind the large stack of cut wood under the stairs and waited.

He couldn't see the double doors of the main hall from his hiding spot. He could only see Aden, but that was who he really needed to see. He would wait for the man to hurry to Aden, then Chauncey would shoot him in the back. Not just once, but with all five remaining shots in Aden's flintlock.

Chauncey waited but nothing happened. No sounds, no movement. Aden struggled to regain to his feet while rubbing the back of his head where Chauncey had struck him. Maybe the man was dead – still inside the main cabin, bleeding out on the floor. Chauncey had shot him in the chest after all.

He *must* be dead.

Chauncey remembered when he'd first taken that step forward to check on the man, the sensation he'd experienced. Chauncey knew that, as impossible as it was, the black-vested man was somehow still alive.

He decided to wait a minute longer and if the man didn't come out . . .

The deck boards creaked on the other side of the stacked wood, interrupting Chauncey's thoughts. The man was here, just feet away on the other side of the stacked wood that Chauncey was hiding behind. He somehow knew it was a trap and instead of going for Aden, he was searching for Chauncey.

Well, fuck this, Chauncey thought.

He needed to motivate the man more. He hated the idea of using his second and last grenade, but it was more important that Chauncey survived. He pulled the grenade out of the satchel with his left hand and pulled the pin. With a smile of delight, he rolled the small steel ball over to Aden.

jewelry and joint bookbindin...

Chapter Seventeen My Side of the Story

November 11, 1814

The riverboat pulled into Baton Rouge before the sun crested the eastern horizon. Benny and I had taken turns sleeping and standing guard. It had been a long, slow slog – the captain had been spot-on about our speed. We'd traveled that morning and all yesterday, but we finally arrived. We made a good three or four miles per hour, but the newer boats kept up a steady five miles per hour, seven if they pushed the boilers hard enough.

The captain slowed the old girl that he called a boat and came along the dock. He grabbed a dirty white cord with a wooden knob at the bottom, the steam whistle, to announce our arrival. I grabbed his arm to stop him and shook my head, letting him know not to do it.

"Don't want to announce your arrival, huh?" the captain said with a thin-lipped smile, his pipe clinched between his teeth. "Sure, sure. Nice and quiet it'll be."

As the boat slowly pulled alongside the dock, barefooted crewman jumped off the boat with ropes in their hands. They hauled the boat towards the docks as the paddlewheel slowed and tied the ropes off to steel mooring cleats attached to the wooden planks of the docks.

"We'll try to make this fast, Captain," I said, respectfully. "As soon as I find my friend, we can turn around and go back to New Orleans, and you can get back to your normal life. But if you leave us," I added with an edge in my voice, "I'll find you and tie you to your own paddlewheel."

"Believe him, Captain," Benny piped up next to me, raising his eyebrows and motioning his thumb my way. "He already had Jacques tied to the anchor of the *Shining Star*. Next time they drop anchor, Jacques goes with it, all the way down to the bottom. I think he's as crazy as a wombat, but he's also mean as a Great White shark."

The captain leveled his gaze but nodded to agree that he would wait, and Benny and I left the wheelhouse. Walking down the stairs, I heard the hardcore gamblers still throwing dice and shouting, but the piano had stopped playing almost an hour ago. When they weren't eating, drinking, taking short rest breaks, and pissing off the side of the boat, these people gambled nonstop.

We stepped off the boat and onto the water-splattered wooden dock. Three other riverboats were moored nearby. One was tied to the same dock as our boat, and two were tied up to the next dock over. The three boats each had three decks instead of two, like the one we were on. Their crews made their way to their main decks to start the long day ahead of them, and most strode around barefooted. Better than a day spent in wet shoes, I supposed. Several were not shy about taking their morning piss right off the side of the boats and into the fast-running river.

We made our way up the muddy bank to dry dirt that led

us to the city. The first rays of sunshine had not broken over the horizon yet, but the glow of the day to come was promising to show itself.

Benny had asked several sailors about the whorehouses in the city and came up with several locations. The first two stops resulted in less than satisfactory results. Annie would be pissed if she found out that I had gone into two *more* houses of ill repute. I still hear about the last time I went into one, in France no less. Lafayette had regaled her one night at the house over dinner and two bottles of wine about the time we'd gone into a French entertainment house to meet with the madam for information. Hopefully, this excursion wouldn't reach her ears.

We entered the third house and were met by an older man who came off as a real dick.

"We're closed," he spat out as he bent over a table and wiped it down with a filthy rag. "Come back tonight if you wanna get your worms wet."

"We're looking for a friend of mine," I said as I glanced around the room. "We were told to come here."

He didn't stop cleaning the table. "As I said, come back tonight, and you can have your pick of friends."

I glared at the man. "We're looking for Chauncey."

The man paused his arm motion and looked up for the first time. His squinting eyes scanned the room and then looked us up and down.

"He's not here," the older man finally said as his voice dropped in volume.

"You didn't say you didn't know him, just that he's not here," I said, taking another step towards the man. "So, you do know him?"

At least we knew we were at the right house.

The man stood upright, and he was near my height.

"Maybe. But like I said, he's not here."

"Where is he?" Benny asked, losing the happy-go-lucky tone he normally possessed. He was all business now.

The man's eyes flicked back and forth. "I don't know. How would I know?"

I gave him the coldest stare I had, one that usually broke a person. After a few seconds of silence, Benny decided to take a different approach and slowly pulled out his kukri, walking past me towards the man.

"Look, mate," Benny drawled. "If he's like a son to you and worth dying for, then God bless you. You're a good man, and I mean that. If he's not worth dying for, then you're a fool."

Benny took one more step forward and the man held up a hand as a shield against Benny. "Wait. He's not."

"Not what?" I asked.

"Not worth dying for," he replied, taking a nervous step backward. "His mother was one of my girls back when Chauncey was just a boy. I let him use a room for the last two months. As a favor to a friend and some coin. But he's gone now. Left about four hours ago."

"Where did he go?" I asked.

"One of the riverboats," he answered, not taking his eyes off Benny. "I don't know which one, I swear."

Benny tipped his head toward me. "There were only three others."

I nodded quickly, and we walked out the door the way we'd come in. As we strode back down the dirt road, the sun had risen several inches above the horizon. Townspeople were awake and moving. Shops were opening, and hawkers stood in the street, shouting to hawk their goods.

We marched quickly, and the boats reappeared. "Split up or stay together?" Benny asked.

"Split up," I answered with conviction. "You check the one we're moored next to, and I'll check the one closest to the shore at the other dock. We can search the last one together."

As we made our way down the riverbank towards the boats, Benny broke off and headed down in the direction of the boat next to ours. I was halfway to the two boats when a man standing on the third deck of the nearest boat caught my attention. I froze in mid step when he stopped what he was doing and stared down straight at me. It wasn't the man I noticed as much as the satchel he carried – a satchel like mine. I was willing to bet the name Nelson was stamped in the leather on the outside of that satchel. The man turned and spoke to a man dressed like a crewman or maybe the captain himself.

I resumed walking, trying to act casually and not like a man who wanted to break into a run. The man who looked like a crewman reeled away from the man who had to be Chauncey, as Chauncey disappeared toward the cabins.

The boat's whistle blew, signaling that it was departing as men untied the boat from the moorings. I broke into a run, trying to jump on board before it pulled away. By the time I reached the dock it was too late, and the boat was already paddling further from shore. It was now pulling past the docked boat a few feet away and disappeared behind it.

I leaped from the dock and over the low railing of the tied-off boat. Without missing a step or stopping, I ran up the stairs leading to the second deck. The boat pulling away was only a few feet off to the side but twenty feet further down the boat. I ran down the catwalk of the second deck at a full sprint. The boat wasn't moving at full speed yet, and I was catching up fast. The boat had not built up enough steam to go more than a couple miles an hour, but it didn't need to. Its paddle wheel was much larger than the boat I had been on, digging into the river with its huge paddles, churning the water, and moving the boat with little effort. I had just past the paddle wheel when I reached the bow of the boat I was on. Running out of catwalk, I was forced to make my leap, diving for the moving boat. I jumped up onto the railing and then held my breath as I leapt across the open water to the next boat.

When I was at a full run, the two vessels only appeared to be four feet apart. Now that I was flying in mid-air, my chest sank when I realized that there was more like six feet of open space between the two boats. I had hoped to land on the second deck of the boat or at least jump from railing to railing, but I came up short and the railing slammed into my chest, knocking the breath I'd been holding out of my lungs. I started to drop straight down towards the water, but my hands managed to grab one of the railing bars.

I hung there for a moment, concentrating on not letting go and forced my fingers to clamp down on the wooden railing. I knew that if I crashed into the water, I'd lose my chance at finding Aden again. Panic built in my chest like a ball of fire. Twisting my body, I swung my legs, trying to find purchase. My foot rammed its way between two railings, and I pushed with my feet while pulling with my arms. I hauled myself up and over the banister and fell onto my back, lying there like a turtle while I tried to catch my breath. I needed to move, but after that sprint, the leap of faith, and having to pull myself over the rail, I took the time to suck in as much air as I could. Finally, I rolled onto my stomach and in doing a semi push-up, I came up on my knees. I grasped the banister with my right hand, pulled myself to my feet, and started my walk down the catwalk of the deck.

At the far end of the catwalk, the man I'd seen from shore ran up the stairwell, followed by six men. He pointed at me and shrieked something to his men as he continued up the next set of steps that led to a third deck. That had to be where Aden was.

Initially, I considered turning around and running for the rear stairwell, but then I would have these men chasing me. The best course of action was to deal with these men first, then go for Aden. We were on a boat – where was this Chauncey guy going to go?

I didn't need to run at them because they were already rushing toward me. The one advantage that I had was that I didn't have to fight all of them at once. The catwalk on the boat was less than three feet wide, so these men would most likely get into each other's way if they tried to rush me as a group.

The first man came in hard and fast ahead of the others, bare-handed and fists up. He swung a haymaker at my head. I ducked the swing easily enough but instead of punching him, I gave him a forward kick with my right foot, directly into his breadbasket, forcing the air out of him and knocking him back into the two men behind him.

The three of them tumbled onto the deck in a heap as the fourth man jumped over them. As he landed in front of me, I kicked out with a side kick to his left knee. His knee gave way as the sound of bone breaking cracked in the air, and he dropped to the deck with a scream. The fifth one didn't jump over everyone in his way. Instead, he jumped onto the back of one of his friends, then leaped in the air at me.

Bringing my right leg back to brace myself, I let him land on top of me. Realizing he made a fatal mistake, he tried to throw a few punches, but without his feet on the ground, he didn't have much power in his swings. I swiveled my body and threw the man over the side. His screams were followed by a loud splash into the water.

The last man, seeing that they were out classed in the

bare hands fighting style, pulled a flintlock from the front of his belt. As he cocked the hammer back on the flintlock, one of my throwing knives plunged into his throat. He flew backwards, landing on his back and firing his flintlock into the deck above us. Blood bubbled out around my blade and dripped down his neck.

The first three men slowly rose and pulled out knives.

I know how to fight with knives, I thought to myself, smiling as I unsheathed my two hunting blades. The first man took a step forward when he saw my smile, which caused him to stop mid-step. The next man didn't stop and shoved the lead man into me. Knowing it was too late and there was no going back, he leapt forward and swung his knife for my throat. I blocked his knife with mine and slashed his arm with the other, making him drop his knife. Then his friends used him as a shield, pushing him forward. I bent at the waist and as he collided with me, he tumbled over my back as I stood up and launched him into the air and over the side.

I didn't have time to watch him go or listen for the scream as the next man had already barreled into me, knocking me onto my back. His arms came at me fast. Dropping my knives, I caught his wrist with both hands as his eight-inch blade swung down for my chest. The man behind him was trying to stab me but the man on top of me was in his way.

I jerked the man on top of me hard to my left, and as his friend thought he had found an opening and plunged his knife at my face, I brought my right knee up hard, shoving the man on top of me to the side. The man bringing his knife down had put all his weight behind the stab and the attack could not be stopped. The man's knife sunk deep into his companion's back that occupied that space above me.

I didn't know who was more surprised by this, the man

with a knife plunged into his back or his friend who had stabbed it there. The man on top of me was dead within seconds but not before bleeding all over my chest and arms. His companion stumbled back, his face a mask of shock, and I shoved the dead man to the side, drew my Tec-9, and fired two shots into the standing man's chest. He crumpled backwards and fell over the side of the paddleboat.

Holstering my Tec-9, I then retrieved my two knives and stood up to address the only man yet alive – the one presently moaning and favoring his broken knee. He managed to stand up on one leg and held himself upright by placing all his weight onto the railing. I took one step in his direction, and he flung himself over the side to the water below.

I paused and watched him splash into the muddy, churning water and shrugged.

Then I slid my knives back into their sheaths and withdrew my Tec-9 again as I made my way to the stairs near the rear of the boat. I stopped at the bottom step and looked up, taking the time to catch my breath *again*.

"Well, like my father used to say," I said out loud to myself. "That whisky's not going to drink itself, so get up and get it."

I then climbed the steps one by one. When my head reached over the top step, I could see a bound Aden being dragged by the collar of his shirt. Aden's hands were tied together in front of him, and a man who had to be Chauncey was dragging him down the catwalk, until he saw me. Chauncey froze in place and fear bloomed on his face while hope showed on Aden's.

"Thomas!" Aden yelled when he saw me.

Then a very large man who stood at least six inches taller and weight a good fifty pounds heavier than me with hands like

283

catcher mitts stepped out of a cabin and onto the catwalk, blocking me. He held two large flintlocks in his hands. I thought the flintlocks were of normal size, but they were actually larger than most. They only appeared to be of normal size in his giant paws. As he raised his flintlocks toward me, I aimed my Tec-9 at him. For a second, my mind's eye, I saw both of us firing our weapons and each killing the other, although I was not convinced I could kill this man with just one shot. Though he had not fired yet, I noticed he came up with the same conclusion as I had.

"It doesn't have to end this way," I told him as I took another step up to the catwalk. "Are you really willing to die for this man?"

"Are you willing to die for your friend?" he responded in a deep, baritone voice that rolled down the catwalk.

"Aye. I am. But that's out of friendship. Why are you willing to die for Chauncey? Jacques told me that Chauncey didn't have any friends."

The large man's eyebrow rose slightly. "You spoke to Jacques?"

His two flintlocks dipped a hair as he looked over them at me and not down the barrels to aim as he waited for an answer. Jacques meant something to this large man.

"Yes," I answered. "Jacques told me I could find him here. Are you the messenger he told me he sent?"

"That I am," the large man said, eyebrows furling with questions. "Why would he send me to warn Jacques, then tell you where he was?"

I had two choices at this point. I could lie or tell the truth. Either choice might backfire on me. I chose to tell the truth and hoped we could work out a deal.

"Because I sacked him last night," I said flatly.

His flintlocks rose back up, and he now looked pissed. Maybe I should have lied. I held up my left hand to try to stop him from firing.

"He's alive," I added quickly, keeping my left hand up to stall him. "He's tied to the anchor of my ship. But he's alive for now. I was planning on dropping him with my anchor and watching him drown, but maybe we could work out a deal."

His eyes narrowed. "What kind of deal?"

"What's your name?" I asked.

"Jim. They call me Big Jim."

Yeah, no shit, I thought. *I bet they do.*

"I was planning on dropping your boss with my anchor," I told him. "I gave orders to my crew that if they were attacked or I didn't return, drop him with the anchor. So, if you kill me, you're also killing your boss."

The big man's face twisted up as if he was trying to work out a complicated math problem.

"But," I continued, getting his attention again, "if you let me pass, not only will I let him live, but I'll let him go and tell him he has Big Jim to thank for his life. I give you my word."

"How do I know you'll keep your word?" he asked, interested in the deal, but needing a small push.

I inhaled my chest fully upright. "Because I'm the real Pale Rider. You can take my word, let me pass, and save your boss, or I'll kill you now and later drop your boss in the ocean. But I need to get by you one way or another, and I need to do it now."

"Chauncey's a pissant," Jim finally said after thinking about his options. He lowered his two flintlocks, shoved them into the front of his belt, and then stepped back into the cabin.

I blew out a lungful of air, relieved that the gigantic man had made the better choice for both of us, and then proceeded to walk down the catwalk. I wanted to run, but after the showdown I just had with the extremely large Jim, I thought it best to compose myself first.

Aden and Chauncey were at the end of the catwalk. Chauncey stopped to glance back at me and then pulled out a normal eighteenth-century flintlock. I kept walking as he thumbed the hammer back. Even from here, I could see his hands shaking. I thought to dive out of the way, but I had nowhere to go. I paused and thought about kicking in the door to the stateroom I was standing in front of. While I was weighing the option, Chauncey fired his flintlock. I was too far away, and the shot smacked into the bulkhead a few feet in front of me, splintering the wood. He then tossed the flintlock over the side and into the water below. Turning, he grabbed Aden and dragged him down the stairs to the second deck.

I grabbed the banister and jumped over it, hanging onto one of the support beams of the railing. I shimmied down the beam to the second level. My feet found the railing to that banister, and I hopped down onto the catwalk. Much quicker than chasing him down the stairs.

Chauncey and Aden emerged from the stairwell, and Chauncey stopped short. Aden yelled out to me again as Chauncey hauled him down to the lower level. I repeated the act and grabbed the banister, jumping over and then lowering myself down to the main deck.

The main deck resembled the other riverboats, consisting of one large main room. Windows lined the wall, so those inside had a view of the river while they sat inside and ate their meals. Unlike the boat I came here on, this one didn't have a gambling hall – it was lined with tables for dining. I moved forward along the main room of the boat when Chauncey popped out from around the corner. I reached for my Tec-9 when Chauncey threw a fist-sized rock at me. Only, it wasn't a rock. I didn't recognize it for what it really was at first, but the very distinct ping sound it made as the spoon flew from the main body was enough to tell me I was in trouble.

"Shit!" I swore as I covered my head with my arms and dove through the nearest window.

I rolled across the table that I had landed on and knocked it over onto its side as I tumbled onto the thick brown rug that covered the wooden deck. They didn't exactly have safety glass in 1814, and my arms and legs burned as sharp broken glass had sliced through my clothes and skin. The grenade exploded and four more of the windows blew inwards in a thousand pieces. I tucked my head, trying to protect my eyes and face.

The upturned table slammed into me as the shockwave from the grenade struck it. The table may have hit me like a car, but it also protected me from the force of the explosion itself. My ears rang and I was seeing double as the world refused to come into focus. I felt like I had gone eight seconds on an angry bull, got thrown and stepped on. I was really starting to hate this Chauncey asshole.

Several crewmen working in the main room also found themselves on the floor. Not knowing what was going on or why, they managed to get to their feet and run for the door at the rear of the room, not bothering to shut the door behind them.

With a moan of pain and significant effort (I was going to feel *this* in the morning), I reached up and grabbed the edge of the table with both hands and forced myself up onto my shaky legs.

A large hole had blown into the thin wooden wall on the other side of the table, and wooden shards of what used to be the wall impaled the top of the table like jagged knives. A thick cloud of dust swirled and filled the air of the entire dining room. The dust clung to the blood on my face and chest in thick layers.

I wiped the sleeve of my shirt across my face, trying to wipe most of the dust off my mouth and eyelids. I coughed out dust from my lungs and spat what could only be described as a light coating of mud out of my mouth.

The boat's whistle bellowed over the ringing in my ears, and I felt more than heard vibration of men running on the catwalk above. A gunshot fired from somewhere outside of the double doors but not at me. *Weird.* Gunshots were usually fired in *my* direction. The ringing in my ears started to fade, and I could hear the heavy footsteps running on the catwalk again, returning the way they'd come. What was going on out there?

I squeezed my eyes closed, trying to clear up my double vision. I wasn't going anywhere if I couldn't see where I was going.

One of the two doors in front of me burst open, and I recoiled. I drew my Tec-9 and pointed it at the twin Chaunceys wavering in the doorway holding the twin Webley pistols, not knowing which one to shoot.

Fire shot out the barrels of the two Webleys as I spun around to my left and was pitched to the floor. I was on my face when I realized that I'd been shot. A tiny cloud of dust sailed up in the dust in front of my face as I blew air out of my nose, which happened to be pressed against the rug. I rolled over on my back with an aching huff and looked down at my chest. My vest had stopped the bullet, and thank God the jell had protected my ribs. They couldn't handle getting broken again.

I aimed my Tec-9 at the edge of the table, waiting for Chauncey to check if I was dead. He had to come check, right? It was only human nature, especially after the trouble he'd gone through to kill me. The men, the grenade, and firing one of his few, precious bullets to kill me. I laid on the floor, pointing my Tec-9 past the edge of the table, and waited for Chauncey to show his face so I could put a bullet between his eyes. But he never came around the table. Sitting up and staying low beneath the edge of the table, I took three quick, deep breaths, forcing oxygen to my throbbing muscles.

I combat rolled out from the table coming up in a shooting stance, but I was alone in the room. Chauncey was gone, and I was looking at an open but empty doorway. On the upside, my vision was clearing up and I wasn't seeing double anymore. On the downside, my head was throbbing from a headache that suddenly appeared.

Keeping my Tec-9 up and ready, I crept to the double doors. Staying behind the door that was still closed, I stole a look out the open one, trying to take in as much as I could. Aden knelt on the deck near the bow of the boat, gripping the railing in front of him.

I didn't see Chauncey, the sneaky rat bastard, but knew he was out there somewhere. If he had run away, he would have killed Aden before escaping and not settled for knocking him in the head and leaving him alive. Aden was bait. Like a staked-out goat with a hunter lying in wait for the lion to step out of the grass and into the open. The terrible thing about these kinds of traps is that sometimes they work, and the lion comes.

But the trap only works if the lion is busy looking at the goat and not looking for the hunter.

Stepping through the open door, I swept my pistol from left to right. So many places to hide, but I still didn't see Chauncey – stacks of hay, several large crates, a pile of wood, and let's not forget the stairs.

Wherever he was, like the hunter, Chauncey was in a

position to see Aden. He waited for me to come out into the open so he could shoot me in the back. I moved slow and quiet, closing the distance between myself and Aden while also trying to look in every direction at once. I froze, cringing as the wooden deck board under my feet creaked.

"Thomas," Aden moaned, lifting his gaze and seeing me. He was attempting to stand.

Scanning every direction except Aden's, I waited for Chauncey to jump out from behind the crates or the stack of wood. Instead of Chauncey was an even worse sight and hair-raising sound. From behind the pile of wood, another distinct *ping* came as the spoon flew free from Aden's second, and I prayed last grenade. It clumsily bounced and rolled across the deck towards Aden.

Before the grenade stopped rolling, I was running full force at Aden. Time slowed down, and I didn't think I was going to make it to Aden in time. Diving in the air, I hit Aden high, like a linebacker, wrapped my arms around him, and shoved him backwards and over the railing. We hit the muddy water headfirst and plunged straight under. Aden slipped from my grip as we twisted in the river's current. I opened my eyes against the churning water, searching for Aden, but the water was too murky for me to see anything.

From under the water, I heard and felt the reverberations of the explosion as the grenade went off on the riverboat above. The water was too muddy to see through, but I waved my arms around, reaching out for Aden as panic rose in my chest. I kicked upward until my head broke the water. Splashing around in the water, I turned my head back and forth, shouting Aden's name over and over. I didn't see any sign of my friend, but the huge red paddle of the riverboat dug into the river ten feet behind me, pushing the large riverboat away from us.

Two hands emerged from the fast-running water for a second. They were tied together and six feet away upriver, then they sunk back down quickly under the dark water. I dove down under the surface, swimming in the direction where the hands had come up and fighting against the current to get there. I thought my chest would burst like the grenade before I found him.

The current slammed Aden into me, and I grabbed at him, but then the current snatched him away so fast I grasped only water. I felt around the water as I let the current take me, hoping it swept me in the same direction as it had Aden. I bumped something and without thought, I grabbed at it. A handful of fabric filled my left hand, and I tugged it my way. My right hand shot out and grasped at Aden, my fingers wrapping around one of his arms in a vice grip. I fought to pull Aden with me upward. My head broke the water again, and as I started to descend, I shoved Aden's head upward with all my might, hoping he was awake enough to get a quick lungful of air.

I only went down a about three feet when I touched the muddy bottom of the Mississippi, then kicked upward, dragging Aden with me again. Aden's eyes were open, blinking as we broke the surface of the river, and his body jerked as if his legs were kicking, trying to help me keep us above the water. Side stroking with my left arm and pulling Aden with my right, I slowly made our way towards shore. My muscles seared with fatigue, wanting to give out on me. My lungs and muscles screamed for more oxygen. My heavy vest and boots betrayed me, trying their best to pull me under, and with every ounce of will I possessed, I had to fight to not get pulled under again.

Then my toes brushed the mushy river floor. After walking on my toes for two steps, my whole foot found a more solid perch. On my fourth step, my foot slipped in the mud, and

I fell forward, splashing under and yanking Aden down with me. The split second I lost my footing, the current drew us back out towards the middle of the river. My muscles were done – I didn't have the strength to pull us back to shore again, and we began to sink under the surface once more. I scrambled with my feet but could not find the bottom of the river to kick off again.

I didn't think we were going to make it – we had come this far only to perish in a river, of all things? It seemed like a cruel joke, and panic burned in my belly again as I began to flounder. Then a hand grabbed the back of my vest and pulled. I was jerked backwards until my head broke the water again and all I could do was keep my grip on Aden to pull him with me, forcing his head up and out of the water. Aden gasped for air and then slipped back under. I somehow found the strength to yank him harder, and again he gasped as his head breached the surface in front of me.

Had air ever tasted so good? Smelled so good? I didn't think so.

"Just stand up," a deep voice behind me instructed.

I paused stupidly and turned my head to see Big Jim holding the back of my vest, dragging me towards shore. The man stood in the water that reached only to his shoulders. I had to walk on my toes again to keep my mouth above the surface, but I could touch again.

I didn't have to go far before my feet found solid foundation on the thick, muddy floor of the river. Big Jim, who was still pulling me, didn't let go until we were beyond the drag of the current and I nodded my head. He let go of me, then thankfully grabbed Aden, hauling him closer to the bank because my arms couldn't do it anymore.

Once we were close enough to the riverbank, I stopped to stare at the back end of the riverboat as it kept paddling. The water was up to my waist as I caught my breath and stared at the riverboat, Chauncey, and the invaluable Webley heading south down river, as they moved farther from my grasp.

Big Jim released Aden when they were next to me, but the big man kept wading until he reached the dry bank of the river.

"Jacques better still be alive," Big Jim muttered under his breath as he continued up the riverbank.

"Thomas," Aden choked out and gave me a strained look. "The Webley."

"I know," I said. "I let it get away. I'm sorry. Let's rest for a bit, then walk back to Baton Rouge. I have a boat there."

I grasped my front hunting knife and cut the rope binding Aden's wrists. We finished wading out of the water and collapsed on our backs in the dry dirt.

Big Jim peered down at us with no readable expression on his face.

"Aden, I assume you already know Big Jim here?" I asked in a manner of introduction.

"We've met," Aden said dryly. "Why did he save us?"

"Saving Jacques." Jim extracted his two flintlocks out of the front of his pants. Water poured from both barrels. Shaking his head, he walked farther inland leaving us where we laid in the grass and cattails.

Aden breathed hard next to me. He ignored Big Jim for the moment. "What are you doing here?"

I tilted my head slightly at him. "Jake."

"Jake!" Aden said, rising on his elbows with a grimace. "Is he okay?"

"He's fine," I told him. "He's on my ship."

"Your ship? What ship?"

"Jake and I acquired a pirate ship," I explained. "And a

riverboat. But the riverboat is more of a loaner."

"I should have known he'd go get you." Aden flopped back down onto his back, blowing out a long exhale of air. "He wanted to get you from the start. I'm sorry, Thomas. I wanted to leave you out of this. I thought I could handle this myself, and you've done more than enough. I'm so sorry that you had to come."

"You're an idiot, Aden," I said, half laughing between deep breaths as a way of accepting his apology. "Jake was right. You should have gotten me or someone else more used to fighting and violence. You're a thinker Aden, not a warrior in the traditional   sense."

"You're right," Aden said, his face hardening at his acknowledgement.   "I   know   that   now."

"Now that you're safe, you and Jake need to leave. I'll get the Webley back. I promise."

"This is my fault, Thomas," Aden countered. "I can't leave. I still have to help General Jackson."

I shook my head, making the grass rustle in my ears. "We will, Aden. First, we get back your stuff, then we help Jackson again."

"Again?" Aden asked.

"We stopped off at Pensacola on the way here," I told him. "Already met the man. Not a bad guy all in all. Maybe a little high-strung. Reminds me of General Washington in some ways. I was able to stop his men from entering Fort Barrancas. He's on his way here as we speak. If he pushes his men, he might make it here before the British instead of after them."

"And Chauncey," Aden stated, changing the subject. "I owe that bastard. He had me chained to a bed for almost two months. *Chained*, Thomas. He seemed to enjoy beating me with a bamboo stick."

"Chauncey will get what's coming to him," I promised, even as my mouth twitched at his protestations of being chained up, as if his very words proved my point about him. Loved the guy, but soldier he was not. "Any idea where the rest of your stuff is?"

"We don't have to worry about my phone or goggles. They were destroyed already," Aden admitted. "Chauncey used both my grenades, as you know all too well. Chauncey has the Webley, but I have no idea about my vest. I do know that Chauncey sold my knife and sword to someone."

"Don't worry about them," I said. "I already got them back. We need to get the Webley and find the vest."

Aden sat up again. "And how do we do that?"

"We know who has the Webley," I said. "And I might know who has the vest."

"Who?"

"Someone named Captain Burlington," I answered. Talking of his vest struck a chord in my mind, and I slapped my hands over my vest.

"What's wrong?" Aden asked as he watched me search my vest.

"I lost one of my throwing knives," I lamented, letting my head fall back down into the sandy mud. "My wife had three of them made for me for my birthday. I left one on the boat. Well, in one of Chauncey's men really, but either way I don't have it and she'll kill me for losing it."

I didn't miss the slight curl to Aden's lips at the mention of my wife. "Sorry about your knife. You mentioned a Captain Burlington?"

"He's a pirate," I answered. "A captain, actually. He's been sailing around the Caribbean, pirating and claiming to be the Pale Rider."

"Burlington?" Aden asked pensively. "Chauncey mentioned him a few times. I think Chauncey was on his crew. This Burlington has been looking for Chauncey. Chauncey was not only hiding me but hiding himself from this Captain Burlington person."

"Good. Maybe we can use that somehow. I have no idea how, but we can figure that out later."

A moment later, we jerked upright to the sound of a steam whistle. Benny stood on the bow of the *Lucky Lady*, waving his arms and grinning widely. The boat slugged down river slower than Chauncey's boat, but faster than we could walk. Captain Mattson was in the wheelhouse, pulling on the rope cord and blowing the whistle.

Captain Mattson slowed the boat and directed her closer to shore. Aden and I reluctantly waded back into the fast-moving water and climbed over the main deck railing. Big Jim stood on land, observing us with baited interest until I waved for him to join us on board.

"Come on!" I yelled. "It's too far for you to walk. I'll take you to Jacques, you big ox."

The big man smiled and waded into the water as Benny slapped me on the back.

"What are you doing here?" I asked Benny. "How did you know?"

"I saw you running down the dock," Benny answered. "I tried to catch up, but you were too far ahead. That was a nice leap you made, by the way. I didn't think you were going to make it. So I ran to the *Lucky Lady* and had Captain Mattson pull away to follow you."

"You did great, Benny," I said, patting the younger man on the shoulder with one hand while helping support Aden with the other. "Thank you. This is my friend, Aden, the man I've been searching for. Aden, this is Benny."

The two men shook hands.

"Benny, please take Aden to the kitchen for some food," I asked. "His ribs don't normally show like they are right now. He'll need your help walking. Maybe find something for him to use as a cane. While you're doing that, I'll ask the captain to increase his speed. We need to catch up to Chauncey."

"It's a pleasure to meet you, sir," Benny said to Aden, as he reached under Aden's arm to assist him. "Come with me, and we'll get you a beer and a big steak."

"Don't bother asking for more speed," Captain Mattson commented as he walked up behind me. "I already have the boat going full speed. This is as fast as the old girl will go. My men have been filling the boiler with wood as fast as they can."

I couldn't accept that answer. "We need to catch that other boat, Captain," I pleaded.

"Not a chance, son," Captain Mattson said. He pointed to the boiler where his crew worked in a frenzy, feeding wood into the fire. "This old girl just can't keep up with these newer boats."

I pinched the bridge of my nose, thinking of my other options. "Assuming they are going to New Orleans. How far behind them will we be when we get there?"

"Well, of course they are going to New Orleans," Captain Mattson said. "It's the last stop on the Mississippi. That's where all the riverboats turn around. It's not like we take these boats out into open waters."

"Very well. How far behind?"

He shifted his gaze downriver. "They might be there tonight. We'll get there sometime in the early morning."

Chapter Eighteen Return

November 11, 1814

I stood at the bow of the boat as the sun broke the horizon off on my left. Benny had woken me a few minutes ago after the captain told him that we were close to New Orleans. Aden and I had stayed up late into the night, talking. He told me about the hell he'd gone through during the last two months – the small meals, lack of company, and beatings. Somewhere in that time, Chauncey had broken my friend, and my chest ached with that knowledge. I wanted to send him back to my farm with Jake and take care of Chauncey on my own, but I couldn't do that to the man. He would never be the same. He needed to get his dignity back and to do that, he had to face Chauncey himself. I was going to have to not only let Aden help get the Webley back but somehow manipulate the situation so that he played a key role in it.

I also needed to buy Aden new clothes and boots. His boots were missing – his feet were a ragged mess – and his clothes were more holes than not. He had eaten three times since climbing aboard the boat and needed to eat more to gain back even some of his body mass that he had lost. Captain Mattson had found a set of less-filthy, baggy clothes and a pair of shoes for Aden that would work for the meantime, but they were too large for him. I had joked with Aden that it looked like he was wearing clown shoes, and that earned me a wan smile.

It was a start. I'd take it.

Big Jim approached us from behind, his huge shadow stretching and covering us long before he reached us. I had expected to see the riverboat that Chauncey used moored to one of the docks when we rounded the last bend to New Orleans, but it wasn't there. Three paddleboats were tied up to the docks, but the one I was searching for was not among them.

"I don't understand," Aden said, as he walked up next to me. "Where's the boat? I don't see it."

"I don't know," I answered. "It should be here."

Aden gripped the railing with one hand. The other held the bamboo pole Benny had found for him to use as a cane. "The captain said it had to be here. It's not like they could go farther. The captain said they couldn't go out into open waters."

"Apparently, the captain was wrong," I said. "Do you have any idea where Chauncey might have gone after leaving the boat?"

"I might," Aden answered, leaning back on his makeshift cane. "He mentioned some islands where he intended to sell the Webley to the British or French."

"Let's just dock and get back to the *Shining Star*," I told him with a bit of impatience as I scanned the docks. "Jake will be worried about us. He won't be happy until he sees you alive. We can come up with a new plan there."

The boat paddled up to the dock, and Captain Mattson

299

tugged on the cord in the wheelhouse, blowing the steam whistle the whole time to announce our arrival. Passengers eager to get back to their homes and families leapt off the boat and onto the dock before the boat was tied off.

Pierre Lafitte sauntered to the end of the dock to meet us and his boat. Four men walked behind him, bodyguards of sorts, I presumed. When they reached the end of the dock where the boat was tied off, they waited.

From my position on the boat, I could see that Pierre wore a sword on his left hip and had a flintlock shoved in the front of his pants. Pierre also had a shiny black cane in his right hand that he leaned on, trying to appear dignified and every bit the southern gentleman that he was not. The man didn't strike me as needing a cane.

There were only three reasons to carry a cane. It assisted in walking, was fashionable, or was a weapon. Why a man with a sword and flintlock required a cane for a weapon was beyond me, but I was betting that in his case, a weapon was the correct answer. The four men behind him had tucked flintlocks in their belts and carried cudgels. Pierre tried to look bored as his men tried to appear intimidating.

"Is this going to be a problem?" Aden asked, eyeing the five men on the dock who were staring straight at us and waiting.

"Not for me," I answered. "It will be for them if this goes wrong. I'm not in the mood for Pierre's bullshit."

Aden's eyebrows flew high on his forehead. "Pierre Lafitte? Chauncey mentioned his name several times. He's afraid of this man. More afraid of the man's brother. I think he was hiding from them as well. He thought they would want in on his deal and take half the coin he got for the Webley."

Stepping off the boat with Benny, Aden, and Big Jim

behind me, I didn't hesitate. I strode up to Pierre, stopping three feet short of him.

"Mr. Lafitte," I said pleasantly in greeting.

"You took my boat," Pierre responded, stating the obvious with a serious look on his face.

"I found myself in need of one," I told him. "You took the liberty of taking the *Shining Star* without permission. I was just returning the favor. I'm sure you don't mind, as it's been returned. Now be a good fellow and move out of our way."

Benny's hand moved to his knife as one of the men behind Pierre lunged forward, evidently not liking the way I spoke to his boss. Pierre held up a pale hand, stopping him.

"Jim," Pierre said, his eyes turning away from me and up to the big man standing behind me. "Do you keep their company now?"

Pierre wanted to know where Jim's loyalties lay.

"Just until Jacques is freed," Jim said with no apology in his voice. I had to admire his conviction and allegiance to Jacques.

"*Oui*," Pierre said, then shifted his narrow gaze back to me. "That was clever of you. I and everyone else expected you to pay me a visit, but you showed up at Jacques's place instead. Why? And why sack him? My men tell me he's a prisoner on your *Shining Star*."

"He had information I needed. The rest is none of your business."

"Everything that happens in New Orleans is my business. And I do mean everything," Pierre said as he leaned on his cane toward me.

I shrugged. "If you say so. You'll just have to live without knowing some things. Or don't. I don't care which."

"What should I do about you taking my boat?" Pierre

301

changed the subject while resting his left hand on his chin as he tapped the first finger of his hand against his lip.

He was trying to intimidate me, that much was obvious, implying there were many different things he could do to me. At the same time, he didn't actually threaten anything, so he was not obligated to take any action presently.

"Fuck you," I said slowly, calling his bluff and surprising the man. "We are not in your office, surrounded by your men. You'll do nothing about it, unless you want to die right here, and right now. Make no mistake, no matter which of your men behind you makes a move, you would be the first to die."

"*Mon frère* has returned," Pierre threatened with rising anger in his voice. "I would take care of you myself, but Jean has asked me to bring you to the shop. He wishes to speak to you. Be happy he doesn't want you dead, yet. You'll come with me to the shop and speak with my brother yourself. He's expecting us now."

"Fuck you," I said again but not as slow this time. "And fuck your brother."

I needed Jean Lafitte and the men he could bring with him. Jackson needed them. But right there, right then, standing on the dock and being threatened, I didn't care. I would deal with the pirates later.

"If your brother wants to talk to me, he can come to the *Shining Star* and talk to me," I told him. "Trust me, Pierre, the last thing either of you wants is me coming to you. That tends to turn out bad for people."

"I'll be sure to tell my brother you said that." The knuckles of Pierre's right hand were turning white from squeezing the head of his cane so hard.

"You do that," I answered with a dismissive chuckle. "That's the second time you threatened me with those words.

For now, either make your move or get the fuck out of my way, you pompous asshole."

Pierre Lafitte's face bloomed red, and his lips thinned. I stared into his eyes, unmoving, but in my peripheral vision, I tracked his right hand and the cane in it. He lifted his cane into the air an inch and my left hand moved to rest on my hunting knife sheathed on my left hip. The cane stopped as if he were trying to decide what to do. Then his cane tapped back down, stabbing at the wooden plank of the dock with a *thunk* which sounded like metal against wood. To everyone's surprise, Pierre stepped to the side with a flourish and allowed us to pass. His men appeared surprised more than I was. After glancing back and forth from him to me and back, they reluctantly followed his lead and stepped to the side and out of our way.

"Oh *oui*, one last thing *Monsieur* Nelson," Pierre called out as I passed him, heading towards the muddy bank. "A platoon of Spanish soldiers led by a Captain Sanchez, I believe, have come to New Orleans. They have been asking questions and describe someone they were most upset with, who much resembles you, black vest and all. I took the liberty of telling him about the *Shining Star*. You may find him waiting for you or he, too, may call on you later."

I ignored his words and didn't turn around to acknowledge him. Captain Sanchez was the commanding officer at the Port of Saint Augustine, where I had killed the four Spanish soldiers. He must have tracked Jake and I here, wanting to kill us or bring us back to Saint Augustine to be hanged.

Pierre may have been trying to frighten me, but I appreciated the warning, nonetheless. I would deal with the good Captain Sanchez in my own time and in my own manner.

"That may not have been wise," Jim whispered to me as we walked away.

I glanced up at him. "Oh? Why is that?"

"Pierre is a powerful man," Jim answered. "But like Chauncey, he's merely a pissant. New Orleans is filled with pissants. Pierre's brother Jean Lafitte, on the other hand, is a man to fear. He's very dangerous, vicious. He's renowned to fight well with sword, knife, or flintlock. He's also the brains of the two. Even though he's the younger brother, his older brother follows his lead. That should tell you a lot. Not a man to have as an enemy. Jean is *not* a pissant. He can also be charming, or so I've heard the ladies gossip. The most dangerous thing about him is his ability to inspire and impress. He has at least ten ships that follow his lead. Their captains follow his orders. He endears loyalty."

"Thank you, Jim. I appreciate your words," I said.

We made our way down the harbor to the *Shining Star* without running into any Spanish soldiers, which made me question Pierre's subtle threat. One of the sailors rang the ship's bell when they saw us, and the entire crew came up on deck to greet us. Jake was the first to welcome us, grabbing Aden in one of his bear hugs.

"Oh, thank God, you're okay," Jake gushed, lifting Aden in the air. "I'm sorry I ran and left you there. I didn't know what else to do, so I rode straight for the alien ship and Thomas."

I was worried that Jake might crack one of Aden's ribs with all the weight Aden has lost. Jake set Aden down on the deck and stood there smiling at me.

"You did the right thing Jake," Aden said, trying to catch his breath.

"You did it," Jake said to me in awe. "You really did it. I knew you would."

"Yes, well, we have some bad news," I said.

"Bad news? What kind of bad news?"

"We lost the Webley," I told him. "Chauncey is planning on selling the weapon tomorrow night to the French or British. We still need to find Aden's vest. Jackson is on the march this way with his men, and other than our ship, we haven't recruited any men for the battle to come. If all of that wasn't bad enough, the British are still on their way here, by land and sea to take New Orleans. Half the town wants to surrender to them before they even get here. And, oh yes, Captain Sanchez is here in New Orleans with a platoon of men, looking for us as we speak."

"Captain Sanchez from Saint Augustine?" Jake asked whipping his head back and forth, searching the docks as if the man was going to jump out of thin air.

I nodded my head. "Yes. Captain Sanchez from Saint Augustine. The same Captain Sanchez whom you were nice enough to inform that we were heading to New Orleans."

"Oh my God, Thomas," Jake said, his eyes wide. "I bet he's pissed that you fed his men to those alligators."

"Alligators?" Big Jim interrupted. "Why would you do a thing like that?"

"Go with Aden to our quarters, and I'll be there in a minute," I said to Jake, ignoring Jim's question. I didn't need to add to the rumor mill. "Benny, go with them and check on your brother."

"I'll stay with you for now, Captain," Benny said, looking directly at Big Jim.

Benny was worried about what Jim's reaction would be when he saw Jacques tied to an anchor.

"All will be well, Benny," I reassured him with a smile. "Go check on your brother. He may need you. Make sure he's recovering. He'll be worried about you. I'll be fine, my friend."

Benny nodded his head slowly as if he was not sure that I would be fine. I must not have sounded very convincing.

"Oh, Thomas," Jake called to me as I started to turn away. "I almost forgot. We received two messages yesterday morning. The first messenger was from the mayor who would like to meet with you as soon as possible. He said it was extremely important and that you should come talk to him before you talk to the city council."

"I wonder why he said that?" I asked more to myself than hoping Jake had an answer. "I would have thought he would want me to talk to all of them at the same time."

"The second messenger was from the city council," Jake continued. "Informing us that, in their words, mind you, that the man known as Thomas Nelson, also known as the Pale Rider, is wanted for the murder of almost two dozen men at the tavern known as Samuel's Tavern."

I grimaced and ran my hand through my hair. "Oh, great."

"It gets worse. They said that you were also wanted for the murder of two dozen more men on the ship known as the *Shining Star*. The fact that those men boarded us and took the ship didn't seem to matter to them. They sent a kid to deliver that message. I think they were afraid that if they sent a man, he wouldn't have left the ship alive."

"They were right," Task said, spitting off the side of the ship.

"Why would the city council care about pirates getting themselves killed?" I asked.

"The Lafitte brothers have a lot of influence over the council. This way they can put pressure on you, causing you to run, or if you stay, no one can object to Jean Lafitte killing you," Task explained.

I threw my hands into the air. "Do you have any good news?"

"Mr. Task had the two lanterns we destroyed replaced with new ones," Jake said with a smile, then he stepped in close to me and lowered his voice. "And the men have all seen the painting, Thomas. First just one of the crew saw it by chance, and then they were all demanding to see it. They all know that you were with Washington at Yorktown."

"Fine," I said, rubbing my head again. I had a lot to do in the coming days. Better to focus on one thing at a time. "Jake, please take Aden to the cabin, and I'll be there shortly. Big Jim, with me, if you please. Let's go free your boss."

As the three men pushed through the crew who had crowded around us, eager to find out what was going on, I motioned with my head for Big Jim to follow me. When the crew realized I was taking Big Jim to the anchor, they suddenly seemed busy working in parts of the ship that were nowhere near the anchor. Big Jim was well known, and no one wanted to be in his orbit when he saw how Jacques had been treated.

As for Jacques, he sat on the deck of the ship, arms outstretched, hands tied to the black steel anchor. Although when I had given the order to tie Jacques to the anchor, I had meant for the anchor to stay in place on the outside of the ship, and for Jacques to dangle from it for everyone to see. Jake, Mr. Task or the crew had misunderstood my orders, and the anchor didn't hang outside of the ship – it now sat on the deck of the ship, leaning against the railing. The rope was still fastened, and it was ready to be pushed overboard if ordered.

Jacques lifted his face at the sound of our approaching footsteps. His eyes locked on me, and fear spread across his face.

"Be easy, Jacques," I said. I flicked my thumb toward Jim. "Your friend has paid for your life. You'll be walking off my ship, not going over with the anchor."

Big Jim came up behind me and Jacques's eyes lit up and

a smile crossed his face when he saw the big man.

"What the fuck is all this about?" Jim asked, pointing to Jacques and the anchor. "I thought you were telling a tale when you said you had him tied to the anchor."

I leveled my gaze him, well as best I could, given his immense size. "You thought I was joking when I said I had him tied to an anchor and was going to throw him overboard?"

"Well, yes. What kind of sick bastard would tie a person to an anchor?"

"The same sick bastard who fed four Spanish soldiers to a bunch of hungry alligators," I said, surprised that I had to voice the answer. Maybe he hadn't heard some of the Pale Rider rumors, or just hadn't believed them. "Make no mistake Jim, if you had not bought his life, I'd be tossing him over the side so that others didn't make the same mistake of crossing me as he had."

Big Jim bent low and opened Jacques's shirt to reveal a slash across his chest that had been stitched up but was still caked in dried blood.

"We didn't do that," I said quickly. "We did the stitching, but his own men did the cutting."

"I may have been wrong about you." Jim went down on one knee, pulled out his knife, and cut Jacques free from the anchor. "It's Jean and Pierre Lafitte who should worry. They would do better to avoid making an enemy of you."

"You're right," I agreed. "They would. But I think it may be too late for that. The water has been poisoned already, and good judgment may be dead. What little chance I had of not needing to kill them may have been destroyed by Pierre."

"For what it's worth, I don't believe you're a pissant either," Jim said, smiling as he looked up at me. Barely. Even kneeling, he was almost my height.

"Thank you, Jim." I was pleased with the back-handed compliment.

"Are we free to go?" Jim asked.

I went down on one knee like Jim and look Jacques in the eyes.

"If you think you've been treated badly here on my ship, ask Jim about my friend, Aden, who has been chained to a wall, beaten, and starved for the last two months, and be happy that you still live." I leaned in close to him. "You took part in his treatment. Jim here has paid for your life, so you'll live to see tomorrow. But if you cross me again, I'll stake you down on the beach and feed you to the crabs. And no, I'm not telling any tales. The crabs. They won't kill you as fast as sharks or alligators, but the suffering lasts a lot longer."

Jacques vigorously nodded his head in understanding. Big Jim eased Jacques to his feet and noticed that his pants were bloody and had been ripped open. Big Jim peered closer and saw the bullet wound to Jacques's leg that Jake had given him.

"You didn't say he'd been shot," Jim said in a growling tone.

"No, I didn't." I stood straight and looked up to face him. "I said he was alive and tied to my anchor. He's alive and was tied to my anchor."

Big Jim licked his lips, then looked down at me and laughed. To my surprise, he stuck out his big paw. I had expected a punch instead of a handshake. I clasped the man's hand, and we shook for a moment. He let go of my hand and then hoisted Jacques up with his arm and they walked away. Before reaching the plank, Jim stopped and slowly turned around to face me.

"Did you come back? Are you truly him?" Jim asked, smile gone and one thick eyebrow curved high on his head. "The real Pale Rider, I mean. The one people used to tell stories about. Are you the bringer of death?"

I kept a straight face as I returned his gaze.

"You're damn right I am."

The End

If you loved this book, please leave a review. And then, get ready for book 5!

Excerpt from *Lafitte's Chance*, the next book in the exciting Pale Rider series!

Chapter One Chauncey's escape

November 10, 1814

Chauncey stood at the bow of the boat in the dark, his right foot resting on the footstep of the railing, his knee up high with his other foot flat on the deck. His right hand, which gripped the Webley flintlock, rested on his raised knee. He was pensive, pondering his next move as the vessel glided through the water, down the Mississippi River. The large steam-powered paddleboat was propelled both by the giant red paddlewheel at the aft as well as by the swiftly running water of the river itself. In the dark night, even from the bow of the boat, only the sloshing of the paddles going in and out of the water in a rhythmic motion disturbed the quiet. It had a soothing effect on his racing brain and stretched-tight nerves.

The moon was up high in the black sky but blocked by the thick overgrowth of trees on the bank. Mosquitos bit painfully at his hands and neck, while frogs croaked their songs from the water and from land. He may have lost his leprechaun, but he had the Webley flintlock, his rainbow that would lead him to his pot of gold, and that was something. In truth, Chauncey knew he was lucky to still be alive. He also knew that he was alive because he had sacrificed his two grenades, using them against the killer, and that was a shame. Those two grenades were not as valuable as the Webley flintlock, but they were worth a fortune in themselves.

The man who Chauncey now truly believed was the Pale Rider had come for him yesterday morning, hunting him like a predator from the depths of hell, yet Chauncey had survived. No, that wasn't entirely true, was it? The man hadn't come for Chauncey – he had come for his friend, Aden, the leprechaun. The Pale Rider had come on like an unstoppable storm, sent by Neptune himself, destroying anyone and anything that got in his way. Like a wave that finally breaks, dragging everything it touches out to sea, so the Pale Rider had swept Aden from Chauncey's grasp. If the Pale Rider had come for Chauncey himself, Chauncey had no doubt he would be dead right now, floating down the river as alligator bait.

Chauncey's body trembled as a quiver coursed down his back at the reminder of the small yet epic battle that had taken place on this very boat. Chauncey had seen the man dive off the boat to save his friend, but no one had seen how the killer had found his way onto the vessel in the first place.

Chauncey's heart still pumped his life-giving blood through his veins only because the Pale Rider chose to save the man named Aden rather than taking revenge and killing Chauncey himself. They had unceremoniously gone over the boat's railing and plunged into the muddy waters of the Mississippi River. Chauncey hadn't seen them surface, but he knew they had to make it out somewhere. He could feel them out there, somewhere in the trees or on a boat behind him. The Pale Rider had cut through the six men Chauncey had paid to protect him.

Then there was Big Jim. One of the biggest and toughest men Chauncey had ever met. He last saw Jim with a flintlock in each hand, standing in front of the Pale Rider as a shield for Chauncey. Jim had stood on the catwalk, an unmovable object, both pistols aimed at the killer. Yet Big Jim had met an unstoppable force in the Pale Rider and was just gone. No shots fired, no screams, no splash of water. After the fight yesterday, Chauncey had the ship searched from top to bottom, and Big Jim was nowhere to be found.

How had the Pale Rider found Chauncey in the first place? Chauncey tapped his forehead, trying to think. So many questions and not enough information. The few answers Chauncey did have only led to more questions.

The paddleboat would be pulling into New Orleans in a few minutes, and Chauncey needed to decide what his next move would be. He was sailing in treacherous waters right now, and one wrong move might cost him his life.

Look for Lafitte's Chance, coming soon!

Excerpt from Book 1 *Chain and Mace*

Descended

Most people seem to believe that angels do not have free will. The truth is that they do. Angels in heaven chose to follow God, just as those in hell chose to follow Satan. When an angel chooses to follow the Lord but breaks one of his commands, he is cast out from heaven, but not all are cast to hell. These angels are known as Fallen Angels. But where do fallen angels go?

August 18

David fled down the grassy hill as fast as his legs could carry him, looking over his shoulder every few seconds. He was breathing hard; his heart pounded in his ears, and he was so tired. *Where were they? What were they?* They were behind him a minute ago, and now they were gone.

He remembered how they silently came out of the darkness, these strange men, *no not men, they were too big.* Animals, or a kind of creatures, *but they walked on two legs, or some of them did.*

Monsters? He tried to think of an argument against using that word but could not. They grabbed Jake, his cameraman, by the throat. Jake hung in the air by that giant hairy hand or paw that shook Jake like a rag doll. There were three of them, that much he was sure of. The first one stood about six and a half, maybe seven feet tall, the biggest bear David had ever seen, but it wasn't a bear. Bears didn't grab people by the throats. He thought perhaps they were wolves. They did look like wolves, but wolves don't walk on two feet.

They must be men in costumes, David thought. After all, that was the reason he was out here in the first place.

His editor had sent him and Jake out to investigate reports of a type of new religious cult. Well, they sure as hell found the cult, or the cult found them. Poor Jake was overweight at least by forty pounds. How could any person just pick up a two-hundred-and-thirty-pound man by one hand? Maybe they were on drugs, PCP, or something. David had done a report earlier in the year about how strong people can get when they are whacked out on drugs. They had heard rumors about a motorcycle gang in the area, maybe they had something to do with this. David's thoughts were interrupted by the rock he tripped on. He fell to the ground and fought to stay conscious as he rolled forward on the grass, the metallic taste of blood filling his mouth.

Kathy! His mind suddenly went to her. *What would Kathy do if he died here?* Crouched in the dirt, he decided he would live. He had to find a phone and call the police, and it was his most unfortunate luck that he dropped his cell phone when he ran. *Maybe a pay phone at a gas station?*

David forced himself to his feet and looked behind him, up the hill that he had fallen down, but it was too dark to see if anyone was still there. He must have run a mile by now. David had played high school football years ago, and he always kept himself in good shape. He thought he could move with decent speed, but these guys were faster. By God, they were fast. It was almost as if they were playing with him. David thought about his cat and how she would pounce on the bugs she would find in the house, only to let them go, then pounce again.

"Stop thinking and just run," David said to himself out loud. He turned to run but was stopped by the very large hand that grabbed him by the back of the neck

Chain and Mace – Book 1

About the author:

Michael Roberts is a Police Officer in Southern California. He also served seven years in the United States Marine Corps, where he operated an Amphibious Assault Vehicle as a crew chief for four years and then served with the Marine Security Guard detachment, guarding American Embassies around the world. He lives with his wife Michelle Deerwester-Dalrymple, a college professor and also an author, and their five children.

Follow him on Facebook and Instagram, or sign up for his newsletter here:

Sign up for his newsletter here:
https://www.subscribepage.com/k8e0d9

MICHAEL ROBERTS

AUTHOR

Also by the Author: